THE CROWN OF WYVERN'S FLAME

THE FORBIDDEN HEIR TRILOGY | BOOK TWO

EMILIA JAE

EMILIA JAE
FANTASY AUTHOR
EM'S BOOKISH REALM

The Crown of Wyvern's Flame | The Forbidden Heir Trilogy: Book Two.

Copyright © 2024 by Emilia Jae. | All rights reserved.

No portion of this book may be reproduced in any form without written permission from the publisher or author, except as permitted by U.S. copyright law.

Front Cover Art: Celia Driscoll

The Map of Velyra: Andres Aguirre | @aaguirreart

Interior Art of Lia & Nox: Eva | @teviense

Editor: Makenna Albert | www.onthesamepageediting.com

Proof Reader: Tabitha Chandler | www.tabithadoesediting.com

First Edition | March 2024.

Paperback ISBN: 979-8-9888968-2-1 | Hardcover ISBN: 979-8-9888968-3-8

Content Warning

Please note that this book is not intended for readers below the age of 18, and may also contain content that some readers might find triggering. This warning is due to explicit language, descriptive violence/gore, mass executions, PTSD, mentions of past child abuse, and mentions of sexual assault.

This series has multiple POVs, including the villains. Please note that these villains are true in their nature. They are wicked to their core and you will see inside of their minds, which can be disturbing to some readers.
Reader's discretion is advised.

VELYRA

VAYR SEA

THE FLORA ISLES

ANERYS

ALAIA VALLEY

EZRANIAN MOUNTAIN RANGE

ELLECASTER

CELAN VILLAGE

VAYR SEA

THE SYLIS FOREST

CETO BAY

TORTUNELE

ISLA

DORAELI

VAYR SEA

to feminine rage.

& all those who have it burning beneath their skin...may you release it with the ferocity of wyvern's flame.

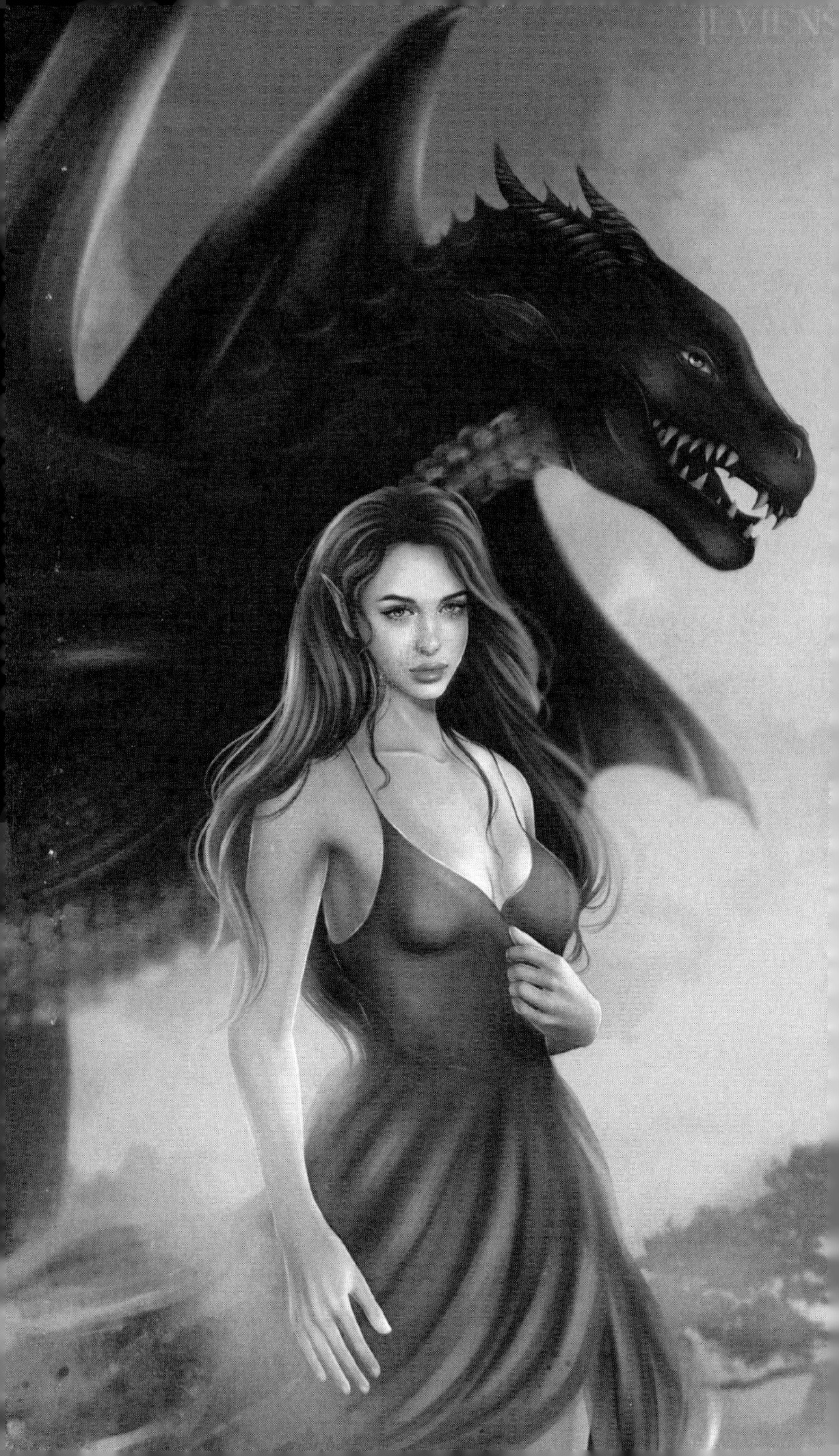

PRONUNCIATION GUIDE

Names:

Elianna (Lia) Solus: Ellie-Ana (Leah) Soul-iss
Jace Cadoria: Jayce Ka-door-ia
Kellan Adler: Kell-an Add-ler
Avery: Ay-ver-ee
Finnian: Finn-ee-an
Lukas: Luke-us
Zaela: Zay-lah
Veli Elora: Vel-ee El-or-ah
Nyra: Near-ah
Nox: Nocks
Idina Valderre: Eh-deena Val-dare
Kai: K-eye
Callius: Kal-ee-us
Matthias: Math-thigh-as
Bruhn: Broon
Agdronis: Ag-dron-iss
Euphoroot: You-for-root
Ruefweed: Roof-weed

Places:

Kingdom of Velyra: Vel-ear-ah
City of Isla: Eye-la
Ceto Bay: See-toe Bay
Ezranian Mountains: Ehz-rain-ian
Sylis Forest: Sigh-liss
Alaia Valley: Al-eye-ah
Celan Village: Sell-an
Vayr Sea: Vay-er
Doraeli: Door-aye-lee

Spells & Language of the Gods:

Tinaebris Malifisc: Tin-aye-bree Mal-if-isc
Venifikas Sussorae: Ven-if-ik-us Suss-or-aye
(The Witch's Whisper)
Umbra Selair: Um-bra Soul-air (Shadow Summoning)
Impyrum Kortyus: Imp-ear-iam Court-ee-ous
(Mind Control)
Odium Embulae: Oh-dee-um Em-boo-lay
(Rift Walking/Portal)
Meritsas Lokoi: Mer-it-sass Low-koi (Truth Speaking)
Ignystae: Ig-nee-stay

Prologue

The Queen

CALLIUS RAN HIS FINGERS through his thick, dark hair in wicked anticipation. He shot me a feral look of farewell over his shoulder, right before the door of my personal chambers clicked shut behind him. My heart raced in my chest as realization settled in that Captain Adler had finally arrived back in Isla with Elianna in tow. Everything was finally falling into place.

I had worked tirelessly day and night since I was a mere youngling, just to prove my worth to my father after he sold me to the Valderres when I was still in my mother's womb.

I stared at the fae looking back at me in the mirror and wondered how disgusted that little girl, once so full of life, would be to see what she had been morphed into at the hands of the males that raised her. I gazed into my own eyes, once pools of warm honey, now darkened by all-consuming rage and grief. Grief for the life I could've had if I had been allowed to.

I had always had a duty to uphold. A duty my father bestowed upon me before he knew what the gods had planned for his own daughter, and after centuries of enduring Jameson...the realm would finally belong to *my* bloodline.

Jameson had survived decades longer than originally planned, and that was due to me not yet giving birth to an heir. My mind raced back to the nights when my father would berate me into seducing the king, who had made it entirely clear that he wanted nothing to do with me aside from parading me before the masses of the kingdom. He thought he had done such a *fine* job of showcasing his false love for me—a fool of a male, always such a wretched fool. I gladly accepted his petty gifts and treasures, which I later realized were gifted out of guilt.

Truthfully, I had always hoped he would eventually find entertainment between another female's legs, but I never imagined that he had the gall to step out on his own queen before an heir was sired.

A hiss left me as the memories flowed. I never wanted his love—never desired it in the slightest and found it entirely nauseating, but what I would always demand was respect. If I would never be legally permitted to love another, the same rule should be set for the king himself, but that was not the realm we lived in. His precious Ophelia not only gained his love, but returned it, and gave birth to the true heir in exchange. My father, may his soul rest in peace among the gods, would've made her end significantly more discreet, but in that moment of discovery, all I could see was *red*.

Fury enveloped me when Jameson stood before me in this very room over a century ago, as he confessed his affair and betrayal to not only his queen, but his kingdom. Years I worked up the stomach to bed the bastard. Years I was flaunted around as if I were a trophy on his arm. And *years* I was relentlessly ridiculed by my own kin for not successfully achieving the one matter I was born to do—take the throne of the Kingdom of Velyra. That was the night I decided I would never again rule from the side of the dais...I would take the entire fucking kingdom by force and fear.

A wicked grin crept up my own lips as I continued to gaze at myself in my vanity's mirror. My father and brother had paid the ultimate price and left me to deal with the future of the realm and their vision for it on my own, but I made sure the legacy that I would leave behind in their name was far greater than what they ever had planned.

My father never could've imagined where we would be now. His lifelong goal and vision was to be at the forefront of ruling Velyra. When Jameson refused his pleading to be named The King's Lord, a new strategy had been forged from the ashes of a once well thought out plan.

And that was that Jameson, no matter how long it may take to appear discreet, wouldn't survive the entirety of his reign.

I stood from my chair and sipped my wine as I strolled over to the window of my chamber's tower that overlooked the Vayr Sea.

I twirled a fiery red curl around my finger as I sucked in a deep breath. My eyes followed the horse-drawn carriage as it was pulled away from the harbor, where Adler's ship had docked, and my stare remained upon it until it vanished into the city.

The setting sun set the realm ablaze, and a wondrous chill ran up my spine as the sweet taste of vengeance coated my tongue.

A wicked chuckle slipped from me as I swirled my wine in its glass. "Welcome home, Elianna."

ONE
Elianna

Sister.

The word rattled through my skull repeatedly since the moment it left my vicious brother's lips. Time had ceased to exist and there was a deafening buzz in my ears as my entire world came crashing down around me. Surely I was just imagining things, and he didn't truly just call me...

"Are you listening to me?" Kai spat at me through the bars of the cell door.

I blinked in confusion, jaw hanging wide as I stared at him. I took in a shuddering breath as my mind tried to process what had just been admitted to me.

He kicked the door aggressively, sending a booming *ting* sound rattling through the dungeon halls. I jumped at the break of the intense silence, which sent a shooting pain through my bloody, carved up back.

"What did you just call me?" I whispered, still refusing to meet his stare as I felt it bore into me.

How could Kai have known that I was his half-sister? Over a century had passed, with the secret being entirely hidden. This wasn't a mere guess—he must have been told by one of the few who had held this knowledge since the night of my birth.

He let out a soft, proud chuckle. "You didn't think I knew."

My eyes shot to his then as my lip curled back. "No. I *know* you didn't know of this until after I left Isla all those weeks ago. You couldn't have."

"The information regarding our kinship was provided to me upon the announcement that I will ascend the throne." A wicked smile formed as he crossed his arms.

Panic consumed me, my thoughts spiraling with the terrifying possibilities of how the realm would be reshaped under Kai's reign.

I tightened my grasp on the overwhelming emotions, determined not to let a hint of fear show.

"So, tell me, little prince," I seethed. "What is it that you think you know?"

He eyed me for a moment, and I was expecting him to throw one of his usual tantrums, but he surprised me and spoke instead. "Just that Father was a fool in love...with someone who was not the queen." He paused as he raised his hand to his face to inspect his nails. "You were the unfortunate result of that."

I eyed him for a moment. "So the queen killed our father over this after more than a century has passed? Why wait that long?"

He pressed his face through the bars of the cell. "You see, it wasn't her revenge that resulted in Father's death. It was *you*."

My heart leapt in my chest at his claim, and my eyes burned with gut-wrenching intensity as our father's murder was so casually mentioned.

"What?! I would *never!* And I wasn't even here!"

"No, you weren't here," he said as he continued to pick at his nails, seeming to have already lost interest in the torment. "You were off fucking the enemy." A malice tainted grin appeared once more.

I bared my teeth in response. "I had nothing to do with his death. You just spoke of the cause, and it was *your mother* poisoning his wine with wyvern's blood."

"You had *everything* to do with it, you stupid bitch!" he shouted at me. "You had been in the king's ear for years! I can only imagine it now. How absolutely *pathetic* the two of you must have been hidden inside his chambers without anyone else's eyes and ears upon you. Tell me, how did it go exactly?" My breathing turned rapid as I tried to calm myself. "How did it go, Elianna? I could only imagine you sneaking in there...'Oh, Father! Won't you please end this terrible war! The humans! They are innocent!' Actually, spare me. Please fucking spare me of the pitiful encounters."

My lip betrayed me and trembled slightly. "Shut the fuck up, Kai!" I screamed back at him, voice cracking. The ache in my gaping flesh wounds from the whip forced a whimper out of me.

His eyes narrowed in on me, and the look on his face sent a shrill shiver down my aching spine. "You will address me as *King* moving forward. And if you ever refer to me as 'little prince' again, I'll see to it that a whip is taken to your back once more."

A sad huff of a laugh left me at his threat. "You're not the king yet." I forced my body to stand, and my eyes met his as I moved to the cell door as quickly as the pain would allow. "You're still just the same, putrid little brat you were as a youngling. A tyrant. A fucking *monster*." His smile faltered. "And if I have anything to do with it, I will make sure that you will *never* be king."

He reached through the bars, grabbing me by what remained of my ruined shirt, and tugged me up against them, up against *him*. "That's another thing, Elianna. We are going to make sure that you never have anything to do with the future of Velyra, *ever* again."

Kai paused for a moment as his eyes roamed over me. "My wedding is in three days' time, moving up my coronation. Mother has chosen a suitable bride, and a marriage alliance was the last requirement for ascension by old Velyran law."

My eyes bulged—a marriage?! Already? They weren't wasting a single moment to pass down the crown.

I clenched my teeth and my lip curled back in disgust, right before he forcefully shoved me away, sending me to trip over my own feet and violently slam down onto the dirt covered floor.

A scream tore from my throat at the agony that ripped through my body. I could feel every grain of dirt and sand rub into each laceration as I forced my body to sit up, dry heaving from the pain that now radiated through me.

When I looked back up at the rusted cell door, Kai had already disappeared, seemingly convinced that he had his fun for the day. I groaned through the intense stinging and begged my body to get up from the ground. I was barely able to crawl over to the sad excuse of a bench in the far corner.

My wounds were now filthy, with not even a drop of water to clean them. I would die from infection down here before they even had time to make actual plans of what to do with me.

But what was the point of living now, anyway? Kai would now ascend the throne and my father was dead. And now, there was a chance my mate was dead as well.

My *mate*. My heart seized at the thought of him—at the vision of him that now constantly replayed in my mind of being forced to watch Kellan take my own dagger to my lover's face. His perfect, beautiful face that I had unknowingly memorized every feature of. His hazel eyes that hypnotized me, and his smile that threatened to bring me to my knees. Now, all I could picture was Jace's body as he dropped to the ground and writhed in agonizing torment, and I knew it was exactly that. I *felt* it.

I dove deep within myself as I sat in my new found prison and reached for that bond—begging the gods to allow me even a sliver of hope that he still lived, but I couldn't differentiate my own emotions from anything else. All I felt was immense anguish—both physical and emotional.

I was the unknown, true heir with barely any claim to the throne. Well, not a believable claim. With the king dead, there was no way to prove who I was. Who I was to the Kingdom of Velyra, and who I was to my father.

A single tear slipped from my lower lashes and down my dirt-crusted cheek as I tucked my knees into my chest and hugged them tightly.

I would die here, and I never got the chance to tell Jace how I truly felt—how I had felt for *weeks* before I even realized it was the mating bond that drew us together.

My twin soul.

My equal in every way.

And now, he would never know the truth of what I felt for him.

TWO
Avery

THE PAST FEW DAYS had been nothing short of horrific. I hadn't seen Lukas since we snuck into my father's old chambers and stole the journal that held all of his secrets. A lifetime worth of secrets. My entire life, Lia had been my *sister*. Anytime the thought of it plagued my mind, I would nearly burst into a river of tears.

All those nights we spent together—creeping around the castle grounds, hiding from Lukas, having secret sleepovers, and smoking euphoroot until we were essentially braindead for the evening. The last sleepover we had, I even told her I had always wanted a sister. And the whole time, she *knew*. She knew that I had one, and it was *her*—my very best friend.

I tried so hard to be angry with her for keeping something like this from me, but deep down, I knew why she did. If anything, I just felt so awful that she had to bear the weight of it alone. Always watching us be able to run to our father openly, or even the occasional embrace from our wicked mother. She must've felt so, so alone.

I frantically paced back and forth in my room while staring at the journal that lay on my bureau when a knock sounded at the door.

"Just a minute!" I yelped as I dove toward the journal and shoved it into a drawer.

I peeked over at my bed where Nyra had been napping, now sitting up on high alert with her ears perked toward the door.

I straightened the creases in my gown and glided over to the door. I opened it with a soft smile to see Finnian standing there, eyes wide.

My smile dropped as I reached out and grabbed him by his shirt, dramatically pulling him into my room, and then slammed the door behind me.

He continued to stare at me, appearing as if he was trying to find the words his mouth refused to speak.

I aggressively clapped in his face. "Snap out of it, Finn!" I shouted, startling him. "What happened?"

He shook his head and cleared his throat as he searched for the words. "There were reports of a hooded prisoner being brought down to the castle dungeons yesterday. I just overheard when I was down in the gardens. Whoever it is, it is being kept under wraps."

My brows furrowed. "And you heard nothing else? Not what they had been brought for or if a trial is to be held?"

"That is all that was said. They are all curious because the dungeon gate now has a guard posted—there has not been one in decades since they have remained empty."

My thoughts raced. "Mother's favorite form of punishment has been a—"

"Noose," he cut me off. "Yes. So who would be down there that they would not kill immediately and also not want the guards getting wind of?"

My eyes flared. "Lukas! It has to be. They wouldn't want him to be seen taken into custody. It would incite chaos among the ranks." I started pacing back and forth in front of him.

"That's what I was thinking, too. We have not seen him since that day at the stables. I assumed he felt the need to flee in order to survive, but that's not who Lukas is," he said as he began to curiously glance around the bedchamber.

I stopped in my tracks as I watched him. "Can I help you with something?" I asked as I crossed my arms.

"What were you...throwing around in here before you opened the door?"

My spine straightened, and I considered showing him our father's journal, but I wanted to investigate its pages further before involving anyone else.

"Absolutely none of your business. Now, let's sneak down into the dungeons." I went to pull on his arm to follow, but he ripped it from my grasp, forcing me to turn back around to him.

"I am *done* going through your creepy tunnels, Avery," he said in a tone that was more stern than I was used to.

"Don't be ridiculous. I don't know *all* the tunnels! That was Lia's job. We are going into the dungeons the old-fashioned way," I responded to him as I waltzed into the hallway outside of my room. "We'll be back, Nyra!"

"Old fashioned way?" he raised a mocking brow as he caught up to me.

"The stairs that lead to them. Obviously."

"You mean the ones in the courtyard? We will be seen," he huffed out, nearly out of breath from trying to keep up with me as I floated through the halls.

"You just leave that to me," I retorted with a grin as we raced down the castle's staircase.

Dusk was upon us as we reached the courtyard of Castle Isla. Hiding behind one of the pillars, I noticed there was only a single guard that stood watch by the slightly hidden door.

"See! I told you," Finn snapped at me, and I rolled my eyes. "There's no way we will be able to get down there. There's a freaking guard at the door, Avery."

"Will you just shut up and let me think?!" I hissed as I tapped my finger on my bottom lip in thought. My eyes shot to his. "Smack me across the face."

"Um. What?" He stared at me blankly.

"I need to make it look like I have been crying. I can fake a damn good cry, but my face needs to look red and puffy. Smack me." I paused and my eyes narrowed on him. "Lightly!"

Finn continued to stare at me, seeming both terrified and amused all at once. "You scare me sometimes."

"Good. Now do it."

Finnian straightened his shoulders and cleared his throat as if he was about to put on a big show. He raised a shaky hand in the air and smacked one side of my face, causing me to let out a soft cry, and then, to my surprise, smacked the opposite cheek immediately after.

My gaze snapped to his. "Hey! What the hell!" I whisper-shouted as I shoved him, causing him to stumble.

He started laughing. "What?! You think one side of your face being red is believable?"

"Asshole." I rolled my eyes. "A warning would've been nice," I said through a snort.

"Go put on a show, sis." He winked.

I nodded at him as I lifted the hem of my dress and snuck around the back pillars to make it appear as if I had come through the side castle gates. I then ran out into view of the entire courtyard and started bawling my eyes out.

"Oh gods! Oh, gods, this is awful. *Awful!*" I cried. I wildly wiped my fake tears as I fixed my gaze on the guard by the door. "Oh, thank goodness you are out here, sir!"

The guard looked around, confused, and then silently pointed to his chest, looking for confirmation that I was speaking to him.

"Yes, you! There is a brawl going on right beyond the castle gates! Slummers somehow made their way here and are in a drunken fit over the announcement of the soon-to-be king's wedding!" I threw my hands out at my sides, but the guard still didn't move.

"Princess Avery, I cannot abandon this post," he stuttered out as I ran up to him.

I grabbed onto his hands, and his body stiffened nervously. "Oh, but you must! They are going to kill each other out there. What if they breach the gates? You're the closest one to it! Who knows who else I will be able to find at this hour and if they would even make it in time."

The guard looked at me hesitantly. *Shit*. This wasn't going to work. I let out another obnoxious sob, tightening my hold on his hand as I bat my kohl-lined lashes at him. "You would be my hero," I said innocently as I gave him a gentle smile.

His eyes softened as he gave a sweet, caring smile back at me.

Sucker.

"Okay, Princess. Please don't cry. I will go check it out. How far are they from this gate?"

I let out a few more fake sobs as I nodded repeatedly and released his hand. "They are around the corner of the gate. They may even be headed to the front gateway."

The fool of a guard gave me a proud nod and made his way to the courtyard's entrance.

The moment he was out of view, Finnian came running from where we originally hid.

He clasped his hands and held them up to his own face, fluttering his eyelashes in mockery of me. "You would be my hero," he teased in a voice that was entirely too high to mimic my own. "That may have been your best work yet."

"Shut up. It worked, obviously. Now let's go!"

Both of us ran for the dungeon's entrance and were surprised when the barred door that led down the stairs was unlocked. We pushed through and glided down the stairway.

"Gods, it's nearly as gross down here as it is in your passageways," he said as he sniffed the air. "It reeks of iron and mildew."

"That it does," I agreed, as I turned my nose up. "At least the halls are lined with torches, so we can see."

I glanced down at my feet and noticed the bottom of my dress was already covered in dirt from the floor that clearly hadn't been maintained in years, or perhaps ever.

We walked for what seemed like miles through the winding tunnels. "What exactly are we going to do once we find Lukas? We don't even know if he is in here. And it's not as if we could just...let him out," Finnian said.

"I just want to make sure he is okay first. Then we can figure out a plan."

We walked past a few cells, peering into each one to find that each had been empty and untouched. Finally, after stalking past another row of barred rooms, I saw a large shadow-like figure hidden within the darkness behind the bars of one.

"Lukas?" I asked in an unsure tone.

The figure stood and slowly made its way into the torchlight. My racing heart finally slowed when I saw that it, in fact, *was* him, but he did not look well.

"Oh, gods," he croaked out. "Avery. Finn. What are you two doing down here? You can't be seen!" he said, his raspy voice full of worry.

I grabbed hold of the cell's door with both my hands and laced my fingers between the rusted bars. "We have been looking for you! We wanted to make sure you were okay...and...and well..."

"Alive," he finished for me.

I briefly slammed my eyes tight and nodded repeatedly, trying to force the tears to stay inside.

He let out a sad chuckle. "Well, I am alive. For now, that is. Have you heard anything about Lia?"

My eyes snapped back to his. "Has there been news?"

"I have been down here since the day I spoke with you in the stables. They threw me in here when a falcon that was meant for me was intercepted. It was from Lia. The letter said that she was safe beyond the Sylis Forest and she wanted me to meet her by the next full moon."

My jaw dropped.

"Who intercepted the letter?" Finnian asked hurriedly.

Lukas pursed his lips and, through clenched teeth, said, "Who do you think?"

"Shit," I murmured. "Well, at least we know she is safe."

"For now," Lukas interjected.

Finnian started curiously glancing around the cells, and I swore if he complained about the view and stench down here one more time, while Lukas had been down here for *weeks*, I was going to lose it.

"Wait a second..." Finn finally spoke. "You said you have been here since we last saw you? That was *weeks* ago!" My eyes widened at the suspicion that Finnian had also clearly just realized. "We came down here because we thought you were brought down only yesterday."

"Weeks?" Lukas repeated, clearly confused. "It appears I have lost all sense of time down here."

"There were reports of a hooded prisoner being escorted here. We thought it was you! So we came running," I cut in.

"Those gods-damn pricks," Lukas spat. "The food they have been bringing me has been laced with ruefweed. I have been sleeping these weeks away and haven't had a choice. My choices are to either starve and die or sleep. And now I know why."

"Lia," I whispered as both Finn and I started anxiously looking around the surrounding cells. "You haven't heard *anything?*"

Lukas sighed. "I am a fool," he grumbled as his jaw locked. He gripped the bars of his cell door tightly in his fists. "I thought I heard screams in my sleep, but chucked it up to the imagination of being down here and alone for so long. These cells haven't been used in decades since trials are barely held anymore."

I couldn't find any words, so I raised my head and peered down the seemingly never-ending hall of prison cells. My lips parted as I stared, and a moment later I took off into a sprint, further into the abyss that was the dungeons.

"Avery! Avery, be careful!" Lukas yelled as Finn ran after me.

"Lia!" I screamed, praying there weren't any guards down here. "Lia, are you here? Please answer me, Lia!" The last of my words ended on an echoing sob.

I glanced through each room we passed as I ran, when suddenly a quiet cough sounded from a few cells down. My run came to a screeching halt.

Finn slammed into me, but caught my body before I fell. "Sorry," he said in a shaky voice.

I straightened as I peered down the dark, eerie hall. "Lia?" I croaked out. "Is that you?"

With caution, I approached the cell that the cough had echoed from and gazed through the bars, but I was only met with darkness.

Finn came up behind me and gently pulled me back by my elbow. "We don't know if that's her in there," he whispered in my ear.

"Who's there?" A desperate, pain-ridden voice called out from within the shadows.

I pulled my arm from his grasp and then we both pressed our faces through the bars. "Lia! It's Avery and Finn. Oh gods, what has happened to you?!"

Movement sounded in the darkness as if she was crawling her way up to her feet, when her face slowly emerged in the torchlight. "Hi, you two," she said weakly, looking as if she could barely take another step.

"Oh, my gods!" I cried as I started forcefully shaking the cell door, desperately trying to pry it open with my bare hands as she made her way to us at a snail's pace.

Tears were now streaming down my cheeks in waves. I couldn't hold them in any longer at the sight of what had been done to her.

"It's okay, Avery. I'm okay," she said in a hushed tone.

I looked her up and down repeatedly. She was not okay. She was *filthy*, clutching the straps of what remained of her shirt to her front. I could see it was covered in dirt and *blood*. So, so much blood. Her blood, I realized.

"What the hell did they do to you?" Finn shrieked in horror. His face mirrored what I felt inside.

Lia now stood face-to-face with us and gently placed her shaking hand atop my own as they rested on the bars.

"Avery, please don't cry," she begged, and then immediately bit her bottom lip as it trembled. She was trying to stay strong for us, to make us not worry.

"Stop that. You stop that right fucking now," I demanded in a surprisingly steady voice. "You do not need to pretend you are okay. I have eyes, Elianna. I can see you are in very, very rough shape." She took in a shaky breath. "What happened?" I asked in a tone much softer.

She smiled. "I'm home. Aren't you happy?"

"Enough!" Finn snapped. Both of our eyes flew over to where he stood, now a step behind me. "I can't see you like this. They broke you. They fucking broke you, Lia! What the hell happened?"

"I know," she whispered. "I...I don't even know where to begin." She hesitated. "The very short version is that I am being tried as a mortal sympathizer."

"What?!" Finn and I both gasped at the same time.

Lia giggled sadly. "I missed you guys." She paused. "Perhaps that is exactly what I am now, though. I've seen the humans. How they are. *Who* they are. Mortals are not all bad and are very much like us. They are just doing what is necessary to survive."

"What are you saying? That you...you support the humans in our war?"

"I support the end of the war, Avery," Lia said sternly, and I winced. "I always have. Now I'm just much more convinced of this decision."

"How did they find you?"

"I, very foolishly, sent a letter by falcon thinking it would be secure. I had no idea the king was dead at that point. I was hoping to bring my new...friends back and convince him to put an end to this."

Friends? Human friends? I couldn't believe it.

I looked her over once more now that she fully stood in the torchlight. Lacerations riddled her body—an open wound sliced across her chest that looked as if it curled from around her shoulder.

"The queen killed our father," I said to her and hurt flashed across her features. "And yes, I mean *our* father."

Her stare slowly rose to mine. "I assumed you were made aware just as Kai." Tears swelled in her eyes once more. "There have been so many times I wanted to tell you. So many times it almost slipped, or I wanted to say, 'fuck it' and just blurt it out. But I couldn't. I had to protect him and his secret."

"I know," I whispered, trying to muster up a smile. "I'm not mad, and I understand why you did it. I just could never have kept that secret. You know..." I shrugged. "Me and my big mouth."

She let out a small, sad chuckle once more, but flinched slightly from the pain, and my heart stuttered.

"What caused these lacerations?" I asked hesitantly, praying that it was not at the hands of our cruel brother.

Her eyes darkened. "Kellan and Callius." She paused, and for a moment, I didn't think she would continue. "They chained me up down the hall and...took a whip to my back."

Finnian and I both let out a quick gasp and my hands flew to cover my mouth.

"And while century old secrets are coming to light, you should know that it is also not the first time." My eyes widened in horror at what she had said. "I didn't fall from wisteria vines as a child. Your mother had Callius whip me for using her hairbrush when I was a youngling. I'm so sorry I had to lie to you."

I was stunned silent for a few moments. My hands balled into fists at my sides as realization hit me how monstrous my mother truly was. She had Lia whipped as a *youngling* for an offense as small as using a hairbrush. One she undoubtedly brushed through my own hair many times. It was becoming increasingly unbearable to know I shared the same blood as someone as cruel as her.

"I will kill them," I hissed through my teeth as my brows furrowed.

"You will do no such thing," Lia snapped. "I don't trust them. Kai has already been down here trying to torment me. I fear for the fate of Velyra with those three males now at the forefront of the ranks, but I mainly fear for the two of you. Do not get in their way. Don't do anything stupid."

"Lia, your wounds are getting infected," Finnian whispered nervously.

"I know," she said with a sigh. "There's nothing that can be done for me at this point, but you two need to be smart about what you do."

What? Oh, gods, she was serious. Lia was giving up.

"What the fuck do you mean there isn't something that can be done?!" I shouted, definitely too loudly, but I couldn't bring myself to care.

"Avery, you have to leave me here."

"No. No, I absolutely do not. *That* I will figure out, but I'm going to get Veli to come treat these wounds. She can at least get rid of the infection."

"They will know I had help," Lia seethed, heaving over slightly in pain.

"I really don't give a shit, Lia. I refuse to let you die. Especially of a preventable infection!" I scolded her. "I will be back as soon as I can, and I will bring Veli. Please don't die on me in the meantime."

Lia snickered. "I will do my best."

Finn reached out for Lia's hand and gave it a gentle squeeze. "I have two sisters. Who knew?" he joked. "And for the record...you would've been a much better suited heir than Kai."

She squeezed his hand back and smiled. "Thanks, Finn."

"Let's go Finn, we don't have much time with her infection spreading."

The two of us then raced down the hall, back toward the entrance of the dungeons.

Elianna

I watched as both Finnian and Avery hurried down the hall from where they came, and I couldn't believe they had found me and were now working to rescue me. While anxiety threatened to take over me at the two of them involving themselves in a treasonous act, I couldn't help but feel some form of pride.

A shuddering, heavy breath of relief left my lungs when suddenly, footsteps sounded from the opposite direction of where they came. The chamber where Nox was kept.

Panic clogged my throat as my gaze turned to the darkness of the eerie dungeon hall, only dimly lit by a few torches, when Kellan's figure leisurely emerged from the shadows.

"Fuck," I whispered, as my head sagged between my aching shoulders.

"Good evening to you too, princess." He smiled wickedly at me as he placed his hands in his pockets. "Now tell me, what did I just hear the prince say regarding you being the true heir?"

My stomach twisted in painful knots as his chuckle echoed through the vacant hall.

THREE

Avery

WE RUSHED PAST LUKAS and promised we would explain everything to him later, right before we raced up the stairs and through the dungeon's still unguarded entrance. Our first deal of business was to find Veli and beg her to help Lia.

Whipped.

I couldn't believe they *whipped* her. It was cruel and barbaric. What other kinds of plans did they have for her? For my sister? Did they plan to drag out her torture before they outright killed her? Or did they want this infection to consume her? I was so nauseous at the slightest thought of it.

"How in the realm are we going to find Veli? We don't even know where she lives! She has barely been seen to begin with," Finnian heaved as he was out of breath, trying to keep up with me once more while we ran through the courtyard.

"Well, how hard could it be? Surely she is around here somewhere."

Veli hadn't been physically on staff at the castle in decades, thanks to our mother banning healers, but I assumed someone would've seen her recently. She was always sneaking in to assist Father when his illness took over, and now it made sense why she could never figure out what had been killing him.

I worked to catch my breath as we wandered through the foyer of the castle's main entrance. Decorations were already being placed on display for Kai's wedding. The staff worked tirelessly to ensure every detail looked perfect, from the meticulously arranged decorations to the spotless marble floors. We then twirled down the spiral staircase that led to the staff's wing.

"Princess Avery and Prince Finnian! How lovely to see you here," a friendly voice called from the corner. I turned my body to see it was one of the handmaidens.

"Hello!" I greeted her cheerfully. "I'm so sorry. I am not sure of your name."

She gave me a kind, tight smile. "Lillian, Princess. My name is Lillian. How can I assist you two this evening?"

I looked her up and down. Lillian appeared to be around my age, but then again, most fae did since our aging practically ceased to a halt during our second decade of life. She had the spirit of someone my age, though, so that I could work with.

"Hi Lillian, so nice to officially meet you. This is my brother, Prince Finnian." I gestured to Finn, and she curtsied at him. "I am wondering if you can help us find someone. Veli. She's a healer that used to work here and is often seen roaming about if help is needed...or if she's just being nosy."

Her eyes darted back and forth between Finn and I. "So-sorry Miss. I mean Princess! I have not seen Veli in weeks. Not since the ki–" She hesitated. "Not since the passing of your father. I am so very sorry for your loss. It is a significant loss felt by all in this realm, Princess Avery."

Shit. Veli hadn't been here since she tried to help my father. Had Kai and the others done something to her, too? Or did she simply run if she suspected foul play?

"Thank you very much, Lillian. And please, call me Avery." I smiled at her. "Tell me, do you know where Veli lives?" I asked innocently.

"Is she in trouble?" Lillian stared at me cautiously, as if she wanted to ask more, but knew her place.

"No, no, of course not. I would just very much like to speak with her. She was a dear friend of my father's and I just had a few questions for her."

The moment the words left my mouth, I regretted them. It wasn't even nearly believable. Veli didn't have friends.

She terrified me as a child, but Father always liked her. Or perhaps he was just afraid of her as well. But she could heal like no other. Wounds that would typically take weeks to heal for fae, she could have healed in a day or two. It was as if she had a magic touch. Rumors claimed that other healers amongst Isla had requested courses and lessons from her, but her answer was always the same.

And that was to "fuck off."

Finnian looked at me like I was an idiot. I couldn't even be mad at him for it.

"Okay, A-Avery," she stuttered out my name. "She has been seen down by the docks many times. Nobody knows where she actually lives, but I would assume in that area."

The docks. That was halfway across the city. The city that I had barely ever been allowed to roam through. I would immediately be lost. I glanced over at Finn and he just shrugged in defeat.

"Thank you very much, Lady Lillian." I went to turn, but she walked out in front of me.

"Oh Miss, I am no Lady. I am just a handmaiden."

"You are a female, are you not?" I asked, but she just looked between Finn and me once more, brows furrowed as if she was trying to study us. I leaned in closer to her. "Never describe yourself as just a handmaiden. A person's title does not define the depths of their character. Also, I think you are lovely. So you are a Lady to me." I winked, and she blinked.

"You are different from the others," she said quietly.

"Yes, well, if you have had some unfortunate run-ins with our brother, Kai, I do apologize on his behalf."

I went to move around her once more but she spoke up again. "I'm leaving my shift in ten minutes, and I would love to guide you through the city if you need it." My brow raised at her in question. "Oh gods, I am so sorry. I just assumed you didn't know your way, judging by the looks you exchanged, but obviously you could just take one of the castle's carriages."

I looked at Finn and gave him a curt nod. "We would like that very much," he said to her as his eyes remained on me.

"Of course. Let me gather my things and I will meet you at the castle gates in ten minutes," she answered, with surprise and something else I couldn't quite pinpoint lingering beneath her tone.

While Lillian went to gather her belongings to leave for the evening, Finn and I ran to one of the staff's closets, desperately searching for clothing to help disguise who we were. We found two cloaks that were both much too large for either of us, but they would have to do.

I draped the dirty brown cloak over my already filthy dress and placed the hood over my head as Finn and I snuck back through the castle to meet her at the gateway.

We made it to the pillars when we noticed the guards patrolling around the battlement's entryway.

"Shit," I murmured.

"Can't bat your eyelashes out of this one, huh?"

I swung out and punched him in the arm.

"It's dark. Maybe if we time it right, we will be able to sneak past them," I said, unconvinced of it myself.

"You give us far too much credit. We aren't Lia." He rubbed at his sore arm.

"No, we aren't. However, she is counting on us, so we need to make this work."

We watched the guards as they patrolled back and forth four times under the darkness of the night sky.

"On the count of three, we make our move and run as their backs are each turned from the gate's entrance," I said to him, and he gave an abrupt nod in response. The guards then turned to move in the opposite direction, their backs facing us. "Shit, now!" I yelped in a whisper as I stood from my crouch and sprinted as silently as possible toward the gate. Finn immediately followed behind me.

I kept my eyes on them the entire time, and as soon as they both went to turn on their feet, I dove past the gate and out of their view. Finnian landed half on top of me on the ground, letting out a grunt.

He scrambled to his feet and aggressively pointed at me. "You said on the count of *three!* Three Avery! You didn't even say ONE!"

He helped me to my feet once he stopped complaining. "Oh relax, we got here, didn't we?"

Murmurs from the guards echoed over to us, forcing us to jump behind the gateway's side tower. Once out of view, we heard, "Have a good evening, Miss."

"Thank you, sirs."

Lillian. Thank the gods.

She strolled through the archway and glanced around.

"Psst," I hissed, barely snagging her attention. "Psst, Lillian! Over here."

She turned to us, and her eyes widened. "What are you two doing on the ground? And are those...are those cloaks from the staff's closet?" She crossed her arms. "Ha, people were just looking for those."

"Ah," I said, as I stood up from kneeling and walked to her. "We will, of course, return them." I gave her an awkward smile. "Now, show us the way, Lady Lillian."

She gave me a suspicious look. "Why are you two sneaking around, anyway?" I glanced at her and her face blanched, "Oh, I'm so sorry, it's absolutely none of my business."

My brows creased as I eyed her warily in return.

"Our mother isn't fond of Veli," Finn cut in.

"Your mother is rumored to not be fond of any healer," Lillian interrupted. Her cheeks flushed as Finn's eyes flared slightly. "I apologize, Prince. That was not my place."

"No, you are correct. And because of this, we just don't want her knowing where we are going, so we would appreciate it if you kept this between us," Finn added, a tiny threat laced between each word.

"Of course, I won't say a word." Her gaze traveled up and down our figures right before she turned on her feet and moved toward the city without another word. We had no choice but to follow her into the night beyond.

FOUR
Kellan

OF COURSE, ELIANNA WOULDN'T say a fucking word about what the prince and princess were talking about. She just laughed at me in her pitiful state she was in and turned away from my view, giving me a glimpse of her ruined back. I wanted to rip the cell door off its hinges and whip her all over again.

Heir? The heir to *Velyra?* What the fuck did that mean? Was Elianna the rightful queen? She must have been the first-born child to King Jameson. There would be no other explanation. In fact, it explained all my previous questions regarding her. The king favored her above all others. The queen absolutely despised her. Lukas protected and defended her as if she were his own flesh and blood...and he was the only one the king trusted.

Mother of the gods, what a nightmare.

I stormed beyond the castle gates and headed straight to the slums, where I knew my second in command, Vincent, would be.

I walked into one of the taverns beyond the Evergreen Belle, and sure enough, Vin had a female holstered on his lap at the bar. I strode up behind him and grabbed his shoulder.

"Aye, Captain! Didn't think I would see you down here tonight," he said to me right before he licked up the intoxicated female's neck until his tongue met her jaw. She forced out an uncomfortable giggle.

"Put her down, Vin. We have business to discuss."

He stared at me dumbfounded and gestured to her. "You're kidding. Right?"

"No. Put her down. I'll grab a table in the back. If she isn't a whore, she will be here when you return."

He furrowed his brows in response, which only confirmed that she indeed was a whore and would make her way into the next lap within minutes.

"I will be back, love." He sighed as he picked her up and placed her down onto the mud and ale covered floor. She let out an annoyed huff of air and immediately turned on her feet.

I chuckled. "They're a copper-coin a dozen, Vin. Quite literally. We can go across the street to Evergreen after."

"Whatever," he grumbled out, as he followed me to the back of the tavern.

We sat in a booth hidden in the shadows at the back of the room. Once the barmaid handed us each a mug of ale, Vin turned to me. "What's this about?"

"Elianna," I admitted, as I sipped.

He grimaced. "Aren't you done with this bitch yet? I thought you were going to kill her once we got back here."

"Well, she definitely received punishment, but it is nowhere near the end. But change of plans. We will not be killing her."

His smile faltered. "Come again?"

I leaned in close to him, making sure there were no wandering ears and eyes in our vicinity. "She is the *heir*. The true heir of the realm. The firstborn daughter and child of King Jameson Valderre. That is why she was favored so highly. That is why the queen hates her. And *that* is exactly why I need to keep her alive."

Vincent stared at me for a few moments, blinking, right before he burst into tears of laughter. Obnoxiously loud laughter.

"I don't see how any part of that is funny," I said through my teeth.

"Captain, did you just hear yourself?" he continued laughing. "Elianna Solus is the daughter of the late *king?* Are you serious? You believe that?" His laughter finally came to a halt when he saw the unamused look on my face.

"Considering I heard it from the mouths of the prince and princess, yes. I absolutely fucking believe it."

"What?" he gaped, choking into his mug as he sipped.

"Glad I have your attention, you fool. I was down in the dungeons. Went in the back way, you know, through the tunnels, when I heard voices coming from the cells. I hid in the darkness and listened. Avery and Finnian found Elianna. They plan to get a healer to help with her wounds, which I don't really give a shit about. Less nonsense I need to deal with now that I need her alive, but they spoke of how *she* was the heir, or should have been instead of Kai."

He stared at me dumbfounded so I continued. "I need to convince the queen to keep her alive. That way, *I* can marry her. And then we can kill the rotten little shit prince..."

"And take the throne," he finished for me.

A wicked smile curved my lips. "Precisely."

"Excellent plan, Captain!" he boomed.

"I thought so."

"It'll just never fucking work."

I spit my ale back into my mug and swung my head back up at him. "And why is that?" I barked, aggravated by his sudden liquid courage.

"Why would the queen let her live?" he asked.

"I have proven myself and my loyalty to the crown. I will just simply convince her that Elianna having a life with me would be a fate worse than death. Which may actually be the case at this point." I shrugged as I took another gulp. "I'll have her push out a few heirs and then get rid of her, too."

He stared at me knowingly. "Why be The King's Lord, when you can simply just *be* the king?" He chuckled.

"Cheers to that." I grinned as we raised our mugs and toasted to the new future of Velyra.

FIVE

Avery

WE CREPT AROUND THE bustling streets of Isla under the cover of the moonlight. I couldn't help but gawk and stare at everyone and everything that passed us by. I had never seen the city like this—so full, so *alive*. I had never been allowed to.

The sights, scents, and sounds of the city lit my soul from within. I loved it. Fae were everywhere—out having fun, fighting in the streets, bartering, walking with their families. Every corner turned had a unique sight and view of all the things that Isla had to offer.

"Close your mouth, Avery, you don't know what floats in the air down here," Finn joked, as I realized my mouth actually was gaping open at everything my eyes fell upon. I snapped it shut.

"We are almost there. Just around this corner," Lillian said, as we followed through the streets.

As we made our way around the winding bend at the end of the brick road, the view opened up to the docks that sat in the Vayr Sea. The sound of the small waves fading in and out in the distance took over the echoes of the active streets.

"I'm not sure where she lives," Lillian chimed in, breaking my trance. "But I'm sure we can ask around."

"Thank you so much for bringing us here." I grabbed her hand. "We will need to move forward alone now. We very much appreciate this. And your silence."

She blinked at me, looking somewhat confused, and glanced around. "Of course. Just be careful out here...people aren't...the friendliest."

I nodded at her, and she turned from us, making her way back through the busy streets.

I turned to Finn. "What now?"

"You're asking *me* that?! This was your plan!"

"Oh, for the love of the gods. Fine! I will ask around."

"If you didn't know what to do, then why did you send her away?" he snapped in a whisper.

"Something felt off," I admitted.

"Well, dammit, Avery, she was nice enough! She was probably nervous. We did ask her to keep a secret from the *queen*, after all."

I brushed him off and took a step in the direction of the docks. The people down here looked significantly less well off than others only a few streets away. They were filthy—some sitting on the sidewalks with cups held out for coin.

I clasped my hood tightly, trying to hide my identity the best I could, and bent down to an older looking male sitting on the sidewalk, leaning against a building.

"Excuse me, sir? I was hoping you may know where—"

"Coin or get fucked, lady," he barked at me through his numerous rotting teeth.

I jumped back, speechless, as I continued to stare down at him. My hand rose to point at the beggar and reprimand him for speaking to me in such a manner, when Finn grabbed my wrist and pulled me away, dragging me along down the street.

"Are you out of your mind?" he whispered nervously in my ear, as he guided me away from the male.

"Maybe we should circle back and try again in the daylight," I answered, and paused as my thoughts flooded me. "No. No, we can't do that. Lia may not have until daylight."

My gaze followed the street that led out to the sea, observing the few dock hands at work. I took a single step towards the water when another hooded figure *appeared* directly in front of us, freezing us both where we stood. It reached out to grab my hand, and I jerked back in terror at the sight of the slim fingers with violet, talon-like nails that shimmered beneath the moonlight.

I lifted my stare to look into the figure's cloak, when the assailant's other hand pulled the hood back slightly, revealing depthless pupils surrounded by two rings of gold and violet.

Veli.

"Gods, Veli," I uttered.

Her eyes narrowed in on us both as her hand remained clutching my wrist. "What in the realm are you two doing down here? I could smell you a mile away."

That was concerning.

"Um, looking for you." I dragged out each word.

She raised a brow and skimmed our surroundings. "You fools. Come. Come before you get us all killed."

We anxiously followed Veli through the darkened alleyways between Isla's buildings, being careful to step over both the males and females alike who were drunkenly passed out within them. At least I hoped they were passed out.

The alleys reeked of piss and whiskey. I turned to Finn, who looked as mortified as I felt.

"You live down here, Veli?" I asked, but she shushed me in response.

Veli finally came to a halt in the middle of an alleyway when she reached into her cloak and pulled out a key carved from bone. She then waved a hand at the dark bricks and a door materialized, forcing me to blink repeatedly to make sure that I was seeing things correctly and it wasn't just a trick under the moonlight. We watched in awe as she started to roughly jiggle the key in the doorknob. The sound of the lock clicking echoed through the small alley.

"What in the realm?" I whispered.

The small door swung open and Veli ducked down and ran inside. We had no choice but to follow.

Veli's home was very...interesting to say the least. Hundreds of different plant species were potted and spread throughout the shelves, tables, and even hung from the ceiling of her dark, eerie space. Ancient-looking books were scattered on almost every surface and a cauldron was propped up in the far corner of the main living area, with a fire roaring under it.

"Veli, it isn't wise to leave a fire going if you aren't..." Her glare felt as if it was piercing my soul as it bore into me. "Home," I finished on a gulp.

"Little Princess Avery, still never minding her own business," she hissed.

Finnian let out a loud laugh, earning an eye roll from me.

She threw the hood of her floor length cloak back, revealing her silver hair that fell to her waist. Her unusual eyes pierced through the barely lit space. "What are you two doing down here? Especially at this time of night."

"I was being truthful when I said we were looking for you. Where have you been?"

She eyed me carefully. "Your father is dead. There is no need for me at Castle Isla any longer."

The way she spoke of the king's death so casually ignited a flicker of rage within me. "My father considered you a *friend*, Veli. Why do you think he kept you so close all these decades?"

She scoffed. "To keep him alive when your psychotic mother banished most of the healers."

"He trusted you," I said, trying to hide the shakiness in my voice.

"Do not speak of things you know nothing about, young princess," she snapped, as she pointed at me with her long nails. "Now, what can I assist you two with? And if it is just for a walk down memory lane, I will have to ask you to leave."

Finn stepped in front of me. "It's Lia. She needs your help. She needs a healer."

Her eyes went wide. "Elianna?" Finn nodded. "Where is she? What happened?"

"She is greatly injured and currently locked within the castle dungeons. Her wounds have become infected. She will die if they aren't treated."

"The dungeons, you say? Looks like your mother finally made her move against her, since the king is gone," she said without facing us.

"You know?" I asked hesitantly.

She turned then. "Oh, I have known since the day after Elianna was born. And the tragic death of her own mother."

"Did our father tell you?" I asked.

"No, but he didn't have to. When I arrived back at the healing quarters the following morning, the palace reeked of death, but also of life. New life. It was slightly overwhelming. Your father sent me away that night but refused to tell me why. When I finally saw him that next day, I knew what happened. The babe's scent had similar notes to his own, though his was much more masculine and was overpowered by musk. Vanilla—sweet and warm. And then another scent emerged. Gardenias—beautiful, pure, and powerful."

My mouth popped open and my fingers flew to cover it as Veli continued, "Rumors of a missing healer spread later that week." She sighed. "She was my friend, Ophelia. She had always carried a floral scent and had also been pregnant but wouldn't tell anyone who the father was. Said she didn't know." Veli shrugged. "Then it clicked once the queen started removing healers, but I never told your father. I watched over the years how much he loved that little youngling, though. And also how terrible he was at hiding it."

I watched Finnian as he paced around the room during her speech, appearing more anxious after each word she spoke.

Tears swelled in my eyes. How had I never noticed the similarities of Lia's scent to our father's? While each fae was born with their own unique scent, we often acquired notes from our kin.

Finn's wandering came to a halt before one of Veli's many bookshelves. He lifted his hand to touch an interesting-looking skull that had been polished and displayed on one of the black painted shelves.

"Don't touch that!" Veli screeched, and in the blink of an eye, she was *in front* of him, blocking the shelf.

Finnian jumped back with a cry, "Gods!" His breathing became heavy as Veli's lip curled back in a small snarl. "Veli, how the...how the hell did you just do that?!"

"Don't touch my shit," she ordered him, as she stalked back toward the cauldron.

Both of our eyes followed her as she made her way around her small, hidden tenement. "Veli," I whispered, but she ignored me. "Veli, what you just did was impossible. How did you just do that? You were in front of me and then in front of him in less than a second. Fae aren't *that* fast. And then the door! One moment it didn't exist and the next it appeared. I thought it was a trick of the light."

"Ugh," she grumbled, as she rolled her eyes. "You two have always been trouble, you know that?"

I crossed my arms and shot her a knowing look, but Finn still looked as if he wanted to crawl out of his own skin.

"I am not fae," she announced, barely loud enough for me to hear. "Nor am I a healer. Well, in the traditional sense, anyway."

"I don't know what you mean. Are you a halfling? I have seen your ears."

She raised her hand gradually and tucked her silver locks behind the pointed ear I knew she possessed. With a wave of her taloned fingers, her ear transformed—the tip disappearing and now rounded.

Finn let out a loud gasp. "A witch!" he shrieked and aimed for the door, tripping over piles of her books as he raced toward it.

Veli waved her hand once more, this time in his direction, and the door simply *vanished*.

"Oh, my gods!" I said, eyes flaring in awe, as I turned to her. "You really are a witch."

"I prefer sorceress, thank you very much," she said, crossing her arms. "I descended from the Elora Coven."

I blinked at her. "The Elora Coven has been extinct for...centuries, no?"

Veli picked at her very long, violet nails. I noticed now that they matched the bright purple ring on her iris. "Most of us, yes. That is a story for another time that I will probably never tell you." I huffed out an annoyed breath at her in response. "If Elianna's wounds are infected, we need to hurry. Bring me to her," she demanded, as she moved around the room, grabbing a few more vials, and picking leaves from her plants, shoving them into her cloak's pockets.

Veli waved her hand through the air a second time, and the door reappeared in front of Finnian. An audible gulping sound left his throat—neither of us had seen *true* magic wielded before.

He practically ran through the doorway, desperate to get out of Veli's home, and we followed closely behind him.

SIX
Elianna

How long had it been since Avery and Finn came down here and found me? I couldn't keep track anymore. The dungeons were so far underground that I would never see a glimpse of sunlight, probably ever again.

I tried to glance down at the open wound cut across my chest. A puss-like, yellow substance formed from the infection and had spread across my injuries. I tried to adjust my body and winced.

"Fucking perfect," I whispered to myself.

I had turned my ripped shirt around in an attempt to cover my sliced open back more than my front since no one else was down here with me. It was useless, though. The dirt and filth of the cell had already dug its way into my injuries.

The sound of multiple whispers and scurrying footsteps filled the dungeon hall beyond, but I could barely move my body from where I sat, hunched over on the small bench, to see who it was.

"Here she is!" Avery's voice echoed from the cell door. "Oh gods, Lia! Are you awake?"

"Barely," I huffed out. My gaze lifted to the door, and I was surprised to see Veli standing with them. "Evening, Veli."

She scoffed. "What have you done to yourself this time, Elianna?"

Oh, yes. This was clearly something of my doing.

"Just the usual, I guess."

"Hm," she mumbled. "Can you walk?"

"No, she can barely sit up!" Finn cut in.

"If none of you know where the key is, I don't think this will work," I said in a shaking, weak voice that I tried to steady. Every rumble from my vocal cords sent shooting aches through my body as if the small hum affected each slice embedded in my skin.

"Uhhh, I don't think that will be a problem," Avery said cautiously.

My eyes flicked back up to them when, all of a sudden, Veli appeared *inside* the cell.

"Wha—" My screech ended on a harsh cough as I leaned away, despite the pain that ripped through me at the sudden movement. "Veli! How did you..."

"No time for nonsense. Turn around," she ordered, spinning her terrifying nails in the air, motioning in a circle.

Nonsense. As if me questioning how she just somehow jumped through a locked door was anything but a damn good question.

She leaned in close as she started to examine me. I watched her curiously, and then my eyes caught on her own. My jaw popped open as it occurred to me why the eyes of the crone back in Celan Village had looked so eerily familiar.

"You're a witch?" I asked in a hushed tone.

"Sorceress," Avery and Finnian announced in unison from beyond the cell bars.

Veli rolled her eyes at them and then looked up at me. "Are you going to remove your shirt or what? I don't have all night."

I went to raise my arms, but the pain made it unbearable. Veli lifted her hands and placed them gently on my shoulders, being careful to avoid the slash that curved over one and across my chest. "Mother of the gods, what have they done to you..." she said, sounding almost concerned. "Allow me."

She slowly brought down the remnants of my shredded shirt, revealing my ruined flesh as I clutched the front of it to my breasts. Avery's hands flew to her mouth in shock, and Finn promptly averted his gaze as more of my skin was revealed.

"This is going to be uncomfortable," she warned.

I let out a rough laugh in response as if I could be any more "uncomfortable" than I was at this moment.

Veli reached into her pocket and pulled out an odd-looking leaf and a tin of salve.

"Chew this. It will help with the pain." I took the dark, orange-tinted leaf and threw it into my mouth. I was surprised to find it tasted of melons. "It is a sedaeyo leaf, a natural substance for pain relief. The queen burned many of the sedaeyo ferns a few decades ago, but I have been growing small amounts in my home to keep them on hand. I had been sneaking leaves to your father the past few months before his passing."

My eyes widened slightly at her admitting that she knew the king was my father. "Who told you?" I asked as I watched her thickly spread the salve across my chest.

"No one. Your father wore his emotions on his face for the realm to see. I knew your mother. She was a talented healer. It was a sad day when her soul left the realm."

Tears pricked at the back of my eyes. "Thank you. I don't know much about her."

Her violet and gold eyes met mine. "Well, you look just like her. Your eyes, as I'm sure your father has told you. Her hair was slightly darker than yours, but as far as I am concerned, you are practically a replica."

Gods, no wonder why my father constantly brought my birth mother up to me, and why the queen despised me so intensely. I truly was a constant reminder.

"Apparently you smell like her, too," Avery chimed in, causing me to raise a brow.

"Your sister has a big mouth on her, you know that?" Veli groaned.

"Oh, I know." I smiled softly.

"The infection is worse than I thought. Your veins around the wounds have already turned black," she cut in, making my smile drop.

Veli looked around the cell and noticed a few of the dungeon's rats huddled in the corner and made her way to them. She plucked one up from the floor as it screeched.

"What I am about to do...you cannot speak of. Do you understand?" I nodded at her, and she turned around to my red-headed siblings. "That goes for you two big mouths as well."

Avery and Finn straightened under the torchlight.

"After what I have seen tonight, the last thing I ever want to do is anger you, Veli. I won't say shit," Finnian stuttered. Avery quickly nodded in agreement.

"Very well," she said dryly.

She placed one of her hands over my heart and started squeezing the wiggling rat tightly in the other. Suddenly, a faint, violet glow slowly appeared between her fingers and was forced into my skin.

The sensation was indescribable, as if a flame had ignited within my chest—not a flame of fire, but of *ice*. I could feel the intense coolness of her magic work its way through my veins from the center of my chest all the way through each fingertip. The magic caused a bit of discomfort, but nowhere near the pain I had been enduring.

I tore my vision from her hand and nearly threw myself back from the witch as I met her *glowing* eyes. The longer she held on, the louder the creature in her hand screamed. Veli then dropped her hand from my body, and I felt the iciness of her power dwindle away.

I looked down at my chest to see the gashes had completely closed, leaving a bright white scar. "How did you?...What the hell just happened?" I gaped at her and then noticed the rat was now foaming at the mouth in her grasp.

She brought the creature to her face and tsked. "Such a shame," she said as she snapped its neck with her thumb, causing its body to go limp in her hold. "The only way to remove disease and infection is to place it within another living being," she announced to us.

I looked over at the door. Avery, for once, was completely speechless, and Finnian looked like he was about to faint.

"There's nothing I can do about the scars. They will remain with your body," she said, forcing my stare back to her.

"Th-thank you," I said to her, still in shock.

"Why didn't you do that for the king?!" Avery shouted at her back. I closed my eyes tightly and pursed my lips, knowing Veli wouldn't take such a question lightly.

Veli whipped back to them and then was once again beyond the cell door, standing not even a foot from Avery. "It would be wise to not ask such foolish questions, Princess. Do you know the risk I just took for Elianna?" Avery shook her head. "I could not detect what was wrong with your father. It was not an infection, and I tested him for every known poison in our realm. I couldn't find shit. I couldn't even sniff it out. And before you ask yet another idiotic question, yes. Witches' senses are even more powerful than the fae's. I was being truthful when I said I scented you out in the city this evening."

"Why was this a risk? And why would you take it for me?" I asked as I walked up to them, wrapping my bloody shirt once more around myself.

She turned from Avery, looked me up and down multiple times, and then sighed. "I have my reasons. However, the Elora Coven, where I originated, has been dissipated for centuries. Only a few of us remain. I would like to avoid running into my lost sisters. Magic calls to its kin, you know."

I blinked. "I think I saw one," I said to her as I clutched the bars of my prison. "In the village I was hiding in. A human village. She was sputtering some riddle at me, but I noticed her eyes. They were so much like yours...except *different*. Her eyes were crimson ringed instead of violet. But the gold remained."

Veli let out a malicious chuckle. "Let me guess, she didn't look like me? She looked like a—"

"Crone," I cut her off. "Yes, she looked ancient. Like her bones would turn to dust at any moment, but I felt very uneasy being near her."

"That would be because of the dark magic," she answered, surprising me. "It is forbidden. Or was anyway. That is the main reason our coven is...no longer. Dark magic took hold of many—the power is nearly infinite, but it comes at a cost. But make no mistake, while they look of brittle bones, they are some of the most powerful beings in our realm."

"You didn't want such power?" Avery asked, and Veli shot her a look of warning.

Veli twirled a lock of Avery's hair around her nail. "I dabbled. Wasn't for me, I prefer my eternal youth." She grinned.

"Was what you just did for me dark magic?"

Veli wouldn't look back at me. "No. I try not to use my abilities since it only draws other witches to me. Small bits here and there are safe, but anything of substantial power runs the risk. I've kept my life in Isla a secret for centuries now, and I would like to keep it that way. I don't play well with others like me," she hissed, but I could read everything she refused to say.

While she was terrifying, like the witch I had met in the village, Veli had a good heart. She must if she chose to be a healer.

"I appreciate what you did for me."

"Don't mention it," she said, a subtle threat in her tone. "I need to leave before I am seen. Things are not going well out in the streets leading up to Prince Kai's wedding and coronation. Take care, you three," she warned, and then she vanished before I had a chance to blink.

I started giggling, mainly from insanity. "What the hell did you two do?"

Both of them looked concerned. "We went out to the docks. A handmaiden said Veli lived out there and she...found us. Apparently from that insanely talented nose of hers," Avery said.

"You went into the city? At *night?* And to the docks, no less? Gods, you two have no idea how foolish that was."

Finnian huffed out a sharp breath. "Well, it was to save you..."

I flinched. "I'm sorry. Thank you. Both of you, thank you so much." I paused for a moment and then remembered

Kellan. "Shit. Kellan knows!" Their eyes snapped up to mine. "He was hiding in the shadows down the hall when you two were here. You need to leave. He heard *everything*."

"What?!" Avery gasped. She then glanced down the hall in the direction I pointed. "Show yourself, Captain Adler!"

I tried not to laugh at her attempt at authority. "I don't think he's here now, but you need to be careful. He knows you planned to heal me, but the look on his face when he realized I was related to the king was...well I'm worried about what he could be planning. So be careful, okay?"

"Okay," Avery croaked. "It's getting late. We need to sneak back into our chambers, but we will come back as soon as we can!"

I smiled gently at her. "I know. Your safety comes first though, so *be careful*. And give Nyra some belly rubs for me, okay?"

She returned my smile and nodded. They then walked back toward the dungeon's entrance.

SEVEN

Jace

It had been nearly two weeks since I had last seen Lia. Also, since I was forced to watch as she was tied up and tortured by her former love, and then dragged away back to Isla, away from me, as I was left unconscious and mutilated on the ground to die.

My face had finally started to heal a few days ago, but I would bear the scar for the remainder of my existence. I stared at myself in the mirror of my barrack's bedroom in Ellecaster, barely recognizing the man looking back at me. My hair had grown out longer than I ever allowed before, and I had a horrendous gash that began at the inner corner of my left brow bone, across the bridge of my nose, halting right below my right eye. Essentially, my entire gods-damn face.

None of that mattered, though, because the part that I didn't recognize in myself, and the part that *terrified* me the most, was the fact that I was a man in love.

The uncertainty of her safety forced me to sit and stew in the overwhelming need to constantly react and lash out. I didn't care what it took...I would burn down the entire continent in order to get her back if that's what it took.

My feelings for Elianna went beyond love and adoration, and these feelings constantly consumed me. Lia was *everything* to me. The universe could crumble beneath my feet, but if I had her in my arms as the realm fell, I would have all I needed. And I didn't even realize it until it was too fucking late, like a gods-damn fool. Too late to tell her. Too late to *save* her.

Waking up in the cinders of what remained of the village to find that she had been taken from me felt as if the ground had been ripped from under my feet, and I'd been free falling in despair ever since. I would take her back from them. I would take her back from Adler and absolutely fucking destroy him, even if it killed me to do so.

We arrived in Ellecaster only a day after the deadly attack in Celan Village. We brought all survivors with us, and Gage and Zaela had been tasked with rounding up volunteers within Ellecaster to host the families for the foreseeable future—until we were able to bring them beyond the mountains.

As soon as we reached our headquarter city, I demanded that we march our soldiers stationed here to Isla to rescue our queen, but they resisted. They argued that I needed time to recover from the effects of the wyvern's blood. There was not an ounce of me that cared that my body was riddled with throbbing pain—I would endure anything needed if it brought me closer to her. I was their gods-damn commander, and they attempted to coddle me as if I was a child.

Every day that passed without finding her was a day wasted. Every day that she was not here and safe by my side was a day that she would inevitably endure torture at the hands of males she once trusted. At the hands of a male she once *loved*.

Bile burned the back of my throat at the thought of Kellan's vile hands upon Lia's body. A body he thought he *owned*, as if she was a possession instead of the absolute goddess of a being that she was.

My hands curled into fists at these thoughts that had constantly plagued my mind, day in and day out. I picked up my glass of whiskey that was on the bureau and whipped it at the wall as I roared in anguish and fury. The glass shattered into tiny pieces that fell to the floor.

A light knock sounded at my bedroom door within the barracks. It was the only home I had aside from where I grew up in Alaia Valley—my mother's small cottage that sat at the edge of her brother's estate. Since I had been appointed commander, my days were consumed by the responsibilities of leading my soldiers, leaving little time for having the comforts of a home. It only made sense that I would bunk with them during my stay in the city.

"Come in," I announced as I cleared my throat.

The door creaked open slowly, and I looked up through the mirror to see a pair of the same hazel eyes that I beheld staring back at me.

"Hi," Zaela greeted me as she glanced around the room. Her eyes widened at the sight of the glass pieces scattered on the floor. "How are you feeling?"

Since we had made it back to the city, while my face had been healing, the rest of my body felt as if it had been overcome with pain, rotting from the inside out. I could only assume it was a side effect of surviving the wyvern's blood. I felt weak and useless, but I continued to press on. I had to. For Lia.

"Fine," I said through my teeth.

She flinched slightly in response. No matter how hard I tried not to blame her for Lia being taken, it felt impossible. She was always at her throat, no matter how hard Lia tried to help or convince her that she was on our side. Zaela always pushed back in that nasty way she was just *so* good at.

In an act of selflessness, Lia attempted to rescue Zaela by sacrificing herself, allowing my cousin to flee unscathed. Zae didn't deserve that kindness from her, and she knew it.

"You're starting to look better." She gave me a half smile as I continued to watch her in the mirror. "We have news."

My attention immediately shifted towards her, my breaths picking up nervously. "And?"

"It isn't about Elianna." My heart stopped painfully in my chest at the sound of her name. "Unfortunately, our sympathizers haven't seen her. However, we have news regarding the coronation and the prince's wedding. It is apparently the event of the century and was announced to the realm just days ago. Everyone will be there. And I mean *everyone*."

I made my way to the bed and sat down, placing my head in my hands. "When is it?"

"In two days' time."

My eyes snapped back at her, and she grinned. "Are you thinking what I am?"

The corner of my lips curled up. "We won't be able to make it there in time, not by a long shot. Do they have enough within Isla?"

"They do indeed believe that it is possible."

I stood from the bed and walked to my small window that showed the view of all of Ellecaster. The towering, ancient buildings of stone and the cobblestone streets were now bustling with more people than usual, with the villagers amongst them.

"Send the fastest falcon we have," I ordered.

I turned and moved towards my nightstand, where the broken shards of Lia's dagger lay scattered. With a gentle touch, I traced my fingers over the hilt, swearing I could feel her through it.

"Tell them to do whatever is necessary, and if Lia is seen, she is *not* to be harmed." A feral grin crept up my face.

After calling an emergency meeting, I stood before my few hundred soldiers stationed in Ellecaster as we all gathered together in the training fields beyond the city's gates.

"Is this everyone?" I asked Gage quietly as he stood at attention by my side.

"Everyone in the barracks knew to be here," he answered sternly.

Our entire family's dynamic had been flipped upside down. My rage toward the fae had morphed into an uncontrollable force burning within me, but now it was directed at those who had caused harm to my Lia.

Zaela, always so harsh and abrupt with her confrontations and actions, had become someone who tiptoed around her own words toward me.

Gage had also grown colder in recent days. In private, he maintained his joking and carefree demeanor, but had transformed into a determined warrior of vengeance. He trained relentlessly day and night, preparing our army for the inevitable while I had been confined to my barracks until now.

Lia wasn't just taken from me—she was taken from all of us.

I stared out at the masses before me as I worked to reel in my irritation. Gage had cautioned me that most of the younger soldiers stationed here were far from ready to ride into battle, and the more I stared out at their faces beneath the light of the setting sun, the more apparent that became. Forcing them to march on Isla in the state they were in now would only doom them to slaughter, and I would need to resolve that as soon as possible if we stood a chance at getting her back.

"Soldiers!" I boomed into the sky. "Something has been taken from me. From all of us. And that is the future of a better, safer realm." I paused as all their gazes fixated on me. "In an unexpected turn of events, we have formed a powerful alliance with a mortal sympathizer who not only has a true claim to the throne, but has also become incredibly important to me. And she has now been captured by the enemy. She is the former captain of their army, Elianna Solus. And unknown to the realm, she should bear her true name of Valderre."

My jaw clenched painfully as their eyes widened, and I wasn't sure if it was because she was the heir, captured, or at my admittance of what she meant.

Murmurs erupted throughout the lines.

"Silence!" Gage bellowed as he stepped out from my opposite side. Their whispers ceased instantly.

Although I was ready to storm Isla and retrieve her with our troops, it was evident that our armada here was not.

A growl rumbled through me in aggravation. I would storm the realm's capital with just Gage and Zae if I had to, but their stance on my well-being went unchanged. I knew that if I were foolish enough to venture alone to the Islan gates in a rescue attempt, my life would be forfeited. But more importantly, I couldn't bear to think of what would become of Lia if I met my fate before she was safe.

"In order to ensure our readiness for war, we require further training in battle strategy for those who appear unprepared. In the meantime, I want scouts posted with a falcon between here and the Sylis Forest. If you see anyone that isn't human, you send word immediately. If they are individuals, capture them after the letter is sent. If it is a group, or gods fucking forbid an army, do not engage. Send your falcon that very moment so we can properly prepare and leave the city before they make their way to us. I will *not* risk the civilians. Am I understood?"

"Yes, Commander," they boomed in unison.

"Nothing remains of Celan Village but rubble and ash, and we will do everything in our power to ensure history does not repeat itself if the fae march on Ellecaster."

I looked to each of my sides and glanced quickly at both Gage and Zaela, who each kept their faces firm and focused.

"Us mortals have never had any sort of royalty in Velyra, and while I command our armies and preach our customs and laws to the best of my ability, I have found a possible future for our race to be protected under the crown. It will not come easy. The battles and journey ahead will be equally exhausting as they will be daunting. The blood to be spilled will serve as a testament to the lengths that we are willing to go for our people's future. Our children's future."

The sky had darkened as the sun completely set beyond the fields of wildflowers in the distance.

"Be well, brave, and safe. You're all dismissed."

EIGHT
Kellan

A DAY HAD PASSED since I learned of Elianna's true lineage, and as the prince's coronation rapidly approached, the anticipation of making my move to strike plagued me.

Tonight would have to be the night I convinced the Queen and her son to give Elianna's life to me. It would be easy to persuade them to believe that a lifetime with me would be far more torturous than having her life simply end. Lia was probably begging for that by now, anyway.

After relieving the guard of his post last night, I watched from afar in the courtyard as the prince and princess snuck out of the dungeons for the second time that day. I could only assume that they had healed her somehow. Luckily, it was one less thing that I had to deal with now that I needed her alive.

It was all too gods-damn easy.

Now, with Elianna and Lukas locked up and controlled, I could slither my way in deeper with the crown right before I ripped it from the top of their fucking heads.

I swaggered my way into the throne room to see only Callius had arrived for the meeting so far and stood at the bottom of the dais.

"Callius, where is Her Majesty?" I asked as I wandered over to him.

He raised a brow at me. "What is the means of this, Kellan? You should know that the queen is under no obligation to be on time to meet with you when she isn't even aware of what this meeting is about."

I tried to hide my irritation. "Yes, well, I have a proposition for her that I believe she will be thrilled to hear."

"We'll see about that. It appears that you are...up to something," he grumbled as the door behind the dais opened wide, with Queen Idina standing in its archway, looking unimpressed.

I ignored Callius as I bowed before her while she sat upon the throne. "Good evening, Your Majesty. You're looking lovely as ever."

She rolled her eyes. "Flattery will do you no good here, Captain. Now, how can I help you? I have been told you have a proposition for me."

My eyes darted quickly around the room. "I do, My Queen, however where is Prince Kai? I thought he would be present as well."

She eyed me warily. "Is this a proposition for me or for the future king?"

"You, My Queen. I apologize if I, at any point, made you assume otherwise."

Clearly, this bitch was in a mood. Fantastic.

She waved a dismissive hand at me. "Go on."

I gave her a half smile and took a single step toward the dais. "My proposition is to barter for the life of the former captain, Elianna Solus."

She leaned down toward me, an intense fire lit beneath her stare that I had never seen before. Not even in the direction of Elianna. "Excuse me?" she spat.

Callius suddenly looked extremely interested in the design that bordered the tiled floor.

I cleared my throat. "Elianna Solus. I wish for her to remain alive and in my grasp. She is my *claimed*, for me to do with as I please. I know you despise her...let me dole out her much-needed punishment." The queen looked as if she wanted to roast my head on a spike. "Think about how miserable of a life she would lead being chained to me. Forced nightly to be with the one she despises most in this realm. An eternity of misery awaits her if you allow her to live."

I gave her my most convincing smile.

Her eyes flicked back and forth between me and Callius and she looked as if she was deep in thought when she opened her mouth and said, "No."

My smile dropped instantly. "I'm sorry, My Queen?"

"You heard me." She straightened on her throne. "No. Elianna will remain in royal custody until her public execution in the city square, the day following Kai's ascension of the throne." She looked past me as if she could imagine seeing through the walls and right at Elianna herself, locked beneath the castle. "I want her to watch."

She began chuckling at her own comment and Callius followed her lead.

I was about to lose my shit.

"Pardon me, Your Majesty, but why?"

"Why?" she shouted at me, forcing me to take an involuntary step back. "Because she is a mortal sympathizer, Captain." She twisted her head to the side in the most predatory move I had ever seen from her. "She was of the highest rank within our guard and committed treason. You believe she should live?"

"I just thought that..."

"Well, Captain," she cut me off. "We do not pay you to *think*. And yes, while the thought of Elianna being your slave for the remainder of her miserable existence is tempting, I am declining your proposition. The answer is no. She will be put to death for her crimes."

The queen knew what she was doing. As long as Elianna was alive, her son's ascension would be threatened. This had nothing to do with her not wanting to be tortured by me. She just needed the bitch to disappear, and she had the perfect excuse to make it happen.

The queen stood from the dais and Callius walked up the few steps to take her hand and escorted her down the stone steps.

"Have I made myself clear?" she asked as they waltzed past me.

"Crystal," I answered, as I forced a grin on my face while my teeth clenched. The hand behind my back twisted into a fist.

"Excellent. I will see you at the wedding tomorrow," she called back to me as Callius walked her out of the throne room.

I stormed through the city streets with a bottle of whiskey in my hand. I took a swig of the amber liquid with each step and reveled in the burn it brought to my chest.

No? She said fucking *no?* I needed to kill something. Preferably her little shit son, but I couldn't do that. Not yet, anyway. We had a long way to go before we were even close to that. I didn't give a damn if he ascended the throne. It would be *mine*.

I searched for Vincent as I stalked down the tavern lined street when I came across a familiar view. A favorite of mine—The Evergreen Belle.

As I stumbled up the steps, a thought occurred to me. I threw the heavy door to the establishment open, and it slammed into the wall on the other side, startling Lorelai where she stood behind her desk.

"Kellan! What in the gods' names are you doing coming in here like that?!" she barked at me.

Once inside, I dropped the half empty bottle of whiskey. The glass exploded once it hit the floor, making her flinch. I reached for the door behind me without letting my eyes leave hers and slammed it shut, encasing the room back into its usual darkness.

"I don't have any females available for you right now, and if you are going to come in here and be a sloppy mess, I will need to ask you to leave," she said, her voice shaking at the end of her warning.

My eyes continued to bore into hers as I slowly took a step toward her, and then another. Before I knew it, I was behind her desk with her. She backed into the wall behind her in fear, trapping herself as I lingered over her. My face was now but inches from her own when I placed each hand on either side of her face.

"I need a favor," I breathed into her ear. A shiver went through her body. The scent of her arousal enveloped me. I also scented a hint of fear.

"Y-yes," she stuttered out.

I buried my face in her neck and then my tongue licked leisurely from her collarbone, all the way up her neck, and then took her sensitive earlobe between my teeth.

She let out a loud gasp at the contact.

"Do you have any more of these pretty little dresses lying around?"

She quickly nodded. "I have many, for myself and the girls," she said through heavy, anticipating breaths.

I lifted my head and smirked at her. "Good, because I'm about to rip this one to shreds," I said, as I lifted her up by her thighs and forced her back against the wall once more. Nervous giggles left her throat as I forcefully claimed her mouth with my own and she responded by spreading her long, lean legs wide for me, locking her ankles around my waist.

I fucked her senseless right in the middle of her brothel's lobby until the sun rose the following morning. And while Lorelai watched me move in her with eyes full of wicked desire, the only thing rummaging through my mind was that I would have Lia *and* her throne if it was the last thing I ever fucking did.

Nine

Elianna

I woke up at only the gods knew what time and found Kellan staring at me through the rusted cell doors.

"Good morning, Princess. You're looking lovely...and *healed*." His knowing grin was ear to ear.

"It's a little early for you to be here to torment me, no?" I rolled my eyes at him as I sat up from the dirt floor.

He eyed me and rubbed his beard. "Change of plans there, love," he said as he unlocked my cage and stepped inside, causing my spine to straighten. "We have business to attend to." He gave me a cold, bone chilling smile.

"What are you talking about?" I snapped.

He chuckled. "Always so difficult. And here I thought you would be excited to leave the dungeons." He crossed his arms.

I wasn't stupid enough to believe that there wasn't a catch to this, but any chance I had of escaping could lie in this moment of being let out of the cell.

"What are you up to?" I asked warily.

"The queen is allowing you to be released as a prisoner, so long as I take you as my wife."

My heart raced in my chest. That would be a fate worse than death. I forced my face to remain calm.

"Hmm, no thank you."

"Pardon me?" he said through his teeth.

"I decline your lovely offer," I said as I brought myself to my feet.

He was in front of me in an instant and grabbed me by the throat, expertly blocking any form of air.

"I think you misunderstood me, princess," he whispered in my ear as he choked me, making my eyes bulge at the sudden loss of breath. "You don't have a choice in this matter."

He released me and I let out an involuntary gasp, my lungs taking in as much air as possible as I coughed uncontrollably.

"What the fuck is going on?!" I spat. "The queen would *never* let me live. She has been waiting for an opportunity to kill me since the day I was born."

Kellan looked me up and down numerous times. "You will marry me this evening." An unspoken threat lay in his words.

"I will do no such thing. I would sooner take a blade to my own throat before I *ever* considered being your wife. Never again. Ever."

Kellan's stare darkened. "There was once a time when you loved me, sweet Lia." He lunged at me once more, aiming to grab my wrist, but I dodged his grasp.

My lips curled back into a snarl and I met his gaze defiantly, as I was flooded with memories of false love.

"I will never understand how I was so blind to your true nature, Kellan, but I assure you, I will *never* make that mistake again. You expertly manipulated me into not only a relationship with you, but to trust you with thinking you had my best interest at heart. That was never the case. Lukas had always been right, and I was an idiot to not listen. He tried to convince me of your true nature for *years*, but I had naively chosen blind ignorance."

He stood over me, the heat of his breath on my nose. "You will do as I say, you stupid bitch!" he boomed in my face; tension written all over his own. "Now come, come, Princess. We don't have all day," he said through his teeth.

My stare narrowed with suspicion as I observed him, my gut instinct warning me that there was something he wasn't telling me about his eagerness to rush me out of the dungeons.

"Oh, my gods," I whispered as my eyes darted back and forth between his. "You didn't get permission for this at all." His lips contorted into a scowl. "What are you trying to do? Marry me and somehow think we would take the throne and you would be king?" I asked jokingly, the last word ending in a small, hateful laugh.

He took a step back from me, and his jaw ticked.

"Mother of the gods. I'm right, aren't I?" I let out a loud chuckle. "You're a fool, Kellan."

"Don't you want to be queen, love?" he asked, his tone morphing to that persuasive way I used to fall for so easily.

"If I am to become queen one day, you are the *last* male that would be my king," I said with a challenge.

He grinned. "And you think your human would have been a great king?"

Any hint of amusement on my face dropped at his mention of Jace. "Do not speak of him," I growled as my lips curled back, exposing my canines.

"Whatever," he spat. "The new plan is to expose who you are at Kai's ascension and kill the little prick while we are at it. The queen too. It won't be difficult to prove her treasonous acts to the realm."

"I am *not* marrying you!" I screeched.

He took a step toward me once more and I matched him by taking a step back, keeping our distance the same.

"I have made many mistakes, Lia."

"Cut the bullshit. I can see what you're doing. It's never going to happen. Your plan will never work. You are acting like a desperate fool."

He got in my face. "My plan *will* work, and you *will* cooperate. Your precious siblings' and Lukas' lives depend on it."

My eyes widened with horror, and his lips slowly twitched up into a grin. My breathing quickened as panic took over me. "Don't you *fucking* touch them," I seethed.

He gave me a fake, gentle smile. "Then it looks like our wedding will be following Kai's this evening."

I followed Kellan back through the dungeons and as we approached the stairs of the exit, a cough echoed from within one of the darkened cells.

Was someone else down here aside from me?

I peered through the bars of the cell door the sound came from and couldn't believe what I saw. Lukas was unconscious on the floor.

"Lukas!" I screeched as I dove toward his cell.

Kellan wrapped one of his arms around my waist, catching me as I was practically midair, and ripped my body back into his.

"He can't hear you, Princess," he said casually.

"What have you done to him?!" I cried.

"He's just taking another little nap. He is a big fan of those recently," Kellan said with a laugh. "We just moved his body into this first cell this morning. Couldn't have you two be too close to each other, after all. Plotting and exchanging secrets."

They were drugging Lukas. Just as they had drugged me on the journey back to Isla.

"I hate you," I whispered as my head sagged between my shoulders.

"I know, love. I know," Kellan admitted as he dragged me up the steps by my chained wrists.

I expected the courtyard to be crawling with guards, but there wasn't a single person in sight.

"Where is everyone?" I asked as my head whipped back and forth in all directions, desperately searching for someone, *anyone,* who could help me.

"Well, I'm in charge now that Lukas is imprisoned." He eyed me. "I relieved them of their stations for the hour. They were given orders to report back midday."

This monster thought of everything. The one who threw me in the dungeons originally was now the one helping me escape. It left an uneasy feeling in my gut, as if I would be better off back down there, rotting in the cell, than in the hands of this evil male.

Right beyond the courtyard gates, there was a standard city carriage waiting for us, and I saw his goon, Vincent, at the head of it.

"Where are you taking me?"

"Well, you need to look appropriate for Kai's wedding, otherwise you will stick out immediately, and we can't have that."

"Wait." I stopped in my tracks, and he rolled his eyes. "You're taking me to Kai's wedding? How is that a good idea?"

He grabbed the chains linking my hands once more and aggressively guided me into the carriage, practically throwing me in before he crawled in after me and slammed the door shut.

Kellan tapped the front of the carriage twice, and I could hear Vincent as he directed the horse to pull us to our destination, wherever that may be.

"It *isn't* a great idea, but the queen ordered for your public execution to be held in two days, and this is the only time to sneak you out unseen. She plans to announce your treason to the realm this evening to those that are in attendance at the wedding, and then Kai's ascension will be tomorrow."

My eyes widened slightly, my hand instinctively reaching to touch my neck at the mention of my execution being ordered.

He pointed his finger in my face as he flashed his teeth. "I am expected to be at the wedding. Half of the gods-damn city is. As you're aware, everyone, aside from the family, is to wear a mask at a royal wedding, so all eyes are to remain on the prince and his chosen wife. You will wait in the back of the crowd and remain unseen. Do not draw attention. I will be required to be in the front, but Vincent will be with you to make sure you don't do anything stupid."

I tried to hide my grin at what he had just revealed. Vincent was as good as dead as far as I was concerned. This would be the perfect opportunity to make my escape.

"Do you understand me?!" he snapped, his sea-blue eyes nearly bulging out of his head as the vein in his neck throbbed.

"Perfectly," I answered.

TEN
Elianna

THE REMAINDER OF THE carriage ride was silent as we were brought through the city, and when the horse finally came to a stop, I jumped up on instinct.

"Easy," Kellan said, holding his hand out so I couldn't take another step. He poked his head out from the door and looked around before he faced me once more. "Coast is clear. Let's move fast," he said as he unlocked the cuffs on my wrists, surprising me.

"Where are we?" I asked. When the door opened fully, the front entrance of The Evergreen Belle appeared before me. "You're fucking joking," I grumbled.

He pointed in my face once more. "No. Funny. Business. Or the cuffs go back on. Got it?"

I stuck my tongue out at him as I flipped him my middle finger in response, earning an eye roll from him. "Fucking females," he huffed, as he jumped out of the carriage.

I followed him up the steps and was surprised to find the lobby completely empty as we entered. I turned back around quickly to see Vincent pull the carriage away from the establishment, right before Kellan shut the door behind us, encasing us in the moody darkness that was The Evergreen Belle.

"Lorelai!" he shouted, his deep voice bouncing off the walls.

"Up the stairs, to the left!" she called from a distance.

Kellan put his hand on my lower back and forced me forward. It took everything in me to not strike him, but if I had any chance of escaping, I needed to play along for the time being.

As we walked up the steps, I stopped short at the sight of a large, beautiful room that was surprisingly brighter than the rest of the otherwise ominous place. Lorelai had multiple rows of colorful gowns displayed and hung throughout the space, along with a large vanity in the center of the room. This must've been where her...*workers* got ready.

"Hello Elianna," she greeted me with a fake smile.

I gave her a quick nod. "Lorelai."

Kellan kicked the room's door shut and made his way to a chair across the room.

"You're having me get ready for the prince's wedding in a brothel?" I eyed him, my tone full of annoyance.

"Finest brothel in Isla," Lorelai chimed in as she stalked over to me. She picked up a single lock of hair that rested on my shoulder. "Gods, Elianna, when was the last time you *bathed?*" She turned her nose up.

"She has been...occupied," Kellan cut in. "And once again, I paid you triple to make sure no one knows that we're here. You will do well to remember that, Lorelai," he threatened.

She threw her hands up mockingly at him. "Of course, Captain. Can't have my reputation for silence tainted."

Lorelai must've had no idea that I was technically a prisoner of the crown then since she was shocked at the state I was in. Interesting.

"The tub is in the next room. Please...scrub. I don't want your filth to destroy one of my gowns."

I rolled my eyes at her and leisurely walked over to the bathing area that was attached to the room we were in. She had nearly as many soaps and scent options as Avery did in her personal chambers.

I lowered my body into the scolding hot water, groaning at how amazing it felt on my filthy skin. I scrubbed my body and hair for what seemed like an hour; it felt so good to be clean and finally bathe. When I stepped out of her porcelain tub, I looked down at the water to see it was nearly black from all the dirt and gods knew what else I had scrubbed off of myself.

I wrapped my body in a towel and made my way back to the main room to find Lorelai in Kellan's lap, straddling him with her tongue down his throat, her back to me.

Kellan made eye contact with me and broke their kiss to give me a smirk. When Lorelai turned around, her smile dropped, but she twisted in his grasp, maneuvering her leg back over his thighs as she remained seated atop him.

"Apologies, Elianna." She smiled as her back pressed into his chest, thinking this would get a rise out of me. "I was not aware that you were into sharing your males. After your last visit here, I assumed it was off limits. Next time, we will wait for you."

I snorted at her, and Kellan's smirk faltered. "You can have him," I said, as I stalked over to the multiple dresses on display.

She cleared her throat as she approached me. "You may choose from these. Hopefully, they..." She looked me up and down. "Fit." She dragged out the word.

I scoffed at her slightly as I rolled my eyes. "It's always a pleasure seeing you, Lorelai."

She could definitely sense the sarcasm in my tone.

I picked up an emerald dress and observed the plunging neckline, that was far more revealing than anything I had ever dared to wear before. My gaze then moved to the intricate gold lacing that was stitched throughout the gown's corset.

I sighed. "This one will do."

"Excellent choice," she said, as she guided me over to her vanity. "The green will make your eyes pop. Now sit," she ordered, as she forced my shoulders down so I would fall into the vanity's chair. "I have...a lot of work to do."

Lorelai fussed with my appearance for hours while Kellan got ready for the evening himself at the opposite end of the room. However, I constantly felt the weight of his stare, as if he was just waiting for me to beg Lorelai to help me escape, but I knew the female was not loyal to her own. The madam was just as ruthless as any male, and her loyalty was to the highest bidder.

She had decided to curl my hair and pin back the top half to reveal the supposed "masterpiece" she performed on my face.

"Take a look," she said to me, as she turned my chair back to the enormous vanity mirror.

I opened my eyes and barely recognized myself. My eyes were thickly lined with kohl, and a light rouge was dusted along my cheekbones and lips. The curls in my hair fell down to my lower back and the front of it had been twisted up intricately and pinned back. She was also right about the dress—my eyes seemed to illuminate, even in the dim light of the room now that the sun was setting.

"You look like a—"

"A queen," Kellan cut her off as he buttoned his jacket, a wicked grin tipping his lips.

"Captain Adler, it is not right to say such things," she hissed, her tone teetering on the line of jealousy.

"Let's just get this over with," I grumbled as I stood from the chair and glided over to the door, the gown flowing around me.

The feeling of it was awkward. I could probably count on one hand how many times I had been required to wear a dress, never mind a full-fledged gown. I felt out of place, like an imposter, to be dressed so extravagantly.

"Perfection, as always, Lady Lorelai," Kellan praised her, as he pressed a soft kiss to the top of her hand, making her cheeks flush.

I was going to vomit.

She let out a quiet giggle in response and escorted us both down the stairs and out the front door of her establishment, where Vincent was already waiting for us with the carriage.

I stepped up into the cabin and nearly tripped over the front of the gown in the process. Kellan caught me and guided me through the door, lifting the dress in the back for me.

As I sat on the cushioned bench, the sound of a whip cracked through the air, causing me to involuntarily flinch, but Kellan didn't seem to notice. My mind instantly raced back to that first day in the dungeons.

As I sat frozen in fear, I realized the whip wasn't intended for me, but for the carriage's horse, as the beast took off into a gallop down the city streets and aimed for the castle.

Avery

My breath caught as my assigned handmaiden tightened the corset of my gown, while I had been mindlessly staring out the window of my bedchamber. My gaze wandered down to the curls in my hair that cascaded down to my waist. The fiery hues burned under the light of the setting sun as it beamed through the opened curtains.

"I apologize, Princess," she said as she moved to loosen the section she just pulled tight.

"It is quite alright, thank you for assisting me this evening," I answered.

She let out a soft hum in response and continued lacing me into the gown.

A few moments of silence passed as a knock sounded at the door. Before I had a chance to respond, the door creaked open, forcing my gaze to snap in its direction.

I was horrified to see the queen standing beneath the arch of the doorway. She stood there with her hair braided and pinned up, a crown sitting atop it, wearing a gown of a deep crimson hue.

"Mother!" I gasped. "Should you not be with Kai as he gets ready for his wedding?"

She clasped her hands in front of her as she took a step into the room. Her eyes moved to the handmaiden. "You are dismissed."

"But she's not yet finished," I interjected.

My mother held up a hand, silencing me. "I believe I am capable of assisting my own daughter as she readies herself for a royal wedding."

My eyes flared in response to her words—she never cared to spend time with me before, so why does she wish to be present now?

The queen's gaze moved back to the handmaiden, who remained at my side. "Do not make me repeat myself."

The poor girl fled from the room instantly, rushing past my mother as if her life depended on it. The door clicked shut behind her, and the air in the room thickened.

My eyes quickly glanced at my dresser drawer that contained my father's secret journal, and I worked to steady my breathing as she moved to approach me.

The queen came to a halt before me and spun me back towards facing the window. I had to fight back the lump in my throat, feeling a mix of anxiety and rage, as I confronted the harsh truth of what my own flesh and blood had inflicted upon those she considered inferior.

The feeling of her touch on my lower back sent a shiver down my spine as she worked to finish lacing the back of my dress.

"Do not slouch, Avery," she reprimanded, tightening the laces with such force that it left me breathless.

She moved to step around me once finished, standing only a mere foot in front of me. I lifted my gaze to meet hers, feeling the chill of her icy hand against my cheek as she cupped it while inspecting my appearance.

"You have been distant these last few weeks, my daughter. Finnian as well. Why is that?"

I blinked, shocked she had even noticed. "We did not want to inconvenience you during Kai's wedding preparations." The lie slipped through my teeth surprisingly easily.

"You are all my children, and I wish for us all to be closer—a more united front," she stated as her hand dropped back to her side. "The distance began long before any announcement of a wedding. It is due to your father's death, is it not? After all, he was your favorite parent." She gave me a knowing, wicked grin.

Anger flooded me as I sucked on my tongue while our stares bore into each other. Desperately trying to keep my face neutral, I opened my mouth to speak. "It has been difficult without Father here, yes. Although I do apologize if I have made you feel as though I favored one of you over the other."

She gave me a tight-lipped smile that did not meet her eyes. "My Avery, do not speak lies to my face. You are my daughter, and you are like me in more ways than one."

I clenched my teeth at her words. I was *nothing* like her, but she was unaware that I knew of her hidden, murderous secrets.

"And what do you know of me, Mother? To think we are so alike."

Her eyes darkened slightly. "I understand that love is what you desire, and an arranged marriage would be suffocating for you." She raised a single brow, and I remembered that her marriage to my father had been arranged before her birth.

"You speak of this, yet still plan to auction me off to the highest bidder."

A genuine smile cracked through her lips, but it was not warm, nor welcoming. It was bone chilling.

"Your tongue is as sharp as mine, too. I know you do not understand this now, for you are still considered young, but one day you will understand the need for marriage alliances. Just as all daughters born to royalty and lords come to learn."

I tore my gaze away from her, but she caught my chin between her fingers and brought it back.

"The love I have for my three children has always been equal, as you are each of my blood. You and Finnian will always be just as important to me as Kai. However, with him being the heir, his ascension takes precedence over all else."

Her words washed over me, and I responded with a gentle smile, realizing that she was trying to convince herself of her claim more than persuade me to believe it.

She released my chin and turned on her heel, moving towards the chamber door. Her hand reached for the doorknob, and she peered over her shoulder, looking back at me. "I will see you at the wedding, my daughter."

And without another word, her steps continued into the hall. The click of the door echoed through my bedchamber, and for the first time in my existence, I was left speechless.

ELEVEN

Elianna

THE CLATTER OF HOOVES filled the air until our carriage ground to a halt amid the parade of Lords and Ladies, all traveling through the city for the soon to be king's wedding.

Kellan stared at me from across our confined space.

"What?" I hissed, as I crossed my arms in annoyance.

"You look beautiful, Elianna."

I threw my head back and rolled my eyes. "You're insufferable."

He chuckled. "Remember our deal. You behave yourself and Avery, Finnian, and Lukas will live to see another day."

"Define behave myself," I said in a flat tone, as I lifted my fingers toward my face to inspect my nails, my attempt to appear bored.

He instantly jumped across the carriage and was nearly straddling me on the bench. One hand at my throat as the other gripped my face tightly, squeezing my cheeks firmly with his rough, calloused fingers. I refused to show him an ounce of fear, although I'm sure the sound of my heartbeat gave it away.

"You know *exactly* what behaving yourself means. Stay hidden and unseen in the back. Do not draw attention and do *not* try to escape at the wedding. You're going to be a good little girl for Vincent while I uphold my duties for the event. Have I made myself clear?" he said through his teeth.

"Yes, now *get off* of me," I choked out.

His hold on my cheeks didn't loosen as his stare bore into my own. Without warning, he then firmly pressed his lips onto mine. My body squirmed beneath his, desperately trying to get out of his grasp and remove his mouth from my own. He tried to slip his wretched tongue past my lips, and I took the opportunity to bite down hard on his bottom lip. The shock of it was strong enough to make him release my face and stumble back onto the bench across from me.

I could taste his blood on my lips, and he watched me as I licked it off, chest heaving as we refused to break each other's stare. Out of the corner of my vision, I noticed even more blood from the bite dribble down his chin. Good.

He wiped his mouth with the back of his hand and snickered. "You should know by now that something like that would only turn me on."

I bared my teeth once again when the carriage door flew open, revealing that we had arrived at the courtyard gates instead of the main entrance to the castle.

Kellan glanced back at me. "It's showtime, Princess. To avoid the guards at the door checking names, we will be sneaking in through the back. I also need to maintain the facade of having been here for the preparations." He reached into his jacket pocket and revealed a golden mask made of lace, handing it to me.

I pulled it on and secured it to my face, covering the majority of the top half, further concealing my identity.

He reached over and tucked a strand of hair behind my ear that had fallen loose from its pin during his tantrum. He then clutched my wrist tightly as he led me from the carriage and into the empty courtyard beyond.

Once inside the castle, Kellan took the main halls to get to the throne room, where the wedding would be held.

Vincent escorted me the long way through the castle, so we would appear by the throne room doors and mix in directly with the enormous, masked crowd.

Lords and Ladies from all over Velyra were still arriving when we appeared, effortlessly blending in with the bunch. I kept my head down as promised while we were all herded into the room for the ceremony by the guards.

I glanced from side to side, looking for any potential escape route if the opportunity were to present itself. Even if I were able to sneak away, Vincent wouldn't be able to make a scene without alerting the other guards, which would, in turn, expose both him and Kellan. As he continued to escort me, his grip on my arm tightened, almost as if he could sense the path my thoughts were taking.

The room looked extravagant. Chandeliers above were beaming with light, reflecting off of all the diamonds and crystals that were brought out for the occasion. Freshly picked flowers from the garden decorated every aisle and corner of the enormous space, filling my nose with their floral scents. The floors were so spotless that I could see my own reflection on the marbled tiles, and banners were hung, lining the walls of the throne room with the Valderre family crest—a large, centered "V" adorned with the antlers of a black stag, and a crown.

Each Valderre ruler chose their own crest, and my father honored his own by incorporating the great black stag that he kept mounted in his bedchamber.

My heart ached thinking of my father. If only he could see what had already become of his kingdom and family before Kai was even officially crowned.

There must have been at least a thousand chairs in the throne room alone. Many people attending wouldn't even be able to see the ceremony itself. Citizens had already been lining the streets beyond the gates to get even a tiny glimpse of the event.

"Lia." I jumped at the whisper of my name. I turned to see it was Vincent. "We will sit here." He gestured to two of the seats at the very end of the last row.

I pursed my lips and stalked past him to take my seat. "You may not call me that. My name is Elianna, and you will address me as such."

He chuckled as he sat down next to me. "How about another whip to the back for being such a feisty little thing?"

My eyes widened slightly at the threat. Bile rose in my throat at the thought of enduring that once more, but I refused to meet his stare as I continued to look straight up at the dais.

Kellan stood at attention on the side as Callius escorted the Queen to her throne. My eyes wandered over to the right, where I could see Avery and Finnian set off to the side, awaiting the bride and groom to appear.

Relief flooded me at the sight of them, realizing that they hadn't been caught after fleeing the dungeons. Finn looked dapper per usual in his suit, while Avery wore an intricate gown of royal blue, the bodice glistening in the light with what I could only assume were diamonds threaded into the dress itself.

"And *that* is exactly why you will watch that feisty little mouth of yours," Vincent whispered to me, making my hand ball into a fist on my lap. He placed his hand over mine. "Easy there. I would hate to see Princess Avery's beautiful face sitting on a spike beyond the castle gate."

My lips parted as my eyes flared in horror, but I couldn't voice any words. I was frozen where I sat. There were so many things I wanted to say; to do. Starting with slitting his fucking throat for voicing his thoughts, but I couldn't. I couldn't do a gods-damn thing without risking the lives of my brother and sister.

The seats in the throne room filled quickly as guests were herded in like cattle by the guards. Some attendees took notice of us, giving a quick glance before immediately looking away. My gaze wandered to Vincent—he was always a rugged, ugly brute, and even dressed in expensive finery, he made the guests uneasy.

The guards surrounding the room were too busy focusing on ushering the guests to their seats, instead of checking under masks to reveal who each of them was, which made it entirely too easy for me to blend in. They were getting incredibly sloppy.

If I were still running this place, I would've kicked their asses, but for now, this worked in my favor.

"I don't know exactly what Kellan's plan is," I spoke softly so only he could hear. "But it's never going to work. Marrying me secretly tonight after this ceremony and coming out of the shadows, trying to convince the realm that I am the rightful heir, will get him nowhere. Except for killed, which I'm quite fine with, actually."

He snickered in response.

I scoffed, and then suddenly, the orchestra's music began, startling me. Everyone in the crowd rose to their feet as Kai appeared beneath the dais at the front of the aisle, while Florence Nilda approached the back.

My jaw dropped in horror. She *hated* Kai. She was one of Avery's few friends that I could actually tolerate, mainly because she could see right through the prince. Her father knowingly sold her off to a monster, and likely didn't give a shit. I'm sure all he saw was the future heir of Velyra carrying on his bloodline—at the cost of his own daughter.

I had never even thought to ask who was stupid enough to marry Kai. I knew that half of the Ladies in Velyra would've jumped at the chance, not knowing how cruel he truly was. Florence knew, though, and I could tell by the look on her face as she sauntered down the aisle that she knew a marriage to Kai was a fate worse than death.

"I was shocked, too," Vincent said to me. "However, her father runs the majority of the spice trade and jumped at the chance of joining the royal family."

I clenched my fists and made a mental note to add her father to my now never-ending kill list. That was, of course, if I would ever be able to get the hell out of here.

"What does the queen want with spice, you may wonder?" he taunted. "Not a gods-damn thing. What she desires is powerful allies with coin. Coin to fund the remainder of her war, to be exact."

Ignoring him, I glanced back up to the front of the throne room and could see the hurt in Avery's eyes as she was forced to watch her friend betroth herself to the vile, soon-to-be king.

Everyone gawked at the bride in admiration as she descended the never-ending aisle. Guests wiped their tears of joy with their handkerchiefs, and all I could focus on was the single tear I watched glide down the bride's cheek as she passed us only a few moments before.

Once she was at the dais, the temple priest lowered his hands, gesturing for everyone to be seated once more. It was extremely rare for the priests to ever leave the temple of the gods. A royal wedding was one of those few occasions.

Once she reached the dais, Kai aggressively took Florence's hands and whipped his gaze to the priest without so much as a smile toward his bride.

It was clear as day that he saw her as one thing and one thing only: the way to ascend the throne. My heart lurched for her.

The priest began his speech and spoke of how the gods were proud of such a match to be made and how they accepted this as the future of Velyra. The crowd remained silent and I could see just a flicker of a grin beneath the mask on Kellan's face, where he remained guarding the left side of the dais.

The priest turned to Kai. "Do you, Prince Kai, take the lovely Florence Nilda, daughter of Lord Stanley Nilda, to be your wife and future queen?"

Kai eyed the priest in a way where he looked annoyed at the question, as if he had no time for the traditional pleasantries. "Obviously."

The priest cleared his throat. "And do you, Florence, take Prince Kai Valderre, son of the late King Jameson Valderre, may his soul rest with the gods, to be your husband and future king?" His voice echoed through the crowded, hushed throne room.

I could see her bottom lip tremble all the way from the back of the room, and mine mimicked the movement as my heart broke for her. Kai's face twisted with fury at her slight hesitation. Confused murmuring echoed among the guests.

She opened her mouth to speak. "I—"

It happened so fast. I blinked, and the scene before me had drastically changed. Blood-curdling screams erupted among the crowd in terror. Everyone in the room was up on their feet, racing for an exit before I could even comprehend what had just happened.

I blinked a few more times to be sure that the sight before us was indeed true.

An arrow now protruded from the center of Florence's chest, straight through the other side of her body. Blood dribbled down her lips and poured from the wound, quickly soaking into her extravagant, white wedding gown. Her body dropped to the floor at Kai's feet with a sickening thud.

Arrows were now flying through the air from the top balconies as the crowd attempted to scatter, but there were too many bodies to move quickly enough to flee.

I could hear Avery's scream above all others at the sight of her friend being murdered right before her eyes. My eyes caught on Callius as he dove and grabbed Kai, ripping him out of the way right before another arrow was shot where his head had just been. He then quickly moved to shield Kai and the queen's bodies with his own as he rushed them back through the door hidden behind the curtain on the dais. Avery and Finnian weren't even a thought to him.

I went to move, but Vincent stepped in front of me. "Oh, no you don't. I'm not letting you out of my sight!" He ducked down from an arrow. "We need to take cover."

I shoved at his chest. "I can't believe you idiots did this!" Whipping my head back to the dais, I watched as Avery and Finn scurried under a table that was off to the side of the room and hid to take cover. I had to get to them so they could escape safely. I *had* to.

Vincent then tackled me down to the ground, surprisingly saving me from an arrow that surely would have gone straight through my skull. "Elianna, this isn't us!" he boomed in my face.

I crawled back to my feet and frantically looked around and watched the chaos unfold around us. Masked soldiers were now parading through the masses, cutting down any Lord and Lady they came across in the crowd. Many were still up on the balconies, shooting their arrows aimlessly into the guests below. The entrance doors to the throne room were now *closed*. Trapping everyone inside.

Sympathizers.

My mouth parted, and I looked at Vincent as he yelled, "Let's go!"

I took a step back from him and, with all my might, swung my fist directly into his face. The sound of bone and cartilage crunching filled my ears, and he howled in pain as his nose was crushed beneath my fist.

I seized the opportunity to take off into a run toward Avery and Finnian, leaping over numerous chairs and blood-drenched bodies. I couldn't let the sympathizers find them, and I had no way of knowing if Jace was okay or if he planned this attack and told them to spare my siblings or not. I had to assume the worst.

I took a step out into the aisle and had to bend backward to dodge a sword that I noticed almost a second too late as it swung at my face. As I leaned back, I slipped in a puddle of blood as it pooled from the multiple corpses that now riddled the throne room floor.

The masked male went to strike me again, and I rolled my body out of the way, tripping him in the process and bringing his body to the floor with me.

I noticed a dagger strapped to the waist of one of the murdered guests and I ripped it free from its sheath. In one swift movement, I rolled back to where my attacker fell next to me and threw my leg over his body, straddling him on the ground as he lay there, disorientated, yet still working to strike me. I lifted the dagger high above my head and started to repeatedly slam the blade into his chest, over and over and over again as a scream tore through my throat. His blood blinded me as it splattered all over my face and torso.

Lost in a haze of fury, I directed a lifetime's worth of rage on this sympathizer who had unknowingly just relentlessly attacked someone that was on their side. An arrow whizzed past me again, but this time the tip of it sliced through the outer part of my arm, causing my stabbing movements to falter as the pain struck me.

I looked back down toward him and the roar of the screaming crowd might as well have been silent, as the only noise I could hear was the masked male gurgle on his own blood as he took his last breath on the floor beneath me.

Tears began streaming down my face at the sight of his mutilated body, riddled with stab wounds I had inflicted. Nausea settled in my gut.

My eyes darted back and forth between his own that were now glossed over. "What have I done?" I whispered.

Blinking out of my trance, I took my fallen attacker's sword and whipped my head back and forth from the throne room door, that was now being kicked down by the living guests as they screamed for help, to where Avery and Finn were now crawling out from underneath the table.

"No!" I shouted as I started running.

I cut down anyone in my path. Lord, sympathizer, a Velyran guard. Their blood coated me as it sprayed—the screams that tore through them reverberated through me, which would surely haunt me later in the night.

I couldn't see. I couldn't see anything but a rage-induced haze of red as I pushed my way through the madness to save two of the only people I had left.

"Lia!" Avery screeched as I made my way to them.

I threw my arms around her neck and Finn then jumped on me. The three of us held the embrace entirely too long for the situation at hand.

"What are you doing here?!" Avery cried as she pushed away from our hug, but gripped my arms tightly, refusing to let me go. "How did you get out?"

"It's a long story. Oh gods, look out!" I cried as I tackled them out of range of the flying arrows. The three of us landed on the table they had hid under, and it collapsed beneath our weight.

We all stayed ducked down there for a few moments. "You two need to listen to me right now. Right *fucking* now, do you hear me?" They both nodded rapidly with nerves. "I think my mate is behind this."

"What?!" Avery squealed, a smile plastered on her face in excitement, somehow forgetting the position we were currently stuck in. "You have a *mate?* Who?!"

"The human commander. There is a lot that I haven't had the chance to tell either of you yet."

"*WHAT?!*" they both yelled. Avery's smile quickly shifted to a concerned, scornful look.

"Listen to me!" I screamed as I ripped the blood-stained mask off my face. "These are sympathizers. They may know not to touch you, but I cannot guarantee it. I had no idea this was going to happen." I paused, trying to think of where I was even going with this. "I don't know what is going to happen to me after tonight."

"What are you saying?" Finn cut in.

"I am saying that if something happens to me, you two need to get the hell out of here. Kai is going to ascend the throne regardless, and you cannot trust him or Kellan. In fact, stay as far away from Kellan as possible."

Once those words left my mouth, my head snapped up. My eyes searched the crowded room, and I watched the throne room door finally burst beneath everyone as they tried to tear it down, and the mob poured through it.

Where was Kellan? Hopefully dead, but I knew I wasn't that lucky.

I rose to my feet and gripped both of their arms tightly. "You must flee beyond the Sylis Forest, to the human lands. They were planning to rally behind me and give their support to take my place as the rightful heir. Their leaders know of you. You should be safe."

"Do you hear yourself?" Avery asked.

"Unfortunately, I know how unbelievable and horrifying this is. I don't know what else to do!" I looked over to see that the crowd was now mostly through the doors. "Let's go!" I yelled at them as I picked the sword back up from the table's debris.

We rushed for the door and I was forced to cut down another sympathizer that blocked our path, refusing to listen to my pleas for him to stop. "Lia!" I screamed as our blades met over and over again, forced to ignore the ache where the arrow had grazed my arm. "I know Commander Cadoria!" A flicker of recognition flashed across his face, but a moment later he tried to strike once again, lost in the blood lust from the attack.

I wanted to burst into tears, knowing that each sympathizer I was forced to kill was one of my own supporters lost.

We finally made it out of the throne room to see an enormous crowd of people fleeing to the front of the castle beyond the main entrance doors that were now gaping open, one of them hanging off the hinges. Sympathizers were now retreating as well.

Kellan then appeared from one of the hallways and pointed at me and my gore covered body. I hissed at him as I reached for my siblings.

"Come on!" I roared as I pulled at both of them and we raced down one of the other halls, Kellan barreling after us closely behind.

"*Elianna!*" his voice boomed, echoing through the castle hall as we anxiously ran from him.

We threw down the decorative tables and their decor as we passed them to slow him down, but he effortlessly dodged them.

We turned a sharp corner, and my heart stopped dead in my chest as we came face-to-face with Callius as he stood there, blocking the remainder of the corridor.

The three of us came to a skidding halt as we were trapped between the two ruthless males.

"Fuck!" I roared, out of breath from the run. I blocked Avery and Finnian with my body. "You will *not* touch them," I seethed, raising my sword at him.

"Callius!" Avery called, her voice stern. "You will let us pass."

"Of course, Princess Avery. You and the prince may pass, and you will then be escorted to your chambers until the castle is secured. Your mother and Kai are safe from harm's way, and now I need to be sure you both are as well. However, Miss Elianna..." He took a swaggering step toward us. "Will be put back where she belongs."

The dungeons. I could only imagine what was going through Kellan's mind right now as he stood behind us.

"You take the prince and princess to their chambers, Callius. I will take Elianna back to her cell," Kellan said as he moved to approach me. If he was nervous, his tone showed no sign of it.

"Absolutely not," Callius said, surprising all of us. "I will take Solus back to her cell, and you will escort the prince and princess to their rooms."

Kellan was now in front of us, all three of our heads moving back and forth with the conversation that looked as if it was about to turn deadly between the captain and his predecessor.

"And why is that?" Kellan spat at him.

"You know exactly why." Callius strode past Kellan and gripped my arm, ripping my sword from my grasp. "I will deal with you later," he growled at him, and Kellan's hand balled into a fist at his side.

A threat.

"No!" Avery yelled back to me as Kellan pulled her and Finn away.

I could feel the tears burning the back of my eyes as they threatened to spill. "I will be okay," I choked out, knowing very well that wasn't the case at all.

Neither of them looked like they believed it for a second.

Kellan then forced them down the opposite end of the hall as Callius painfully gripped my two wrists together and twisted them, making me hiss. "You've become a giant pain in my ass once again, Elianna."

"Go to hell," I said through my teeth.

He then forcefully escorted me through the castle.

TWELVE

Elianna

Panic-fueled fury took over me, and I kicked and screamed the entire way back to my prison. Callius didn't have any cuffs to restrain me, since everything had erupted in chaos. He was forced to throw me over his shoulder to contain me, and I cussed him out the entire time he dragged me through the castle corridors and out into the courtyard.

Lifting my head up to get a better look at my surroundings, I was horrified to see the sympathizers that had been captured were being executed right where they knelt on the ground. No trial. No hanging. Just beheaded right there.

"Put me down, you ugly prick!" I screeched as he descended the dungeon stairs.

He shifted his weight and slammed my body into the stone wall in response, forcing a grunt out of me.

"Honestly, Solus, do you ever just shut the fuck up?" he boomed, as he pushed his other hand through his now tousled hair in frustration.

"You would like that, wouldn't you?" I retorted.

"How did you get out anyway?" he asked as we arrived at the bottom of the staircase.

"Lia?" A familiar voice hesitantly sounded from the shadows.

My head snapped up as I continued to hang over Callius' shoulder. "Lukas!"

I tried to violently wiggle my way out of his grasp, ignoring the ache that still radiated down my arm, but it was no use.

Think, Lia.

My eyes flared as the thought hit me, and I then rested my stomach to be flush against his back and reached my hands up between his legs, nearly gagging in the process. In an effort to flip over his body, I hurled my legs forward with all my might, and forced him to come crashing down backward on top of me on the ground.

Ow.

I pushed as hard as I could to get him off of me as he started mumbling curses at me. "Get off me, you brute!" He rolled his body off of mine and I frantically crawled across the floor to get to Lukas' cell.

I grabbed onto the bars and pressed my face between them. Lukas stepped into the dim torchlight and the sight of him rocked me to my very core.

He looked so much thinner beneath the light. Gods only knew how long he had been down here, wasting away with sleep from the drugs.

"Lia," he whispered as he bent down and cupped my cheek with his hand. His gaze then returned to Callius, anger contorting his features into someone I barely recognized. "What the fuck are you doing to her?!" He roared through the rusted, flaking bars.

Callius then grabbed my ankle out from behind me and ripped my laying body back towards him. The dirt and tiny rocks that covered the floor dug into my skin.

I moved to kick him in the face, but he dodged it as he got to his feet and then thrusted his boot into my ribs. All the breath held within my lungs blew out of me instantaneously.

"Get off of her!" Lukas shouted in fury through the bars, unable to do anything to help me.

Callius then took ahold of both of my legs and started dragging my body on the ground back towards my cell. "I have no idea how your whip marks healed, Solus, but we're going to fix that."

"Whip marks?!" Lukas boomed as he tried to rip his cell's door off the hinges. "I will kill you! I will *kill* you for touching the king's daughter! Every ounce of pain she has felt by your hand will be given back to you tenfold!"

I could barely hear him in the distance as my body was violently dragged away from the only remaining parental figure I had left. And he was a prisoner, just as I was.

Lukas

I couldn't believe this. I couldn't believe this was happening. How had everything gone to shit so fast?

The king had passed not even two months ago, and the kingdom was already falling apart—his daughter and friend trapped beneath his own castle and imprisoned in its dungeons.

Callius' footsteps were approaching once more, coming from the direction of where I watched him drag Lia's body.

"You stupid prick," I spat at him. "What is wrong with you?!"

He stopped in his tracks before me, but wouldn't turn his body to face mine. "It's not my fault that you have always been on the wrong side of this. You chose your fate. Not me."

He then continued up the steps and out of my sight.

I called out to Lia for what seemed like hours, but received no response from her. For all I knew, she was unconscious in her cell. The thought of it made me nauseous. I could only imagine what she had been enduring since she was dragged back to Isla.

My breathing quickened as anger flooded me at the reminder of her being whipped upon arrival. The true heir of the realm had been whipped in her own dungeons. How had everything come to this? Jameson kept this secret from the moment she was born. Everything he had done was to protect her, but it had only doomed her once he met his end.

My empty stomach growled, and I peeked over at the stale, nearly moldy bread on the floor that I had been given that morning. I couldn't eat that. Not now, knowing that I would just fall back asleep and be clueless as to what was happening with Lia.

An idea hit me then.

There was no way Callius or Kellan would be standing guard at the top of the stairs. That would be beneath them. They would have one of the newer recruits handling that.

I had one shot at this, and it better work if I had any chance of helping her.

I cleared my throat, ready to put on the greatest performance of my life. "Guards!" I yelled. "Something is wrong and I'm in need of a healer!" I rolled my eyes at myself.

I pressed my ear through the bars to hear better, but nothing came.

"Gods take me! Help!" I dragged out the word as I threw my head back in frustration.

Take the bait, dammit. *Take it.*

Finally, the sound of the dungeon's iron gate creaked open from the top of the stairs and hurried footsteps followed.

A young male stood before me a moment later, eyeing me warily where he stood beyond my cell.

"Thank the gods. I need help."

"S-sir Lukas, you know I can't do that," he stuttered.

I got a better look at him in the torchlight and saw that it was one of the young males I had brought on not even six months prior. He went from receiving orders from me, to getting orders to keep me locked up. He didn't know what to believe, and I could see it on his face.

I made it a point to look hunched over in agony as I pushed my body flush against the bars. Glancing down at his side, I noticed the skeleton key hanging from his hip.

Perfect.

"Come here, boy. You have this job because of me. You at least owe me this."

The guard looked hesitant, but he took a small step forward. That was all I needed.

In one swift movement, I reached my arm out between the bars and grabbed him by the back of his head. I slammed it into the rusted iron that separated us continually until I felt his body go limp in my grasp, unconscious.

His body dropped to the ground as I released my grip on his hair. I got down on my hands and knees and reached through the bars once more, this time to grab the skeleton key that hung from his belt.

I stood back up and my eyes darted from the key down to the guard's limp body. I couldn't believe that it was that easy. However, the hard part would be escaping, and getting Lia out safely.

Maneuvering my arm through the bars, I stuck the key into the hole on the outside of the door and contorted my wrist to twist it awkwardly. A small sound popped, and the door cracked open.

I pushed it open fully and took a small step out, glancing up the stairs to see that the guard had closed the door behind him. My gaze then moved to the seemingly depthless passageway before me.

I had to find Lia and quickly.

THIRTEEN
Avery

Kellan's grasp on my wrist as he escorted me through the castle halls was far too tight, and entirely too inappropriate for a guard and the princess he was supposed to be protecting.

"You're hurting me," I hissed, trying to keep calm. Lia told us to stay as far away from Kellan as possible, and Callius handed us over to him only moments later.

He turned back to me. "Now, now, Princess Avery, we are almost at your chamber. Can't have you slipping from my grip and running off like your darling sister has a habit of."

My eyes widened at how he carelessly admitted to me that he knew about Lia. I had nothing to say in response, but I continued to try and tug my wrist from his bone crushing grip.

We finally arrived at the door to my chambers after he brought Finnian to his first, where a guard had already awaited to barricade him in there. Kellan opened my chamber's door and guided me through it. I was relieved to see Nyra lying on my bed, letting out a yawn. I turned back to face him to speak, but he beat me to it.

"How in the realm did Elianna get out of her cell?" he asked in an accusatory tone.

I blinked at him. "I am not sure."

"Well now, Princess, don't play coy with me." He took a step toward me, and I took a matching one backward. "I heard about your little maneuver of telling my guard to leave his post at the dungeon's entrance a few days ago. And then Elianna's wounds were magically healed the following day? Interesting, to say the least."

I straightened my spine. "Surely you aren't accusing the princess of treason, Captain Adler."

Nyra jumped down from my bed and trotted over to my side as she growled at Kellan, showing her teeth ferociously.

He looked down at her, gave a soft chuckle, and shook his head. "Your mother will be so disappointed in you when she learns of your treachery to the crown. Elianna escapes from her prison and somehow ends up at the prince's wedding in disguise. The wedding that was necessary for him to ascend the throne, and then it is ambushed by sympathizers with his beautiful bride-to-be murdered in front of the crowd?"

"How dare you!" I shouted at him. "Florence was my *friend!* I never would have taken part in something like this. And I didn't help Lia escape. I wish I could take the credit for it, but it was not my doing!"

He eyed me. "I wish I could believe you, Avery, but since you were spotted seducing the guard at the dungeon door, things are not looking good for you here. Now, you will need to sit in this room to think about how you will somehow try to make this up to the queen and future king. I would hate to see his first task at defending his crown be sentencing his own kin to death for treason."

Lia's words echoed in my thoughts as I remembered her saying that Kellan had heard everything said in the dungeons the day we found her. Tears burned my eyes as I realized what he was doing.

"Oh, my gods..." His eyes glanced back to mine. "*You* let her out, didn't you? You had something planned, and it didn't work. Now she is back in her cell and you are trying to pin this on me! Lia told me to stay away from you, but she didn't get the chance to tell me why! You are proving yourself to be the vile male I was warned of."

He smirked and gave me a quick wink. "Goodnight, Princess Avery."

He then shut the door behind him, and the sound of a soft *click* echoed through it.

"What the?"

I ran to the door and went to open it, but the handle wouldn't budge. Nyra started scratching at the bottom.

I raised my fist and aggressively pounded on the door. "Kellan! You let me out of here this instant!" I yelled as I stomped my foot down onto the tile floor in a tantrum.

"Apologies, but the skeleton key was given to me upon taking over Lukas' position. I believe you to be a threat to our future king. You will need to stay put until the castle is secured," he said tauntingly through the door. "And don't try to kick it down, either. I will be sending a guard up immediately."

"I hate you!" I screamed through the door.

A small laugh left him. "Aye, well, apparently, that is a common Valderre female trait."

And then I heard his footsteps slowly walk away.

"UGH!" I let out in frustration. "He can't pin this on me," I said to Nyra, but she just started panting.

I anxiously looked around the room and then ran over to my bureau. I ripped the drawer open and was relieved to see that my father's leather-bound journal was still sitting where I left it. "Thank the gods," I whispered to myself.

I leaned my back up against the bureau and slid my body down to the floor. Tears burned the back of my eyes as I stared down at the front of my ruined dress. Blood stains of the fallen were splattered across it, and I took in a shuddering breath as the vision of my dear friend being shot with an arrow replayed in my memory. Nyra crawled up next to me and rested her giant, fluffy head on my lap.

"How did everything come to this, Nyra?"

After swiping away the escaped tears, I started scratching her ear and then opened the journal to read another entry.

This page didn't have a date, but since it was one of the last entries, it must've been recent. It caught my attention. *Today, Veli was speaking in riddles. She seemed more...odd than usual today, but I couldn't say that to her. I would never want to make her feel uncomfortable around me, especially after our unspoken agreement to not speak of the otherworldly power she possesses.*

Truthfully, while most feared Veli for the oddness she exudes, I quite enjoy her company. She has never held back her feelings to me, and while most would be wise to toward their king, Veli treated me as if I was any other creature she was treating or speaking to. It was refreshing.

Since I fell ill, she has come every day to run tests, but so far, she can't figure out what is causing it. However, her speaking in riddles made me slightly uncomfortable. I can't get it out of my head.

"Beware of the day the pillar falls, for an heir will rise from blood and malice, and when the moment comes that the enemy weeps, a stranger of kin shall forge the way for the one who was promised."

It makes no sense. I can't figure out what it means, even now still, but it seems ominous. When I asked her, she shushed me, which was typical of Veli. She just handed me more sedaeyo leaves to chew on for the pain and left.

What the hell? What did any of that mean? And Father *knew* Veli possessed magic?! I had to find a way to get back to Veli and her secret home to demand she tell me what this meant.

Actually, I would definitely need to ask nicely. She still scared me.

My curtains flowed from the wind that was let in through the window, catching my attention. I leapt up and ran towards it. Sticking my head out the window, I peered down at the dizzying plunge to the ground below my tower. I let out a disappointed huff, realizing that there would be no possibility of escaping through there—not unless I was brave enough to scale the tiny ledge of the tower, but that would be a death sentence.

"Wait a second," I said, whipping back around, and the wolf curiously tilted her head. "We were able to find secret doors in the king and queen's personal chambers!" I glanced at each corner of my large bedroom. It had always been covered in tapestries from ceiling to floor for as long as I could remember. "There must be one in here," I whispered.

I tiptoed over to the door and peered through the keyhole to see the shadow of the guard who was indeed silently guarding me. I would have to be quiet.

I started to run around the room and ripped out the tapestries, peeking behind each one of them, and was met with nothing but solid brick walls. I searched my bedroom, the closet, and even removed all the large wall hangings in the bathing room. Nothing.

I stormed over to my bed and dramatically threw my body onto the mattress and screamed into my pillow. Nyra jumped up next to me and started kissing my cheek.

"We have to get out of here, Nyra. Lia needs us and I don't know what to do." She let out a small whine and my lips thinned. If I missed Lia, I could only imagine how Nyra felt. She hadn't seen her in months.

I looked up, back to my bureau, and then noticed there was one tapestry I hadn't checked yet. The one hung behind the dresser.

I got up and sauntered over to it. I tried to peel the fabric back, but it was no use with the enormous mirror that rested on top of the bureau. I glanced back at the door. "Get ready to run," I whispered to the wolf.

With all my might, I heaved the dresser to the side, and the sound of it sliding across the floor was far too loud. The tapestry still clung to the wall behind it, likely from it being pressed up against it by the bureau and mirror for over a century, but as I slowly peeled it back, my lips twitched up in a grin when an aged wooden door revealed itself.

"You alright in there, Princess Avery? I heard an odd noise."

I jumped at the sound of the guard's voice. "Everything's perfect. Please remain at your post, for I am going to bed and do not wish to be further disturbed," I called back to him in a cheery, yet firm voice as I took my first step into the tunnel.

Nyra and I ran through the dark passageways with only a single lit candle that I was able to grab from my room. It seemed as if she could see far better than I could in the darkness, so I was more so relying on following her.

Winding down the tunnels, I tried to keep track of my steps and how many turns had been made, hoping that they followed the halls of the castle.

"Nyra," I whispered, and she tilted her head back up to me. "We need to find Finn." She started panting and then sniffed at the stale, dusty air. "Yes, good girl! Finn! Find Finn."

She took off in a run.

"Shit," I muttered as I started following her, trying to cover the tiny flame of my candle so it didn't flicker out with the wind, leaving us in complete darkness.

I followed her through the winding passageways when suddenly she came to a complete halt, and I skidded to a stop right behind her. She started sniffing the air once again, but there was a door right next to us.

I slowly opened it and prayed the hinges didn't squeak, revealing myself to anyone who could be on the other side of the wall. I opened it just enough to get my arm through and tugged slightly at the tapestry that blocked it. Peering out, I noticed we were only down the hall from Finn's bedroom door, the guard still blocking him in.

"Shit."

I closed the door silently.

"Nyra, we are so close." I tiptoed down the tunnel another thirty feet and a much smaller door revealed itself. It resembled one built possibly for a youngling. "Interesting. This must lead to his room."

I pried it open and heard Finn stir on the opposite side. A piece of furniture was blocking this door, so I knocked on it lightly.

"Who's there!" Finn screeched.

I paused at the tone of Finn's voice. He sounded terrified. I tried to suppress my laugh.

"Pssssst, Finn!" I whisper-shouted. "It's me!"

"What?!" he cried in an octave higher than his typical voice.

Mother of the gods, this male.

I started tapping on the bureau that blocked the mini door and got down on my hands and knees to try to push through. Nyra wiggled her way under me.

"It's Avery, you idiot! I'm behind the dresser, but *be quiet*."

Footsteps slowly sounded in my direction, and he struggled to shove the dresser out of the way. When he moved it just enough to sneak through, he peered down at me and Nyra.

I gave him a little wave with my fingers. "Hi."

He started rubbing his temples. "I'm not going to like whatever you are up to. I can feel it."

"Sh!" I hushed him as I crawled through the small door and slid out from behind the furniture.

"Why is Nyra with you?"

"We have to run."

"Run?! You cannot be serious."

I slammed my hand over his mouth to silence him. "We have to get out of here. It isn't safe for us. Lia was right. Kellan is up to something and he is trying to pin Lia escaping the dungeons on us by telling Kai and Mother that we are committing treason."

His eyes widened, but I kept my hand over his mouth for a moment longer because I didn't trust him to not scream again.

"We need to find Veli and get to safety," I said as I cautiously removed my hand from his face.

"I was right. I don't like what you are up to at all."

I rolled my eyes. "It's either run, or risk being trialed for treason. And personally, I am not taking my chances," I whispered as I placed my hands on my hips. "We have to get out of here, but your door is being guarded. I didn't see Kellan lock it, so we might have a shot to run."

He stared at me blankly. "And how exactly do you plan to get rid of the guard? Why can't we just go back through the tunnels?"

"I have an idea for the guard, but it will only work if you play along. I don't know the way through these tunnels to get back down to the garden, and we can't take the tunnel back to my own chambers because Kellan locked my door from the outside *and* there is also a guard. We have to try to sneak back down to the passage door that is a hallway down from my room and do it quietly so we can escape through the gardens."

He shook his head. "We can't do this. It isn't going to work. We will be caught. Surely Kai and Mother won't believe—"

"Don't even finish that sentence, Finnian Valderre!" I pointed at him. "Mother killed the king. She killed our father. I wouldn't put it past her to either lock us up and throw away the key or have us suffer the same fate he did."

He audibly swallowed. "So, what do we do?"

A wicked smile crept up my face.

Finnian mumbled a curse at me in response.

FOURTEEN
Elianna

Frantic footsteps sounded through the dungeon hall, racing back toward me. I assumed it was Kellan coming back to rip me out of this prison cell and place me in a separate one of his own, when suddenly, a different, familiar voice echoed through the dungeon, calling out my name.

"In here!" I shouted, as I shot up from the bench and tried to peer through the shadows to see beyond the bars when Lukas appeared in front of me.

"There you are!" he said as he started fumbling around the cell door with...was that a *key?*

I glided over to the door and watched him curiously, having a hard time finding words.

CLICK.

The door popped open, and I leapt out, throwing my arms around the back of his neck as I began sobbing uncontrollably. He matched my embrace, and I could hear a few sniffles coming from him as well.

"How did you get the key?" I asked, voice hoarse.

"Don't you worry about that," he said as he pulled away from me and gripped me by my shoulders. His eyes bore into my own as he continued, "I need to get you out of here."

My brows furrowed. "I am not leaving without you!"

He gave me a sad look and gripped my hand. He glanced down at the front of my blood covered gown and sighed. "What the hell happened?"

"Kellan knows. He had this grand scheme to force me into a marriage and then try to convince the realm of who I was so he could become king. It is ridiculous and the most desperate attempt at power I have ever seen from him. Kai's wedding was attacked by sympathizers. His bride is dead. So...*so* many are dead. A river of blood was flowing through the castle halls when Callius dragged me back down here."

He just stared at me, and I watched as his jaw ticked. It was so very rare that Lukas lost his temper, but I had a feeling that was about to happen.

"I was going to come back to convince the king to end the war. I was going to come back for the throne and claim what is rightfully mine. The humans...they are just like us. Some are kind and incredible beings, while others are rotten. They are no different from us. The queen needs to be stopped. I was ready to do what he had always secretly wanted me to. It was so foolish of me to try to communicate with you the way I had. I just never thought that..."

"You thought your father would still be alive," he cut in. "You had no way of knowing what was happening here, Lia." He wiped a single tear that fell from my cheek. "You cannot blame yourself for this."

Shouts sounded from down the hall. My jaw dropped as our necks craned, snapping towards the noises. I could hear Kellan's voice above the others as he realized Lukas was out of his cell.

Lukas tugged on my wrist. "We need to move. Now!" he shouted, and we both took off down the opposite direction of the hall. I didn't know what we would do when the only exit I knew of was blocked.

The shouts were getting closer when we came to a sudden stop in the large, open cavern at the back of the dungeon's chamber. Nox was chained in his usual spot. I glared around the room, flinching at the sight of the chains that were still laid across the floor where I had been restrained and whipped upon my arrival.

"What are we going to do?" I whispered, my eyes darting back and forth from Nox to Lukas, who was now storming up to the beast.

"Be careful!" I shouted to him as Nox raised his enormous, horn covered head.

"I need you to do me a favor," he said to the scale coated creature that stood nearly as tall as a building before him. "I need you to get her the fuck out of here. Can you do that for me?"

Nox curiously tilted his head to the side. If we weren't about to be captured again, I would have let out a sharp laugh at how much it reminded me of Nyra.

My heart ached thinking that I may never see her again after this.

"And don't eat her!" he shouted at Nox, who let out a huff of hot air through his nostrils in response. "I've done a lot for you, beast. Please do this for me."

He turned back toward me and handed me the skeleton key he somehow had come across.

I looked down at the key in my hand and then lifted my gaze back to his. "No," I whispered. "I am not leaving without you."

Tears slipped from his pride-filled eyes, and he cupped my cheeks with both hands. "Your father and I are so proud of you, Lia."

An agonizing sob broke through my lips. "Stop this! Come with me!"

He looked at the wyvern and back at me. "He's never flown before. I would weigh him down, and a distraction needs to be made for you to get out of here."

I peeked over his shoulder right as Kellan and Vincent appeared through the cavern's opening, followed by a dozen other guards at their backs.

"Elianna!" Kellan roared, the sound of my name reverberating through the open space.

Lukas pressed the key further into my hand. "It is a skeleton key and will work on his chains. You need to go!" he shouted at me in desperation. "Now!"

I could barely see through the flood of tears pouring from my eyes as I took off into a run toward Nox, and Lukas did the same in the opposite direction.

I stopped short in front of the wyvern, noticing that my running made him uneasy. I threw my hands up to show him I was unarmed. "Easy, boy. I'm not going to hurt you." He huffed out through his nostrils once more. A warning. "Please don't turn me to ash. How does getting out of this prison sound?" I asked as he tilted his head in understanding at me.

He lifted his tail to reveal the area on the wall where his giant chains connected to—trapping him there.

I carefully took a step forward. His gaze followed me as I tiptoed around his body, back pressed against the wall as I made my way to the far corner.

"You stupid fuck!" I heard from behind me and I whipped around to see Lukas had picked up a metal rod he must've found down here and impaled it through Vincent's thigh. He ripped it out, seeming unphased as he punched Lukas in the face. Vincent's sword was on the ground, feet away from where he must have been disarmed, and Lukas reached for it as the other guards moved to swarm him.

"He's mine!" Vincent boomed at them.

My eyes then locked on Kellan as he stalked toward me and Nox.

"Shit, shit, shit!" I frantically fumbled around with the key as I slammed it into the keyhole on the chain, but it wouldn't turn easily. I let out a loud scream of frustration as sweat dripped down my brow while panic took over me, when I heard a rumble from Nox's chest. I could see out of the corner of my eye that Kellan was horrifyingly close to us.

Finally, the lock clicked, and the heavy chain fell to the ground at my feet.

My eyes met Kellan's as he stood in a fighting stance, his gaze leisurely moving between my own and Nox's. He rose his sword in the air and pointed at the wyvern.

"Now, princess, don't do anything foolish. You know I would have come back to rescue you. We have plans, after all."

I looked back toward Lukas and could see he still held his own against not only Vincent but also the others, as he courageously swung the sword at each of them as they circled him.

"I will *not* go with you and I will *never* be your bride!" I shouted at him.

I took a giant leap onto Nox's side, desperately gripping onto his black, iridescent scales, as I carefully climbed up onto his back.

Oh gods, what in the realm did I just do?

"Woahhh," I said out loud to myself, as Nox's body swayed beneath me. I was expecting him to retaliate at the sudden weight on his back, but instead, Nox lifted his head up higher and stood his ground against Kellan.

"Elianna, get back down here now!" Kellan shouted at me as he raised his sword higher, threatening the beast beneath me.

Nox then lowered his head to Kellan's eye level, and for a fraction of a second, I watched pure fear creep into his eyes. It was the most beautiful thing I had seen in weeks.

I straightened my spine and leaned down toward him, clutching the wyvern's back tightly between my thighs to keep balance. "Never," I whispered to him, but I knew he was aware of what I said based on how his eyes flared with challenge in response.

He took a single step forward, and Nox let out a deafening roar directly at him. Kellan was forced to drop his sword to cover his ears, and I could see even Vincent and Lukas' fight had faltered at the sound.

I lifted my head up to look at the ceiling of the small nook in the cavern, which seemed like an endless stretch upward. I had no idea where it would lead to, but the tiniest speck of moonlight shone through a hole in the top.

"Up, Nox! We have to go up!"

The wyvern lifted his gaze to match mine and then moved to *crawl* up the tunnel-like wall to the ceiling above us.

"Wait, what?! No, Nox! Fly! We need to...oh gods!" I slammed my torso down to rest at the base of his neck and held on for dear life as he continued to climb up the rocky wall, using the tips of his clawed wings and his taloned back feet.

Small pebbles of rock broke off the structure from his wings at the weight of us and one smacked me in the face, moving my line of sight in the direction of Lukas for a final time. His eyes found mine, and he gave me a soft, loving smile—right before Vincent got one last punch in, sending Lukas' body slamming down into the ground at his feet.

"NO!" I cried.

Then I lost sight of them as the tunneled ceiling closed in around us as Nox continued to climb.

A rock somehow flew up from beneath us and slammed into Nox's head, triggering his grip on the wall to stumble. I almost lost my own hold on him when he faltered and glanced down to the ground once more to see Kellan throwing the fallen pieces of stone back up at us. Nox let out another roar, making the cave we were desperately trying to climb out of tremble.

Nox's head leaned back slightly too far, and my thighs' grip loosened. I was only holding onto him with my arms wrapped as far as they could reach around his thick neck, and I was thankful the gash from the arrow had already begun to heal. I let out a terrified screech as my legs dangled and swung around in the open air. My stomach dropped when I peered down at the floor below.

He finally leveled out once we reached the top, and to my own horror, the hole was entirely too small to fit us through.

"Fuck," I uttered. "Nox, what are we going to—"

My words failed me as Nox swung his head back, his neck nearly crushing me in the process, and slammed his head into the small hole within the stone directly above us.

The hole widened as pieces of the rocks chipped off and tumbled all the way to the floor below.

He did it again. Nox slammed his horned head back into the partially enclosed ceiling three more times before the hole opened up to show the view of the crystal-clear night sky.

"HA! YES! Yes, Nox!" I boomed.

I tightened my hold on him once more and then he took the tips of his wings and pulled us through the exit he had created. I tucked myself in as close to his back as possible, trying to avoid the protruding jagged rocks as they sliced into my skin while we squeezed through the exit.

His talons dug into the crumbling granite wall and he pushed the lower half of his body up with his hind legs, thrusting us entirely out of the cavern.

Suddenly, we were resting at the top of a small hill that lay just beyond the back castle gates, toward the sea.

The wind blew the bottom of my dress up and I quickly grabbed it and slammed it back down onto Nox's back. What I wouldn't give to be wearing my fighting leathers or armor right now.

I peered down through the hole we had just climbed through. Once the dust settled, Kellan looked like an ant storming around all the way down at the bottom.

I chuckled softly and awkwardly patted the back of Nox's neck. "Excellent job, my friend."

A purr-like sound rumbled through his chest, earning a smirk from me.

Nox suddenly extended his wings, freezing me in place just as I was about to jump down. The wind picked up and caught onto them, driving his body upright onto his hind legs.

"Woah!" I shrieked as I clutched his neck once again.

I tried to peek around the beast's shoulder and looked up at his face. He looked curious. Excited. And honestly a little scared.

He flapped both wings in unison a single time.

My heart stopped.

"Oh, no. No, no. Nox! Don't you dare."

His wings flapped a second time. Then a third.

I witnessed the moment the thought crossed his mind. His eyes thinned into slits as he violently started flapping both wings together in tandem at his sides.

"I'm going to die," I muttered to myself as I braced for take-off.

Before I had the chance to blink, we were levitating in the open air to the beat of his unsteady wings. Occasionally, one would flap without being in tandem with the other, causing us to drop every few feet as we climbed higher into the sky. Each time it happened, my stomach would sink, and my grip on him became impossibly tighter as I involuntarily yelped in terror.

"Take it slow, please," I begged, voice trembling with nerves as I watched the moonlight shine off of his amethyst-reflecting, onyx scales. The sight was so beautiful. I had never seen anything like it.

Nox gradually started flapping us even higher above, away from the castle and into the lightening sky that was about to break into dawn.

FIFTEEN

Avery

"I don't want to do this," Finn said to me as I hid in the shadows of his bathing chamber with Nyra.

"Stop being a pussy and just do it!" I hissed.

"Fine!" he shouted at me in a hushed tone.

Finn cleared his throat and moved to his bedroom door. He opened it, startling the guard.

The guard whipped around. "Prince Finnian. Do you need something?"

"I, uh, yes. I need you to adjust the window in my room for me. I cannot close it and it is quite brisk in here."

I watched from the shadows as the guard raised his brow at him and sighed slightly. "Of course, Prince."

He took a few steps into the room and once he was beyond the opening of the bathing chambers, I silently snuck up behind him and shut the door he came through.

His back stiffened, and he went on alert immediately, so I grabbed a candelabrum off of the small side table and smashed him over the head with it, in an attempt to knock him unconscious.

"Ow!" he screeched as his hand flew to the back of his head, where a tiny bit of blood appeared.

My lips parted, and I was frozen where I stood as he slowly turned around and saw me standing there. Weapon in hand.

How did Lia make stuff like this look so easy?

"Princess?" He looked at his hand and saw the blood. "What in the realm are you—"

His question was cut short when Finn, to my surprise, punched the guard right in the side of his face. His body dropped to the ground and a fleshy smack filtered through the air.

I dropped the candle holder as my jaw dropped. I lifted my gaze to Finn, who looked just as shocked as I felt about what he had just done.

A smile spread across my face. "Holy gods! You badass!" His lips kept opening and closing, but he couldn't find the words. "On second thought, don't think too much of it. I still need you to be alert." I smacked his cheek lightly. "Let's go! Nyra, you too."

The three of us cautiously walked through the door and when we saw the hall was empty, aside from us, we all took off on silent feet through the castle.

We got lucky and didn't run into any guards during our trek through the never-ending, twisting halls. We arrived at the hidden door I had gone through with Lia so many times before. I wanted to check to see if the guard was still in front of my chambers, so I carefully tiptoed to the corner that would reveal my door and cautiously peeked around it. My eyes landed on the guard, who had fallen asleep while standing up, leaning against it.

Perfect.

I jogged back over to Finn and Nyra as he was pulling the tapestry back.

"He's asleep in front of my door. Seems like he didn't suspect a thing."

"Thank the gods," Finn huffed out as he opened the old door and walked right through it, surprising me once again.

Nyra and I followed him through it, and it suddenly hit me that there was no going back. This was it. Our lives would never be the same again.

We carefully crawled through the vines that covered the garden's hidden door, and I had to untangle them from Nyra as they wrapped around her. She started growling at them in frustration, and I let out a short snort of amusement as I tried to shush her to prevent getting caught.

"What now?" Finn whispered to me.

I looked around the garden, which was thankfully empty. We got lucky once again, and I was wondering when our luck was going to run out. I glanced up at the sky and saw that dawn was on the horizon. The castle would typically be flooded with staff and guards at any moment. We had to hurry.

"We have to get to Veli. There's nowhere else for us to go and I have a lot of information I need to get out of her."

"Did you just hear yourself?" he asked, looking completely unamused. "Demanding information from Veli would be about as wise as approaching a wyvern in the wild. It's just something you don't do."

I rolled my eyes at him. "Come on. Lukas told me he snuck onto the castle grounds that day a few weeks ago by a small breakage in the back of the battlements that had never been repaired. We can sneak out through there and get into the city."

Hunched over, we carefully snuck through the gardens. I took in the smell of the roses, lilacs, and wisterias, trying to not remind myself that this would be the last time I ever walked through my favorite place. The garden I would read in every day or lay with Nyra in its grass.

I halted in my tracks for a moment and glanced around, taking the sight of everything in. I could almost envision a younger version of Lia and myself sneaking around here at night as we tried to catch fireflies, with not a care in the world nearly a lifetime ago.

The vision was lost as Finn stepped on the back of my ankle, not realizing I was no longer moving.

I let out a small hiss and shot him a warning look.

"Sorry," he muttered. His gaze then was fixed beyond my shoulder. I whipped around to see what he was watching when I noticed the shadow of a male reflecting in the candlelight through the stable window.

Finn took off into a sprint toward the barn.

"No!" I warned. I caught up to him quickly and grabbed his arm. "You don't know if that's Landon." I started shaking my head with concern.

He glanced back at the stables. "It's him. I can't leave him."

Finn shook out of my grip and stormed toward the structure, Nyra trotting at his side. He carefully opened the door, and I walked through behind him.

Landon stood on the far side of the room, separating hay into buckets for the horses.

He looked up at us, surprise stretched across his features. "Prince. Princess. How can I help you?"

Oh gods. He was clearly still upset with Finnian.

Finn glanced down for a brief second at Landon's chest, where Kai had branded him, and then took a hesitant step in his direction. "I don't have much time to explain," he started. I looked over to the window and saw that dawn now illuminated the sky with its swirling purple and pink hues. "We need to get out of here."

"I don't know what you mean," Landon said as he brought his attention back to the hay.

I walked over to him then. "Look at me." His eyes met mine reluctantly. "We are fleeing. We have to. Kai's wedding was attacked last night by sympathizers. Lia somehow escaped from her cell and they are trying to pin it on us. It's not safe here anymore. The Velyra we have always known is no longer what it once was. If Kai can't find us, he will come after you in an attempt to get to Finn. You *must* come with us. You could be killed if you don't."

Finn started nodding in agreement. "Please," he begged. "Come with us. If you're still upset with me, I will accept that, but I can't just leave you here to die." His voice cracked on the last word.

Landon's eyes darted back and forth between us. I watched his gaze drift down my ruined gown that was still covered in dried blood and gods knew what else from the massacre.

"Mother of the gods," he let out in surprise. "Is that from the wedding?"

I nodded as I bit down on my lower lip.

"The two of you can't run around Isla like that. You will be spotted immediately by city guards." He went to move to a closet on the opposite wall and pulled out three large, black cloaks and handed one to each of us.

All three of us threw them onto our backs in unison as we stood in a circle.

"If you come with us, there's no coming back here. I just want to make sure you realize what this means," I said to him as gently as I could.

He looked around the stables and let out a loud sigh. "Things around here have gone to shit, anyway." He paused for a moment, and his tone saddened. "I will miss the horses, though."

I closed my eyes tightly at the thought of leaving Matthias behind, but there was no way we could sneak him out.

"I know," I croaked out. "I will too."

We moved toward the back door of the stables and I glanced out the window just in time to watch as guards poured into the gardens.

Kellan was at their front, making my eyes flare. "Not one fucking word of this to anyone! Am I understood?"

"Shit," I hissed. "Come on!"

We all snuck out the back door and crept up to the battlement wall. We kept our bodies low as we followed it until a few gray bricks resting on the ground appeared from where Lukas must've snuck in. No one was ever on this side of the castle, so it made sense that it had gone unnoticed all these years. There was nothing back here.

I poked my head through to see there was a steep, rocky hill that led down toward the sea. We would have to carefully walk that path and go into the city that way. We had no other choice.

I dove through the hole, and they all followed suit. I made sure my recognizable red curls were tucked into my cloak's hood and looked at the boys.

"Are you ready?" I asked, and they all nodded. I looked down at Nyra to see she was sitting at my feet and smiling at me, which tugged at my heartstrings.

Before I had a chance to take a step to move, an odd *whooshing* sound echoed on the wind, catching all of our attention.

We all glanced up at the vibrant, flame colored sky and were left in awe as we watched the far-off silhouette of a wyvern soaring through the air, a rider with long hair flowing through the breeze on its back.

"What in the..." Landon started as he lifted his hood to look up into the sky. "What is that?!"

"She got out," I breathed. "Mother of the gods. She did it!"

"Is that the wyvern from the dungeons?!" Finn whispered frantically.

"It must be," I answered softly.

"Wyvern in the dungeons..." Landon echoed in confusion. "Does this have anything to do with the wyvern's blood you had mentioned in the stables a few weeks ago?"

"Yes," I answered, turning to him. "We will explain everything, but we need to leave and find shelter first before we are caught."

Our three gazes shifted to the sky once more, following the wyvern's flight toward the mountainous landscape in the distance. Genuine smiles spread across all of our faces as we quickly descended the hill to head into the city beyond.

SIXTEEN

Elianna

I HELD ONTO NOX'S neck as tight as I could as he roughly attempted to fly for the very first time—while I was on his fucking back.

He seemed completely out of his depth, flapping wildly as we ascended further and further into the clouds. The wyvern looked down, and I watched from the side as one of his eyes widened. I had known for some time now that wyverns could feel fear, and it was clearly written between the scales on his face.

"Nox!" I shouted over the wind. "Stop going higher! We need to go forward, toward those hills in the distance!" I pointed, realizing a moment later he likely couldn't see what I was doing.

He shook his head from side to side as if he was telling me *no*. The movement jolted me, making me lose my balance and slip down his massive body. I flailed my arms around as I searched for anything to grab onto and was lucky that I caught myself on one of his wings.

I let out a loud scream, startling him, and he sent us even *higher*.

"Stop!" I screeched.

I was now dangling from the area where the joint of his wing met his body, holding on for dear life with both hands when he turned his long neck to contort his head to face me.

Could wyverns smell fear? Because I was about to shit myself as I was now nose to nose with the fire breathing creature.

"Listen to me! I know you can somewhat understand me." He huffed out a breath directly at me and the heat of it made me woozy.

I risked letting go of his wing with one hand, praying the strength of my arm that now held all of my weight didn't falter. "Stop going up." I started shaking my head as I raised my hand to imitate us levitating in the sky. "And start going forward." I then took that same hand and started gliding it out straight as I nodded.

Nox tilted his head to the side as he tried to comprehend the instructions.

He tilted his torso forward and flapped his wings, shooting us forward faster than I expected.

"Ah!" I yelped as I grabbed him once again with both hands. "Yes. Yes! Very good," I said as I heaved myself up, carefully crawling up onto his back, and sat down at the nape of his neck.

I awkwardly tapped his neck. "Good, now, let's try that again."

Nox shot forward and before I had a moment to blink, we were shooting across the sky as the sun rose.

"Ha!" I shouted, but it was lost in the air from the roar of the blowing gusts. "Yes, Nox! Hell yes! *Woah*." Adrenaline rushed through me as he veered left without warning, but I was finally getting a sense of balance.

We were going incredibly fast, and the wind sent my hair flying backward. I ducked my head down to hide behind his neck, so the air we rushed through wasn't so harsh on my eyes.

"Don't push yourself, Nox. You have never done this before."

A thought then occurred to me.

"Stop flapping! We can glide on the wind gusts now that we have momentum."

The wyvern listened to me, and literally just *stopped* flapping entirely. He tucked his wings back into his sides and we were frozen midair for a fraction of a second. A moment later, we both started to freefall down to the unforgiving ground below.

A scream tore through my throat as my grip on him slipped, and we both started plunging to our certain deaths.

My stomach dropped as I watched the ground rapidly approach us from below.

Gods, I was going to die.

Nox was falling next to me, and I watched as his eyes flared with determination. He pointed his nose down, angling his body to dive under my own, and then flipped himself upside down.

"What the?" I shouted to myself.

He shot his wings back out, slowing his fall, and I dropped onto his belly. A moment later, he forced his wings inward and wrapped them around me as we violently crash-landed into the terrain.

I hesitantly opened my eyes as I felt Nox's wings leisurely lift off of me.

I raised my head and blinked through the dust that now surrounded us in the air. Nox lifted his head to look at me. His body was easily five feet deep in the ground, forming a massive crater in the otherwise untouched field.

"Are you okay?" I croaked out as I crawled up his belly to get closer to his face.

He blinked his luminous golden eyes at me, and I realized how silly it was that I expected him to answer.

"Well, you aren't dead, so I am going to go with yes," I said as I wiggled my body down and jumped off of him.

I crawled out of the small crater we created and looked back toward Isla, which appeared to be miles behind us now. We were right outside of the farmlands.

I turned my body back toward Nox as he spun his body over and shook off the dirt and debris from the landing. A tiny smile tugged at my lips at the sight that was so similar to how Nyra would shake herself off when it rained.

I looked up at him. "Thank you," I said, but he just continued to stare. "For saving me from that fall. I probably wouldn't have survived otherwise."

I went to take a step and felt the need to add on, "Although it *was* your fault that we fell in the first place." He let out a low growl toward me. "Oh, do not give me attitude!

You shouldn't have tucked your wings in. I told you to *glide* on the wind. Not freefall to the ground!" My leg stomped childishly on the last word. I was exhausted, and it showed.

His lips pulled back in a small snarl at my tantrum, and I realized I was arguing with an overgrown lizard.

A small gulp left me, and I quickly changed the subject. "We have a long way ahead of us. And, personally, I don't feel like going back up in the air quite yet." I pointed to the sky, and he looked up, almost sadly.

"Come on. Let's get moving before someone sees us," I said, as I picked up the front of my destroyed gown and strutted forward.

Nox then balanced the top half of his body on the front joint of his wings and followed behind me, guarding my back. We then embarked on the seemingly never-ending journey north to Ellecaster, where Jace had planned to go the last time we saw each other.

I was headed back to my friends.

Back to *my mate*.

My mate, who appeared to have organized an attack on my brother's wedding. Had there been orders to not harm my other siblings, or even me? When I demanded the false guard to halt, only a fraction of recognition appeared, and he tried to assault us, anyway.

Perhaps Jace wasn't behind the attack at all, and these sympathizers acted without the mortals' knowledge. It was the best I could hope for, given the circumstances, because the thought of my mate betraying me, or ordering an attack on me, was just one more thing I couldn't bear.

SEVENTEEN
Kellan

THIS WAS A FUCKING joke. In a matter of hours, the prince's wedding was ambushed, Callius caught me trying to sneak Elianna off, and to make everything even fucking worse...she *escaped*.

On the back of a wyvern.

Typical Elianna bullshit.

Now I would have to deal with Callius, the queen, and Kai about how the guards didn't sense sympathizers amongst the wedding guests. Luckily, Elianna being out of her cell, I could easily blame on the annoying princess and her little sidekick prince. However, my entire plan was now shot to shit.

I left Vincent to deal with Lukas and made my way back into the castle as dawn rose in the sky. I looked far out on the horizon and could still make out the tiniest outline of the wyvern in the distance.

"Luck was on your side this time, Princess," I muttered, shaking my head furiously as I went to turn a corner and came face-to-face with Callius.

Fucking *perfect*.

"And where did you just come from?" His arms were crossed, and I didn't appreciate the fact that he was addressing me as if I were a youngling. "You were to bring the prince and princess back to their rooms."

"I did," I said in an unamused tone as I shouldered past him.

"Oh, I don't think so, Adler." He palmed my shoulder and spun my body back in his direction. "Why were you just down in the dungeons? Why was Elianna out of them in the first place? The queen is ready to put all our gods-damn heads on the chopping block."

I eyed him and gave him a knowing look. As if the queen would kill the one male brave enough to lend her his cock these last few decades. His eyes flared as recognition flashed across his features—he thought I didn't know. *Everyone* knew, at least anyone with two eyes and half a brain.

"How am I supposed to know how she got out? The princess was seen running around in the dungeons earlier this week." I paused and met his stare, inches from his slightly aging face. "Perhaps she wanted her friend to play tea party with her one last time."

Callius grabbed me by the collar of my buttoned shirt and slammed my back up against the castle's courtyard wall. Gods, this fucker was old, but still stronger than I anticipated.

"Don't play coy with me, you little shit. Don't forget who gave you your position of power."

He aggressively released me and I straightened my clothing as I eyed him, a snarl on the cusp of leaving my lips.

"I was down in the dungeon for...reasons." I was about to inform him what happened with Elianna, but he cut me off instead.

"The queen is requesting our presence."

"Well, I—"

"Immediately," he seethed.

He turned his back to me as he walked into one of the outside corridors that contained the castle's courtyard door. I flipped my middle finger to him as I clenched my jaw so hard that I thought my teeth would crack.

If I had any chance of saving face, I had no choice but to follow him inside.

The throne room was still a disaster. Staff anxiously ran around us as we stepped over puddles of blood and the last of the dead bodies that had yet to be disposed of.

The queen was perched on her throne and the little shit prince was at her side. Both their faces mimicked the other, riddled with rage.

I took a careful step around a discarded limb on the floor. "Highness."

"Don't you fucking *Highness* me, Captain," she cut me off, leaving me speechless. "What. Happened."

"I wish I could say, My Queen," I responded.

"You wish you could say?" Kai interrupted. It took every ounce of my internal strength to make sure my facial features stayed neutral. "My bride is *dead*. My ascension is *postponed*. Sympathizers were within the castle walls. And you dare say you do not know?" His veins strained against his neck as he stared me down, huffing.

I cleared my throat and clasped my hands behind my back, rocking on my feet. "Well, I would say there is a traitor among us." I gave him a wry smile. "We will sniff them out."

"You. Will," he seethed as he started pacing. He turned his head to the queen. "My mother informed me that due to Velyran law, now I won't be able to be crowned king until another bride is chosen."

"Well, my son," she said, tone so soft it was hard to believe it was her who spoke them. "We will find you one as fast as we can. The ceremony will be private to ensure that doesn't happen again."

The prince didn't give a shit about his bride—he was just annoyed he wouldn't be crowned king as soon as he wanted. Kai was nothing but a gods-damn brat throwing a tantrum.

"Whatever," he spat viciously. "I will just take a little stroll down to Solus and pay her a visit to pass the time." He laughed maliciously.

Fuck. Fuck. *Fuck*.

I sucked on my tongue for a moment in thought and when I looked up, the queen's eyes were boring into me. "Do you have something to say, Captain?"

My eye twitched.

"Yes, your Majesty." I hesitated for a moment. "Unfortunately, there's no easy way to admit this to you. However, Elianna Solus was seen escaping earlier this morning, just before dawn."

Her face contorted into something truly horrific. Something that looked as if it was conjured by the dark gods themselves. I watched as a blaze of fire danced within her eyes as they continued to stare through me.

"What?!" Callius roared, as Kai balled his hands into fists at his sides, barring his teeth at me.

"You see, she was in attendance at the wedding," I started. "The princess was seen sneaking down into the dungeons, visiting her the past week. Perhaps it isn't a coincidence at all that sympathizers ambushed the wedding the same night she was let out of her cell."

"If you saw her at the wedding..." she started.

"I personally brought her back down to her cell," Callius cut in. "I don't have a single clue how she could have escaped after that."

"Callius..." she started, concern mixed with something I couldn't place in her tone.

"You had demanded I collect Adler the moment I saw you, My Queen." He gave her a look with pleading eyes. "I was going to bring it up in discussion in private to avoid wandering ears and eyes."

My brows furrowed as I watched them before I turned to observe the surrounding room. Staff kept their distance from us as they worked to clean everything, mopping up the stains of gore.

I cleared my throat, bringing their attention back to me. "Salvinae lured the dungeon door's guard down to him. He somehow was able to knock him unconscious and get his keys from him, letting both himself and Elianna out."

"And?" the queen hissed through her teeth.

"We were able to recapture Lukas. Elianna is gone."

"How?!" Kai boomed from the dais.

I turned my attention to him. "The wyvern. She flew up through the caverns on the back of your little blood bag pet." My tone was entirely too misplaced to be speaking to the royals, but I was losing what little patience I had left for them.

The queen instantly rose to her feet, standing over us from the top of the dais. "Let me get this straight. In a matter of twelve hours..." She began to pace as she rubbed her temples. "My son's wedding turned into a blood-soaked massacre, my daughter supposedly released our treasonous prisoner, and then said prisoner escaped on the back of our greatest *fucking* weapon?!"

I blinked. "It, um, it appears so, Highness."

She let out a furious scream that echoed and bounced off of the throne room walls. "Callius! Fetch my lovely daughter. *Now*."

Callius nodded to her and quickly left the room. Surely they wouldn't believe the princess when she came in here claiming I lied. They all knew how much she admired Lia. It was entirely believable.

I hoped.

Callius was gone for an unbearably long twenty minutes of uncomfortable silence, and when he finally arrived back in the throne room...he was empty-handed.

My heart seized in my chest. Where the hell was she?

"My Queen...The princess was not in her guarded room. Nor was Prince Finnian. They...they've vanished. Nobody has seen them."

Her already overly arched brows flew up her forehead. "Excuse me?" she screeched. "How did they leave guarded doors without being noticed?!"

"That is still being determined. But they are not in their rooms and have not been seen since being escorted there. We believe Avery discovered a tunnel behind her dresser and used that to escape." He shot me a look of disgust.

Gods-dammit.

"Listen to me, all of you idiots," the queen demanded. "Nobody outside of this circle and the two guards at their doors learn of their disappearance."

"Understood," Callius and I both answered in unison as we stood at attention.

"Good. Captain, you are dismissed for now," she said to me and then turned to my predecessor. "Callius...I have some plans for the lovely traitors amongst us. Round them up. Everyone. And if my lovely children are found among them, bring them here to me." She gave him a sweet, bone-chilling smile.

EIGHTEEN

Avery

By the time we had made it into the city, the streets were bustling with life and gossip. The three of us kept our heads low as we made our way through the busy roads.

Whispers about the evening's events could be heard at every turn, but to me, it had already felt as if it had occurred a lifetime ago.

"Did you hear the prince's bride was murdered last night?"

"There was a massacre at the castle. So many lives lost. Is this what we are to expect under the new king?"

"I escaped by the skin of my own teeth. We were barricaded in the throne room. Chaos. It was chaos."

And it was. It had been nothing but pure mayhem last night. Brutal, bloody madness.

Every time I thought of it, all I could see was the crimson river that flooded the marble floor of the throne room, threatening to turn my stomach. I shoved those visions as far into the back of my mind as possible, letting the adrenaline push me forward until we found sanctuary at Veli's—and that was if she would even let us in.

I did my best to look at landmarks we had passed with Lillian who had guided us through here only a few days prior, but everything appeared different in the daylight. As we turned the street corner that revealed the docks in the harbor, I felt a flutter of relief as I realized we were finally close to Veli's home.

People on the streets took notice of us, glaring down at Nyra as she trotted alongside us.

We needed to find the witch, and fast.

We made our way down, closer to the docks, when trumpets sounded through the air, catching everyone's attention. I peered up the street to see multiple guards atop their warhorses as they turned the corner, looking to be searching for something—or someone. They stared down at every individual as they passed.

"Remove your hood!" a guard ordered, and then a young male quickly ripped the hood of his cloak from his head, his arms shaking with nerves.

I glanced over at Finn and Landon. "Come on, we can't be seen."

We ducked our heads and quickly waded in and out of the crowd that grew smaller and smaller as we worked our way through hidden alleyways, much like the one Veli's home had been in.

After traveling down what seemed to be the ninth alley, I was about to give up hope of finding her when I noticed a small dark hued doorknob on the side of a building.

"Holy shit. There it is," I said in a hushed tone.

We walked up to the nearly invisible door, and I raised my fist to knock when Finn immediately forced my hand back down to my side.

"Is this really a good idea?" he asked nervously. "I just feel as if we have pushed our luck with her."

I scoffed at him. "Well, I think we are out of options aside from this, don't you think?"

"What if she turns us away?" he asked, and Landon watched us through furrowed brows.

I rolled my eyes. "Listen! Both of you. She is the only person we can trust right now, aside from Lukas."

I went to continue my rant when the door flew open, revealing a very irritated looking Veli.

Smiling nervously at her, I wiggled my fingers in greeting.

"Do you three have any idea how loud you're being? Gods, it was like you were yelling. I heard everything." Her brows rose.

One of my own rose to match hers, considering she just described our hushed voices as yells.

I carefully looked in both directions of the alley we stood in before I met her gaze once more. "We need your help, Veli. Last night—"

She lifted a hand to cut me off. "I heard. I heard all about it. I want no part in any of it."

She went to close the door, but I shot my arm out and stopped it before it could fully close.

Veli looked as if she would strike me. "You are going to help us. You know something, and I *know* you do."

She cracked the door open further, squinting at me with curiosity. "And what would that be?" She crossed her arms.

I sighed, and reached into a fold of my dress, where I had hidden my father's journal. I pulled it out and showed it to her.

"What is that?" Finn asked.

"I would like to know as well," Veli chimed in, unamused.

I glanced between the three of them and then down to Nyra, who was sitting on my feet. "It's the king's journal." I looked at my brother. "I'm sorry I have kept this from you. I've had it since that day Lukas and I went into Father's chambers, and I should have shown you then."

Hurt flashed in his eyes, and I had never felt like a worse sister in my life, but we didn't have time for this.

Turning back to Veli, I said, "He wrote in it throughout his life when something was of importance."

"And why would it matter to me that the king had a diary?" she hissed.

I stood my ground and leaned in slightly closer to her. "Because there is a very intriguing passage involving you...and the otherworldly power you possess."

My teeth clenched as irritation snuck up on me. Conveniently, she left out the little detail of our father knowing that she could wield magic.

Her brows rose, her features softening slightly.

"The passage also speaks of a time when you were rambling regarding an heir of blood and malice."

"Mother of the gods," she whispered. "That fool. Ugh. Come in. This can't be discussed out here. Come in quickly."

A small smile crept up my lips as she gestured for us to come inside.

The small space was just as dark and moody as I remembered. I laughed while glancing at Finn, who stood perfectly still, making sure he didn't touch or brush up against a single relic in the room.

Landon looked confused as his eyes wandered over everything in the space, but he kept quiet.

"Sit. Sit down," Veli commanded as she fanned her arms at the settee in the middle of the room while sitting in a matching chair across from it. The furniture was a deep purple in some velvet-like material.

"We're allowed to touch the settee?" Finn asked from behind her, still standing near the doorway.

Veli whipped around to face him. "Watch it, boy."

"Yes, Lady," he said in a panicked voice as he rushed over to the couch and sat between me and Landon.

She chuckled wickedly. "I am no 'Lady.' I am much more powerful than those feather-brained merchant's daughters." She crossed her arms once more and gave us a terrifying grin.

Finn audibly gulped. "Sorceress. Not Lady. Got it."

I tossed the leather-bound book onto her glass table that was between us all. "This holds all of my father's secrets. Including Lia's true identity and how he wished he had made her his heir. This could be the key to removing Kai from the throne."

"Regardless of what the king wanted, he did not voice this. Kai is the known heir. There is nothing we can do now to change that since the king is dead."

My jaw locked, lip curling back as I tried to reel in my anger towards her dismissing me. "I will not accept that and you shouldn't either!"

Her violet eyes roamed over me for a moment, and then she huffed out an annoyed breath through her nostrils. She reached down and picked the journal up from the table.

"I folded the tip of the page to mark the spot," I said to her.

"Foolish girl. You should never crease the pages of a book. Can they not afford bookmarks in your castle?" she sassed.

"I was on a limited time crunch," I retorted through clenched teeth.

Finn snickered beside me, likely happy that Veli's negative attention was now off of him. I shot him a warning look.

Veli opened the book to that exact page and sighed. She then read the small passage aloud.

"*'Beware of the day the pillar falls, for an heir will rise from blood and malice, and when the moment comes that the enemy weeps, a stranger of kin shall forge the way for the one who was promised.'* I can't believe he remembered all the words," she huffed out. The three of us sat frozen.

"Well, what does it mean?" I asked nervously.

"It's a prophecy. Obviously," she hissed, as if prophecies of the gods were common in today's realm. Nobody had believed in them or spoken them for centuries.

I tried a different approach. "Can you explain what the prophecy means?" She raised a brow at me. "Please?"

Veli's gold and violet eyes slowly moved across all of us and then back down to the book. "The pillar falling. That is the king. His death set everything in motion." She stopped for a moment, but none of us interrupted her. "The heir from blood and malice. Obviously Kai. He is a malicious little thing, is he not? The blood part never made sense to me until I learned of the king being poisoned with the blood of a wyvern." She let out a loud sigh. "Stranger of kin forging the way for the one who was promised. Looks like that is you two redheaded idiots." She pursed her lips.

My jaw popped open at the blatant disrespect she just spat at us until the excitement took over me. *I* was part of a prophecy?

"But what does 'stranger of kin' even mean?" Finn asked, shaking his head in thought.

"You two didn't know she was related to you until recently. You had no idea you shared the same blood." My eyes widened. That actually made sense. "However, the part I do not quite have a grip on yet is the enemy weeping. Why would our enemy weep, causing you to forge the way for her?" Veli scratched her head as she stared off blankly at the wall.

"Oh, my gods." Everyone's eyes shot over to me. "Lia said she found her mate. The commander of the human armada."

Veli scoffed. "That isn't possible. A fae cannot mate to a human. The gods wouldn't allow that." I contemplated about it for a moment before she said, "Unless he had fae heritage somewhere in his bloodline, a halfling perhaps. Still, it would be a long shot."

I leaned down, getting as close to her as the table between us would allow. "Think about it, Veli. She found her mate amongst the enemy. Lia found her mate and convinced the humans to fight for her chance at the throne, and then she was ripped away from them. She was *their* way to stop the bloodshed and save their race."

Veli blinked. "Hm. Interesting."

"Interesting?!" I spat. "That is all you have to say?"

She looked very unamused as she stood up from her chair. "What do you expect me to say? Does it make sense? Sure. It surprisingly does. That doesn't mean I know entirely what to do with said information. The king overhearing my muttering and then foolishly writing this into a journal doesn't mean I have all the gods' answers regarding it."

"How long did our father know of your magic, Veli?" I snapped at her, and then remembered what Lia had said in the dungeons. "And why were you and some crone across the continent murmuring riddles, anyway?"

Her neck whipped in my direction. "Your father and I never outright spoke of it, but I knew he had put the missing pieces together over the centuries, especially once healers were banned and I was able to travel through the castle unseen. Your father was a fool when it came to love, but not necessarily one of all sorts."

She clicked her nails together impatiently. "And it's rare, but the gods have been known to use the magic-possessed beings of the realm as mere puppets, conduits, and tools to get what they want. Occasionally, even to provide themselves with entertainment. They spoke the ancient prophecy to us, placing it into our minds. Witches were bred to be servants to them and their desires—just as all other beings."

Her gaze drifted over us before she continued. "Unfortunately for me, I was in the presence of the king and couldn't help what was said once the words were whispered to me."

The air was thick with tension for a moment, and then I finally leaned back in the settee and let out a long breath. A second later, Veli's spine straightened, and she angled her ear to the door, snatching all of our attention.

Veli's eyes flew back to mine. "Something is happening in the city square." She rushed over to the door. "Put your hoods back on and follow me. We can't be seen."

Nineteen

Avery

We left Nyra at Veli's home, which Veli didn't approve of, but if we were going to be discreet, we wouldn't be able to have a giant white wolf casually walking around with us in the crowd.

The sun was now high in the sky and the streets were packed with civilians. Males, females, and younglings alike were eagerly pushing through each other to try to get closer to whatever was going on in the city square. Whispers of captured traitors echoed through the streets, making all four of us uneasy.

"Serves them right!"

"How dare they betray the crown! New king or not, they swore their lives to Velyra."

"Sympathizers. In our own guard. Disgusting."

My heart sank at each passing murmur I heard as we pushed our way through.

Did our own guards really let in the sympathizers? Or were they just all disguised as guests that no one thought to give a second look?

At this point, I didn't know what to believe. Lia had admitted to being one herself, so that had to count as something for them. I had never met a human or a halfling. All I had to go on was the rumors of what they had done to my uncle and grandfather that I had never met, and the bloodshed they caused on our side of the war.

However, Lia was smart, she always had been, and if she trusted the mortals, then we should, too. Given everything that I had learned about my mother and her wicked tendencies, it made it that much easier to side with the sympathizers. I just wished they hadn't gone about it in such a bloody manner, but this was war.

While I was new to the ways of it, I couldn't imagine an enemy sitting down with the queen for tea and having a civil conversation about ending the one thing she had set out to do since before I was born.

As we forced our way through the throngs of civilians, we finally caught sight of what was causing the commotion. A never-ending line of individuals extended beyond the stage in the center of the square, their wrists tightly bound and their mouths gagged with cloth.

I recognized some of them. Then, as my eyes went down the line, I realized I recognized nearly *all* of them. It was almost the entirety of the castle's staff.

My gaze whipped back to the center of the square to look up at the wooden stage, where twenty nooses hung before the crowd. It was about fifty feet in front of where we stood within the masses. Guards were stationed across the front of the platform, making a barrier in case anyone was dumb enough to try to stop what was about to occur.

A second massacre was about to take place in Isla within twenty-four hours. And this time, it was at the hands of the crown.

"Holy gods," Veli whispered. "Keep your heads down. Both of you. You cannot be seen or recognized out here." She gestured to me and Finn.

My eyes met his, and pure terror was etched into his features.

"I know them. I know *all* of them." Landon's hushed voice was riddled with pain, bringing all of our stares to him. "I...I think I would've been up there with them if you hadn't forced me to come with you."

"I think you're right," I admitted, right before I bit my lower lip.

Callius appeared then and the murmuring voices in the crowd went silent. Nothing could be heard except the flowing water of the square's fountain, and a small babe crying off in the distance.

He stopped in the center of the stage and then the guards off to the side moved to guide the first set of people up onto it, placing each individual in front of a noose, wrapping it around their necks.

My heart felt as if it was going to beat out of my chest.

"Attention!" Callius' voice boomed across the city, as if he didn't already have every individual's attention already. "As many of you are aware, the castle was under attack last night. The king's bride was murdered in cold blood before the wedding attendees. In addition to this, many of the guests themselves were also slaughtered in the throne room."

Muttering erupted through the city at the news that he had just confirmed.

"*Quiet!*" he yelled. Silence immediately answered him. "The future king is...devastated at the loss of his beautiful queen-to-be."

I whipped to Finn. "Lies. Nothing but lies!"

"Shh," he hushed me, his eyes darting back and forth between me and the stage before us.

"Sympathizers have been popping up far too often in Isla, and actions must be made. Some have revealed themselves in the castle's own staff and guard. Due to it being impossible to weed through them all and expect the absolute truth to be told, severe actions must be taken. The castle's staff and known sympathizer guards will be executed *today*."

Small bursts of cheers erupted through the city. *Cheers*. They were excited to witness the deaths of their neighbors, peers, and friends.

I glanced around and felt some relief to see that many of the faces in the surrounding crowd looked just as mortified at the situation as I felt.

Perhaps the people cheering just didn't want to expose themselves by not looking fond of what was about to occur.

"I can't watch this," I whispered, and when I went to turn, Veli caught me.

"No. It's too late now. If they see us wading through everyone, we will be caught."

My eyes flared as I realized that she was right. I *hated* that she was right.

The ropes were tightened around everyone's throats and when Callius gave the signal, a masked guard to the side pulled on a wooden lever, dropping the floor beneath their feet away in an instant. The sounds of necks and bones snapping filtered through the air. Nausea climbed up my throat. I was going to be sick as I was forced to watch their bodies dangle lifelessly from the ropes.

The floorboards were raised once more, and we were made to watch as they repeated this numerous times. They took the lives of countless fae, never knowing if they were truly innocent or guilty. Some sobbed as they stood in line, waiting for their fate. Others held their heads high as they accepted it.

I had never been so horrified by something in my entire existence. Murder—there was no other way to describe what was unfolding in the heart of the city—cold-blooded, mass murder, and it was by the *crown*. My heart was shattering for them and their families.

Out of those hanging from a noose, how many were innocent? How many of them were guilty, but only seeking revenge for what had already been done to someone they cared for?

Sniffling was now heard through the crowd as they gazed at their friends or loved ones being hung by the neck until dead.

The last of the staff was escorted onto the stage and lined up with their nooses.

My face blanched, and I almost let out a cry when I noticed that Lillian, the fae who had helped us sneak out and find Veli that night, was among them.

"No," I whispered as I took a step forward, but Finnian caught my wrist. "No. No. No. Not Lillian."

A single tear fell from his lower lashes. "I don't think there is anything we can do."

I focused on Lillian's doll-like face, but what I expected to see there wasn't present at all. There was no fear. No regrets. She held her shoulders back with a knowing grin plastered across her features as she gazed back at the thousands that stood before her. She looked *proud*.

Callius went to raise his hand to give the signal for a final time when another voice echoed through the air, stopping him.

"This will not end with us!"

It was *Lillian*.

"My mother was a halfling, and she was murdered decades ago by order of your cunt of a queen!" she spat. Gasps of shock surrounded us. "This will not end with us. The gods have spoken of a better future. Your tyrant prince will doom Velyra as we know it."

I was frozen where I stood; my jaw hung open in disbelief. Was it her who had let the sympathizers in? *Lillian?* The female that helped the queen's children only nights ago? I couldn't believe it.

Then I remembered what she had said so quietly before offering us her help...*'you are different from the others.'* Had

Lillian aided us that night because we had shown her kindness?

"I believe in a better realm. I believe in a better people. And I believe that the *true* monsters of Velyra reside within its own castle walls!"

Callius took a step toward her. "We have a confession! A shame you let all the others die before you." He snickered.

"I had help. And we don't have a single regret other than the prince surviving the ceremony. The bride's killing arrow was meant for *him*."

More gasps of shock rang out.

Callius' expression turned into that of fury as he struck her in the face. Lillian's head whipped to the side at the force of the blow.

Blood lined her teeth as she gave him an eerie, crimson-stained smile. Her eyes began to wander over the crowd, and my heart sank as her gaze paused on me, somehow finding me in the masses beneath my hood. She gave me a subtle nod, and my lips parted.

Her gaze moved back to Callius, looking every bit the defiant prisoner, full of pride.

Callius didn't waste another second as he gave the signal, and the lever was pulled. Bodies fell and more necks snapped, including Lillian's.

Her satisfied grin clung to her face even in death.

I audibly swallowed as my lip trembled. "I can't believe this."

"I can't either," Landon chimed in. He had been silent the entire time as he was forced to watch his friends be murdered.

"There is one more traitor to be dealt with," Callius announced as the crowd began to disburse. Everyone's movements stumbled to a halt. "Our late king's very own personal guard, Sir Lukas Salvinae."

Bile clogged my throat. My eyes snapped up to Finnian to see that his were so wide I thought they would pop out of his skull.

"Mother of the gods," Veli whispered. "This...this is not good."

No. No, it wasn't at all.

Gasps of shock echoed on the wind as Lukas was physically dragged up the stage's wooden steps.

His body looked to be teetering on the edge of death already. His eyes were so black and blue that they were practically swollen shut. He had cuts all over him, including an enormous gash down his arm that was still leaking fresh blood.

Lukas was brought to center stage, directly next to Callius. When the guard's grip on him loosened, his body swayed as if he could barely keep himself upright.

"The former Captain Elianna Solus has been discovered to be a traitor and newly self-proclaimed mortal sympathizer!" Callius shouted at the crowd. "She was in the custody of the castle guard awaiting execution when Lukas set her free, allowing her to escape from our grasp. This offense will be punishable by death."

Uncontrollable sobs ripped through my chest. I couldn't help it. I couldn't control it as we were about to be forced to watch our friend be killed in front of us for doing something that we all planned to do together.

"Any last words, old friend?" Callius said as his head whipped back in Lukas' direction.

Lukas lifted his head to meet Callius' stare. The voice that came out of him seeped with rage and power. "Long live the *true* heir of Velyra. Princess Elianna Valderre!" he roared in his face, his words reverberating through the city.

My jaw dropped. Gasps of shock ripped through the crowd at what Lukas had just declared in front of everyone in Isla's streets.

Callius' features contorted with wrath at what Lukas had just announced to the realm. A moment later, in one swift movement, he unsheathed his sword and ripped it clean through Lukas' throat.

An unbearable scream of agony tore through my own as I watched Lukas' severed head fall to the ground at his feet and land with a fleshy smack. Blood poured down the front of his torso as his body dropped a moment later.

Finnian vomited next to us and the entire city was shouting with horror, disbelief, and grief.

"Get ahold of yourself, boy. This is not the place or time. Be strong. Be strong *for him*," Veli said, as she placed a hand on each of our shoulders.

She was right. We were drawing too much attention, but at this point, it seemed as if chaos was about to erupt all over again.

"What did he mean?!" one person yelled to our right.

"True heir? The captain was the *true* heir? Why did he say her last name was Valderre?!" another person shouted from behind us.

Roars of agreement echoed all around, and the guards stormed into the masses to take back control before they lost it entirely.

"Enough!" Callius boomed once more. "Get the fuck out of my sight. Everyone!"

The guards unsheathed their swords as they continued to head into the crowd, and turmoil truly erupted then. We each held our hoods in place tightly as we disappeared into the mob of Isla's citizens and ran as fast as we could back to Veli's hidden home.

TWENTY
Elianna

WE HAD BEEN WALKING north for hours and were lucky that we hadn't been seen by anyone, as Nox followed me silently through the endless Velyran fields.

All I could think about with each step forward, and farther from Isla, was Lukas. He had sacrificed his own chance at escape and I knew he would be thrown right back into his cell, and only the gods knew what else Kellan had planned for him since he helped me flee.

My heart ached now for both my father and the father-figure I had all of my life.

Lukas had said he was proud of me. *Proud.* As if being foolish enough to be caught multiple times was something to be proud of. How could he or anyone else think I would be fit to rule? Not only would the realm never accept me, but I wouldn't know the first thing about leading them into a better world.

A rumble skid through the dirt beneath my feet, causing me to stumble. I looked back over my shoulder to see Nox was now lying down on his stomach, panting like a canine.

"What do you think you're doing?" I asked him. "Nox. We need to go north. Meaning we can't just stay here and...lay." I gestured to the ground with my hands.

He didn't budge, and I scoffed.

I stormed up to him and wrapped both arms around one of his hind legs, and attempted to pull him to get him to move. When he still wouldn't budge, I released my hold and fell to the ground, flat on my ass.

Nox let out a short few huffs, mimicking what seemed to be laughter.

"Are you serious?" I grumbled, squinting up at him through the rays of the sun. "I don't have time for this. Let's go!" I dragged out the last word.

His eyes thinned into slits as he looked down at me. My heart skipped a small beat, thinking he could blast me to ash at any moment, but honestly, if he wanted to, he would have done it by now. He definitely wouldn't have saved me from the fall this morning, either.

A few tiny birds started fluttering around the horns on his head. The wyvern looked at peace as he experienced nature for the first time and was enjoying the songs they sang to him.

A small smile crept up on my lips.

"Fine. We will rest for a little while. It will be much safer to fly at night when you blend in with the sky, anyway."

His giant eyes flared again, and he looked down at me, almost looking confused.

"What? I mean, we will have to fly at some point! It would take weeks to get to Ellecaster on foot! Maybe even more."

He didn't look convinced.

I pushed myself to my feet and crossed my arms, looking up at him. "Don't tell me after walking around all day you prefer this." I gestured to the ground. "To the skies." I gestured back up into the air above.

He let out an irritated growl.

"Ugh. Fine. We will rest here until dusk, but we will be taking to the skies at some point. Do you understand me? I have no weapons...aside from you. Being down here is dangerous, especially at night. So rest up."

Nox slowly lowered his head to rest on the ground, the chickadees following him. His eyes closed tightly as the small birds continued to sing to him, lulling him to sleep in the middle of the grassy field.

I sat back down next to him and warily leaned my back up against his side. I glanced back at his head and noticed he didn't even flinch. He was comfortable with me for some reason. After everything he had been through at the hands of Kai and Callius, he trusted me enough to be vulnerable and sleep. That had to count for something.

So, I leaned my head back to rest on him and allowed myself to doze off for the first time in what seemed like days while I watched the clouds pass over us in the sky above.

I awoke to Nox's body jolting out of nowhere, scaring the shit out of me.

I leapt up to my feet in an instant and automatically reached for the non-existent dagger at my thigh on reflex.

Dammit.

I looked up to see it was past dusk, and the sky was pitch black. The only light provided was by the beaming moon and surrounding stars.

Shit. How long had we been asleep?

Nox was lashing out and snapping his jaws at the small bats now hovering around his head that replaced the birds. He let out a growl of annoyance and caught one in his mouth.

"Nox! Let it go! It might be...dirty."

The wyvern whipped his head at me and gave me a look that resembled raising a brow, if he had any.

I rubbed my temples. "I...I don't know. But it probably won't taste good."

He contemplated my words, which I honestly couldn't tell if he understood them or not, and then he spat the bat out at the ground.

The little creature bounced off the terrain and flew away, shaking off Nox's saliva with each flap of its tiny wings.

"Beautiful," I said. "Are you ready to try to fly again?"

Nox lifted his gaze to the stars and then brought it back down to me and shook his head.

I threw my left foot down in a dramatic stomp. "What? What do you mean 'no' you don't want to?"

He lowered his head completely to the ground, resting it in the grass.

"Oh, no you don't," I said through my teeth as I stormed around his enormous, scaly body and climbed up his side to get onto his back. "Look, I'm not thrilled about this either, and please, for the love of the gods, don't drop me again. But this is our only shot at making it where we need to be."

His giant golden eye narrowed in on me as he turned his head backward, contorting his neck to get a better look at me.

"We're going to figure this out together," I breathed.

Together. Just as Jace and I had promised each other months ago. Remembering those words and the scene that followed them caused an ache to radiate through my chest.

I let out a shuddering breath and put all my focus into diving deep into the bond—the tether to him and his beating heart. Yet still, all I felt was anguish, and I dismissed it as my own.

I pursed my lips. "Alright, start flapping those wings, Nox."

With a loud *whoosh* sound, both wings shot out from his sides and flapped down toward the ground.

"Good. Very good. Now again."

He continued to flap his wings, but it was too slow. We were still on the ground.

"What if you started running to get a head start?"

He twisted his long neck and looked back at me, unamused.

"Oh, I'm sorry! Do you have a better idea?"

He huffed out a breath of hot air again and then took off into a *sprint* on his hind legs. I clutched the fin on his neck as tightly as I could as he started flapping his wings in unison.

"Yes! Yes, Nox!" I shouted as I glanced down to see that we were now off the ground and hovering higher with each flap.

Soon enough, we were soaring through the night sky. I loosened my grip and sat up, my thighs tightly clenched around his spine, and my core muscles worked to keep my body in place atop him.

I brought my hands out at my sides for balance and looked around the skies. The stars glistened even brighter from up here. Nox's scales shimmered beneath them with their amethyst hues.

I quickly glanced down and realized it was a mistake when I saw how high up we were now. We passed over villages, fields, and small forests. It was so much faster to travel this way. We had already gone miles in merely a few minutes.

Nox left his wings out and glided on the wind, just as I had tried to instruct him to the previous night.

The biggest, genuine smile of joy spread across my face. I felt so free up here. The wind blew my hair back, the warm air danced around my face and the tail end of my gown fluttered on it.

I let out a loud screech of triumph that filled the night sky and bounced off the distant hills.

I could live up here. Just me, Nox, and the moon.

All I was missing was Jace.

We flew under the display of twinkling stars for hours, and whenever I got cold, I would huddle behind him at the nape of his neck.

I wondered how far off dawn was, since I had no idea how long we had woken up after the sun had set.

I twisted around to look down at the ground and noticed a farm in the distance. Cows were already being let out to graze in the field, which meant it couldn't be far off.

The herd of cattle snagged Nox's attention a moment later.

Without warning, he swooped down straight towards the field, aiming right at the farm animals that we were now hauling at full speed.

"Nox! No!" I screamed, but my words were lost in the air.

I screamed "no" over and over again, but it was no use.

He tucked his wings in sharply and dove, wrapping his talons around one of the cows, and then immediately took back off into the sky...with the fucking cow.

The poor creature let out a sound of distress.

"Nox, what are you doing?! Put it down!" Glancing down at the ground, I realized that we were already soaring to great heights again in only a matter of *seconds*. "Wait! Don't drop it. We need to place it nicely dowwww—"

My instructions were cut off when he dove once more toward the terrain.

Nox released the cow from his grasp when we were about fifteen feet above the ground, and then we landed, extremely ungracefully, right beyond that.

I jumped down from his back and couldn't hold in my scolding for a single second. "No! *Bad!*"

Was this how you spoke to a wyvern? Had anyone ever truly spoken to one before? I highly doubted it was like this if they had.

I glanced back down at the now very dead cow.

"Ugh. Well, it's dead now. Might as well go make use of it," I said, as I slumped down to the ground in defeat.

Nox waddled over to his dinner and didn't waste a moment before he dug in. The scene of it was...disgusting, to say the least, yet my own stomach growled. When was the last time I had eaten? I honestly couldn't remember.

At the sound of my grumbling abdomen, Nox's head lifted up curiously from the carcass and stared at me, blood dripping from his jaw. He then ripped off a piece of meat with his teeth and sauntered back over to me.

He dropped it onto the ground at my feet and looked down at me with concerned eyes.

"I appreciate it," I said as I hesitantly patted his nose, that was now mere inches from my face. "But I can't eat that. It's raw. I'll figure something out. You need the strength, though. Go enjoy your food."

He took a large step back from me and his eyes darted back and forth between me and the chunk of meat.

Nox then took in a large breath, and my eyes widened. A moment later, he blew a tiny burst of fire directly toward me and I dove to roll out of the way as I yelped.

I lifted my head from the ground and peeked over at the meat to see that it was now charred on the ground.

...He...did he just *cook* that?

Nox gave me a small nod of his head.

I hesitantly crawled back toward him. "I don't appreciate having fire blown at me without warning, but... uh, thank you." I cleared my throat.

He blinked at me and then turned on his feet to head back to the feast that awaited him. I eyed him warily as I watched him.

Maybe Nox knew how to control his flames after all, and all of those mishaps in the dungeons were really just him nervously extinguishing his greatest defense too quickly to rid himself of those pricks.

I ripped off a piece of the meat and took a bite. I let out a small chuckle as an involuntary moan left me from the food hitting my empty stomach.

"Maybe this wasn't a death sentence after all," I whispered to myself as I shoved the food down my throat and gazed out at dawn as it spread across the horizon.

TWENTY-ONE

Jace

My days had become a constant loop of the same bullshit. I would wake at dawn and go for a run through Ellecaster, making sure I greeted all the citizens who resided here as I passed. Fake smiles aside, I had always believed it was important to know your people personally. While I knew it was impossible to know each individual by name, I always made an effort to stop and make small conversations when I could. While I was burning on the inside with grief, I put on a strong face for them, which seemed to make them feel more at ease, given the growing issues down in Isla.

Once my morning run was complete, I ran down to the drill fields beyond the city and trained with the men until sunset. We would train all day, perfecting our fighting skills, archery, and line stances.

My soldiers here grew more confident daily. I could only hope that my general in Alaia was managing things as efficiently, ensuring that we could function seamlessly together when the time came. In my heart, I knew that the time was drawing near.

Today, the sparring was not going as smoothly as it had been the last few days. The men were tired from the constant training sessions, and I was growing angrier by the minute.

Angry that they were tired, even though they had every right to be. Angry that I still hadn't heard a single thing about Lia. And absolutely furious that we weren't any closer to winning this gods-forsaken war.

Every single second of the day, I contemplated slipping out from the barracks in the middle of the night, taking a horse, and riding down to Isla alone. I would trade my life for hers in an instant, and with each passing day, the thought of going out to find her on my own became more appealing.

I didn't care if it was a death sentence for me—as long as she got out.

"You!" I pointed to one of the scrawnier soldiers, his nervousness evident as he shifted from foot to foot. That wouldn't do. He had to learn not to show his fear, especially on the front lines. "What is your name, son?"

He took a single step forward, past the line of soldiers. "Garrett, sir," he said in a shaky voice that I could tell he was desperately trying to calm.

"Come here, Garrett."

The boy walked up to me. I glanced back and forth between him and the small unit behind us.

"Do you fear death, Garrett?"

"N-n-no, sir. I mean Commander!"

I eyed him. "I don't believe you. Do you want to know why?" He nodded nervously. "It's because I can sense your fear. It's written in your body language."

Murmurs erupted down the lines, so I redirected my attention to them all.

"Fearing death is normal. Our souls leaving the realm is an unknown, terrifying thing that looms over us mortals day in and day out. However, fear will not help you out there! Fear is not on your side. Do you know what is? Anger."

I paused for a moment as the murmurs came to a halt. "Rage is on your side. The fury we feel inside of ourselves at how our kind has been suppressed for over a century. How we have been slaughtered by the tens of thousands, our women and children suffering horrifying fates. Our homes and villages destroyed. Use *that* as fuel. Do not shake in your fucking boots at the sight of the masses that march here to destroy us. Use that anger, that *rage*, and turn it back on them. Fight for survival. Fight for the lives our parents should have lived. The lives you want your children and grandchildren to have."

I was met with silence as a few hundred pairs of eyes bore into me.

"Tell me, men, is *that* something worth fighting for?"

"Yes, Commander." A roar of agreement sounded from them.

"You are all dismissed. Go home and kiss your wives. The end of the war is near, but you should cherish these moments leading up to it with your families."

My heart lurched as I said the words. To go home to their wives. Would I ever have that? The thought of having that with anyone else but Lia repulsed me. I never wanted that.

Never desired to have someone at home waiting for me. But Lia...Lia would never be at home waiting. I would have to try to knock her out and tie her to a gods-damn chair or some shit to have her stay behind. And I would bet all my coin that she would still find a way to get there and fight with me at my side.

A sad smile tilted the corner of my lips as I watched the men disperse in front of me, all seeming to be much more relaxed than only moments ago.

"That was one hell of a pep talk, brother," Gage's voice sounded from behind me.

I turned to him. "They were getting sloppy. That kid looked like he was going to shit his pants just from drill." I rubbed my temples with one hand. "I can't even imagine him on a battlefield. Perhaps he is too young."

Gage let out a chuckle. "You and I were fighting on the front lines when we were much younger than him. He will get used to it. His eyes lit up while you spoke to the army. They just need to know *you* believe in them and what they are fighting for."

I clenched my jaw in response. I didn't know what to say. Perhaps he was right, but I couldn't lead my men out to battle if they were terrified during training. It would be a fucking massacre.

He looked me up and down. "How are you holding up?" he asked warily.

I snickered as I kicked a rock at my feet. "How does it fucking look like I'm holding up, Gage?" I replied, refusing to meet his stare.

"It looks as if you're constantly furious and on edge."

My gaze snapped up to his then. "Should I not be?" I couldn't control the bitterness in my tone as I lashed out at Gage, even though I knew it was uncalled for.

He walked up to me and placed his hand on my shoulder, shaking me lightly as he looked into my eyes. "We will get her back. She is the toughest girl we know...aside from maybe Zae." He paused for a moment. "Actually, don't even tell her I said that. I don't feel like getting my ass handed to me." A small laugh left me without permission at the thought of that. "The point is, Lia is a survivor. We are doing everything we can to get to her in a way where it will make the most sense and be successful."

I hesitated before I spoke what had been plaguing my mind. "I'm leaving in the morning, Gage. I can't wait here any longer. It's eating me alive. I need you and Zae to handle things here until I return with her, and I won't risk the two of you." He shot me a look as he rolled his eyes, scoffing at me. "Don't give me that," I growled.

"Give you what, brother? You cannot go there alone. It would be a death sentence. You are no more easily controllable than Lia is—you are mirrors of each other, especially in that sense. However, if I have to barricade you in your own gods-damn barracks, I will. You sacrificing yourself would only piss her off, anyway—and then she'd be after me and Zae."

The corner of my lip tilted in a smirk. "But be that as it may, I *will* find a way to keep your ass here, and I don't care how upset you are with me for it. You've barely given yourself enough time to heal as it is, and you need your strength back. It would be best if we at least had *some* form of armada with us. Also…I'm insulted you would try to leave us behind in this."

I sucked in and bit down on my inner cheeks, annoyed that he was right. "I miss her. And I'm worried about her." Gage smiled at my admission. "I don't want to hear it," I grumbled at him.

"Listen, I just can't believe you admitted something like that, even though we all know exactly how you feel. I miss her too, brother. Just obviously not in the same sense."

I snickered and looked up to the clear afternoon sky. "You better not." My smile fell, and I looked back at him. "I just don't know if she is truly okay."

"What do you mean?"

I blinked a few times, trying to think of the right words to describe what I felt. "I…I kept getting these phantom-like aches that often lingered, and it made me feel like she has been hurt. And the last few days, my heart will begin racing, and then I'll be slammed with an overwhelming sense of nerves and adrenaline out of nowhere."

He raised a brow at me. "Uhhh, I'm not sure I understand."

I went to speak again, but our conversation was cut short by a voice calling to us from up the hill.

"There you two are!" Zae said as she ran down to us. We were now the only three left in the training field.

She placed her hands on her knees as she bent down, trying to catch her breath.

"Out of shape, Zae?" Gage asked with a laugh.

She stood back up and punched him in the gut without hesitation, forcing a grunt out of him, but he laughed through the pain.

"Gods, you two," I said as I shook my head, not in the mood for their shit.

"I am *not* out of shape. I just ran all over the city looking for you. The soldiers were already out in the streets, so I didn't think you would still be down here."

"What's going on?" I asked, confused.

She turned to me and met my stare. "A falcon arrived from Isla. We have news."

I had never run so fast in my life. I ran through the city streets, not bothering to stop for the small talk that the people were so used to. I could faintly hear Zaela and Gage behind me telling me to slow down, but I couldn't, even if I wanted to. All I could think about was if the falcon had news of Lia.

I skidded to a stop in front of the post and stormed in. The woman behind the counter looked nervous at the sight of me as I stood there, sweat covered and disheveled.

"I'm so sorry to barge in like this, Miss. You have a falcon letter for me?"

"I do. Let me grab it," she said as she strolled to a basket behind the counter.

She came back and handed it to me. I ripped it a little too aggressively from her grasp and apologized as I ran out the door. I then stood before my co-seconds.

"What does it say?" Gage asked while trying to catch his own breath now.

The parchment had been sealed to avoid being tampered with after what had happened with Lia and her letter to the king. With shaky hands, I ripped open the wax seal, unrolled the paper, and began to skim over the letter.

"Holy gods," I whispered as my breath caught. I looked back at them, both looking like they were about to slam me with questions. "Not here. Let's get to my barracks."

The three of us ran to my quarters, and I slammed the door behind me and immediately clicked the lock in place.

"What the hell does the letter say, Jace?" Zae asked as she hesitantly sat down on my bed.

Gage was nibbling on his thumbnail nervously, his eyes darting back and forth between the two of us.

I unrolled the letter once more and read it aloud.

Commander,

The ambush was mostly a success. While the prince unfortunately survived the attack, the bride did not, thus delaying the coronation. We took down as many crown supporters as we could.

The following afternoon, the prince ordered a public execution of all suspects, some of which had assisted with us entering the castle for the celebration. Others, though, were entirely innocent.

Right before the execution of a castle guard, he screamed to the entire crowd present, "Long live the true heir, Elianna Valderre." Whispers traveled of his admittance, and people are wondering what secrets the castle has been keeping all these years. She has been announced as public enemy number one, and there is a hefty reward on her head for whoever captures her and brings her back to the crown.

Once I know more, if deemed safe to, I will send another falcon as soon as possible.

Take care.

"Holy shit," Gage breathed.

"She got out!" Zaela confirmed as she jumped up from the bed.

A smile grew on my lips. A genuine smile. The first time in weeks since I had last seen my rightful queen. "It appears she did."

"What do we do now? Do we wait for her, or do we go try to find her?" Gage asked, reaching for the handle of his sword.

He was ready to go save her. My best friend was just as loyal to her as he was to me.

"We'll wait it out until next week. She could be anywhere and the letter was dated a few days ago. If she doesn't turn up or send word, we go out and find her and bring her home."

"Home," Zae repeated without a hint of the lip that normally accompanied her tone.

I gave her a single nod. "We bring our future queen to her awaiting army beyond the mountains, where we will finally figure out how to end this once and for all."

TWENTY-TWO

Avery

THE FOUR OF US and Nyra had been holed up in Veli's tenement for days. Guards and soldiers constantly patrolled the streets of Isla, inspecting every individual face they passed, which made it impossible for us to leave. I was beyond thankful that Veli was able to make her door vanish.

Once we snuck back here after the public executions, all of us were silent for nearly a day. I had no words for what I felt. I was forced to watch someone I had known since I was a child be decapitated in front of the entire city. The most loyal guard to the crown and to my father, gone. Murdered in cold blood. In the blink of an eye.

Every time the scene of it flashed across my mind, a sob would involuntarily escape me, which I could tell was irritating Veli.

Or maybe she was just irritated that we were all stuck here with her.

"Must you sob continually?" she asked with a sigh from across the room.

I sat up from where I was sprawled out across her settee. "Well, I am *trying* to be quiet! It's not my fault you have annoyingly sharp hearing," I snapped back at her.

"Watch it," she said through her teeth as she pointed at me with one of her incredibly sharp talons.

"How do you even do anything with those, anyway?" I asked, my voice riddled with attitude. I was absolutely pushing my luck with her.

She gave me a wicked grin. "Would you like to find out, Princess?"

I gulped down my retort and laid back down as Finn paced back and forth across the room and Landon sat across from me in the settee's matching chair. They had still barely spoken to each other. I couldn't tell anymore if it was because Landon was still upset with Finn for what Kai had done or a lack of what Finn did to help. Perhaps Landon was just as shocked as the rest of us and was left speechless.

I glanced under the small, round glass table that was positioned between the couch and chair and noticed there was a pile of ancient-looking, dusty books under it. My gaze drifted over to the witch, whose back was turned, and then my curiosity got the best of me as I reached under the glass and grabbed the top few. The layer of dust on them made me believe they hadn't been touched in decades, and the books just sat below her tea table.

I was glancing at them when the third caught my eye. It looked significantly older than the rest, and I was drawn to it for some odd reason. After placing the other two back, I dropped the third book onto my lap and let out a small grunt, not expecting it to weigh as much as it did. I traced my pointer finger down the spine. The material the book was made out of was…interesting, to say the least—like leather, but not quite the same.

I turned my attention to the title that I squinted my eyes to read in the dim candlelight. Her home didn't have any windows, and with the walls painted a shade resembling onyx, it was difficult to see in here with even my fae sight.

The book was titled *Tinaebris Malifisc*. I shrugged a shoulder after trying to pronounce the strange words in my head for nearly a minute and opened the book.

The edges of the pages were frayed and archaic looking, no longer a light beige, but stained and yellow hued. A shiver ran up my spine as I turned each page, revealing more phrases in a language that I couldn't comprehend, but the pictures accompanying them were even more bothersome.

Before I could blink, the book slammed shut in my own hands. I was partially frozen in fear, thinking the book shut itself, when I looked up through my lashes and noticed Veli staring at me—anger written into her features.

"Put. It. *Down*," she seethed.

I sat up and placed the book on my lap, covering it with my arms. "What is this, Veli? It feels…"

"Ancient? Malicious? As if it were crafted from wrath? Well, that would be because it was, and it is written in the ancient language of the gods. So put it the fuck down before you hurt yourself," she demanded. I eyed her but didn't move. "It is also bound with the skin of the gods' children—the deities." She shot me that terrifying grin of hers once more and I frantically threw the book onto the table.

"Ew." I shuddered.

Veli glided over to us and sat next to me, lifting the book into her lap effortlessly with her magic that I was desperately trying to get used to.

"This book solely possesses dark magic. It was bound a millennia ago. You shouldn't have even touched it. Never mind open it, you stupid, reckless girl."

My eyes narrowed in on her, but I kept my mouth shut for once.

"What is in there?" Landon asked. "What can that magic do?"

Veli let out a sigh. "How am I the one that got stuck with you three?"

"Everyone else is dead," I said flatly, staring off into nothing.

Veli shrugged her shoulders, but I didn't miss Finn wince in the corner of the room at my morbid reply.

"The book allows its wielder to do incredibly wicked things. It covers blood magic, shadow summoning, breaking mental shields, and much more. It's dangerous, sinister. Especially in the wrong hands."

"What does all that mean?" I asked, even more confused now than when I originally picked up the book.

"It is none of your concern, girl," Veli hissed, but I continued to stare at her, refusing to move on until she explained what all of this meant. "Fine," she huffed. "Have nightmares for all I care, but do not come crying to the witch that tried to warn you."

Veli blinked several times as if looking for the right words to say before she spoke. "In the realm of blood magic, a witch can harness the power to manipulate your body by controlling the blood coursing through your veins. They could make you move or mimic what they desired, or even just stop your blood from pumping into your heart. All they would need is a drop of your own blood in a vial, or for you to have an open, bleeding wound."

My eyes widened slightly, but she continued. "Shadow summoning should be self-explanatory, and it is the only form of the sorcery that I have ever manipulated. The wielder can summon shadows to be concealed from something, and the cover of them will move as they do—making you essentially invisible to the untrained eye. Shadows work in mysterious ways. On any given day, I am able to summon them as a shield to not be seen, but when they move in unison with me, it delves into the realm of forbidden, dark magic, as they often possess a mind of their own when utilized by a malleable, easily manipulated witch." She let out a sharp cackle. "Or one with wicked tendencies."

Veli's focus returned to me, but I had nothing else to say aside from, "Is that all?"

The corner of her lip tilted. "Could not be further from being all. In fact, it is just the very tip of the surface. Breaking mental shields is...well, it isn't pretty. Essentially, the witch could deteriorate their victim's mind from the inside out. It is gruesome and painful. If the wielder is strong, they could even manipulate the mind of another to do unthinkable actions. Ones they would never typically do on their own, and this is not just limited to fae or humans, but all sorts of creatures alike."

Veli's pale face blanched even further as she spoke of the magic, all signs of her previous amusement gone.

"And these are the types of spells that witches of your kind have used? Lia said she saw one," Finn chimed in.

"As I said before, not all the Elora Coven partake in such wickedness. However, many chose that path, yes. It's why the coven has dissipated over the centuries. I, myself, was the first to leave, as my views no longer aligned with that of my High Witch."

"Is a High Witch your...leader?"

"Indeed," she said abruptly, as if not wanting to speak of her.

"Well," I started. "What happens once that magic is used?"

"After a witch gets a taste of that kind of power, it is nearly impossible to not constantly crave it, bend to it. Give your very soul to it. Once the book is utilized and a spell is cast, the witch gains eternal control over that magic. The book is no longer needed in order to cast the spell. The more spells a witch consumes, the more they will wear on her physical body."

"And the cost is only your youth?" I asked.

"Only?" Veli spat. "Witches are immortal, girl. All we require is the essence of a beating heart."

I raised a brow at her and her riddle. "So?"

"I would prefer to not live my existence as a crone. However, our eyes can change quickly—it does not matter how many enchantments are learned. With only dabbling a few times, our irises can morph into the crimson that Elianna said she had seen. It gives us away to our prey, making the wielder look as untrustworthy as they truly are. It allows whoever the creature is on the opposite end of the power a fighting chance to escape. That was a gift from the gods given to the realm. A chance to see dark witches for what they truly are."

"Why wouldn't the gods just put an end to dark magic?" Finn asked from the corner he still stood in, his arms now crossed.

Veli let out a small cackle as her gaze lifted to him. "Not all gods are benevolent, boy."

That sent a shudder through my entire body. I couldn't imagine being brave enough to risk upsetting the gods, never mind one of them that wasn't...friendly.

"Oh, my gods," I breathed.

"Yes. Those would be the ones," Veli said, sounding annoyed.

"Shadow summoning. That's how we can get out of here! You said so yourself that you have wielded them before," I announced in a near yell as I stood from the settee.

"Excuse me?" she hissed. "What part of I don't touch that shit with a ten-foot spear did you not understand?"

"You fear this dark sorcery then?" I asked.

"No," Veli stated. "In the realm of magic, everything hinges on the power of intention and will. What I fear is it being in the wrong, taloned hands." She crossed her arms as her violet gaze narrowed in on me.

"Then listen to me! People believed Lukas in the square the other day. Some people would follow. Some people would *fight* for Lia to take the throne. We just have to convince them it's the truth."

"And how do you expect us to do that?" Landon chimed in.

I walked over to the small table in the kitchen and picked up my father's journal.

"With this." I showed them. "It's in his handwriting. It has his wishes for what he truly wanted. The journal contains Veli's creepy prophecy." She rolled her eyes in response. "With this, plus Lukas' words to the realm before he died, we may have a chance at helping Lia. We just need to sneak out of the city somehow and find her. She told us where to go the night of the wedding if we fled. It's obvious that would be where she is headed."

"And you somehow expect me to just summon dark magic and cloak all of Elianna's supporters in shadows to help them sneak out of the city?"

Landon and Finn walked up next to me, and all three of us slowly nodded our heads.

"No. Absolutely not. I won't do it," Veli said as she tore her eyes away from us.

I quietly approached her. "Veli, you just said so yourself that magic is about intention, dark sorcery or not. If Kai ascends the throne, the realm will fall. It will rot away just as he has, and our mother. The realm we know will cease to exist. You have a chance to be a part of something big."

She whipped to face me. "I have *always* been doing something big. I'm an Elora witch disguised as a healer. I help people and have been for centuries. I *have* made a difference. That doesn't mean I'm meant to do more," she said, her tone teetering on the line of anger and pleading.

"But wouldn't you want to, given the chance?" I asked her, voice soft.

She carefully looked me up and down and then glanced over to the tea table, where *Tinaebris Malifisc* still sat, power radiating from its closed pages.

Veli let out a loud sigh and closed her eyes tightly as she rapidly tapped her foot on the floor. "You have no idea what you're asking of me," she stated, but we all continued to stare in silence as we watched her mind race regarding what to do. Her eyes snapped open abruptly and then flashed over to the book. "Fine. Just know that I hate all three of you."

I turned back to the boys and gave them a tiny, closed lip smile.

Neither of them returned it.

TWENTY-THREE
Veli

THESE GODS-DAMN BRATS. THEY just stormed in here a few days ago after running from me practically their entire lives whenever they saw me in the castle halls. Now, they nearly demanded me to use dark witchcraft? As if it were something so simple, easy, and *safe* to do?

They were in for a rude awakening. Not everything could be done at the drop of a hat, as I was sure they were used to. It takes years to master dark sorcery. And I hadn't even touched it in...centuries.

I watched as the three of them mingled with each other on my couch, their forest mutt sprawled out on the floor by the door. The wolf was more well-behaved than they were, that was for sure. It didn't rummage through my things and demand I piss off the gods.

"How will we get people to meet us or know where to go? It's not as if we can just hang flyers or run out of here and risk getting caught whispering rumors of a meeting on the streets. Guards would ambush us immediately," Avery said to them.

Neither of the boys answered her. It was abundantly clear from the start that she ran the show.

I waltzed over to them and shooed them off the settee, taking my seat on the center cushion, and crossed my legs. My focus turned to the bossy red head. "Where and when do you want to meet?"

"What?" she asked hesitantly.

My brows furrowed. "Don't make me repeat myself."

"I...I don't know where we could have people meet us. I'm hoping for as many people as possible, but it's not like anyone can move around freely without the city guards questioning them."

I couldn't believe I was about to offer this.

"I can put a whisper out. It's simple, decent magic. It will reach the minds of anyone who supported the king, was fond of Elianna, and those who believed Lukas with his last attempt to support the rightful heir. Of course, it will run the risk of them opening their mouths and speaking of it to others."

"H-how..." she stuttered out.

"It's magic, girl. Don't question it and its uses. Do you want it to happen or not?"

"I mean, of course I do!" She glanced at the others. "We. Of course we do, but where would we meet?"

"The city square is easily accessible," I answered as I placed my hands on my hips. "I would suggest the slums, but some may choose to not attend if we chose a location as such."

"What about the—"

"Guards? Leave them to me. I have had a bone to pick with some of them for a long time, anyway," I said with a snicker as I inspected my nails. When my gaze lifted back to theirs, they were eyeing me warily. "Don't worry, I won't kill them. Now, when do you want this to occur?"

"Tonight," Avery answered immediately. This foolish girl.

"Typical." I paused. "Impatient, but I understand we are on a time crunch, so we shall have them meet us at midnight when the moon is highest in the night sky. I cannot promise the magic will work as long as we need it to, but I will try my best. If the guards' mental shields are too strong and the spell drops, we run. Do you understand?"

The three of them nodded in unison. I glanced at the wolf that had woken up from her sixth nap of the day, now yawning into the air.

I focused on a lit candle across the space and had it float over to me, which freaked the prince out.

I thoroughly enjoyed it.

"None of you make a single peep," I warned.

The candle levitated above my crisscrossed legs and I raised my hand, holding my palm directly over the flame. My eyes fluttered shut as I muttered the spell *venifikas sussorae*, which in the tongue of the gods translated to The Witch's Whisper.

My mind was no longer my own. I could feel the souls throughout all of Isla, their innermost thoughts regarding the subject woven into the spell—Elianna Valderre.

I received a mix of emotions all at once from the tens of thousands of residents within the neighboring walls.

Repulsion.

Admiration.

Wariness.

Amusement.

And, to my own surprise, a significant amount of *hope*.

I cast out the whisper of the whereabouts and time of the gathering to all that seemed susceptible to it, and when I snapped back to reality, I opened my eyes to see three very terrified looking fae.

"What?" I snarled.

"Your eyes..." their companion started, his voice shaking. "The lids were glowing gold!"

"I don't think I will ever get used to that," the prince whispered.

Huffing out a breath, I admitted, "Ah. Yes, that does happen. The gold in our irises will glow brightly when manipulating a spell."

"Could you sense much?" Avery asked.

I hesitated for a moment to process all that just tore through my senses. I sucked on my tongue before I said, "Support. More than I expected. So now we wait."

"Now we wait," she repeated as she continued to stare at me in disbelief.

As if that wasn't what I just said.

The time had come for us to meet with those who had accepted the whisper. I had told them it would be best for them to hide within the shadows I cast upon them while I made my own way to the roof to get a better look at the surrounding areas. If there were any guards near, I would take their fragile little minds in my grasp and hold them in place until otherwise necessary.

I held *Tinaebris Malifisc* tightly in my grasp as I looked at the three before me. The power of the book radiated through my body as I held it in my arms. Its presence sent an unwelcome shiver down my spine, knowing that I held unlimited, ancient power at my fingertips.

However, just because it was there didn't mean it was right to use it. Even knowing that I didn't plan to use it for malicious reasons, this went against everything I had ever stood for in my life. This book was the reason I had separated myself from my coven all those centuries ago and had been in hiding ever since.

But desperate times called for desperate measures.

I flipped the book open to the page concerning shadow summoning, tracing the tips of my fingers over the only spell I could already wield and trusted myself to use. As I exhaled, memories washed over me, reminding me of the immense struggle it had been to part ways with my shadows all those centuries ago.

I then held my sharpened nails out to the three meddling idiots before me.

"Is this going to hurt?" Finnian asked, voice shaking with nerves.

Of course it was the prince that asked.

I didn't lift my gaze from the book. "Perhaps."

I heard him let out a small gasp when Avery cut in. "She's kidding." A pause. "I hope."

I slammed the book shut between my palms. "Will you two knock it the fuck off so I can concentrate?!" I turned to the other boy—Landon. "They truly are always like this?"

"Indeed," he grumbled. He was quiet, this one...I supposed that made him my favorite of the three.

I tucked the book under one of my arms and concentrated, keeping my eyes open as I held my opposite hand out to where the shadows would cast.

I held my breath nervously, still unsure of whether this was a wise thing to do, but we were running out of time. "*Umbra selair,*" I whispered into the chilly night air. A faint, golden light cast out onto my held-out arm.

Three sets of widened eyes bore into me as my own began to glow, and shadows burst from the palm of my hand, surrounding them.

"Holy gods," Avery breathed. "It's working."

"Hello, old friends," I cooed softly as a small smirk crept up my face.

As the shadows' eruption ceased, the glow from my eyes faded as they moved to hover over them. My gaze shot to the moon. "We don't have much time. The people will flood the streets shortly and I need to take care of the guards. Stay quiet. The shadows only cover so much if I'm not present with them."

Stepping away from them, I gave them a menacing wink and vanished before their eyes, mirroring the way I had disappeared in my home when they first barged into my life. A second later, I reappeared on the roof of my building.

"Veli!" Avery shouted, a little too loud for comfort.

I whipped my head back down to her, a scowl across my face. I could barely see her, but I knew she could see how unamused I was by her outburst. "Your eyes. Why aren't they glowing anymore?"

"Do you not understand the meaning of quiet?! The spell has been cast, and they will do what needs to be done. They move as their own entity until I either summon them home or take back control. Now, go wait on the outskirts of the city square before I change my mind!" I ordered in a hushed voice.

They took off into a sprint, shadows hovering over them like a darkened mist beneath the moonlight.

Once I stood in the center of the roof, I cast out my mind to travel the streets of Isla and seek out the guards. To my surprise, there were only fifty currently on patrol throughout the entire city.

I placed the book down at my feet, and as if it expected what was next, a gust of unsummoned wind violently flipped the pages to the one desired.

I audibly gulped as I stared down at the spell book that desperately ached to be used, whispering my name viciously on the night breeze. Raising my hand out in front of my body, I imagined those patrolling guards in my mind. How easy it would be to break them. Melt their minds from within. The temptation radiated through me—as if the book *wanted* me to destroy them.

"*Impyrum Kortyus.*" The words slipped from my lips without warning.

Power. Absolute, certain, and devastating power erupted throughout my body. The magic felt dangerous, addictive, and all-consuming. The force of it flooded my veins inch by inch while I took hold of each of their minds and gripped them between my taloned fingers.

I lingered within their thoughts longer than originally planned, but I could see *everything*. Their darkest secrets and deepest desires. Their entire souls and beings, who they were to their very core, right there on the surface for the taking.

Unfortunately, I had a job to do.

I ripped their consciousness from them and felt as each of their bodies dropped to the cobblestone streets below their feet.

I let out a large breath and peered down into the roads that were already overcrowded with people heading to the square.

Were they coming for support? Or just curiosity? There were so many of them.

Regardless, we were about to find out.

I carefully leapt down from the roof, summoning a small gust of wind to slow my fall until I landed on my feet. My hands lifted to fasten my hood over my silver hair, and then I silently slipped through the masses, avoiding eye contact at all costs as I worked to keep the guards unconscious.

TWENTY-FOUR

Elianna

Nox and I were both physically and mentally exhausted. Nights of nothing but constant flying and days of trying to sneak in naps here and there were finally catching up to us.

To make matters even worse, I still didn't have a weapon aside from Nox.

I lay sprawled out across his back, gazing up into the sky above as we continued to fly north. I had lost count of how many days had passed since we escaped the dungeons of Isla.

Out of nowhere, clouds fanned out below the stars, blocking the one joyous view I had for the night.

Then thunder sounded.

Nox's wings faltered, and our flight dropped about twenty feet. A scream tore from me during our short freefall.

I wiggled myself around to sit back at the nape of his neck. "What the hell!"

He continued to flap his wings and move forward, but he turned his head slightly back to look at me.

My eyes softened as I noticed he looked scared.

"It's just thunder! It will be okay!"

Another loud crack exploded through the sky, this time accompanied by lightning. Rain then poured down on us, soaking us both.

Gods-dammit.

"Alright, Nox. We have to land!" I yelled to him over the rain, and he dove toward the ground. "Gently!" I reminded him.

He then leveled out his wings on each side, gliding us safely to land.

It was down pouring at this point. I was absolutely drenched, and the gown that I was still stuck wearing weighed me down as I tried to take a few steps through the thickening mud.

"Shit." I looked off into the distance and, for a moment, thought I could see lights flickering through the wall of rain.

"Come on, Nox. Let's go see what that is up there," I said as I marched toward the dim torch lights up ahead.

As I took a few more steps, I noticed not nearly as much rain was coming down on me. I looked around, but it was still pouring.

I tilted my chin up to see Nox was covering my body by hovering his head over me, blocking the majority of the heavy rain that poured down.

I giggled. "You don't have to do that!" I shouted up to him, but as I continued my steps toward the lights, he balanced his giant head right over me, making sure I stayed somewhat dry.

"Fine. I guess I'm not mad at you anymore for being afraid of thunder," I teased.

An odd purring sound rumbled through his chest, directly behind me.

A hushed laugh left me. This journey across the realm was anything but enjoyable, but at least I had him.

Once we were about a half mile from the lights, I could see enough through the rain to notice that it was a small village, and in the distance, a forest lay a mile or two beyond it as well.

A village meant there would be post. Perhaps I could send a letter to Ellecaster to let them know what happened, and that I was safe. I had no idea how far we were from there still, and a falcon could be faster than us. However, a village also meant people, so I would have to be extremely careful.

"Nox." I turned to him. "I need you to stay hidden and unseen." He narrowed his eyes at me. "I need to go do something quick in the village over there, but I will be right back. Stay here and I will come get you." I still had to shout at him due to the storm.

He looked annoyingly unconvinced. "I mean it, Nox! Stay here, okay?"

He let out a loud huff and sat on the ground right where we stood, his landing splashing mud out from beneath him. He lowered his head to me. "...Good boy," I said as I patted above his large nostrils.

I set off and made my way to the village, peeking back at Nox every now and again to make sure he was listening to me. To my surprise, he was. At least for now.

The rain turned frigid, and I hugged my body tightly with my arms, trying to control the shivers that traveled through me. I stomped through the sludge in my finery slippers that I had worn to the wedding, soaking my feet in the process.

To my surprise, when I arrived at the outskirts of the village, I realized it was small enough to not require a gate.

The rain slowed slightly, and I hid behind one of the buildings that lay on the outskirts of the town. As I peered around its edge, I noticed there wasn't a single person on the streets.

Strange, but it wasn't uncommon for smaller settlements to have curfews to prevent drunken chaos. Judging by the placement of the moon as it peeked between the storm clouds, it was nearly midnight.

Keeping myself tucked into the shadows of the building, I took a single step out from my hiding spot and then deemed it safe enough to walk along the dirt road.

The street was lined with wooden buildings that had lit torches next to each door. The roofs covered their flames, blocking them from the rain, which must've been the lights I saw.

Something didn't feel right. The deeper I walked into the eerily quiet town, the more uneasy I felt. There weren't any taverns, inns, or shops. All the buildings I passed by looked exactly the same as the one before it.

Once my body refused to take another step forward, I moved to turn around and head back to Nox—and then my heart leapt in my throat.

Males. Many of them. Staring at me through windows and doors that quietly creaked open.

This wasn't a village at all.

It was a war camp.

Of my own fucking armada.

"What do we have here?" one of them said as he sauntered out of what I assumed to be his barracks.

Think, Lia. Think.

"Looks like the gods declared us worthy of a treat tonight."

Oh, gods. Okay, looks like I need to pull rank.

As far as I knew, the crown hadn't announced their former captain's betrayal yet.

"Is that any way to speak to your commanding officer, soldiers?"

Many of them now poured into the streets, but I held my ground firmly. I knew it would be over the second I showed them an ounce of fear.

The one who spoke squinted at me through the light rain that still drenched the streets. "Is that you, Solus?"

"Who else would it be?" I took a swaggering step toward them and then realized I was unarmed and in a rain-soaked gown that was significantly weighing me down.

"Well, boys, it looks like the gods really *did* find us worthy of something tonight." Any hint of amusement dropped from my face. "Are you aware of the bounty that's on your head, *Captain* Solus?"

Fuck.

I had no idea what to do. I let out a nervous giggle, trying to distract them. "Ha. Well, you know, the funny thing about that is..."

A moment later, I took off running in the opposite direction, my knees lifting so high they nearly touched my chest with each stride as I focused on not tripping over the front of my gown. Honestly, it must've been quite the sight to see. I almost had to laugh at myself. All I needed to do was make my way back to Nox and we could escape.

This caught them off guard for only a second, and then they followed suit.

I ran as fast as I could, but they were on me instantly. I couldn't fight them all, but I would die trying before I let them cage me and drag me back to Isla.

One of them grabbed me by my sopping wet hair and yanked me back into them. I used the force of his pull to wind my arm back and swing around, punching him square in the jaw.

He let out a grunt and released my hair on impact.

Another lunged at me and I dove out of the way, landing right in a puddle of mud. Luckily, that was on my side as another came up from behind me and gripped my ankle. I thrusted my leg away from him, and my slick, muck-covered skin easily allowed me to slip from his grasp.

I forced myself to stand, and three came at me at once. I punched one in the face and then dropped my body back down to the ground in a crouch and swung one of my legs out, tripping the other two.

Ha. I still had it.

Once standing again, I flung my arms out at my sides as I watched too many males to count as they approached me. "You assholes still want some of this? Don't forget who trained you!" I screamed through the storm.

Before I had time to react, a shadow cast from the torchlight behind me. The cool touch of a blade was then on my throat.

"Still cocky, I see," the male said. He pressed the blade tighter to my skin. As I glanced down, being careful not to move my body, I witnessed drops of my blood falling, blending with the raindrops that were trickling down my skin.

I would rather rip his blade across my own throat than deal with the torture that I knew awaited me if I were to end up back in Kellan's hands. As the thought of it crossed my mind, a very large, terrifying shadow loomed over us all from one of the rooftops.

A vicious grin grew on my face. "You all are so fucked," I said in a hushed, raspy voice I barely recognized as my own.

The group that faced me hesitantly turned and followed my gaze to the roof that hovered over them. Each one of the males let out a gasp in shock once their eyes fell upon Nox, who was now leaning out over the street, gripping the building with his taloned wings. His growl rumbled through the air, mimicking the thunder off in the distance.

"Nox, I told you to wait outside!" I yelled up to him jokingly. "But, you know what? I'm feeling generous. Do your thing." I gestured to the crowd of soldiers in front of me that all looked as if they were about to shit themselves.

I realized the blade was still on my throat, so while I had the distraction, I stomped hard on my captor's foot and lifted my arms to shove his away from me. I slipped out from beneath him.

Chaos erupted as Nox leapt from the building, his landing rumbled the structures surrounding us. He was now in the middle of the street, ripping my attackers apart. Some began to flee, while others stupidly tried to charge at my wyvern.

I watched as a male with an arrow across the way had one aimed directly at Nox's face.

"Nox, look out!" I screeched as the soldier released the arrow. My eyes anxiously followed the arrow as it flew through the air. A scream was working its way up my throat when I watched as it hit him...and *bounced* off his thick skull.

Huh. Well, *that* was good to know.

The distraction cost me when another soldier lunged at me with his sword. I jumped backward, but not far enough, and was met with a small gash on the outskirts of my arm.

I peered down as the blood trickled down my forearm. I looked back and forth from the wound to the attacker. "That was rude."

Nox had witnessed the entire ordeal and let out a deafening roar into the storming sky. The surrounding soldiers had to cover their ears.

Without warning, Nox then shot an enormous blast of fire at my attacker, melting him where he stood in his boots.

"Mother of the gods," I muttered as I ran backward away from him. I watched in awe and terror as the male who had just been before me turned into a puddle of boiling guts and shards of bone.

However, Nox didn't stop there. He unleashed a blaze across the entire camp. Buildings caught fire and were engulfed in the blaze within seconds.

Soldiers ran by me as their clothes went up in flames, and a wicked chuckle left me as I listened to them as they cried and prayed to the gods for help.

The gods wouldn't save them now.

Nox was about to make sure of it.

I looked up and watched the magnificent creature that came to my rescue tear through the last of his fire.

Screams of anguish and suffering continued to sound off around us and in the distance as the entire war camp came crumbling down into ash.

As I admired his beauty, I suddenly found myself surrounded by the flames, trapped within them myself.

"Nox!" I shouted into the smoke-filled air.

His head whipped in my direction and he flapped his wings a few times, sending the surrounding blaze outwards as he levitated above me. He opened the foot of one of his hind legs and gently wrapped it around my body, lifting me into the sky with him.

    We flew away into the night toward the forest in the distance as the storm cleared, and I watched as the remainder of the buildings crumbled to the ground.

TWENTY-FIVE

Avery

I COULDN'T BELIEVE THE turnout. There had to be hundreds of people in the street, maybe even a few thousand. All here because they believed Lia was the true heir of the realm, showing that their loyalties no longer lay with the queen or our brother.

Could Veli truly keep the guards distracted for the amount of time needed? Gods, I hoped so.

I watched her appear from within the crowd as she shoved her way to the front, earning many disgruntled looks.

I could see she was trying to hide her glowing eyes as she waved her hand in our direction and the shadows dispersed from around us. It was time.

I took a step out from the side of the building we hid against, aiming towards the fountain centered in the square, when I felt a tug on my wrist. I turned to face my brother.

"What if they don't want to listen to us?" he asked, genuine concern in his eyes.

"We make them listen," I answered as I forced my feet forward and out in front of the masses that curiously faced us under the moonlight.

Whispers and small hushes could be heard as I walked to the front of everyone, but I knew not many would be able to see me, so I took a step up onto the fountain, grabbing the attention of those who had remained speaking amongst each other.

"Who are you?"

"Why are we here?"

Phrases I could easily make out among the murmurs. We had decided to keep our hoods on to protect our identities in case this went south, but fuck that. If we had any chance of them listening to us, we had to prove who we were and what we truly believed.

Finn and Landon climbed up on the fountain on either side of me, and I gave each of them a quick glance before slowly lowering my hood.

"Is that the princess?!"

"Princess Avery!"

"Is she even considered a princess after the ascension?"

"What the hell is going on?"

I almost laughed out loud at the sound of the last one I chose to listen to. As expected, the whispers were turning to shouts, so I raised my hand in an attempt to quiet them down, but they weren't paying attention.

I cleared my throat. "As you all are aware, my name is Avery Valderre. I am the daughter of the late king, Jameson Valderre." I swallowed thickly, trying to not let the tears come at the mention of him. The crowd, to my surprise, finally went silent. "As some of you heard days prior, I am not his first daughter." I watched as people looked side to side at each other in confusion. "The king's first daughter, and *rightful* heir, is Captain Elianna Sol–...Elianna Valderre."

I paused for several moments, looking at each face in the crowd I could make out before me. I was shocked to see so many recognizable soldiers among them. It made me nervous to speak about this in front of them, but their presence was good. It meant I could bring more than just support to Lia. If I was lucky, maybe I could bring her a small army.

"My father made many mistakes, but his biggest regret was hiding her from the realm. Hiding who she truly was from all of you."

"Why?" a woman shouted from within the masses. "Why would he hide his true heir? And why should we believe you? Perhaps you just want the throne for yourself."

Gods, that didn't even make sense. I thought these were all supporters, but I guess their concern was understandable, given the circumstances.

"Because of this," I said as I reached into the pocket of my cloak and pulled out his journal, opening it to the last page written in. The page that stated all he felt about the queen, prince, and Lia.

I read it out loud to them and became anxious when I was met with a deafening silence.

"I know some of you may not believe this, but I need you to know that my brother is not fit to rule this kingdom. He is not fit to sit upon the Velyran throne. He will doom this realm and every being in it."

The masses began muttering amongst each other. People were nervous, as they should've been.

I was internally panicking. What if they didn't listen? What if they didn't care? We never planned to mention this, but I had to do whatever was necessary, and who knew how long we had left before Veli's spell wore off...

"The king was never sick—he was discreetly murdered by the queen. My mother is an awful female, and it sickens me to think that Prince Finnian and I come from such a being. My father wanted to end the war. He wanted what Elianna does, and that is peace in the realm."

Nobody interrupted, and I seemed to have grabbed most of their attention again, so I continued. "The queen will stop at nothing until every last mortal is destroyed. Every halfling and sympathizer. Anyone that wishes to treat humans with any form of decency and respect. She raised Kai to be the same way, and she tried to do the same to us."

It became eerily quiet once more. Clouds covered the moon, cloaking the streets in darkness, but I could still feel thousands of eyes on me. All that could be heard were a few coughs and mutters in the farthest reaches of the crowd.

"My point is that we blindly followed her view on this, and until recently, I believed everything she said regarding the humans in our world. My sister, your rightful queen and heir of the realm, fully supports and will fight for the end of this war. I know you are all tired of sending your fathers, brothers, husbands, and sons off to battle, never knowing if they will return. We can *end* this."

"You wish to end it with even more bloodshed!" a man yelled.

"I'm not saying it will be easy, but at least this way, we would fight for what is right. We would be fighting with and *for* the true heir of the Valderre line, someone who is truly *worthy* of carrying such an honor."

Murmuring arguments broke out among the masses, turning to full on shouts of rage, as the citizens of Isla panicked about the unknown of the realm's future.

"This isn't working…" Finn whispered as he leaned into me.

I turned to him, still balancing on top of the fountain. "Oh, I'm sorry. Would you like to add anything to this?" I hissed.

"I have something I would like to say," Landon said as he pulled off his hood, revealing his identity to the crowd. "I was the castle's stable keeper. I have been in the presence of every individual mentioned to you and I can confirm that what she speaks is true. Elianna is kind. When I met her, the circumstances were…" He glanced at Finn quickly. "Far from normal. However, what Princess Avery speaks is the truth. Kai is vicious and has the potential to be even worse than Queen Idina ever was."

I watched in awe as he slowly unbuttoned the shirt beneath his cloak, exposing the ruthless scar he bore from

Kai's actions. The mark on his skin was mottled and jagged, showing the true brutality of our brother's assault on him.

My gaze shot to Finnian, who wore nothing but devastation at the sight of his lover's bare chest.

"One day, Kai walked into the stables and wanted to brand Elianna's horse, knowing it was against her wishes. I advised against it, considering he had no say over such actions, and in retaliation, he branded *me*. He lunged at me and held the brand to my chest for triple the amount of time necessary to mark a war horse. I was denied access to a healer and was told he would kill me himself if I tried to seek one."

Shouts and gasps of horror could be heard throughout the streets, bouncing off the buildings and echoing through alleyways.

"If this is what the king-to-be does out of boredom to his own castle's staff, what will he do to his citizens? What will he do if he even suspects retaliation or disrespect? Gods-dammit, what will he even *define* as disrespect?" Landon paused for a moment and looked to me and Finn. "However, what I do know is that these two...they are...they are *good*. I will follow them to Elianna. I will give her my sword and my support." He faced back out to the crowd, and Finn released a shuddering breath at his words.

"And lastly," Landon continued. "I will do whatever it takes to make sure the fate of Velyra is in the right hands. Even if it kills me. I would want that for my future younglings, and you should all want the same."

A male I recognized as a soldier took a step forward, separating himself from the others before us. "She has my sword always. Captain Sol–... Elianna has always been someone I deeply respect. I was glad to fight by her side in the war, and I will gladly continue to, so she can claim her place as queen."

Queen. Gods, that felt so bizarre and...incredible to hear.

I nodded at him, and he took a step back into his original place. "There is a safe place for us to flee in the meantime, beyond the Sylis Forest. The journey will be long. It will be difficult, but we must leave at this time tomorrow," I announced to everyone.

"Tomorrow?!" The word was gasped out over and over again throughout the city.

"How will we leave? Surely the guards won't allow such a thing!" someone shouted.

"We have..." I glanced down at Veli, who looked entirely unmoved by all of this. "A way that no one will see us." I bit down on my bottom lip at the extremely vague answer I had to give them.

My heart sank as I noticed people leaving. The edges of the crowd were dispersing, either from no longer deciding to support Lia, or thinking that doing so was a death sentence.

Veli stepped forward then and climbed up onto the fountain next to me, shoving Finn to the side.

She gazed out at the crowd and removed her hood, revealing her captivating, glowing eyes.

"A witch!" someone screamed.

"Will you all just shut the fuck up?" she roared. I blinked at the back of her silvery head of hair in shock as she faced them. "We are running out of time. I took care of the guards in the city on patrol tonight. They are...currently taking a nap."

A snort left me at her lie.

"I cannot keep them in such a state much longer. However, you will all listen to me and listen well, for I will not repeat this. Tomorrow night at this time, we will meet in the lower fields and leave this city behind in hopes of coming back to it once deemed safe. I will cast shadows to cover us and our trail until we are out of the city's view."

Veli lifted a taloned hand, and shadows danced between her fingers. A few horrified gasps rang out from the masses.

"They won't see us so long as you listen to my instructions. Pack light. Pack food and water and anything you know you can actually carry on the journey. And if any of you decide to betray us and let the guards or castle dwellers know of this plan...do so after tomorrow night. Or you will be dealing with *me*."

Her eyes glowed even brighter in response to the words she spoke. A few individuals in the front row shook with nerves at the haunting sight of her.

"Now go." She gave a slight gesture with four of her fingers, a signal to leave. "Speak of this only to those who you know were present. We leave at midnight tomorrow when the moon is highest in the night sky."

The crowd immediately dispersed in slight disorder as they all scattered back to their homes. Murmuring whispers of doubt and fear echoed among them.

"Do you think anyone will show?" I asked my three companions as I watched the citizens leave.

"Well, we'll find out, won't we?" Veli answered as the glow in her eyes slowly dimmed.

"The guards will be waking. We need to get back."

Her eyes looked...different. I tried to squint to get a better look, but she scoffed at me and turned her face away.

"They're bloodshot. I'm tired. Now let's go," she announced over her shoulder.

We quickly followed her back to her home and prayed that the gods were on our side.

TWENTY-SIX
Elianna

Nox and I sat at the edge of the forest beyond the war camp until dawn. I watched the flames reduce to cinders as they turned the entire camp, and everyone in it, to ash.

These were once males under my own command, and they so willingly were about to give me up. Had I been a fool to think some would follow me as I took my claim to the throne? Perhaps I was.

I wiggled out from beneath the cover of his membranous, leather-like wing. "Ready to go?"

He gave me what seemed to be a nod of agreement and stood up as he shook off the remaining wetness from the storm.

I peered up into the new day's clear, cerulean sky. "If that camp was here, there may be others around. I'm not sure exactly where we are, but to be safe, we may need to walk through the woods for a little while."

Nox looked entirely unimpressed.

"Oh, relax, you big baby," I said, taking a step beyond the tree line. "We can launch into the air once I feel we won't be spotted by any possible enemies on the outskirts of these woods. It's only until we are deep enough between the trees—just a few miles."

He reluctantly followed.

The further we hiked into the forest, the darker it became. The sun was blocked in most areas by the leaves that encased the forest's ceiling.

There was a sinister feel to it—familiar one at that.

We walked for a while, following the moss on the trees. I chuckled to myself, thinking about how different this situation was only a few months ago—when I was the one unwillingly following Jace through an enchanted forest and making fun of him for following the direction of the moss.

My heart ached as I thought of him, but the farther north we traveled, the closer we were getting to him—to my mate. This time, when I reached down into the bond, something bright was peering through all the lingering anguish—it felt like *hope*.

Blowing out a breath, I whispered to myself, "Gods, Lia, get your emotions under control."

I looked back at Nox, who had a scowl on his face, his scaly lips pressed together tightly. He growled at twigs and branches as they scraped his wings, that he now kept tightly tucked into his body.

I let out a soft giggle as I went to face forward again, but I clumsily lost my footing as my ankle twisted in an unexpected drop in the ground. I fell flat on my face into the dirt.

Nox huffed out what seemed to be a laugh. Perhaps I deserved the karma for laughing at him a second ago.

"Oh, yeah! Hilarious." I rolled my eyes at him as I peeled myself up.

I observed the terrain that I had fallen into and my eyes widened at the sight of the deep, unique looking impression within the forest floor.

I climbed to my feet and stepped up out of the giant hole.

"You've got to be fucking kidding me," I mumbled as I took in the sight of what was an enormous footprint.

I glanced back and forth from Nox to the footprint in the ground. I stomped up to him and gently grabbed the outer joint of his wing, pulling him up toward the footprint.

"Do me a favor and put your foot in that thing," I said to him. He looked at me and seemed very confused.

"That!" I pointed to his hind leg. "Put it there." And aimed back at the dirt.

He let out a sound that resembled a sigh, as if he were sick of my shit, and placed his clawed foot into it. The hole swallowed it up.

"Well, that's unfortunate." I looked up at him. "Looks like my nightmare came true for a second time in my life. We are in the Sylis Forest," I announced to him as I spun slowly in a circle, observing our surroundings. "And you are *not* the biggest thing in here, either."

He removed his foot from the hole and looked up at the leafy canopy, letting out a snarl.

"Don't get mad at the trees," I joked as I pressed onward. "The sooner we are out of here, the better. Perhaps we will be able to find a gap in the tree's canopy before nightfall," I said to him as we made our way north once more.

It had been hours, and luckily, we hadn't run into any mammoth-sized trolls, or only the gods knew what else could've made that type of footprint in the hard forest floor.

Every now and again, Nox would find a small critter in the trees and would snap at them. Sometimes, it was just to taunt them, and other times, it was to fully commit to the act of taking the poor creatures as snacks.

Gods, what I wouldn't do for a snack right now myself. Food had been scarce, to say the least, and my body felt weak from the lack of it. I kept my mouth shut, though. At least one of us was eating, and he would need his strength once we were able to fly again.

Suddenly, the forest went silent. The leaves were no longer rustling in the wind, birds halted their singing and Nox went as stiff as one of the trees.

I gazed off into the distance and moved my eyes around to take in the area. "Please don't be a troll. Please don't be a troll. *Please* don't be another freaking troll," I whispered.

A moment later, an arrow whizzed right past my face and embedded itself into a tree a few feet from where I stood.

My jaw popped open in shock as I stared at it for far too long. "Oh, for fuck's sake!" I huffed as I whipped back at my wyvern. "Nox! Run!"

The two of us took off, arrows flying all around us. I glanced back, worried that one would hurt him, but remembered that the night before one bounced off of his head.

I took the risk of looking over to each side of us and saw…horses? Running along with us as the arrows now came from every direction, except from straight ahead.

I tripped over the skirt of my dress and toppled to the ground, tumbling through the path and over the roots sticking up from it. Nox came to a screeching halt as he barreled through the woods behind me.

I screamed loudly as it looked like he was about to accidentally run me over, but instead, his body came to a stop directly above me. He hovered over me protectively as he let out a ferocious roar, whipping his neck in all directions, making it clear that it was directed at our attackers.

The stampeding sound of hooves ceased, and I peeked out from underneath Nox's belly to see it wasn't horses that were running along the side of us.

They were supposed to be a myth. Though, I supposed it made sense that all "myths" lived amongst these woods.

Centaurs.

The odd combination of man and horse. There were at least twenty of them, and we were surrounded. Arrows nocked in their enormous bows and pointed directly at us.

"Come out," one of them demanded.

"No, I think I am good, actually," I responded, trying to buy some time to think of how to get out of this.

"Kill the wyvern," I heard him order.

"Wait!" I screeched. "I'll come out. Just don't hurt him."

I shimmied out from underneath Nox and pushed myself onto my feet. Nox pressed his chest into my back, reminding me that he guarded me from behind.

"State your name," the centaur said.

"You first." I gave him a sweet, antagonizing smile.

He took a few steps toward me, and I unwillingly tried to take a step back, but was blocked by Nox. The unique creature's threatening movement towards me was unsettling. So much like a warhorse, but larger, and with a humanoid torso and facial features.

"You think this is a game?" he barked at me.

I was honestly shocked they spoke the true Velyran tongue.

I cleared my throat. "My name is Elianna."

"And what are you doing in my forest, *Elianna*?"

I blinked at him. "I'm not sure how you own the entire forest, but we were just passing through, so if you don't mind, we will be on our way." I went to take a step but heard the tight pull of a bow from one of the centaurs off to the side.

"It has a mouth on it. Kill it, Bruhn," the one pointing the arrow at me said.

I clenched my teeth as my nerves threatened to consume me—I had to be smart about this, and I didn't have any weapons. I cursed myself for not thinking about grabbing one of the soldiers' swords before Nox plucked me up from within the flames the night prior.

"Hi, Bruhn. Nice to meet you and your...herd." I gestured to them. "Anyway, like I said, we were just passing through."

He looked me up and down. "Kill them," he ordered, and then half turned his body from me.

"I don't have time for this shit," I said, loud enough for them all to hear.

I charged at one of the unsuspecting centaurs toward the side, who was too close to me to have time to react. I took a step up onto a boulder to the right of him and leapt up with all my might, coming down with my fist held high in the air, and punched him in the side of his face.

A few of them let out a gasp as my victim dropped his bow, and I dove for it.

They all started shooting their arrows at me and I continued to roll out of their way, down a small hill, while clutching the oversized bow to my chest.

Gods, this thing was nearly as long as my entire body.

Nox let out another rumbling sound of frustration and was hissing at them. He snapped at the herd with his pointed teeth, since his body still hadn't restored the flames he spent at the war camp.

With a small lull in arrows shooting toward me, they all suddenly *charged*. I ripped a few from the ground they protruded out of and fired back at them. My arms were barely strong enough to pull the giant bow string taut to shoot them.

Most of them veered out of the way and moved to circle me once more.

I pulled myself to my feet and slung the bow over my shoulder as I took off into a sprint back toward Nox. One of them galloped toward me and I veered out of his reach. My arm stretched out as he moved to pass, but I wrapped it over his hip, swinging myself up into the air. Time slowed as my body twisted above the centaur and came down, landing directly on his back.

The others had no choice but to stop firing their arrows, not willing to take the chance of hitting one of their own.

I ripped the bow over my body and slammed it down onto the centaur's shoulder blades. I heaved it toward me, forcing the curved wood of the weapon to form around his throat, suffocating him. He took a few steps back as he desperately worked to get air into his lungs until he came to a stop beneath a willow tree—its vines hovered around our faces.

"Any of you take another step closer and I will snap his fucking neck!" I roared into the forest air.

The centaur squirmed beneath me, trying to contort his fingers to fit between the bow and his neck to sneak in a breath.

"Release him!" their leader's voice boomed.

My eyes snapped in his direction, and I gasped when I noticed two of the centaurs standing on each side of Nox, their sharpened spears pointed straight at his eyes.

"Don't. Touch. My. Wyvern," I hissed through my teeth.

"Who are you exactly, Miss Elianna? Release my friend and then we can talk about your beast," Bruhn declared.

I eyed him. The leanness of his horse-like body curved around him and worked its way up his abdomen. His arms, thick with muscular strength, were clasped behind the humanoid part of his back.

I didn't loosen my grasp on the bow. "My name is Elianna Valderre, and I am the *rightful* heir to the throne of Velyra," I snapped at him. "I'm sure it is...secluded out here, to say the least, but a war rages on beyond the walls of this forest. I'm trying to stop it. I have allied with the human armies and plan to take back my kingdom."

It was silent for a moment before the herd of them erupted with laughter around me.

For the love of all the gods. "It's the truth."

"Sure it is, and I'm Lord of the Wood," Bruhn mocked through his laughs.

"Well, you said it was your forest earlier, so maybe I would've believed that," I muttered, barely loud enough for him to hear.

The centaur below me took advantage of my distraction and dug his fingernails into my forearm, right atop the barely healed gash from the war camp. I let out a hiss from the unexpected slice of pain and he shook me off his back, forcing my body to fall to the ground.

My gaze snapped back up to him as he removed the bow from around his neck and worked to catch his breath.

I glanced at my forearm and watched as small drops of blood pooled from the crescent-shaped wounds and dripped down onto the terrain.

"Bastard," I growled.

He took his reclaimed bow and pulled an arrow through the string, aiming it directly at my face.

Nox was thrashing and snapping his jaw at those who stood guard in front of him as he watched me intently through his narrowed gaze.

I stared down the wooden arrow, greeting death the way any soldier would, when the unthinkable happened.

Vines.

The whispering vines came alive from the willow tree that hung above us and wrapped themselves around the centaur's arms and throat, choking him once more—perhaps even more violently than I had been.

Everyone let out a gasp of terror.

My eyes flared in confusion as I scooted my body back a few feet on the ground, watching in horror as the tree attacked the creature.

"The willow," Bruhn started, taking a hesitant step toward us. "It's...it's responding to your *blood*."

"What?" I whispered and looked down to the ground, where a few tiny drops of my blood had seeped into the forest floor.

"Agdronis, drop your bow," Bruhn ordered the centaur who was about to kill me.

On command, he released his weapon, and we watched as the vines leisurely unraveled themselves from his body in a serpent-like manner.

"Mother of the gods," I breathed.

Once the vines retreated from his body, Agdronis swiftly galloped out from under the tree.

"You were being serious," Bruhn stated quietly as he turned to me. "You're the true heir of the realm."

"Why would I waste my breath and make that up?" I hissed as I stood from the ground.

"It would've been a ridiculous lie."

I raised my brow. "No shit. Now drop your weapons from my wyvern." I pointed to Nox, and placed my other hand on my hip as I sized up Bruhn, who stood at least three feet taller than me thanks to his horse-like body.

The centaurs that held the spears obeyed, and a growl rumbled through Nox's chest.

I strode up to him and he lowered his head down to me so I could pat his snout. I turned back to the herd of centaurs with a scowl on my face, and they all stared at me warily.

"You are one of the...oddest things we have ever encountered," Bruhn said. "It is not every day you see a young, combat-trained fae princess with a pet wyvern."

I didn't feel that it was necessary to bring up the fact that I wasn't raised as a princess.

"Yes, well, I guess you learned something new today." I went to awkwardly walk away from them, hoping that would be the end of this ridiculous encounter, but of course, it wasn't.

"Heir of the Realm," Bruhn stopped me. "We are not the worst things lurking within these trees. If your wyvern can fly, I suggest learning how to ride him."

A serpentine smile crept up my lips. We had been walking for miles—surely we would be safe from enemy eyes in the air now.

Without a word, I crawled up Nox's side and onto his back. I positioned my legs around the nape of his neck and looked down at the herd that now stared up at me, gaping. As they all gawked at us in awe, or maybe it was shock now etched into their faces, I gave them a menacing wink.

"Learning won't be necessary," I answered, and as if he took it as a command, Nox launched up into the air. Our bodies blasted through the canopy of the forest's treetops and we were then out in the open sky.

I peered down into the hole we created through the leafy covering and observed the centaurs as they continued to stare up at us.

I surveyed the surrounding sky, and doubted we would be spotted out here, so high above the Sylis trees.

"Let's go, Nox. Let's go find Jace."

He let out a small chirping sound and shot out full speed without warning, forcing a laugh from me.

I lifted my hands out towards my sides for balance like that very first time I had ridden him while we escaped. Only this time, it was to fearlessly enjoy the exhilarating sensation of gliding through the sun-filled, open air.

TWENTY-SEVEN
Avery

NIGHT HAD FALLEN. It had been a week since both the wedding massacre and Lia's escape. Veli said she heard whispers throughout the streets today while she was out getting supplies for the journey ahead. Rumors regarding guards searching specifically for me and Finnian.

Deep down, I always knew they would be, but it was unnerving to hear of it actually occurring just beyond her hidden door. Prince and princess turned wanted criminals for treason, though I doubted our mother would have labeled us publicly as such—it would've embarrassed her.

"It's time," Veli announced to us as she fastened her cloak and grabbed her few bags of supplies. "You all know the plan. If the magic drops and our cover is blown, we will need to leave some behind and make a run for it."

That just didn't sit right with me at all, but I supposed it was the only option we had.

I looked down at Nyra. "Ready, girl?" She nudged at my hand with her wet nose in response.

Veli went for the door and looked back at me, Finn, and Landon. "I'm going to head back up to the roof and get a feel for the guards once more. Once in control, I will absorb their consciousness so we can all get the hell out of here. I will send the shadows for you then, so keep this door cracked so you can sense them. Head to the fields. The shadows will expand onto anyone you find and welcome them in," she reminded us all. "Be careful."

She blinked a few times, looking as if she was going to say something else, but instead snuck between the crevice of the door and its frame.

This was happening.

We were really doing this.

The moment the tendrils of darkness drifted down from Veli's roof, we all raced out the door and through the alleyways under the cover of the shadows.

I wasn't sure what I was expecting, but it certainly wasn't this. The streets became flooded—*flooded* with people ready to flee with us.

Fae of all ages, some hesitant, rushed alongside us as we ran toward the Islan gates. They leapt out from their homes, shops, and corners of every passing street, joining us in our race toward freedom.

"I can't believe this," Finn said in a hushed tone through his heavy breathing. "All these people are here to support Lia."

I went to speak but was cut off by someone directly behind us. "We may not know all the details exactly, but if there is a possibility of a future that removes Prince Kai from the throne, many of us will take that chance."

I glanced back without losing my pace to see it had been a male who looked as if he was in his fourth decade of life in human terms, meaning he was most likely at least nine centuries old.

It brought tears to my eyes.

"And if she has the support of the known siblings of the current heir, then that was good enough for us. We all saw the fear in your eyes when you spoke of him." He paused for a few moments, trying to catch his breath through running. "If those who grew up alongside him are afraid of what he may bring to the kingdom, then that was answer enough for us with where our loyalties should lie."

"Thank you," Finnian called back to him. "For listening to us." I peeked over and watched as he smiled at Landon, but the gesture was not returned.

Those two really needed to figure their shit out.

We ran through the never-ending winding streets, picking up hundreds, if not thousands, of more individuals and even families along the way. As we were about to turn the last stretch that led to the city gates, Veli appeared out of nowhere and ran up next to us in the front.

She looked nervous, even with her glowing eyes.

"Is something wrong?" I tried to whisper to her through each stride.

I glanced down to make sure Nyra was still next to me, but she looked as if she wanted to run ahead of us. She hated the shadows and snarled every time a haze of them got too close—it was almost as if they were taunting her.

"Guards just arrived at the gate," she admitted, barely loud enough for me to hear. "They were not here before, but I can sense them now. There were...*significantly* more soldiers on duty tonight."

My head whipped to her as my heart skipped a beat. "I'm sorry?"

Holy gods, were we betrayed?

She shot me a look, and it sent a shiver down my spine as I looked directly into those fierce eyes. "I'll take care of it," she mumbled. "It just won't be pretty."

"What won't be pretty?" Finnian practically shouted at us.

Both mine and Veli's heads snapped in his direction. "Shh!" I forced through a nervous breath.

I slowly turned my attention back to the witch that led us. "What are we going to do?"

We were about to turn the last corner of the street that would lead us all out into the open and in front of the gates.

"I cannot summon the spell again while I'm still trying to keep the current one. If I drop it, those other guards throughout the city will wake up," she snapped, but I knew it was more from nerves.

The turn was upon us.

"Do what you have to do. We won't stop in the fields. We will run straight through and keep going until we can no longer see the city gates." I said to each of them beside me, not realizing that the front of the crowd following our lead could also hear.

"We will pass the message down the lines. If they want to live, they will do what is necessary," the male behind us announced.

I turned my neck back towards him and mouthed the words *thank you*.

"The guards currently down will be disoriented when they open their eyes. That will delay them, but we will still have to move as fast as possible."

Our front lines rounded that last corner and we all came to a sudden halt, alerting those at our backs to do the same.

Twenty additional guards stood across the gateway, staring us down as if they could see right through us. Then I realized that what they saw was most likely nothing more than a ghostly black haze of darkness coming directly for them.

"Show yourself!" a guard bellowed into the air. "Yesterday evening, guards awoke on the streets without any recollection of what had happened to them. And now we have found several of our officers unconscious in the middle of their stationed streets once more. I believe we have found our culprit." His tone turned menacing.

That explained why there were several more on duty tonight.

Murmurs erupted from behind us. The shadows covered us visually, but not the sounds. I tried to shush them, but they continued to just get louder as nerves rattled through them.

We were about to be caught. Chaos would surely ensue, and we would never be able to escape.

Gods-fucking-*dammit*.

My eyes flicked over to Veli, and she gave me a quick nod. I watched her as she confidently stepped out from the cover of her shadows, a small haze of them following her and hovering around her silver hair as if they were her guardians. She sauntered toward the soldiers before us under the moonlight.

All twenty of them unsheathed their blades.

"Shit," Landon bit out.

I nodded rapidly in agreement as I bit down on my bottom lip.

"Hello, soldiers," Veli started, appearing bored while examining her taloned nails. "Do you value your lives?"

"I know you," the one in the middle shouted at her. "You're that old castle healer. We searched for you on execution day by orders of the queen, but you were nowhere to be found. Pity." Laughter traveled down their small line of guards.

She giggled maliciously. "I will take that as a no, then."

Her shadows swirled around her as she lifted an arm towards them, lazily pointing a talon in their direction. They all raised their blades higher in confused anticipation, becoming more wary of the situation. I could see a faint, golden glow casting out from her eyes.

"Witch!" the same guard shouted.

She then voiced her enchantment in the language of the gods and we all watched as each of the guards dropped their weapons and stood stiff as boards alongside one another.

"Veli," I called out, but she raised her other arm behind her, halting me.

We all stood in uneasy silence for what seemed like an eternity, but it was merely a minute. I turned and peered through the bodies in the crowd to see *hundreds* of people who had been following us were now scattering back through the streets behind us, retreating to their homes.

"No!" I shouted down the crowd, but it was no use. I went to chase after them, to beg them to stay, but Landon wrapped his arm around my waist, keeping me where I stood.

They were scared, whether it was of the guards and being caught, or witnessing the use of Veli's magic, I wasn't sure. Both reasons were valid, but they were dooming themselves to a far worse fate by staying here. I watched as hundreds more continued to retreat, dwindling our crowd down to a fraction of the size it was only minutes before.

My stare refocused on what was occurring in front of us, and I observed the hand that Veli had halted me with as it balled into a shaking fist. Was she searching through their minds? Whatever she was doing...whatever she *saw*, she didn't like it one bit.

I blinked, and suddenly, all the guards that had been frozen collapsed to the street beneath them.

Power, pure and raw, emanated from the witch.

I took a cautious step forward as Veli half turned to face us. Her *eyes*. They weren't violet anymore. They were shifting from that beautiful purple to a fiery fuchsia, and back again, swirling around the golden glow.

"We need to move quickly," she said on a breath.

Veli's shadows that had been weaving between her locks of hair expanded out and moved to drape themselves over the guards.

I arched a brow in confusion, and the remaining army behind us marched forward.

Once we were caught up to Veli, she whispered to me, "Do what was said before and move beyond the fields. Don't stop until you can no longer see the city gates. I will wait here in case more come to stop us."

The boys nodded in unison and went to move, but Veli reached out and grasped Finnian's hand. "Don't look at them," she warned. "The bodies."

Finn gulped loudly, and the masses rapidly funneled around us and through the city gate.

I crept up next to Veli and stood beside her as they passed. "They aren't unconscious…are they? The guards," I guessed, voice shaking.

"If you saw what was in their minds, you wouldn't have let them live either," she stated in a tone I never wanted to hear again. My entire body trembled in response to the energy that radiated from her.

We stood there until the last of the shadows passed us, covering the runaways from sight.

"It is done, then," she voiced after a long period of uncomfortable silence between us. "Let's get the hell out of this gods forsaken city."

She strode through the gates and I trailed her steps, refusing to allow myself to look back and grieve for the only home I had ever known.

TWENTY-EIGHT
Elianna

NOX FLEW THROUGH THE night, even after I fell asleep cradled on his back at the nape of his scaly, ridged neck. I had luckily learned how to maneuver my body up against his to block the constant, rushing wind that surrounded us.

I rubbed my sleepy eyes open and noticed that dawn was on the horizon. I shifted to sit upright, earning his attention as he twisted his neck to look back at me like he always did.

"Good morning," I said with a yawn. The corner of his lips tilted upward, resembling a smile, earning a soft chuckle from me. "Eyes on the sky there, Nox. I don't feel like colliding with a flock of birds again."

Which had happened.

Twice.

He swiveled his neck to face forward once more while I tried to blink the sleep away from my eyes.

I peered out over the side of him and noticed we were no longer above the Sylis Forest. My eyes flared as nerves took over me.

"We better still be flying north!" I called out over the breeze. He huffed out an annoyed breath, so I whipped around and realized the tree line at the end of the woods was only a mile or two behind us.

Thank the gods.

I blew out a breath of relief. "We should get back down on the ground, Nox. We could be spotted up here again." He ignored me. "I'm serious."

He peeked back at me and continued to fly straight. "Um, excuse me! I know you can hear meeeee!" My last word ended on a drawn-out shriek as Nox lazily flipped his body upside down midair, sending my own free-falling through the sky and toward the ground below.

A girlish squeal unleashed itself from me as I descended through the air, my hair flying upwards, practically blinding me. Nox dove directly below me and leveled out his wings, forcing me to painfully land on his firm back with a grunt.

I twisted my body to be upright again and crawled as far up his neck as I could, holding on for dear life. His jaw hung open in what seemed to be a gaping smile.

"You thought that was *funny?!*" I shrieked. "You could've killed me!"

He glanced back at me, giving me a knowing look, as if it were ridiculous to assume he would allow me to hit the field below us.

I scoffed. *Wyverns*.

Sliding back down his neck, I perched up in my usual seat when I noticed what resembled rundown buildings in the distance.

Oh gods, Celan Village.

"Nox, okay, this time I'm very serious. Do you see that village up ahead?" He moved his head up and down once in a nod. "We need to land there."

The wyvern gracefully swooped down toward the ground, and my heart started racing rapidly as the wind rushed at my face in our descent.

We landed on the outskirts of the nearly disintegrated buildings, and any form of joy had fallen from my features.

The village was *destroyed*.

I slid down the majority of Nox's body and leapt out once I got closer to the ground. I glanced over at a familiar wooden beam that stood out from the terrain. As the memories flooded my thoughts, a shiver ran up my spine. I could vividly recall the feeling of being bound to it, forced to watch in horror as Kellan mercilessly slashed my mate's beautiful face.

Nox waddled up to it, almost hitting me with the outskirts of his wing as he passed. He sniffed the blood-stained post.

I walked up to him and examined it closer, realizing there actually was a large, nearly black, old blood stain smeared across it.

I reached up as high as I could and patted his side to comfort him. "That's from me." My voice was barely above a whisper.

His horn-covered head whipped toward me, nearly knocking me over in the process, and to my surprise, I didn't even flinch. He nuzzled his nose on my chest and I could hear a low growl rumble through his own.

"We'll get our revenge." I stroked under his chin, staring blankly at the stain of my own blood. "Those males will get what's coming to them," I promised softly.

Peeking up at his face, I watched as his golden eyes narrowed in on the pole, and then suddenly, his tail lashed out from behind us and swiped at it, sending it to the ground. A grin snuck up on me as his rumbling growl morphed into a light purr.

"Thank you," I whispered to him as I looked up into his eyes.

A moment later, I turned from him and he quietly followed as I moved to explore the ruins of what was left of Celan Village. For a brief moment in time, this tiny place felt like home, and now it was destroyed. I couldn't help but feel responsible for the death and ruin that was brought onto this settlement.

I stopped short in front of what was left of the building that I had barged through to save Zaela. The vision of the burning sky as I fell backwards onto this cobblestone street flashed through my memory, stunning me.

Nox gave the arch of my back a light tap with his snout, reminding me that he was there.

There was truly nothing left here. How many people had escaped? How many had met their fate? Another flash from the horrific night appeared before me as we turned the corner of the structure where the family had fled from me, terrified, believing that I was there to harm them. They thought that I would've hurt their children and loved ones just because I was foolish enough to forget to hide the tips of my ears in all the chaos.

My heart thudded in my chest at the vision of them fleeing from me and unknowingly rushing into the blades of Kellan's soldiers.

The sun was now high in the sky and birds chirped their songs as they flew through the air above us. Nox gave me a look that I now knew all too well. He wanted to be back up in the sky with them.

"Soon, Nox," I assured. There was nothing here that remained, anyway. I assumed Jace wouldn't still be here, but for all I knew, they could've started rebuilding. However, now that the whereabouts were compromised, it made sense that they wouldn't.

My eyes widened as I remembered how Kellan had snapped my dagger before hauling me back to Isla. I whipped around and ran back to the post that we originally came from and anxiously searched the ground for any sign of the only gift I had from my father.

I couldn't find it anywhere. I roamed about the entire area, lifting debris, sorting through the dirt, and retracing every memorable step made. It wasn't here. My dagger had vanished.

I kicked at a rock on the ground angrily, forgetting that all I still had on my feet were the now shredded slippers from the night of Kai's wedding. I pulled at the ends of my hair and forced my stare to the open sky above, letting out a booming scream of frustration and anguish.

I dropped down to my knees and watched as Nox came up and sat before me, staring down at me with hurt in his eyes. Hurt that I realized was stemming from me, and what he watched as the recollections of the worst night of my life swallowed me whole.

I looked up at him and observed his amethyst scales as they reflected in the sunlight. "What do you say we make the final stretch to our new home, huh?" I said to him as I pulled myself to my feet.

He lowered the side of his body closest to me by leaning on one of the joints of his wing, allowing me to easily climb up and take my riding seat.

"I've never been where we are headed. All I know is that we need to travel north to Ellecaster," I reminded him as I got settled.

I wondered if it would even be possible to get there in a few hours by flight. I remembered Jace had said that the journey would take around a day by horse, which meant it couldn't be far by the beating wings of a wyvern.

My heart fluttered rapidly in my chest for a moment as I thought about Jace. I was *so close*. The anticipation of finding him, seeing him, and holding him within my grasp once more was almost unbearable. I reached deep down within the very makings of my soul and felt him there—the bond between us.

What terrified me the most was wondering whether he would accept or reject the mating bond we now shared—which would inevitably bind our souls together for the remainder of our existence.

A moment later, Nox stretched out his enormous wings and sent us soaring through the skies above.

TWENTY-NINE

Kellan

I GLARED DOWN AT the *twenty* dead bodies of city guards as the sun rose behind the Islan Gates. My jaw locked as fury rampaged through my veins. I balled my hands into fists as I watched Vincent round up the remaining guards who had been on patrol last night. What the fuck happened?

I counted down the line as they all stood at attention. It was clear they were unaware that half of them were shaking in their fucking boots as they waited for me to erupt.

One hundred and eighty guards were on duty patrolling and the additional twenty tasked with securing the entrance to the city ended up dead at the foot of the gate.

So it left only one question. Were the attackers entering the city or leaving it?

I stood in front of the silent lines of guards, and Vincent appeared at my side once all were gathered. My eyes roamed up and down, lingering on each individual face so I could take in the absolute failures that somehow slipped through the cracks of my training.

"So," I started, a few of them blinked at the sound of my voice as it interrupted the quiet, hazy morning. "What the fuck happened?"

Silence continued. Nobody spoke, and that only served to piss me off more.

I unsheathed a dagger from my boot and pointed it at my own soldiers. "This *will* get ugly if one of you doesn't start talking. And fast."

"M-ma-magic, Captain." My stare whipped to the stuttering young male toward the end of the line. If I thought he shook in his boots before, he was full on trembling in them now.

I stalked over to him and raised a brow. "Come again?"

"Th-there's no other way to explain it, Captain. We were all knocked unconscious with no foul play. One moment I was patrolling, and the next I was waking up without any recollection of what had occurred. I had to peel my face from the cobblestones."

I took a step closer and watched as pure fear settled into his features. I tilted my head to the side as I gazed into his wide-set eyes and tsked. "Soldier, do you take me for a fool?"

"What!" he gasped out. "Of course not, Captain."

I lashed out and seized his face with both of my hands, squeezing his head between them. "Then why do you speak to me as such?!" I roared in his face.

I glanced down and watched as the young soldier pissed his pants.

"Oh, for fuck's sake," I grumbled as I gripped my dagger once more and, in one swift movement, sliced the blade across his throat. Blood poured down his torso as I watched the light leave his disbelieving eyes. His body dropped to the street with a loud *thud*.

I had zero tolerance for liars, and absolutely *none* for males that wet their gods-damn pants just to be receiving orders.

"Now," I started. "Anyone else have any better guesses as to what happened? Or will I be forced to move down the line in this manner?"

Not a single one of the remaining pairs of eyes looked my way.

A monstrous roar was working its way up my throat when it was cut off.

"The guard was telling the truth." A small voice echoed from down the road.

I turned to look in the interruption's direction and noticed a young boy, no older than the age of ten, holding the hand of an even tinier youngling—perhaps a sister. She clutched her brother's hand tightly with one hand, and in the other she held a stuffed animal.

I approached them in the most calming manner I could muster up. "What is your name, boy?"

"Reign, sir. And one day, I will be a guard, just like you," he answered, exuding confidence in his statement. A smirk formed on my face. This kid had more balls than one of my own gods-damn soldiers.

I lowered myself in a crouch to be at eye level with the boy. "Your name suits you." I paused. "I am Captain of the Guard and Seas, Reign. And I would be honored to have someone as assured as you join my ranks one day."

He gave me a firm nod, his grip never loosening on his sister's hand. "He was telling the truth, sir. Many fled the city last night. My parents refused. I refused. We are loyal to our kingdom regardless of who sits on the throne."

My eyes widened briefly at what the boy admitted. "Magic has not been in the city for centuries, boy. There must be some other explanation for what occurred."

"There was a witch among them," he stated, with no room for argument in his tone. I continued to listen. "She called out to all willing to support Elianna Solus. Our cousins fled. They tried to drag us along, but we would not leave our home. They informed the supporters within the city that the witch would allow everyone to flee under the cover of darkness."

My brows furrowed as I watched the boy and looked back over my shoulder at the bodies that lay in the streets.

"Say you're right. A witch did this. Why are they dead while the others lived?" I gestured to the husked bodies on the ground.

The boy shrugged. "Perhaps the magic didn't reach them and they had to fight through to leave."

I stood up from my crouch and strode back to the bodies. I pushed one of them over with the tip of my boot. The male's face looked...drained. As if his soul had been ripped from him before it was his time.

I bit the inside of my cheek and glanced back from the boy to the guards who still stood at attention in line.

I let out a sigh and combed my fingers through the top of my hair. "Anyone aware of who the mastermind behind this supposed mass exodus was?" I asked, trying to contain my temper in front of the brave lad.

Silence down the line once more.

"It was the prince and princess," the boy called over, and my jaw dropped without permission.

His statement caught me off guard, but it made sense as to why we couldn't locate them. They had apparently been in hiding while committing treason against their own mother.

"That is a...very big accusation, young Reign," I said back.

He gave another stiff nod. "I was told it was Princess Avery who spoke to the crowd of her thoughts regarding the throne. Her and the silver-haired witch healer."

Realization flashed before me, and my neck swung back in his direction. "Veli?" I asked in almost a whisper.

"It must've been, sir." The boy exuded a courage that should make whoever his father was very proud. However, I could feel the weight of his sister's damning stare, piercing through the strands of her blonde hair as it fluttered in the wind around her face.

Vincent approached me. "We never found the king's healer when we went looking, or the stable boy that Kai ordered to have his head brought to him. They must've all worked together to do this and support Solus."

"It would appear that way," I confirmed. I turned back to the younglings, who watched me intently. "Thank you for your insight, Reign. I will not forget this and your loyalty." I shot the line of my piss-poor guards a look. "At ease, soldier." I gave him a wink and patted him on his back as I turned away from him.

"Get back to your fucking posts!" I shouted to the line, and they immediately dispersed.

"What do you plan to do?" Vincent asked, catching his breath as we stormed toward the castle.

"If the princess and Elianna want a real war, they're about to fucking get one."

I stood in the center of the throne room as Callius fetched the queen and her son. It seemed that every time I entered this room now, I was about to get my ass handed to me.

"We need to know if any of our soldiers left with them," Vincent whispered to me as the queen appeared on Callius' arm.

I watched as he led her up the dais and to her throne, no longer appearing as *just* a sworn protector, as a gleam in each of their stares hinted at something else entirely—something they no longer cared to hide. Prince Kai followed behind them, appearing bored per usual.

"If soldiers left to support Elianna, they are weak. They are not who we want in our ranks. Let them support a throneless queen. Watch where it will get them," I answered just as quietly.

"What is the meaning of this, Captain?" Queen Idina spoke from the dais. "I do not enjoy being summoned to my own gods-damn throne room." She arched a brow at me, her face riddled with annoyance.

Fucking fantastic.

"Apologies, Your Majesty, but we have some...interesting and upsetting news to report," I announced as steadily as possible.

"Well, are you going to tell us, or just dance around it, Adler?" Kai spat from the side of them, his arms crossed and lips curled into a snarl.

I wish I could strangle that little shit.

"It appears that a mutiny took place amongst our own streets the past few nights, and hundreds of citizens have fled the city," I reported.

Neither of them spoke. I watched as Kai's eyes widened so large I thought they would bulge out of his face. The queen's jaw locked and her eyes flicked to Callius.

"The patrolling guards?" he asked calmly, but there was a sense of unease.

I let out a frustrated sigh. "This is where it gets...odd. They were all knocked unconscious."

"All of them?!" the queen roared at me through seething breaths. "How."

Not a question.

"Yes, My Queen. A witch has supposedly been living among us for...well, centuries."

"Come again?" Her tone morphed into curiosity, but still a sense of lividness lingered.

"Our late king's favorite healer. Veli," I answered, looking up at her through my brows.

"Veli?!" she snapped as she jolted forward. She leisurely leaned against the backrest of her throne and looked to the ceiling for a moment. "I should've known. There was always something off about that female," she hissed, and it ended in a terrifying cackle.

"So you mean to tell us that Veli, the dismissive healer, organized an escape for citizens she probably couldn't stand to be around in the first place?" Kai questioned.

"Unfortunately, that is only part of what I must tell you, Prince," I began. The queen leaned forward once more. "Veli was rumored to have handled the magic aspect of the escape. It appears that she somehow took away the consciousness of the guards on duty and cloaked everyone who fled in darkness to be hidden from sight. The escape was organized by your siblings. Princess Avery and Prince Finnian."

Any hint of the shit-eating grin Kai typically wore dropped from his face, and I watched as his head whipped towards his mother, jaw gaping.

The queen stood from her throne and let out a ferocious, deafening screech. It took every ounce of effort I had left to either not cover my ears to block out the noise or make a face of repulsion.

She looked back down at us then, her flame lit eyes moving between me and Callius. "Find them. Kill all the traitors that left. Especially that witch bitch," she hissed as she aggressively pointed at me. "Bring my children back to me by any means necessary. Alive."

Without another word, we watched as she picked up the front of her ruby gown and stormed back out through the side door of the throne room where she came from.

THIRTY

Avery

We never stopped. We ran through the night and past dawn. Our troop didn't falter for a single, panic-stricken moment as we raced away from the city of Isla and refused to look back.

It wasn't until the city was a tiny speck in the distance, even with our fae sight, that we deemed it safe enough to rest and debrief.

With the sun now high in the sky above, I was finally able to get a good look at the citizens who placed their trust in us to flee their homes.

A few hundred fae braved the journey. Significantly less than what was in attendance the night we exposed our plan to all who dared to show. I couldn't blame others for staying, especially the hundreds, or thousands, who retreated from the lines as we rushed toward the city gates, thinking we were about to be caught. How could we expect them to just take our word for everything and choose to uproot their entire lives and families with so many certainties unknown?

If we were caught, they would've been executed immediately. All it would take was one single soul to break under the pressure of the crown for everyone's allegiance to be exposed.

It surely would've been another mass execution, and we all would've been made an example of. I wasn't foolish enough to think that Finnian and I wouldn't be included amongst them. Even if our mother tried to spare us, once Kai ascended that throne, his word would be law.

People sat to rest on the grassy field in circles, murmuring amongst each other. I walked through the clusters of them, listening in on what they discussed. Despite the majority holding onto a glimmer of hope, I overheard several conversations that only heightened my anxiety.

"This was a mistake."

"We'll never be able to go home again."

"The witch murdered those guards. What have we gotten ourselves into?"

The guards. I still hadn't spoken to Veli about them since we silently stood in front of their fallen bodies while our rebels moved through the city gates.

A shiver ran down my spine as I recalled looking down at them. Her magic hadn't just ripped their consciousness from them; it ripped out their *souls*. Would they ever even be able to pass on in the afterlife now? Or would their very beings cease to exist from being consumed by the dark magic?

I brought my hand up to cover the tops of my brows, blocking out the blinding sun as I searched for Veli in the masses. Luckily, she wasn't too hard to find, thanks to her long, silver hair. She was offering aid to a young boy whose ankle was injured during the madness of the escape.

I gently approached her from behind. I went to reach out my hand toward her, but she twisted around to face me, her hand clutching my wrist that I was reaching out with. She caught me as I quickly glanced at her eyes, that had now returned to their usual violet hue.

"I am in no mood to be snuck up on," she muttered as her brows furrowed.

"I wasn't trying to. I was coming over here to che—" I stopped myself as I peered over her shoulder, and at the mother of the young boy who was practically seething at the mouth behind us.

"Is there a problem?" I asked, pulling my wrist back from Veli. I crossed my arms at the female, who looked like she was now more likely to *attack* us than help us continue to flee, as a male sat on her opposite side, looking apologetic.

They looked to be a small family of parents and their two younglings. The boy with the wrecked ankle and one that appeared to be a toddler in his mother's arms, squirming around for freedom.

The male gave his wife a scornful look. "Apologies, Princess. I was just trying to explain to my wife that we made the right decision to follow your lead and pledge our allegiance to the rightful heir."

I raised a brow.

"And *I* was just trying to explain to my husband that I do not want a *witch* touching my child with her cursed, murderous hands," the female chimed in before I could even open my mouth for a single word.

Ah. Well, that wasn't good. And judging by Veli's face, I could tell she was already looking impatient.

"Well, while I understand that being in the presence of a..." I paused to peek over at Veli and was met with her damning stare. "Sorceress...may be slightly unnerving. I will have you know that your son is in the hands of Isla's most talented healer. She served the castle for over a century and the king trusted no one else but her." I gave her a soft smile and hoped that I was convincing enough, for everyone's sake.

The female glanced over at Veli with a stare that could've rivaled the witch's own. "Thank you, Princess Avery," she said without removing her gaze from Veli. "But many of the hidden healers fled with us since the queen does not support them. My son's ankle can wait until one has time to assist."

Oof.

I gave her a curt nod and sighed as I looked down at the boy, who had a sour look on his face. "Very well, then."

Peering over to where Veli had been standing, I noticed that she was now storming off into an area in the far-off field where no one had stopped to rest.

I lifted the hem of my ugly, itchy, ankle-length tunic that Veli had lent me, and chased after her.

I stopped a few feet behind her as she threw her hands out at her sides in frustration, and I observed her curiously for a few moments. She wouldn't turn to face me, but I knew she could sense my presence.

I tried to give her some personal space, but we couldn't linger out in the open field for long, so I needed to pick through her mind while we had the chance of being alone.

Glancing up into the sky, my eyes squinted from the sun as a flock of birds flew overhead. "Do you want to talk about it?" I asked to her back.

She let out a harsh, short laugh. "It is becoming abundantly clear that you are not giving me an option, Princess."

I was quiet for a moment and then pursed my lips. "I guess you are right. We have many people counting on us and if you are going to just storm off…"

She aggressively spun her body to face me, and it took everything in me not to flinch in response. "Storm off? How about *you* work as a healer for centuries, helping and secretly saving the people of Isla against the law, then assist them in escaping the new, rotten king-to-be, and have them look at *you* like a monster!" She pointed her taloned nail merely an inch from my face.

My heart stuttered and the stern look I had forced upon my face vanished. "Veli, they don't think you're a—"

"Wyvern's fucking shit, Avery. That is *exactly* what they think I am now!" she snapped. "I ran from this. This isn't the first time I have been forced to start my life over, and originally it was to run from the very thing you forced my hand into doing. You know nothing, Princess. Not a gods-damn thing about me, where I come from, what I have escaped or endured."

I blinked at her. "Be that as it may, I didn't *force* you into anything! You're a healer. You help people. It only made sense that you did this."

A sad smirk twitched at the side of her cheek. "At what cost?"

I placed my hands on my hips as my brows furrowed. "What exactly did you see in the minds of those guards, Veli? Why did you kill them in front of everyone instead of knocking them unconscious, as planned?"

She immediately looked away from me, her eyes darting to the ground at her feet with a grimace on her face. "I didn't plan to kill them, and I considered ordering the shadows to suffocate them if they continued to block our path...but I knew that all hell would break loose if the people cloaked in that very darkness were forced to watch its essence slither down the throats of those who stood in our way."

"You were going to suffocate them with the shadows?" I whispered, eyes darting back and forth as I watched a tiny wisp of them peek out from her silver hair. "Perhaps that magic is too dangerous...or sinister."

"Do not blame them for the darkness I chose to use. The shadows are only as cruel as the witch that commands them," Veli defended her conjured shades as if they were living beings. "However, it is not safe to have them constantly in use. Magic always calls to its kin, and while I have used small bursts over the centuries, the amount of power I was forced to use these past few days would have undoubtedly alerted others of my kind." She sighed.

Her eyes flashed gold as the swirling haze of darkness that hid beneath her locks moved down her arms in a serpent-like manner and then vanished into the palms of her hands.

I stood there, eyes wide, and unable to speak as she continued.

"What I did was to try to prevent being looked at as a monster, only for it to happen, anyway. I was going to knock them all out as we said, but then their...their *thoughts*. They were drowning me. One minute I was in my own mind and the next I could barely find myself in the midst of their plans as they ravaged through me. Not just their plans, but their beliefs."

I took a hesitant step forward and wasn't entirely sure that I was even breathing. "What were they, Veli?"

"To put it in a way you could probably somewhat stomach it...a lot of *death*. Gruesome, bloody, unnecessary death and destruction that would be brought upon Velyra with the support of their new king. Younglings being honed into fierce, brainwashed weapons to destroy anything Kai deemed a threat. The assaults of unwilling females. The guards of high rank that supported him would be entitled to whatever they pleased. And that is just his plans for our own realm."

Nausea consumed me. If that was the *gentle* version of what she saw in a matter of seconds, I didn't even want to know what the true, uncensored version was.

"He plans to challenge other continents?" was all I could muster up from everything she just threw at me.

She smirked. "That is the very basis of that tyrant's plans. He will not settle for what his mother has set out to do. Kai will end what is left of the humans brutally, and once they are nothing more than a species written in a historical text, he will move on in the realm. He seeks all world power, just as your mother."

I forced down a swallow. "And how would those guards know of this?"

She raised a brow and gave me a knowing look.

I closed my eyes tightly and sighed. "Callius."

"Precisely," she answered.

I looked back at her, *really* looked, and she appeared so...defeated. Very much at odds with the Veli I had grown up fearing out of pure, youngling foolishness.

"Callius would never do anything against my mother. So, if he truly spoke of this to Velyra's soldiers, then it must be true. He and the queen are..."

"Inseparable," she finished for me. "Makes you think about a lot of things, doesn't it?" She crossed her arms.

Holy freaking mother of the gods.

"You can't be suggesting..."

"I'm not suggesting anything. However, I am dying to know how one child out of three turned out as cruel as those two. You were all raised the same. I was around enough to see that."

I could barely put my thoughts into words. "She loved Kai differently," I admitted in a hushed tone. "She loved us all, but he was...special to her. I think Finn and I always assumed it was due to him being the heir."

"And that could be it as well. However, I wouldn't put it past those two to push a false heir to the throne, trying to end the true Valderre reign for good."

I watched her eyes flare as she glanced over my shoulder, and I froze where I stood.

Finnian jogged up next to us. "What are you ladies up to out here? Everyone is asking when we will be leaving. We can't linger for long."

I cleared my throat and met his gaze. "Has everyone eaten and rested?"

He shrugged. "As much as they could."

"Excellent." My eyes flicked back to the witch. "We were just having girl talk."

I regretted the words that left my mouth immediately. Veli and girl talk? I doubted even my gullible brother would believe that.

Instead, he just raised a single brow as he gave me a peculiar look and walked back to the gathering that awaited us in the distance.

Veli went to move past me. "Don't say anything to him about that," I called to her. "It would upset him and we don't know the truth."

She gave me a quick, pitying nod and continued back to our small army.

THIRTY-ONE
Jace

Unwelcome nerves settled in the pit of my stomach. Tomorrow would mark the last day of our weeklong wait for Lia's anticipated arrival, and there had been no sign of her. No letter from her. No sightings were reported to me. Nothing.

Absolutely fucking *nothing*.

I slammed my fist onto the table of the tavern that I had stopped in for lunch after sparring with Gage all morning. I clenched my teeth and refused to look up at his stare that I could feel on me from across the table.

What had happened to her? Nausea climbed my throat, threatening to suffocate me, as thoughts of her being recaptured rippled through me. It felt as if my anxiety was slowly devouring me from the inside out.

"We need to get a troop together to leave in the morning," I said to him as I reluctantly looked his way.

He appeared as if he was about to ask me something when Zaela barged in out of nowhere.

"Hey, shitheads," she greeted as she shoved Gage aside and scooted up next to him in the booth.

She grabbed hold of my mug of ale and sent it down her throat, making an audible, irritating gulping sound.

"To what do we owe the pleasure?" I growled.

"Moody today, huh?" she said after her last swallow.

I sighed. "Well, the week I gave her is over. It's time for us to figure out what the hell happened and try to find her."

"She'll turn up," she stated confidently as she put her dirty boots up on the table, crossing one ankle over the other.

"Oh? And what makes you so randomly optimistic?" I threw at her with the bite she normally possessed.

She shrugged. "Maybe you're not giving her enough credit. Isla is far from here."

I was not in the mood for this. I leaned back in the booth and sucked on my front teeth, unable to find words that wouldn't result in me lashing out at my cousin.

"Oh, for fuck's sake, Jace. Snap out of it. I'm just trying to make you not look miserable for a fraction of a second!" she spat as she ripped her legs back down and leaned across the table toward me.

I ran my fingers frustratingly through my hair. "I just...I thought I could feel her before. I haven't felt anything in a few days and it's driving me gods-damn crazy. All I feel is a constant surge of rage that is often followed by grief...and fear."

Gage looked between us as Zaela eyed me curiously. "Is this about what you said a few days ago down in the fields? Thinking you felt that she was injured?" he asked.

"I'm sorry, but what?" Zae practically shouted, the last word ending in a laugh.

"I don't know what I felt or how to explain it!" I snapped, and I watched a flicker of panic flash across her face. "Gods, I'm sorry. I don't know what's come over me. Every day without her, I feel like I can't fucking breathe. I feel like the air is torn from my lungs. My chest aches. I've been getting phantom pains, and it's like I can *sense* her in the back of my mind, but not knowing if she is okay, or if she is even alive, is killing me, Zae. The uncertainty is destroying me."

Her eyes roamed over me.

"You love her, Jace. It is okay to admit that," she spoke in a tone so much softer than I was used to.

"I never even told her," I muttered under my breath as my head bowed.

My heart felt like it was about to explode at my admittance of what I felt for her, and at the grief that now tore through me with the possibility of her soul having left this realm and never knowing the truth of it.

"I should have told her. Even when I was certain that I was about to die on the ground at the foot of the village, and she desperately screamed for me while she was tied to that pole."

My mind flashed back to the scene that I would do anything to have wiped from my memory. The vision of her begging Adler to spare me. The arrow protruding from her bloody, torn up abdomen. The look of devastating fear in her eyes as she watched me fall to the ground when her body had been decimated just as brutally.

"I should've told her then. I should have told her so many gods-damn times." My voice cracked on the last few words.

Zaela reached out and gently grabbed my hand from across the table. Gage placed his on top of hers and I looked up at them.

"She knows," she whispered. "Lia knows what you feel for her."

I looked into her hazel eyes that were so similar to mine. The Cadoria eyes, her father would say. He took care of those he loved above all else. My uncle was the kind of man I aspired to be. So how did I end up so fucking broken when it came to love?

Unfortunately, I knew the answer.

Before any of us said another word, screams tore through the air coming from outside of the tavern, immediately flashing me back to that horrific night that I would do anything to forget.

My eyes flared. "No, not again," I seethed as I gripped the hilt of my sword on my hip. I would not let them decimate another one of my cities.

We sprang to our feet, sending our booth toppling over behind us, and raced out of the tavern's door to investigate the commotion out in the city's streets.

We raced through the streets, and the masses of people as they frantically scattered, screaming that we were under attack. We shouted right back at them, demanding they state who was attacking us and from where, but it was useless. Everyone was desperately searching for cover.

I encountered a soldier who was supposed to be on duty at his post, but he was also desperately searching for a place to hide.

"What is happening?" I demanded as I stormed up to him, grabbing the collar of his tunic as my temper took over.

"The sky! We are about to be under attack from above!" he reported.

The four of us craned our necks to look up into the air and observed an enormous black mass in the distance headed directly toward us.

My lips parted and eyes flared as my gaze found my two closest friends. "Oh, my gods," I breathed.

"Do you have orders, Commander?" the soldier asked, shaking me from the trance I had fallen into. He was putting on a brave face that he certainly hadn't been wearing when I found him only a moment ago.

"Don't engage!" I accidentally roared in his face, as my eyes snapped back to the figure that was rapidly approaching the city. "Follow my lead and don't you dare shoot a single arrow at that wyvern!" I ordered. "Pass it down the lines. Make sure every single soldier and guard here knows it."

He nodded and rushed off.

"It must be her!" Gage shouted while he let out a booming laugh, a massive smile taking up the majority of his face.

I couldn't find any words; I just took off running.

I pushed through the city dwellers that ran the opposite way. I forced my way through the streets, around every corner and bend that popped up in front of me, leaping over carriages and carts that had been abandoned in the middle of the roads.

I could faintly hear Gage politely shouting orders for people to remain calm behind me, and a laugh snuck out of me when Zae chimed in, yelling at them to "calm the fuck down."

Glancing back up into the sky, I could see the wyvern was much closer now, descending directly beyond our city gates.

This was it. It had to be. This was the moment I would finally reunite with Elianna—*my Lia*.

I would get to feel the softness of her skin, comb my fingers through her hair that flowed with each step she took, and look into those pale green eyes that had me entranced with her the moment I first gazed into them. Mostly, I couldn't wait to kiss her menacing smirk that made me weak in the knees every time she shot it in my direction.

My body couldn't move fast enough. Every step forward felt as if I took three steps back, but I finally made it beyond the stone gates of Ellecaster at the same moment the wyvern landed a few hundred feet beyond them.

The creature was *colossal*. That wasn't even the right word. It was terrifying and fierce, but nothing short of breathtaking. Its eyes were fixated on one thing—*me*.

Movement caught my attention at its shoulder, and I somehow managed to tear my eyes from its gaze. My heart stopped painfully in my chest as the other two flanked both of my sides, their run coming to a screeching halt.

I knew they witnessed exactly what I had in that moment.

Climbing up the back of this magnificent, assumed to be extinct beast, was my queen.

THIRTY-TWO

Elianna

I MUST'VE BEEN HALLUCINATING. I was either dead or hallucinating because I just refused to let my heart believe that my mate was standing before me. My mouth fell open, and my fingers rose to touch my parted lips as his stare bore into me from across the small meadow.

Jace was alive. I sucked in a breath that nearly shocked my lungs as I took in the sight of him. All the agony I had felt over these last few weeks vanished and was instantly replaced by an overwhelming sense of relief.

My back straightened as a short growl rumbled through Nox's chest. I gently patted his shoulder, comforting him. "That's him," I whispered, barely believing it myself.

I slid down Nox's body as gracefully as I could manage and cautiously walked around his wing that half-rested on the ground.

I stopped and stood in front of my wyvern's chest as I stared out at the small army that was now forming around Jace. Nox's rough, scaly chin brushed my shoulder as he lowered his head to be next to my own, staring at them just as keenly as I was.

I couldn't stop blinking, fearing that one of the times my eyes opened once more, he would disappear before me. But no matter how many times I blinked, he remained.

Our gazes were locked on each other and we stood there frozen. I was chained where I stood in disbelief, in awe at the sight of him—alive.

Was he anchored in disappointment, or in disbelief, just as I was?

A moment later, he broke out of his rooted stance and sprinted towards me. It was unfaltering, desperate, and rapid, as if he couldn't get to me fast enough.

A small whimper broke from me, clogging my throat as I rushed forward to him. I felt every crevice in the hard, unforgiving ground on my nearly bare feet. The tiny pebbles tore through my skin as I passed over them. The wind blew my hair back as I soared toward him, as if I was still high in the air, flying on Nox's back.

Time ceased to exist. The world around me slowed and melted away. All I could see, all I could sense and focus on, was Jace.

He was closer now, and I could make out the features of his perfect face. His hazel eyes that I dreamed of being able to gaze into again, his hair that had grown slightly longer, begging me to run my fingers through it, and his *smile*. The smile that had so rarely appeared, making it that much more precious in this moment. Lastly, I noticed the scar that now marked him permanently from my own blade.

The moment I knew I could make the distance, I stretched my arms out and dove toward my mate, jumping directly into him. He caught me effortlessly.

I wrapped my legs around his torso and buried my face in the nape of his neck as he enclosed my entire body in his arms. Jace fell to his knees while holding me firmly to his chest, and let out a sob.

A *sob*. The man who refused to show me even a flicker of emotion, aside from resentment, the first few weeks I knew him. The man who led armies and devoted his life to killing any fae he crossed paths with was sobbing. I sat there in the arms of my mate as he wept. For *me*.

I couldn't hold it in for a moment longer and burst into tears as I tightened my hold around his neck even more. The saltiness of them coated my lips as they slid down my cheeks and onto his skin that my face was buried in.

I had no idea how long we remained in that position, desperately holding onto each other. As his grip slowly loosened, the feeling of timelessness slipped away, leaving me disoriented and internally begging for him to hold me tighter once more.

I peeled my face away from his neck and looked up at him. His eyes peered through mine and into my soul as I felt his hand gently cup the back of my head and pull me into him, only this time, his lips were on mine.

The kiss was all-consuming. A fire ignited within me, the blaze tearing through my very being. His mouth claimed my own in a sense of urgency that radiated his need for me. I never wanted it to end. I couldn't fathom anything feeling better than this moment between us.

He broke away from the kiss and pressed his forehead to my own. "You're home," Jace croaked out, and a sob left me in response.

Our gazes bore into one another as we remained in each other's arms. "I love you," he confessed, voice cracking, as his eyes focused on mine intently.

My lips parted at his admission, and then I realized that I was so very wrong. Nothing would ever feel greater than *this* moment, right now.

Before I could respond, his lips were on me again, and he kept his grip tightly around my thighs as he rose to his feet.

I reluctantly unwrapped my legs from him and he leisurely lowered me to the ground, but we both refused to let go. We stood there in a silent, serene embrace until a roar of cheering erupted from behind us.

I had completely forgotten that we had an audience, and gods, if we didn't just give them a show.

We stared into each other's eyes for a few more moments before allowing ourselves to settle back down into reality.

"I thought I lost you," he whispered to me as his thumb brushed over the swell of my bottom lip.

"Never," I breathed, earning a smile from him.

"Thank the fucking gods." A faint chuckle left him, and I answered with a laugh that matched.

Both of us were here, together, and defying all the odds that had been stacked against us.

Jace had survived the wyvern's blood-soaked blade. I had escaped the dungeons beneath the castle and traveled across the realm to find him.

We were here. Both of us. And I would bring hell bound fury upon the gods myself if their fates ever tried to separate us again.

"Alright, you've all seen enough. Now, back to your posts," I could hear Zaela bark at all the onlooking soldiers.

I let out a small giggle, but my eyes never left Jace's. That was until my attention caught on the shadow of a figure running toward us at full speed from over his shoulder.

"Incoming," I whispered with a smirk to him.

"Brace yourself," he answered with a wink.

And with that, I took a single, giant step away from him as Gage tackled me down to the ground.

"Gods, Gage, don't break her," Jace joked from above us.

Gage squeezed his arms that were wrapped around me still and rolled off of me into the dirt, laughing hysterically. "Oh, shut up, Cadoria. She's tougher than you are."

"You got me there," Jace grumbled, earning a laugh from both of us.

Gage got to his feet and offered me his hand to help me up. He then enclosed me into another bear hug, this time allowing me to stay on my feet. "I missed you!" he boomed. "Jace is an unbearable mopey bore without you around. Somehow, even worse than before he met you."

I let out a noise that was half laugh and half sob. "Gods, that must've been *awful* to deal with."

"You have no idea," he said with a grin.

Jace reached out and jokingly shoved at the chest.

"Hey!" I shouted. "Don't you hit my best friend."

"Oh, *your* best friend, huh?" Jace teased.

"Yes, exactly." I smirked as Gage threw his arm around my shoulder.

"I told you I was her favorite."

"I wouldn't say that," Jace said, crossing his arms.

Zaela appeared next to us then. The last vision I had of her was the look on her face as I fell to the ground from the burning building—when I had taken an arrow to my side to save her life. The truth was that I had forgiven her for her words before my body even hit the street.

She had still believed that I betrayed them in that moment. Was that what she still thought?

"Lia," she greeted me with a tight smile and a cheerful lilt to her voice that stunned me slightly.

"Zae," I said, matching her tone and gave her a tight-lipped smile in return.

She awkwardly reached out and rubbed the outskirts of my arm. "I, um," she began. "I'm glad you're okay."

This was her attempt at effort. I would take it.

"Thank you. I'm glad you're okay, too."

Jace reached out to me and pulled me back into his body, kissing my forehead. I gladly snuggled up to him.

"Gods, I don't know how you can do that quite yet," Gage retorted at us. "Sorry, Lia, but you smell horrible."

I burst out laughing into Jace's chest as he let out a grumble I couldn't understand.

I turned to face Gage, but Jace's arms refused to let me go, so I stood with my back pressed firmly into him as his arms crossed over my chest.

"Listen, next time you escape an underground dungeon by the skin of your teeth and are forced to travel on the back of a wyvern across the continent for weeks straight, you let me know how terrific you smell."

Nervous giggles left me, but none of them found my attempt at humor funny. My smirk dropped as I watched looks of horror take over each of their features.

I cleared my throat. "I believe we all have a lot of catching up to do."

"That we do," Jace said right before he leaned down and gave me another quick kiss.

A huff sounded at our backs, and I realized I had completely forgotten about Nox.

The four of us turned toward the wyvern, and I gave my boy a smile. "Everyone, this is Nox." I gestured to my flying companion. "Nox, this is Jace, Gage and Zaela. Our..." I looked at my friends and mate for a brief moment. "Family."

Jace's body stiffened behind me. I couldn't help but wonder if I said the wrong thing until I felt his fingers caress the small of my back in gentle, comforting circles.

Nox gave a loud purr of approval, and Gage looked beyond excited. Zaela looked...well, she looked like she was seeing a giant, flying, fire-breathing lizard for the first time. Jace's eyes just remained wide as he stared up at Nox, perhaps in shock at the sight of him—or maybe in shock that I flew here on his back.

"Do you have any sheep here?" I asked.

Jace arched a brow. "Of course. May I ask why?"

I shrugged a shoulder and angled my chin up at Nox. "He's hungry. He likes cows, too."

I watched as all three of their faces blanched, and I had to suppress my grin.

"We have a few small farms here. We can make arrangements for tonight, but I can't promise they'll be too keen on giving their livestock to a..." Zaela hesitated. "Actually, never mind. I'm sure they would rather lose a few cows than risk becoming a meal themselves."

Gage let out a chuckle. "I like steak, too. Nice choice, my new flying friend," he said, looking up at the wyvern.

Nox tilted his head curiously to the side.

"Hear that, Nox? We'll find you some food for tonight. In the meantime, stay out of trouble...and sight if you can help it for now."

He huffed hot air towards us and I just raised a brow. "We really need to work on your attitude. I will call for you when we have a plan." I lifted my hand to my mouth and let out an ear-shattering whistle. "Next time you hear that, you come find me, okay? Stay close, please."

And with those words, and a few beats of his wings, he launched into the sky and soared above, taking off towards the enormous mountains behind the city.

"He understands you?" Gage asked.

"Gods, I hope so," I joked nervously as I watched him fly away. "He more so...*reacts* to things."

I turned back to my friends and all three of their jaws were practically on the ground, eyes wide in awe of him.

Jace snapped out of his trance first. "Come on, let me show you the city."

I cleared my throat. "Would, um, it be too much trouble to get a bath first?"

Both of his brows rose. "Gods, Lia, I'm so sorry. Of course, you can have a bath."

His face looked like he wasn't entirely convinced. "Are you...sure?"

He looked panicked for some reason.

"He probably just realized that he has been living in the barracks since we arrived. You can go to my place and get cleaned up. I will find somewhere else to be tonight," Zaela announced, and Jace looked more than relieved. "Just don't...I don't want to know what goes on. Keep it to yourselves, please."

"Gods, Zae, I haven't had a need for my own place until now," Jace shot back at her, but then his voice softened as he turned to me. "If I had desired a permanent home here before now, I would have obviously had one ready for you."

My heart skipped a beat and a hint of a smile tilted the side of my lips as the four of us turned and walked towards the gates of Ellecaster—the once great, beautiful city of stone built into the base of the Ezranian Mountains.

THIRTY-THREE
Elianna

As we rounded the bustling, winding streets of Ellecaster, the sounds of chatter and footsteps filled the air. My nerves threatened to consume me as I glanced in every direction, considering the last time I had seen other humans, they had run from me and straight to their deaths. Regardless of my worries, I couldn't hold my smile in—Jace had built this, or worked to rebuild it, making sure its citizens within were safe at all times.

He kept his arm around my shoulder the entire trek through the city, and I couldn't stop sneaking glances up at him. My breath snagged at the sight of him—he was so beautiful. The daylight reflected off his sun kissed skin, and the wind tousled his hair as I caught him looking down at me, flashing his perfect teeth in a grin that rocked me.

His dimples. How had I never noticed those before? Perhaps because I had never seen him smile so often, especially in such a short amount of time.

My stomach dropped as I realized that while he may have confessed his love for me, that didn't necessarily mean he would commit to, or want any part of, a mating bond.

He hated the fae his entire existence, and any connection that his blood had to it. The very idea of a mating bond could feel like a cruel twist of fate to him, forcing his soul into a betrayal against everything he ever believed.

I snapped out of my panic when I noticed all the busy citizens stopping to wave at him, warming my heart. They adored him, and it was clear that they knew he dedicated his life to protecting them here.

Jace leaned down to my ear, his arm never moving from my shoulder. "They're waving at you, too. Not a second of our time here has been wasted."

"They support me?" I whispered on a shaky breath.

"They do. They don't know all the details, as I wanted you to speak of what you plan to do yourself, but they're aware that the true heir of the realm was coming to aid us. Many are nervous, as anyone would be regarding the unknown, but they trust me. And I will trust and believe in you until I take my last breath. They go where I go. And I go with you."

My heart fluttered in response and I leaned into his warm body at my side.

Most buildings we passed near the front gates were made of wood, but some in the distance were made from stone, resembling Isla.

"Have you been expanding what was already here?" I asked.

"Yes and no," Zaela answered as we strolled up a hill toward those solid buildings. "This was one of the first places decimated by the fae armies over a century ago. It was once very prosperous and beautiful. Most buildings were destroyed, but we salvaged what we could. We didn't have quite enough manpower in the beginning to recreate what it once was, but the wooden structures work all the same."

I flinched at the thought of my own armies coming here and leveling out this beautiful city. "I'm so sorry. I hadn't heard of Ellecaster until Jace said it when we first met."

Jace smirked at the charming version of how I portrayed that interaction all those months ago.

"It wasn't called Ellecaster back then. It was Silcrowe," Gage chimed in.

My chin rose to look up at Jace. "Yes, that's what you referred to as the human lands when you spoke of it. You said it was named after the original city of Silcrowe."

"It's what us mortals refer to as everything on our side of the Sylis Forest, up until the Ezranian Mountains, in honor of what happened here that day," he responded. "It has been kept secret for a reason. If the queen was aware that Silcrowe was rebuilt as Ellecaster—"

"She would destroy it again," I finished for him.

A guard came jogging up to us from one of the side streets and then came to a halt before us, stopping our own strides. "Commander," he greeted. "This just arrived for you." He handed Jace a piece of rolled parchment.

Jace gave him a nod, dismissing him, and opened the letter as the man turned around to head back from where he had come.

I looked to Jace as his nostrils flared, but a smirk twisted his face. "I was wondering why we hadn't received any reports from our scouts regarding you crossing into our lands. It appears that your wyvern is faster than our falcons."

"Oops," I said with a wink, and we all continued our march up the street.

Once we reached the top of the hill, we came to a stop outside of one of the stone buildings. The structure was unusually wide and stretched halfway up the street with multiple arched doors lining the sides of it. Bricks of a slightly lighter shade of gray were stacked from the ground to the roof every twenty or so feet from each other, and a door lay between each.

"This is my townhouse," Zaela announced, startling me from my trance as I stared at the building.

"Townhouse?" I questioned.

"Yes, the building has ten units in it. Each door is someone else's home in the structure."

I raised a brow. "From the ground to the roof?"

"Yes...do you not have these structures in your city?" she mocked teasingly.

I contemplated for a moment. Perhaps we did, and I never noticed. "It seems like a tenement, only instead of the homes stacked on one another, they are side to side. We have many tenements in our city, but they are often in the less wealthy areas of Isla," I answered, squinting from the sun as I looked up at the high roof.

"Ah, well then, yes. It is like one of those, then," she said as she made her way to the archway of the end unit, the three of us following behind her.

The door opened, revealing a small, slightly furnished living room. I took a step in after and glanced around the area. Zae walked up to the windows in the front and pulled back the navy-blue curtains, letting the bright sunlight in.

There was a small fireplace in front of the new-looking settee that matched the curtains she had just pulled back. The fireplace was filled with ashes and half burned wood, likely from the night before.

"Sorry, it isn't much yet. We have been busy and furnishing this place wasn't exactly a top—"

I held up a hand, stopping her. "It's perfect. Thank you so much."

"Great. Well, you are more than welcome to stay here as long as you wish. I have offered it to Jace and Gage time and time again." She crossed her arms. "There are five small bedrooms upstairs and one down here on the first level, but Jace wanted to stay in the barracks with his soldiers, and well...Gage goes where he does." I didn't miss her rolling her eyes on the last sentence, and I held in my smirk.

"Damn right," Gage let out from across the room as he played with a decorative candelabra on top of the fireplace.

"Honestly, Zae, you say that as if you aren't annoyed with being with us the majority of your days, anyway. And you wish to *live* with us?" Jace teased.

"Good point," she chimed in. "However, I'm sure Lia would rather stay here than the barracks."

I went to open my mouth, but Jace spoke before I had the chance.

"Obviously. That is why we are now taking you up on your offer. Congratulations, Zae. You just got yourself three new roommates for the time being." He winked at her and I let out a quick burst of laughter.

Zaela grumbled something I didn't care to decipher while Gage waltzed up to her and wrapped his arm around her shoulder.

"Come on, let's give these two some privacy." He turned to us. "We'll catch up with you later. Don't do anything I wouldn't do."

I gave him a wicked grin. "You'll need to be a little more specific than that."

He wiggled his eyebrows at Jace and then guided Zaela back out the front door, leaving me alone with my mate for the first time since I arrived.

The door clicked shut, and the room went utterly silent. I wasn't even sure I was breathing as Jace's presence consumed me. His scent of cedarwood and steel mixed with crackling embers wrapped around me like a cloak.

His calloused hand lightly fell against my shoulder from behind me a moment later, startling me.

I slowly turned to face him. His eyes bore into me with so many emotions hidden beneath them. Fear. Regret. Longing. *Love*.

He brushed the few locks of my dirt-crusted hair that rested on my chest to the side, revealing part of the new whip scar that curled over my shoulder.

His jaw ticked, eyes narrowing in on the marks he knew didn't exist the last time we were together.

He refused to meet my eyes as his fingers lightly traced over the small swirl from the tail end of the whip. "Which one of those fucking pricks did this."

A demand.

I swallowed and flinched, but remained silent until his eyes then lifted to my own. "The same one who gave me the original scars," I revealed in a hoarse, hushed tone.

Jace clenched his teeth so hard I thought I would hear them crack. "I will kill him for that."

The corner of my mouth tipped upwards. "I know."

I went to move in closer, but stopped when I noticed his eyes were lazily lowering down the front of my filthy, shredded gown.

"You escaped at the wedding. You were there, weren't you?" His question wasn't accusatory, just honest curiosity.

"I was," I answered softly as I watched his gaze roam over me.

His eyes halted on my mid-section, at the dark, crimson stains that covered the front of me. "You were covered in blood." His tone darkened.

"It wasn't mine." I smirked.

A breathy laugh left him. "That's my girl."

My heart fluttered at his words.

He pulled me into him and kissed my forehead, resting his chin on the top of my head as he held me there for a few moments, lightly swaying side to side. "Let's go get you cleaned up."

I followed him as he led the way up the staircase.

THIRTY-FOUR
Elianna

AT THE TOP OF the stairs, the hallway opened up to multiple doors. He peered into each room until we discovered the bathing chamber behind the third door on the right side.

Jace snickered. "Of course, she made sure she furnished this room."

I nearly shoved him aside from excitement so I could see what awaited beyond the doorframe, and the sight of it didn't disappoint.

A porcelain tub large enough for two lay in the middle of the chamber, sitting on top of the marble-tiled floor. The walls of the room were lined with wallpaper that had intricate designs of silvers and blues. It appeared that this was one of the few rooms in Zaela's home that she cared to decorate.

Jace went to pull back the window's curtain, but I stopped him. "How about we just light a few candles instead?"

He eyed me curiously, walked over to the tub and turned the faucet's knob, allowing hot, steaming water to pour into it. I was a little surprised this city had running water.

Only the extremely wealthy could afford such a luxury in Isla.

I observed him as he then made his way to the far wall that was lined with candle sconces. He reached for the small stack of friction igniting wood near the sink and worked to light them.

Once the room was intimately lit by candle flame, he approached me once more from behind. He twirled the entirety of my hair around his hand and gently draped it over the front of my shoulder. A chill worked its way up my spine at the contact.

I felt his fingers as they undid the laces of the corset that was built into the dress and worked them all the way down my back. Once finished, both of his hands took hold of the tops of the gown's sleeves and pulled them down my arms, revealing my breasts as the fabric slipped from my torso.

I took in a shuddering breath, not realizing that I hadn't been able to breathe so deeply in over a week. The corset had loosened over time, but I doubted I would've been able to get out of the gown on my own without slicing it open with a blade.

I resisted the urge to turn and face him as his fingers traced over my scars once more, the newer scars that lined my back. The trembling in his hands became more prominent as he worked his way around them.

"Eight," he whispered, voice shaking. "They whipped you...Eight. Fucking. Times." His hand balled into a fist as it rested between my shoulder blades. "I know every inch of your body. Every mark. Every curve. Every dimple."

My spine shivered at his confession. "This never should've happened. I should've protected you."

My eyes flared, and I turned to face him. "This was *not* your fault."

Fury settled into his features, but I knew it wasn't directed at me. "It wasn't? If I had gotten there earlier. If *I* went into that building to look for Zaela, I—"

"You would've been killed. Both of you could've been. I have many regrets in my life, but rushing into that building will never be one of them."

"But if I had found you before they tied you to that gods-forsaken pole…"

I leaned up onto the tips of my toes and kissed his lips, attempting to get him to stop blaming himself.

He broke the kiss and looked down, deep into my eyes. Without a word, he tipped his chin toward the tub that was now filled with glorious, steaming water.

His hands traced down the sides of my body until they reached the skirt of the gown that had caught around my hips. I sucked my lower lip between my teeth as I watched him lower himself onto one of his knees and carefully wiggle the fabric down my thighs until it finally fell to the floor.

"Beautiful," he whispered, and I whimpered as he stood up and took my hand, guiding me into the tub.

The second my body was submerged in the water, I let out an involuntary groan. My muscles ached so wonderfully in response to the warmth of the bath.

I leaned my back up against the side of the cool porcelain tub as Jace grabbed a small tin trough that sat on the floor and filled it with water. He tipped my head backward slightly and poured the bathwater over my hair, soaking it.

The gesture was so dangerously sweet—it made my heart swoon.

Jace lathered soap into his hands and began washing the dirt, blood, and only the gods knew what else had embedded itself into my hair.

"You're going to wash me personally, Commander?" I asked softly, teasingly.

Jace was silent for a moment. "Please let me do this for you, Lia."

There was so much pain in his voice that my lip trembled in response. I was grateful that he sat behind me and couldn't see it. The agony he felt erupted down the bond.

The chamber was filled with unnerving silence for what seemed like an eternity as he washed the gore and grime from my body.

"I believe I got all of it," he said, breaking the torturing silence.

"Thank you." My voice cracked on the last word.

He kissed my left shoulder blade, the one the whip had slipped over. I suddenly became aware of every bead of water that slid down my skin where he kissed. Warmth rose in my stomach as one kiss led to another, and then three more after that.

I then felt his tongue slip between his warm, soft lips and travel along the scar that draped around me up until he reached the nape of my neck, where his tongue was replaced once more by a gentle kiss of his lips.

Heat pooled between my thighs the more his body touched mine.

"I'm sorry you'll have to see more scars. I can try to co—"

He whipped around to the side of the tub faster than I could blink and took my chin between two of his fingers, making sure my focus was on him.

"Listen to me right now, Elianna Valderre." The racing pulse of my heart intensified at his use of my true name. It nearly took my breath away.

"There is not a single part of you or your body that I do not find exquisite. Not a single thing that I wouldn't happily drown in. I have kissed every inch of your body before, and I will do it again. Over and over for the remainder of my existence. Because you are *mine*. Those scars are nothing but a reminder of how strong you are. How resilient and powerful you have become. Regardless of the outcome of this war, you are my queen. From now until my dying breath."

On impulse, I reached out and pulled his body on top of my own and into the tub with me, splashing the sudsy bathwater over its edges as I pressed my lips to his.

The kiss was endless. It was ravenous. And I was insatiable.

I couldn't get enough of him. Not enough of his hands on me, his lips on my own, or the feel of him between my bare thighs. It would *never* be enough.

He pulled his mouth from mine and I almost lashed out in need until I felt his lips press a kiss to the center of my throat. His arms locked together behind me, arching my back upward and my breasts into his face. Before I knew it, his mouth was on those too.

It still wasn't enough.

I needed *more*.

I wrapped my legs around his body, and he lifted us from the tub effortlessly. His hands wrapped around the underside of my thighs, holding my naked body in place as he stepped out of the bath.

His clothes were drenched from the water, soaking the floor as he traveled across the chamber with me held in his muscular arms. Neither of us cared.

We had just made it out into the hallway when he slammed my back against the wall, kissing me fiercely as he kept me levitating in the air. I tried to lower my legs to the ground, but he held them firmly in place.

I needed to tear his clothes off, and I needed it *now*.

I tried to rip the fabric near his neck, but his shirt clung to his body. "*Get. It. Off,*" I growled onto his lips and I felt a wicked grin form on them.

A moment later, I felt my back rip away from the wall and before I knew it, he was kicking down one of the bedroom doors.

He slowly bent forward and lowered me to the bed that lay in the center of the otherwise unfurnished room. He stood up and licked his lips as his eyes grazed down my body torturously slow.

Jace tried to pull his shirt over his head, but it still awkwardly clung to his body as it dripped onto the floor. I glanced down at his hip and quickly sat up, unsheathing the dagger that was strapped there.

I took the blade and sliced it up his shirt, effortlessly tearing through it, revealing the mouthwatering, solid body that hid beneath it.

He stared down at me as he unbuttoned his pants, eyes kindling with need. "That was…" he groaned. "Incredibly sexy."

I grinned as I leaned towards him and licked from his lower abdomen up to the base of his neck, my tongue climbing his body inch by inch.

He was on me again instantly, our mouths colliding in neediness and desire. His knee nudged my own to the side, allowing him easier access to me.

I impatiently waited to feel the sensation of him inside me, but it never came. I was growing more desperate by the minute, and when I reached down to guide him into me, I felt his hand grasp my wrist firmly.

My eyes flew open to see that his were an inch above my own. "So greedy," he whispered onto my lips. His tongue then slipped down the side of my neck, sending goosebumps throughout my entire body.

He made his way to the center of my chest, between my breasts, stopping there for a second before hovering over one of my nipples. I looked down and watched as Jace teased it with his tongue before sucking it entirely into his mouth while his thumb caressed the other.

My back arched at the contact, and I was about to lose any sense of control I had left. I let out a soft moan and before I knew it, his tongue was traveling down my center once more, only now his body was crawling down to the floor.

Onto his knees.

"Jace," I said on a breath. "What are you doing?" I barely recognized my own voice.

I glanced down toward him and all I could see were his hazel eyes hovering between my thighs. The flecks of gold within them shimmered in the setting sunlight that peeked through the curtains.

"Now, what kind of man would I be if I didn't kneel before my queen?"

Before I had time to even process his words, his tongue slipped between my thighs, swirling and circling around my throbbing bud.

"Oh, gods!" I cried out in a near scream.

The heat from his tongue left me for a brief moment. "The gods aren't here, Lia. It's just me." And he returned to devouring me.

I threw my head back against the bed as the pleasure from his mouth erupted through every vein of my body.

After endless, glorious torture, and with a final, agonizingly slow sweep of his tongue, he crawled back up my body and smoothly slipped into me—his thick length spreading me wide. My eyes flared as my insatiable need for him swallowed me whole.

A blaze ignited within me. There was nothing greater than this—than him. Nothing would ever be greater than him and I together.

I watched the beauty of him as he claimed me as his with every thrust into me. I couldn't get enough of him as my hands roamed his chest, his arms, and then clawed their way down his muscular back.

He gave me a malicious grin as he grabbed the back of one of my thighs and folded it behind my head, his rhythm never faltering.

His brow rose slightly in surprise, and I winked. "I'm flexible."

A growl of desire rumbled through his chest.

He then leaned down and kissed the scar over my own and then took my mouth once more. "You're fucking perfect," he whispered on my lips.

And with that, I came undone. I lost all sense of control as my back arched and I erupted around him. The flames blazed through my core, taking me soaring over the edge of climax.

I opened my eyes and found that he was watching me. Observing how my body reacted to his and what he was doing to me. Jace looked at me as if he was in awe at the sight of me beneath him, as if he couldn't believe this was happening or that it was real.

I reached up and cupped his cheek softly with my hand as he continued to move in me. I lifted my finger and carefully traced the scar that slashed across his perfect face.

I didn't miss the small wince the caress caused.

"Beautiful," I whispered, and his eyes flared with affection. My own eyes darted back and forth between his. "I love you."

And with those three words, Jace groaned as release found him; admiration carved into his features as it sent his body crashing down onto my own.

I gradually intertwined my fingers with his at our sides as he nuzzled his face into the nape of my neck while his heavy breaths slowly evened out.

I wasn't sure how long we lay there tangled with each other, but when sleep claimed me, I dreamed of our future.

Of a better realm with him and I at the center of it.

THIRTY-FIVE

Jace

My eyes fluttered open at the sound of birds singing to each other from beyond the open window, and then I realized we had locked ourselves in this room significantly longer than intended. I could barely see straight when her scent enveloped me, and my eyes flew open at the realization that last night hadn't been a dream. It was real, and Lia was finally here with me, wrapped tightly in my arms.

Her back was toward me and I tightened my grip on her slightly, praying to the gods that I didn't wake her in my need to hold her as close to myself as possible. As my hold tightened around her, she let out a soft giggle, letting me know she was indeed awake.

"There she is," I said softly, my voice still hoarse from sleep. I wrapped her in a hug and playfully pulled her onto me, her giggles turning into a full-on laugh.

She wiggled her way around to face me, struggling against my hold on her that I couldn't bring myself to loosen yet.

"Good morning." Her voice was just as groggy with sleep as mine had been. I couldn't even begin to imagine how exhausted she must've been. Escaping the Islan dungeons and flying across the realm on the back of a *wyvern*.

My Lia was fearless, and it was just one of the numerous things that I loved about her.

"How are you feeling?" I asked.

"Tired." She chuckled. "But otherwise, great." Lia smiled gently at me and I couldn't help but return it. "Gods, I don't think I have ever seen you smile this much."

I raised a brow at her. "Is that such a bad thing?"

"No!" she gasped. "I'm quite a fan of it, actually, so if you stop doing it, it will probably make me a little stabby," she joked as she twirled a piece of my hair between her fingers.

"Stabby," I huffed out. "When are you not?"

Her lips parted as she tried to hide her own smile. "Last night." She winked.

I couldn't hide my grin as I leaned down to kiss her. "Thanks for that reminder," I said on her lips.

She stared into my eyes for a few moments and lifted her fingers to trace the scar that ran across my face. Any smile I had fell as her touch followed it, and my heart began to race in my chest.

"Does it still cause you pain?" she wondered aloud.

"Not anymore." I cleared my throat. "I'm sorry if it bothers you. There wasn't much we could do."

Her brows furrowed, and she grabbed my face with one hand, squeezing my cheeks and forcing my gaze to remain on her.

"Don't do that. What did you say to me last night?"
She paused for a moment and my memory flashed back to

when she apologized for her own fresh scars. "These are the markings of a warrior. What Kellan did could have killed you. It would have if you were fully human. I am beyond grateful to the gods that this is all you were forced to walk away with."

Her grip on my face loosened, and she leaned up and pressed a gentle kiss to where the scar crossed the bridge of my nose. "And I think it's sexy." She grinned.

I chuckled and shook my head as relief took over me. "Of course you do."

"I'm also a big fan of this." She went back to combing her fingers through my hair that had grown since she last saw me.

She sucked her bottom lip in between her teeth as she continued to play with it.

"I was going to cut it," I admitted with a small laugh, and her grin fell into a frown.

"I swear to the gods, Cadoria. Don't you *dare*. Let me at least enjoy it first." Her tone bordered along the lines of teasing and an actual threat.

"My apologies, *Valderre*," I said back to her with a smirk.

Her face looked solemn. I thought she would appreciate hearing her father's name attached to her, but it looked as if she felt anything but that.

"It's so strange to hear," she whispered as her eyes darted back and forth between my own. "I wanted it my whole life, but now he's gone, and Kai is about to be crowned. We're really about to go to war over this." Her voice went soft. "A war between kin."

"The realm has been at war for over a century, Lia. You cannot help the acts of those who share your blood." I paused as I observed her for a moment. "And now, us mortals finally have something worth fighting for on our side."

"I'm worth fighting for?" She turned her face, refusing to meet my gaze.

I leaned over her and grabbed her chin, but when I searched her eyes, all I could sense was hopelessness.

I didn't know the extent of what Kellan and the crown had done to her when she was captured yet, but something within her had snapped. I could feel the grief radiating off of her, and it was clear as day right before me, written into her fresh scars and the darkness that lingered beneath her stare. I would do anything to mend her back together.

"You are absolutely worth it. Regardless of the outcome, I will always feel this way, and I will defend you and your honor until my soul leaves this realm. You are the possibility of a better future, and that will *always* be worth fighting for."

She finally beamed at me again. "Who knew you were such a sweet talker?"

"Well, I've had nothing but my own horrendous thoughts to stew in for the past few weeks, and I thought you were..." I couldn't even bring myself to say it.

"Tell me what happened," I begged instead. My tone was as gentle as I could make it through the anger that rushed through me at the thought of all she had to reveal.

"It doesn't matter now," she said as she traced my lips gently with her fingertips. I reached up on impulse and halted her wrist, my grasp light to avoid startling her.

"It will *always* matter."

She blinked at me and sighed. "Very well. I watched you fall and all I can remember is screaming for you as your body squirmed in the dirt at Kellan's boots. He then turned to me and ripped the arrow from my gut, and as I screeched from the pain, he poured a substance down my throat. I was unconscious for days after that. Nearly the entire trip back to Isla."

My hand balled into a fist next to her head, where it rested on the pillows. "They drugged you," I said through my teeth.

She nodded. "Once we docked, they threw a bag over my head, so anyone within the city couldn't see who I was. I was brought down to the dungeons then."

She wasn't giving me everything, and I knew I shouldn't pry, but I had to know. "And the whipping?"

She flinched, and I immediately regretted bringing it up. "Lia, I—"

"Shh." She pressed her finger to my lips. "It's fine." Her eyes wandered around the room that was now filling with sunlight as dawn turned to day.

"When I was brought down to the dungeons, I wasn't immediately placed in a cell. I was dragged all the way to the back cavern where Nox was held. They chained me up and ripped my clothing off of me."

My jaw locked as my vision turned hazy with red. I was going to be fucking sick.

"The chains came from the opposite walls of the space, so they held my arms straight apart. Callius took the whip to my back and Nox was forced to watch. He looked at me with sympathy in his eyes. He knew exactly what they were doing to me because he had endured torture by those same hands."

"Is that when you escaped?" My voice was barely above a whisper.

"Gods, no." She let out a harsh, nervous chuckle as if this was funny. "They threw me in a cell to rot. Kai visited to torment me, and to let me know he knew I was his half-sister." She shrugged. "And then I was sitting there dying from an infection until Avery and Finnian found someone to help...but that is an entirely other story."

Infection. She had been sitting in a dirty cell with exposed wounds that went unattended and began to decay with infection. She could have died, probably would have if her siblings hadn't found her in time.

"And Adler?" I asked, knowing he couldn't have resisted involving himself with any of this.

She sucked on her teeth and blinked as if trying to find a way to dance around the subject. "Oh yes, how could I forget?" Her eyes met mine. "He had overheard Avery and Finn when they plotted to rescue me from the dungeons and learned of my relation to the king."

"Lia..." The word was barely audible.

She snorted, but there was fury in her eyes. "He is the reason I attended the wedding. Kellan snuck me out of my cell, dressed me in a disguise, and planned to marry me himself."

I was clenching my jaw so tight I thought every single one of my teeth would shatter. "What," I bit out, feeling my veins as they bulged in my neck.

"His elaborate, and extremely moronic, plan was to marry me, and take the crown for himself. Kellan was going to try to usurp the throne by forcing me into a marriage and becoming king."

My breathing turned heavy as my hand balled into a fist. "I have never looked forward to killing someone more in my entire existence," I admitted, tone dark with fury. "Here I had been, sick with fear that he had killed you, but instead, he was trying to steal you away from me in another manner."

She smiled softly up at me, instantly easing some of the rage, and lifted her hand to brush my hair back from my face. "It's okay. I'm here now, and that's what matters. I always wondered the same about you, but deep down, I knew you were alive. That you had survived. I could feel it in my very soul."

As I stared down at her, my mind started racing. She said she could feel it? Like how I had told Gage I thought I could feel something horrible was happening to her? It was more than a gut feeling. It was as if my body was reacting to the torment and suffering she had been enduring herself.

I searched her eyes as she finished her story, but all I could see was contentedness. She had accepted what had happened to her, but that didn't mean I had to. I never fucking would.

"When you were gone, I was overwhelmed with worry and grief. I didn't know what was happening to you, but I just knew it was something awful. I was puking, my body ached, and I just *knew* that whatever you were going through, you were forced to suffer. The others believed the pain to be entirely from the wyvern's blood, but I wasn't convinced."

Her eyes widened right before she tore her gaze away from mine.

"What is it, Lia?" I asked cautiously.

"I have to tell you something," she answered.

My heart stopped in my chest at her tone. What could she possibly be worried about having to tell me after everything she already shared?

"I think...there is a reason we knew what was happening with each other."

"What do you mean?" The words flew out of me before I could stop them.

She cleared her throat again as she sat up next to me and refused to meet my stare. "I mean that...there is a reason why I knew you had survived." She paused. "And why you knew my body was...harmed." She gulped.

I stared at her in response.

Lia took in a deep breath. "I think we are...no." She paused again and the anticipation of whatever she needed to say was eating me alive. "I don't think that we are...I know it. We are mates." She slammed her eyes shut on the last word and her hand flew to cover her mouth.

My lips parted, and she opened a single eye to peek over at me to see I was still staring.

"What does that mean?"

Her eyes flew open then, and she faced me nervously. "It...it is something that can happen among fae."

Heat rushed through my body. What could she possibly mean, *something among fae?* The only trait I inherited from the fae bastard who sired me was my healing capabilities, and that was all I could mentally handle.

"What do you mean by that? Among fae?" My voice was harsher than I intended, but I couldn't help it. What was she even saying?

"Nothing! Forget I said anything."

She went to turn away, but I grabbed her arm and tried to pull her into my lap, but she could sense the false calmness I was trying to portray.

"No, I need to know," I said.

"I didn't even think it was real. My entire life I never believed in mates. I made fun of Avery for saying she wanted to have one!" Her words were frantic.

"Elianna, I'm not following."

A shuddering breath escaped her as she stared intently at the bedroom door that, for a second, I thought she would make a run for.

Her eyes finally snapped to mine, and she huffed out a breath through her nose. "Mates are a bond between two fae. It goes deeper than any other bond known to fae-kind. It connects their hearts, their very souls. Even their scents."

I blinked at her in confusion. "And you think...that is what we are?"

Hurt flashed across her face for a brief moment. "I don't think it. I know it. We are mates." She hesitated. "However, you don't have to accept the bond," she rushed out, the words barely understandable.

It felt as if the walls were closing in on me. Mates? What the hell was a mate? Were our lives now linked? What did she mean by "accept" the bond?

"You should have told me." Once again, the words were coming out more clipped than I intended.

"I couldn't have. I found out when you were unconscious on the ground." She anxiously gripped the sheet from the bed so tightly that her knuckles turned ghostly white.

My gaze lifted to hers. "And who even decides this?"

I watched as her eyes lined slowly with silver as tears flooded them. "I believe it would be up to the gods, or their fates."

I sat there silently for a moment.

"You know what, never mind. Forget I said anything." She frantically stood up from the bed, clutching the sheet to her front.

"Woah." I rose to my feet on the opposite side. "What the fuck does that mean?"

"It means to forget I said anything, Jace."

"Well, that won't be happening, *Elianna*."

Her brows furrowed, and she threw one of her arms out at her side. "You clearly don't want this!" Her voice was cracking.

"How can I know if I want something if I. Don't. Know. What. It. *Means?*" I snapped at her.

"You don't want anything to do with the fae or your heritage regarding our kind, so why would you want this?! I was a fool to even bring it up!" she spat.

I jumped onto the bed and dashed to the other side. I swung my legs over the edge of the mattress and stood before her.

Taking hold of both of her arms, I admitted, "I don't want anything to do with my fae heritage, yes. But I want *everything* to do with *you!*"

She whimpered. "You don't mean that." Her voice was so soft I could barely even hear the words. "I don't want to force this onto you. Our scents have blended and I think that means the bond formed when we first made love." Pure anguish lay behind her stare. "But if you don't want this..." She paused, taking in a breath. "You can reject the bond by rejecting me."

Was the love I felt for her really mine? Or was it because of this bond? I thought about it for a few moments as Lia searched my face with her unbearably shattered looking stare.

I thought of every moment spent with her. How at first I couldn't stand the sight of her, and then I couldn't help but laugh at her sass-filled remarks. And then how I stood in awe of her once I finally allowed myself to get to know her beyond just the surface level. Her bravery, honesty, and beauty within—she was selfless.

Elianna was everything I never knew I needed. Did I initially not kill her on the several occasions I had because the mating bond wouldn't allow me? Honestly, most likely yes. But was it the mating bond that made me fall so deeply in love with every miniscule detail about her? Absolutely fucking not.

And she thought I was about to stand before her and *reject* her. Discard her as if she were a piece of rubbish in the city streets. Deny her as if she was anything other than the incredible, perfect soul that she was.

"I mean it with every fiber of my being, Lia." I lifted her chin gently so she would meet my stare. "I don't know exactly what all of this entails, or what it means. However, if this bond ties our souls together for the remainder of our lives, then I would consider myself the luckiest man in the realm."

A ghost of a smile appeared on her full lips as I leaned down and pressed my own to them. When our kiss broke, I watched the tears stream down her flushed cheeks once she finally allowed them to fall. Lia wrapped her arms around me and squeezed as tight as she could, placing her forehead onto my sternum.

We sat there in silence, holding each other while my mind raced about what all of this meant for us.

"It's why you could feel my pain when I was captured. That's how I found out. As I was forced to watch Kellan rip the blade across your face, I screamed in agony. And when my voice went hoarse, and the scream halted, I realized that I physically *felt* what you were feeling. It all came to me at once. The realization of it."

I tilted my head to the side as she peeled her face from my chest and looked up at me. "What do you mean?"

"I always felt your pain. Physical and emotional. When I shot an arrow through your calf that first day, I thought I strained a muscle somehow when I jumped from the tree. What I felt was your pain. When you told me about what happened to your mother, I was ready to burn the realm to the fucking ground for you. For her. And then, when I watched you collapse to the ground by what I thought would surely be your death...something inside of me snapped. All I could think was that I had a mate, and I loved him, and he was dying right in front of my eyes. I would've done anything, *anything*, to save you, but—"

"Shh," I cut her off. "I know, sweetheart. I know." My arms wrapped around her tightly once more before stepping away from her. "We will have our revenge on them. And I can't wait to see *my* queen sit upon her throne."

She smiled widely at me, a hint of wickedness beneath it, and I could feel my face move to mirror hers.

"Now, what do you say we *officially* accept this bond?" I suggested to her with a grin.

"I like the sound of that." She giggled as I swooped my arms down and lifted her up to me. Our tongues collided with a desperate force, and a groan snuck out of me.

I was about to lay her back on the bed when her eyes shot over to the bedroom door, right before it swung open and slammed into the wall behind it, startling both of us.

Lia let out a loud shriek as she shoved out of my grasp and frantically wrapped her naked body in the sheet she had dropped and dove onto the bed.

My eyes whipped to the door and saw Gage standing there with an infuriating smirk on his face.

"Gage! What the fuck!" I roared at him. "How about a knock?!"

He leaned his back up against the door frame and crossed his arms. "Oh, hell yeah. I was hoping this was what was taking you so long. No time for knocking, unfortunately."

"Ew, they better not be in my room!" Zaela shouted from downstairs.

I rubbed my temples at the headache I knew was about to brew from whatever these two were up to.

"Relax, brother, I saw nothing." He gestured to the bed. "And she's covered," he added with a wink, and I almost knocked his ass out right there.

"Hi Gage!" Lia chirped from behind me on the bed. Her embarrassment from only a moment ago had clearly vanished.

He waved his fingers at her as he continued to lean on the frame. "Hi Lia."

I rolled my eyes. "Someone better be dying," I said through my teeth.

"Uhhh, yeah, about that. It's definitely possible. While being wrapped up in your escapades last night, you forgot to feed the wyvern." He gave an awkward smile as he threw his thumb over his shoulder.

Lia leapt off the bed. "Shit!" she shouted, as she threw on my torn shirt from the night before and ran past us both and out the door.

I reached for my pants, that were still damp from being in a pile on the floor all night, and quickly pulled them on over my undergarments that I had been standing there in, and we both ran to follow her.

THIRTY-SIX

Elianna

I burst through the front door of Zaela's townhouse and immediately looked to the sky, and to my annoyance, there wasn't a single sight of wings or the sound of them beating through the air.

"Gods-dammit, Nox," I breathed as I jumped down the front steps beyond the door.

Jace, Gage, and Zaela came flying through behind me the second my foot reached the brick path that led to the road.

I whipped around, clasping Jace's shirt tightly to me. "Where is he?"

A bunch of screams sounded from far off in the distance.

"This may seem slightly obvious," Zaela answered with a raised brow. "But I would follow the screams."

I turned from them to hide the laugh that escaped me through my panic.

Another scream rang out.

I swear to the gods, if I found Nox with a person in his mouth, he would be in *so* much trouble.

We all raced down the street, running as fast as we could. I had to dodge people, carts and wagons, all while trying to keep the shirt that I had sliced off of Jace last night closed.

He caught up to me then. "You're lucky my shirt is long enough to go down to your knees," he said through running, and I glanced over at him. "Otherwise, I would have to kill all these innocent bystanders for accidentally seeing what's mine."

I let out a loud cackle in response as we rushed forward in tandem.

Before I knew it, we were at the front gates of the city, our run ceasing. Citizens were hiding between buildings and in nearby alleyways, but Nox was still nowhere in sight.

I moved towards one of the women who was nearest as she pressed herself against the cool stone of the gate's tower, hiding beneath its shadow. Her body trembled with fear as I carefully approached, while the others stood back and watched me curiously. I took one of my hands and gently fluffed out my hair, hiding my ears just to be safe.

"Hi, my name is Lia. I'm so sorry if my wyvern frightened you." Her eyes flared slightly, but her trembling eased. "Where is he? I'll make sure whatever he did doesn't happen again." I offered her a soft smile.

"He was last seen flying off back towards the farms," she answered.

Pursing my lips together, I whispered, "Thank you, and I truly am so sorry about this. You don't need to fear him. I give you my word. Please tell as many as you can, as well. I would hate to have the city living in fear of him as he lurks beyond its gates."

Her gaze softened, and she gave me a subtle nod as she emerged from her hideaway, warily glancing up into the sky before she slowly crept back into the city streets.

"Where are the farms?" I asked, turning back to the others as they continued to observe.

"They're about a half mile around the bend once we are beyond the gate," Gage announced as his eyes widened.

"Ugh, well, that won't do," I said to myself as I looked down at my attire.

Lifting my fingers to my lips, I let out an obnoxiously loud whistle, summoning him to me as I walked through the gates and out into the field beyond it. The others followed my lead.

My gaze flew upwards to the sky as the sound of Nox's powerful wings filled the surrounding air only moments later. The wyvern came in fast, landing barely ten feet in front of us, and the ground rumbled on impact.

I stood at attention and crossed my arms as I stared up at the wyvern.

He lowered his horn-covered head slightly towards the ground and let out an irritated huff.

"What. Did. You. *Do?*" I demanded in a voice more stern than I had ever used with him before.

Jace went to move in front of me, and I watched as Nox's head rose, his lips curling back in a snarl.

I stepped around Jace. "Don't worry, he won't hurt me. But if you do that again, he might try to hurt you. So let's not do that, okay? I'd rather not have the two of you hate each other."

He raised a sarcastic brow at me in response.

I made my way to Nox, with Jace silently following behind me as if he couldn't help it.

My steps halted directly before him, and he lowered his snout to be next to my face.

"Did you eat somebody?" I asked, brows furrowing.

His giant gold eye flared, and he violently waved his head to the side in frustration, as if it was completely irrational of me to ask him such a thing.

I turned back to face Gage and Zaela, who stayed farther back near the gate, keeping their distance from him. "Okay, well, at least it wasn't a person!" I shouted cheerfully as I gave them a thumbs-up.

I could hear an abrupt snort leave Jace, and a smirk curved my lips.

"You did eat something, though." I tilted my head in a knowing manner.

I hadn't felt like this since Nyra was just a little pup, and I had to constantly watch and monitor what she put in her mouth. Any gods-damn thing she found on the floor of the castle, she would try to eat.

I narrowed my gaze to the side of his lips that barely covered his enormous, dagger-like teeth and noticed streaks of fresh blood.

"Ah ha! I knew it!" I shouted up at him as he raised his head above us. "I'm sorry about last night. I know you were hungry, but I told you I would find you food. Which farm was it?"

He looked down at us, and then his stare moved to the city behind us that was built into the foot of the mountain range. A moment later, he launched into the sky above. The intense wind that his wings sent around us almost knocked the two of us over.

"That went well," Jace mocked as he coughed through the dirt that was floating through the air.

"Shut up," I hissed in annoyance as we both turned back toward our friends. I shrugged and threw my hands up. "Sorry for the scare, I think it was just a—"

The ground shook beneath our feet once more and the rush of air sent my hair flying in front of me, over my shoulders. I peeked over at Jace as he tried to turn towards me, and I started chuckling as I tried to imagine what we were about to face behind us.

"Holy gods!" Gage shouted.

I turned around and watched as Nox dropped a cow at his feet. He looked up at me, his eyes softening. I'm sure to some, no matter how loving his vibrant eyes looked, his vertical pupil was a little unnerving.

"Nox," I whined, dragging out his name. "Why did you kill another cow?!"

He bent his neck down and nudged the carcass toward me with his snout.

I shook my head at him, trying to hide my amusement at his peace offering. The very thing I yelled at him for, he did it *again*, but he brought back the evidence to share with me.

"Nox, that wasn't what I—"

Before I could continue my sentence, he took a step back, stretching his wings out for balance and sent a blaze of flame directly at the deceased cow, charring its body.

"Meant..." I finished as the fire winked out.

I let out a sigh as I turned around and saw all three of my companions standing behind me, looking terrified. Their jaws hung open so intensely it seemed as if they'd reach the ground, and their eyes spread wide enough that you would think they were pinned open.

I couldn't help myself. I burst into a fit of laughter at the sight of them.

I turned my head back to Nox and crossed my arms, admiring him as he stood there proudly. This gods-damn wyvern.

"Did...did he just..." Zaela started.

"Cook it? Yeah. He does that for me," I said through a few more chuckles as I shrugged and shook my head. I looked up at him. "Thank you, Nox."

The wyvern let out a chirp and flew off once more to the fields beyond the city, leaving us alone in the mess he had created.

Jace approached me again. "Looks like I have some groveling to do with some farmers," he said as he rubbed the back of his neck, staring down at the scorched animal.

"Might as well all go!" Gage chimed in as he snuck up behind us and threw an arm over each of our shoulders.

Once Zaela caught up, the four of us sauntered off into the morning daylight to apologize to some terrified citizens regarding Nox's poor manners.

THIRTY-SEVEN

Kellan

I HAD SPENT THE last few days rallying up troops to get the hell out of Isla and on the road to search for those who fled the city.

Everyone is to be executed except the prince and princess. The queen's orders were clear.

But what if we came across Elianna? I would have to find a way to hide her in plain sight of everyone in order to keep her and her claim to the throne in my back pocket for when we could take over the crown.

At this point, we were days behind the mortal sympathizers and nearly two weeks behind Elianna. We would have to move quickly across the land if we had hopes of catching up to them—wherever they were going.

I swaggered through the castle's gardens to make my way to the stables when my name was called in the distance.

I reluctantly turned and saw Callius leaning up against the brick of the exterior castle walls, motioning for me to approach him before I took another step further away.

I glanced back at the barn and fixed my face, attempting to remove the scowl forming at the sight of my predecessor.

The male I once admired as a father figure had now become a giant pain in my ass with all of his meddling suspicions.

When I turned back around with the fakest, most convincing smile I could muster up, I watched as he rolled his eyes while I moved to approach him.

I could feel the grasp I had always held so gods-damn tightly on my position of power loosen as these days passed on. Decades I had worked to infiltrate the castle. Years I had climbed the ridiculous fucking ladder to sneak my influence into the crown. And all of it was being ripped out from underneath me. All because Elianna was stupid enough to try to run off into the chaos after I had given her freedom.

I broke her out of her cage. I snuck her out of the dungeon. *I* was the one willing to kill the little shit prince in order to give her and me all power over the realm. And how did she repay me? By running the fuck off and leaving me in this disaster.

Ungrateful little bitch. I didn't care if I was the one who put her in there in the first place. I was trying to get her out of it now.

I stopped a few feet in front of him. "What can I do for you, Callius?"

He raised a brow at me and did a quick glance up and down my body. "Where were you headed?"

"The stables." I gestured to the building behind me with my chin. "I need to account for as many horses as possible if we have hopes of catching up to those who fled."

"Ah," he started. "Very well then. I do have news regarding the journey."

Now, I was the one raising a brow at him. "Let me guess, you're joining us?"

He gave me a knowing look. "Not just me."

My mind began to race. The tone of his voice indicated that I wasn't about to like who else would be accompanying us on this trip. My eyes thinned as I continued to stare at him in anticipation.

"The queen believes it would be best to bring Prince Kai along so he can witness what it's like beyond the battlement. See for himself what happens to those who commit treason against him," he stated. "And I believe it would be wise to have him experience the reality of what is dealt with beyond the Islan gates. Kai is to be crowned king. He must be prepared properly. Be sure to account for a horse for him."

My jaw ticked the second the prince's name left his mouth. He had to be fucking joking.

"Queen Idina will be choosing a bride for him in his absence so he can focus on learning the ways of being a true ruler," he added.

Of *course* Mother Dearest was choosing his new plaything to parade around the city. She would likely choose one just as shy and obedient as the Nilda girl had been, right up until she was murdered at her own wedding.

"You're kidding…Callius, he will only slow us down. If the queen truly wishes for us to catch up to at least those who fled, we need to move quickly. Has the prince ever ridden a horse beyond the city gate?"

"I knew you would be thrilled by the news," he said with a mocking grin, and my eye twitched. "The queen's word in the matter is final."

"And will you be leaving your beloved queen unattended and unguarded in your absence?" I challenged him. "There is not a time in recent decades that I can recall seeing one of you not accompanied by the other for more than a few minutes."

Callius rose a brow at me and scoffed. "While I do not trust many with her, I have promoted Braynon as her personal guard in my absence. He is a good male and soldier." He looked me up and down. "Though I have been questioning *some* of my decisions recently."

My jaw ticked at his remark towards me. Also, I never liked Braynon, he was always a fucking bore. A rule follower that was never a candidate for my own small fleet that Vincent assisted with. We often had our own agenda.

Callius went to turn away, but I reached out and clutched his arm, forcing him to turn back to me.

"What the hell is this really about? Surely you don't think this is a good idea," I said, losing what was left of my patience.

His brows furrowed, and he ripped his arm from me. "I support whatever our queen decides. The prince comes with us and it is *your* job to make sure he is protected if he leaves my sight at any time. Do you understand?"

A flash of a vision whipped through my mind of unsheathing the sword from my hip and gutting my predecessor where he stood.

"Perfectly." I grimaced.

"The queen's stance on certain ordeals has shifted. On our journey, if we are to come in contact with any mortals, they are to be killed on sight. Once we are back in Isla with the queen's children and Solus in hand, we move the remaining troops back out and seek what remains of the humans. This will be after the public executions of those who fled the city. Our queen wishes to make an example of them." The corner of his lip tilted up. "That is, of course, if there are any survivors left after we are through with them."

With that being said, he turned from me without another word and headed through the castle's garden door.

By the following morning, I had gathered over two thousand soldiers within Isla that we could spare for the journey, leaving the vast majority behind to guard the city in our absence. We didn't have time to collect soldiers posted throughout the realm for this.

While we knew that only a few hundred had fled, it was likely that the majority were unarmed, untrained or were females and younglings.

We certainly didn't need the full two thousand collected to get this done, but I had to put on the show of the century for the queen in order to get back in her good graces.

Dawn was on the horizon, and I watched as our soldiers formed their lines in the fields outside of the city gates. War horses stood at attention next to their riders and were packed with supplies. A few of them were attached to wagons set off in the back of the formation, carrying additional items, such as extra food and weapons.

Standing in front of the fleet, I observed Vincent's gaze, along with a few others', shift behind me. The rolling wheels of a carriage sounded immediately after.

I slowly turned to see one of the extravagant royal carriages, pulled by two white mares, headed toward us as it passed through the gates. Braynon sat next to the coachman as he steered the horses in our direction, looking every bit the obedient guard. I nearly snarled at the sight of him atop the carriage.

And here I was thinking that perhaps the queen had changed her mind and I wouldn't have to babysit on this little escapade.

I fixed my face into a friendly greeting as the horses came to a halt before me.

The door to the cabin opened, and Callius leapt out, gently offering his hand to the queen. She gracefully placed her dainty hand in his as she stepped out from the safety of her carriage. He then pressed a kiss to the back of her hand, making my eyes flare.

Their eyes were intimately locked on each other as she gave him a knowing smirk while he guided her from the wagon, never loosening his hold. They weren't even trying to hide their affection from the realm anymore—even while everyone had guessed; it was entirely different to see their intimacy on display, and so soon after King Jameson's death.

Prince Kai leisurely followed closely behind his mother as she exited, looking less than pleased to be joining us.

I eyed the three of them warily but kept my face neutral as they approached.

"Captain Adler," Queen Idina greeted me.

"Your Majesty." I bowed.

She nodded, confirming I could rise. "I suspect Callius spoke to you of the news regarding Prince Kai joining you all on this journey. It will be beneficial for him to witness the end of the treasonous acts that occurred within our own streets this past week."

I cleared my throat lightly. "He did, Your Highness."

The rising sun in the distance reflected off her ruby colored hair, making it appear as if it were ablaze.

"Excellent." She turned to Kai and cupped his cheek in a tender, mothering way that I only ever witnessed her use with him. "Stay safe, my boy. I will have a new bride picked out for you upon your return."

"I wish to be crowned that day," he hissed. "The day I return, I will take my new bride and then ascend my throne. These interruptions have become entirely too irritating."

She bent to kiss his cheek. "Of course." The queen turned back to me then. "Protect my son, Captain. He is the future of Velyra."

I bowed to her in response, mainly to hide my jaw ticking at her words as I bent down. Protect her son? As if I didn't have enough to do. The male should've been raised properly and not need protecting to begin with. Even the late king had once been a great warrior before he was crowned.

Callius then took her hand in his once more and escorted her back to the carriage. I observed them as she whispered something close to his ear, but I couldn't make out what it was. The gesture was odd enough for not only me to take notice of it, though, as I glanced around to see other curious, wandering eyes.

Once Callius closed the door to the carriage, we all watched as the coachman ordered the mares into motion and pulled the queen back to her castle within the protection of the Islan gates.

He stalked back over to us. "Prince Kai, it appears that you will be riding Matthias." He pointed to Elianna's warhorse that I pulled from the stables the prior night.

The prince's face blanched, and I peeked over at the warhorse that appeared to be staring him down in recognition.

I tried to hide my smirk. "Don't worry, Prince. Matthias is large, but he is one of the best in the fleet. If you need assistance getting on him—"

"No," Kai interrupted me, his tone as stern as his mother's. "I want a different horse."

"Is there a reason, Prince?" I asked, trying to hide my annoyance.

"That is Elianna Solus' horse. I am no fool," he answered. I raised a brow, curious about how he would know that this horse belonged to her. "I will not ride a traitor's beast."

Oh, for fuck's sake. He wasn't even looking at the stallion with disgust. I could practically smell the fear radiating from him as he stood before us.

"Very well." I walked over to my own horse and escorted him to the prince. "You may ride my horse, Gallo. Though he's just as large as Matthias."

"The size of the beast isn't the issue, *Captain*," he spat.

I took a step back from him and threw my hands up in innocence as I backed up toward Matthias. "Of course not, Prince." I turned from him as the sides of my lips kicked up into a smirk as my eyes met Vincent's in the line.

I mounted Elianna's horse and watched as Callius assisted him onto Gallo. Once Kai was settled, he then headed toward his own.

I faced my soldiers as they continued to stand at attention. The morning sun now brightly lit the sky above us.

"Let's go show these traitors what happens when they fuck with the Velyran Crown, boys!" I bellowed to the masses.

A roar of cheering followed, and then we set off to march north.

THIRTY-EIGHT
Finnian

THE DAYS THAT HAD passed since we fled Isla had been torturous. Everyone among us was constantly at each other's throats from a deadly mixture of fear and starvation. We had to scavenge for scraps of enough food to feed the amount of us, and on top of that, most were still terrified of Veli.

She kept to herself most of the journey, only really speaking to Avery or myself. After the first day, when no one would allow her to assist their injuries, she stopped caring about helping them. I felt somewhat sad for her, even though she still scared the shit out of me, too. Although, I was thankful that she hadn't brought out her shadows since we left Isla.

Veli had been a healer long before I was even born, and the people who once trusted her to save their lives now thought she would rip it away from them like she had with those guards at the gate.

A shiver rocked my body as that scene flashed across my memory.

All of this was happening around me, but the worst of it all was that Landon had still barely spoken to me. He only acknowledged my presence if it was absolutely necessary. He would walk alongside others, laugh with them, eat with them, and enjoy their company. However, the second I approached, or we made eye contact, any hint of a smile that had been on his face would turn into a scowl, sending my heartbeat into a thunderous tantrum.

Up ahead, a forest came into view; we had been able to avoid any on the way so far—deeming it easier to travel in open land—but when my gaze followed along the sides of the trees, it seemed as if they were never ending.

"Excuse me!" a squeaky voice called from up ahead. "Honestly, everyone, please *move.*"

I didn't have to follow the trail of the voice to know it was coming from my sister.

A moment later, the top of her red hair appeared as she pushed back through the crowd to me as we all continued to march forward.

"There you are!" Avery practically yelled in my face. "It looks like remnants of an old village are up ahead before the forest," she informed me as she walked at my side.

"Remnants?" I asked her.

"Veli is leading at the front. I could kind of see from where we were at the time, but she said that some buildings looked half destroyed. We will probably be there within the next hour or so."

"Great," I answered.

She eyed me for a minute. "What's gotten into you? You haven't been walking with us for two days now, just moping around back here." She pursed her lips.

I threw my head back and sighed. "Can you just leave me alone and not pry into every single one of my thoughts for once in your life?"

"Sorry, but no. I'm your sister. It's what I do." She gave me a charming smile that would typically make me give in and unload my feelings onto her, but I wasn't in the mood today.

I couldn't find the energy to respond to her.

She scoffed at me and pulled on my wrist. "It's Landon, isn't it?" she asked entirely too loud in an army full of *fae*.

I shot her a warning look and continued to walk forward.

She stopped in her tracks and stomped a foot into the dirt in a ridiculous attempt at a tantrum. Everyone surrounding us moved to walk around her. "Maybe if you grew some gods-damn balls and went up to him, he would start talking to you!"

I whipped around to her, ignoring the irritated looks that were flashed my way by the small crowd around us. "I *have* tried!"

She crossed her arms. "No, you haven't. Not enough, anyway."

I reached for one of her arms and pulled her forward into a stroll once more, so we could stop being a roadblock of bickering siblings. "What do you suggest I do then, Avery?"

"Have a conversation with him alone. Don't let Veli, me, or even Nyra be present. Stop hiding behind us, giving him a half-assed apology, and tell him how you really feel." She fluttered her eyebrows at me mockingly.

"He obviously knows how I feel," I hissed through my teeth.

"Yeah, sure," she sassed, and it was accompanied by an eye roll.

"You're infuriating," I muttered.

As we continued to stride through the open space, I could now clearly see the ruins of what was left of this small village before us. It appeared that most of the buildings had been burned to ashes.

Avery seemed to take notice the moment I had, and she tugged on my wrist, silently asking me to follow her as we pushed our way back up to the front of the crowd where Veli led with Nyra.

"There you two are," she started, and then nodded at the scene that we were quickly approaching. "Looks like some trouble may have found this area not long ago."

I gulped, hoping neither of them could hear it, but they both threw me a knowing look, causing me to wince.

"What do you think it was?" I asked.

"Well, we are about to find out, aren't we?" Avery answered.

We stopped a few hundred yards from the demolished village and turned to the crowd that followed us. Each face I quickly focused on looked more miserable than the last, forcing me not to linger on any of them for too long.

"We will rest here for a little while!" Avery shouted out to them. "A few of us are going to go check out the scene ahead. Everyone, please stay here where it's safe."

I glanced over at her admirably as the masses began to drop to the ground where they stood. Since we left Isla—no, actually, since Lia fled and we decided to follow—she had taken on the role of a leader, a commander in her own right. The princess I grew up with, who adored her pink gowns and tea gatherings yet always secretly craved adventure, was finally getting what she always wanted. And she was a natural at it.

A ghost of a smile formed on my face, and she caught me staring.

"What?" she hissed.

"Nothing, it's just that you're reminding me so much of Lia right now." I started to follow Veli forward as her eyes beamed with joy.

We walked through the piles of debris that still coated the ground that once held the demolished buildings surrounding us.

Nyra trotted over and sniffed at the ash, causing her to sneeze uncontrollably a few times. She then growled into the air, annoyed at what she brought onto herself.

"What do you think happened here?" I asked to no one in particular.

Veli bent down and swiped her finger across a half-charred board that lay at her feet. She rubbed that finger with her thumb, examining the blackness that now stained her skin.

"Wyvern's flame," she answered casually, still observing her fingers.

"Wyvern's flame?" Avery and I echoed in unison, earning the usual glare from the witch.

She sighed. "That's what I said."

She straightened herself and strode forward once more through the rubbish.

"How do you know?" Avery called after her.

Veli stopped and rotated toward us, raising a single brow so high that I thought it would touch her silver hairline. "The giant footprint you are standing in would be the first indication." She tsked and turned away to inspect what lay ahead.

Avery's eyes met mine, and we both looked beneath our feet to see that we truly were standing in a small indent in the ground, resembling the footprint of a massive, clawed creature.

"Why would Lia burn a village to the ground?" Avery whispered, her eyes darting back and forth as I watched her mind race.

"She may not still be with the wyvern she escaped on. Or perhaps she has no control over it and it just decided to do this on its own," I offered.

"Maybe it was a different wyvern. A...a wild one," she suggested, eyes widening slightly.

"Doubtful," Veli called back to us. I peeked over at Avery just in time to watch her stick her tongue out at her.

I chuckled as her eyes shot over to mine, and she rapidly slipped her tongue back into her mouth, looking guilty. Was it bravery or stupidity that ran my sister? Probably the latter.

Nyra whined at our feet, and I glanced down just in time to watch her paw at a marking on the ground. As my eyes narrowed in on it, I noticed it resembled a female's footprint, but the imprints stopped there. As if whoever had been standing there vanished.

"I don't think this was an actual village," Veli announced as she approached us from where she had wandered to.

"Then what would it be?" I wondered aloud as I glanced over the surrounding area.

"I think it may have been a war camp. One of our own. I can't be completely sure since every building caught fire, but it would appear that way. They were all wooden, makeshift buildings. Barracks, essentially, it seems."

"I doubt Lia would attack her own soldiers," Avery warned.

"Unless they attacked her first," I chimed in. "There is a bounty on her head, remember?"

"Exactly," Veli responded. "So that means I have good news and shitty news for you both," she said as she crossed her arms.

Avery eyed her warily. "Good news first."

"We are on the right track. I am quite confident that this was Elianna's wyvern, and that they were indeed here. I can smell her." She gestured to Nyra. "Her wolf can, as well."

Nyra continued to whine, staring at the same spot in the terrain where the footprints, that I now assumed were Lia's, were left.

My gaze moved back and forth between the two of them. "And the bad news?"

She gestured behind herself by throwing her head back slightly, keeping her arms crossed. "That's the Sylis Forest. We have to go through it. It travels coast to coast, and there isn't a way around it except by sea."

"Mother of the gods," I breathed. "You're serious?"

She gave me a wicked grin. "I am."

My gaze flew to Avery and saw that she was looking back at our crowd. She took in a deep breath. "I have heard the tales of what lurks between those trees. We are without a substantial amount of weapons. We have younglings among us. This is a death sentence. I thought we would be able to travel around it!" She looked back at Veli.

Veli nodded in response as we all went to make our way back to our troop.

Memories of being a youngling and listening to ancient stories of the terrifying beasts from the Sylis Forest flooded me. A shiver worked its way up my spine.

I glanced up into the sky and saw that dusk was already settling throughout the realm. We would have to rest here for the night, for traveling through the Sylis Forest was deadly enough in the day, never mind with whatever crawled on the forest floor in the late hours of the evening.

I whispered just that to them both, and they agreed with me for once.

"Everyone!" Avery boomed. "Please listen to me."

Her voice echoed through the open valley we stood in, and everyone's eyes flew to her. She gulped, and I watched as her mouth began to open and close repeatedly as nerves consumed her with what she was about to reveal.

"The journey ahead is far more difficult than what is behind us." Murmuring immediately erupted throughout the crowd.

My eyes flared as Avery's speech halted because of it. "You will all listen to your princess!" I yelled as loud as I could, a hint of authority in my tone that hid the shakiness of the words.

She gave me a gentle, thankful smile.

"The woods behind me are not just any old trees. It is the Sylis Forest." I watched as everyone's faces paled one by one. Her voice was softer this time as she spoke to them, a plead in her tone more than a demand. "We are unable to travel around it. We must go through it, and on the other side lies our future. On the other side lies our true queen of the realm." She paused as shouts started to ring out.

"We can't go through there!"

"We have younglings, Princess! Surely you can't be serious!"

"We should have stayed in Isla."

"Enough!" Veli screamed at Avery's side, startling us both. "You imbeciles have two options before we continue to head north in the morning. You can stay here with us, and we will all protect each other to the best of our abilities in the woods. Or you can flee and head back to where we came from and face certain execution. The choice is yours. You all knew what you were getting yourselves into."

Everyone exchanged quick glances with one another. Whispers of families asking others what they planned to do traveled through the air, wondering if the unknown on the other side of those trees was worth the risk.

My heart fluttered rapidly when Landon slowly approached us. He looked exhausted, no doubt from the journey it had taken us all to get here. His eyes were bloodshot with unrest, his lips chapped from the dryness of the air, and his clothes were just as filthy as the rest of ours.

He gave me a small, awkward nod as he walked past me and directly to Veli and Avery.

I turned to follow.

"Some of the other males are discussing going hunting for food as the females make camp," he announced to them. "Am I needed here, or should I go with the group of them?"

Avery peered over Landon's shoulder at everyone behind us. "Go with them." She gave him a tight-lipped smile and squeezed his upper arm. "We have everything covered here. Make sure everyone stays safe."

"Of course," he said to her as he turned away.

We made uncomfortable eye contact once more and as he passed me, I accidentally blurted out his name, causing him to halt. I froze where I stood.

He rotated back around to look at me with a single brow raised in confusion. "Yes, Finnian?"

My heart sank. Not a "Finn," but a full "Finnian."

I cleared my throat. "Stay safe out there."

As the words left my mouth, I sent up a silent curse to the gods for making me so ridiculously awkward.

However, to my surprise, the tiniest hint of a smirk tipped up the corner of his lips. "It's just to look for some food. I will see you all later."

And then he was gone.

My eyes caught a glimpse of Avery and Veli as they exchanged a look, likely regarding the uncomfortable encounter.

"I don't want to hear it," I huffed at them, and then I turned to help set up camp.

I awoke the next morning to Avery shaking my arm. "Get up," she demanded. "People are missing!"

My heavy eyes flew open, and I stared at her. "What do you mean they're missing?"

"It's past dawn. Landon woke up and went around trying to get everyone awake, and noticed that about fifty people were no longer here with us. Come on!" she urged, and I forced myself to sit up, blinking away the sleepiness that still hadn't left me.

I got up and ran after her, nearly tripping over my own feet as I tried to pull on my boots. When I finally caught up, both Veli and Landon had joined her.

"What do you mean they *left?*" Avery whisper shouted.

"That's what everyone is saying. Last night while we slept, some people decided it would be safer back in Isla than with us. They took their belongings and turned back," Landon answered.

"Fools," Veli hissed.

"We have to go after them!" Avery cried.

"Absolutely not, you reckless girl," Veli snapped at her. "It will cost us time we do not have. They chose their fate."

"But they'll die!" Avery shouted, lip trembling.

I reached my arm around her shoulder and tucked her into me in an attempt to console her, but for once, I agreed with Veli.

"We can't risk it, Avery. I'm sorry, but she's right," I whispered.

I watched my sister while she looked around as if she were trying to take a head count of people, which would still be impossible with the hundreds that accompanied us.

"They had younglings, didn't they?" she asked, a hint of rage in her tone. "They brought their children back with them to be slaughtered." Her fists began to shake with fury at her sides.

Veli took a step toward her. "That's none of our concern now. I'm sorry, but we really need to get moving and start our voyage into the forest."

My eyes widened. I had somehow forgotten that we now had to enter the enchanted forest, where the scent of moss and ancient magic lingered in the air, according to the bedtime stories that used to haunt our dreams.

"Is there no way you can guarantee us safe passage with your sorcery?" Avery snapped at Veli, chest heaving. "You're a *witch*, for gods-sake! I've seen you vanish and reappear seconds later, across a room."

Veli's violet stare flashed back to my sister. "I am very well aware of what I am, *Princess*. You should do well to remember that." The gold flashed in Veli's eyes for a fraction of a second. "I am able to travel by teleportation on my own, never with others."

"So there would never be a way to move the masses safely in that sort of way?" I asked, trying to ease the tension between the two females who looked as if they were about to claw each other's eyes out.

Veli's face barely softened, and she sighed. "There *are* portal rift spells that exist, but to move an army through would be impossible with only a single witch. The power is too great to hold a portal open for many to cross through—multiple witches would be needed for such a task, and even then, it's a risk."

"How does that work?" Landon asked.

"Well, to start, you cannot open a portal to an area you have never been. The witch's memory must have access to the exact location. When a portal is opened, it acts as if it is a rift in the realm just waiting to be stepped through."

"But you cannot do this for us," Avery whispered, defeated.

"Correct," Veli answered, refusing to look at my sister.

"And this...rift portal walking you speak of...it is different from when you are able to vanish and then reappear across a space?" I asked.

"It is," Veli answered. "That is referred to as wisping. Also, I know what you are about to ask next, and the answer is no. Another cannot be taken with me. The act can only be done with the witch's body itself—we are built to handle it, for our bodies travel faster than light through time and space. It can be disorientating, even for us."

My gaze wandered over the three of them that stood with me, each looking defeated.

Landon took one look at Avery, and I could tell that he knew she couldn't bring herself to rally up those who remained.

Her teary eyes met his, and he gently placed his hand on her shoulder, making my heart pang in my chest.

"Alright everyone!" he boomed into the hazy morning sky, earning their attention as he approached the awaiting crowd. "The time has come to enter the Sylis Forest. Nobody is to wander off alone. Stay together in at least pairs of two. If anyone sees anything, announce it. Stick together. Protect each other. We don't know what's in those woods."

I looked at him in admiration. These past few weeks, he had put on such a strong face for those who traveled with us. He barely remained the skittish stable keeper that I once knew and loved. Now, as I watched him look out for everyone as if they were his own flesh and blood, I somehow grew to love him even more.

THIRTY-NINE
Elianna

SLIPPING BACK INTO THE usual routine with my chosen family was incredibly easy. The last few days had consisted of planning our next moves, training the soldiers, and sneaking kisses with Jace every second I could.

It didn't matter how many times I felt his lips on my own; my stomach would flutter with butterflies the moment our bodies connected in any way.

After groveling to some extremely upset and terrified farmers over Nox's little buffet, Jace had taken me into the city to show me around. It was nothing short of extraordinary to see—all that they had managed to rebuild with such little resources available over the years.

Everyone pitched in to help, no matter their age or rank. The sense of community was admirable among these people, and I was incredibly proud to consider them mine.

After I received the tour, Jace took me to a few of the shops to get fitted for some new clothing. It made sense, considering I had arrived in a destroyed gown and was later forced to run through the city in nothing but my mate's shredded shirt.

Zaela had offered some of hers that I could borrow, but I couldn't even get a single pair of her pants past my knees. I frowned up at Jace as the disappointment of it struck me, but he just met my gaze and stared as if he were drowning in lust and desire.

Since then, we had all been working on furnishing Zaela's townhome. Or *our* townhome, I should say. After a very heated discussion over a few ales at their favorite tavern, we all officially took her up on her offer of living together while we stayed in Ellecaster. There were more than enough bedrooms, and every time I had brought up not caring about sleeping at the barracks, Jace looked as if he was going to be sick.

Gage thought it was because Jace assumed that one of the other men there would try to sneak off with me behind his back. He then proceeded to tease him that if that were possible, he would've done that himself long ago.

Such a flirt.

We still hadn't brought up the fact that we were mates to the two of them yet. It didn't feel like the right time, and the idea of it was still so incredibly new to the both of us. We just wanted the knowledge of it to be between us and the gods for as long as possible while we adjusted to the bond ourselves, trying to learn and understand this connection we now shared.

We were both navigating through something entirely new. I, myself, had no idea what to expect from this or what it would entail. Was there more to the bond than just the connection we felt? We couldn't even research it while we were here, for the mortals did not carry any fae texts within their lands.

Regardless, that didn't matter. What did matter was that I was here with him, and we would figure this out together.

And now here I was, over a week later, sprawled out across the settee in the living room waiting for Jace to pour each of us another glass of wine as Zaela whittled a small wooden figure with her hunting knife in the chair next to the roaring fireplace.

A smile beamed on my face as my mate approached me with another full glass. He effortlessly lifted my legs where they were stretched across the cushions and sat under them, placing them back down on his lap gently.

I reached over and started twirling a small wave of his hair around my finger as he lovingly caressed my thigh, sipping his drink. This scene felt entirely *easy*. Entirely normal. As if it were always meant to be this way.

I glanced over and noticed Zaela watching us intently with an expression I couldn't place. Was she irritated at our display of affection now that it was completely out in the open? Or was that just...her face?

"Are you excited to make our way to Alaia?" Jace asked. "I have so much I wish to show you there."

"I can't wait. I'm intrigued to see this mystical land of unknown beyond the mountains," I answered.

"It truly is a breathtaking sight," Zaela chimed in. "The views are unlike anything I have ever seen. Essentially untouched by man, aside from our settlement areas."

My eyes lit up as I looked at her and then back to Jace. "It sounds incredible."

"It is," he said as he reached up to scratch his chin. "You have many people to meet once we arrive. General Vern to start. He is in charge of those in the valley in my absence and worked alongside Zae's father."

"Ah, yes. Leon Vern. The old man who refuses to retire," she said with a hint of affection in her tone. "However, he *did* convince the hesitant masses of your promotion."

A low chuckle rumbled from his chest as his gaze wandered across the room to his cousin. "That he did. Your mother will be pleased to see us."

"I hope you're mentally preparing for the annual speech of complaint regarding our constant absence." Her eyes drifted over to me as she halted the carving of her wooden figure. "My mother has remained in my family's estate in Alaia. As lovely as she is...she can be a bit overbearing." She smirked.

"She's just a lonely older woman now, Zae. I'm sure she'll try to fatten us up the moment we walk through the door," Jace teased.

Zaela chuckled. "I'm not quite sure she'll let us leave this time. And I'm definitely telling her you referred to her as old."

As they joked about her mother, my thoughts instantly flowed elsewhere, to my own family and their well-being. Had Avery and Finnian been locked away in their chambers or in the dungeons with Lukas once I escaped? Were they now prisoners in the only home they had ever known? Had they fled, or fought back? It was disorientating, feeling such serene peace yet simultaneously being consumed by guilt for my family.

Silence suddenly blanketed the room, and I glanced back up at my mate to see that his eyes were boring into me—concern etched into his features.

"Everything alright?" he asked softly.

I gave him a curt nod as I averted my gaze from his. "I'm just worried for Avery and Finnian. I feel so guilty being here, with you, safe...while they could be enduring anything under Kai's command. I doubt the queen would harm them, but I don't trust the prince."

"Should we put our plans for the valley on hold and search for them instead?" he asked.

I swallowed as my mind raced. What good would a handful of us do if we marched up to the Islan gates, if that's even where they still were? We had to be smart about this, and I would not risk my mate or siblings on a whim.

"First, we need to find out where they are. When was the last time you heard from Islan sympathizers?"

"Not since we learned that the attack on the wedding was a success," Jace answered.

My brows furrowed as I stared at him, his eyes flaring with concern from the look I shot him. "Many people died. Not just terrible lords, but good, *innocent* people, as well, Jace. My siblings and I could have been among them."

He flinched, and I felt his guilt ripple down the bond, making my features soften.

"I'm sorry," I whispered. "I just worry for them, and sitting in the unknown has been awful. It feels as if I traded one family for another, but I just can't let them go."

"You will never have to trade one family for another, my Lia." He gripped my knee and leaned toward me. "Your family is ours."

The corner of my lips tilted at his words as I brought my glass of wine to them once more. Suddenly, the front door to the townhouse swung open. It slammed into the wall behind it, startling all of us and putting us on high alert.

My heart raced in my chest and my breathing turned heavy as I worked to calm myself down—reminding myself that I wasn't in the dungeons, I wasn't Kellan's prisoner, and that sound was not the cruel crack of a whip against my skin.

Jace eyed me, looking every bit concerned, but I gave him a gentle nod, letting him know I was okay.

Gods, Lia. Pull yourself together.

Gage stood in the doorway, nearly out of breath. "Brother! There you are!" he shouted in the small space.

Jace's brows furrowed, but he remained sitting beneath the blanket of my thighs. "What is it, Gage?"

"The men are all at the taverns celebrating a successful formation at training today. It's boys' night, fucker!" he announced as he swaggered across the room with a grin that stretched ear to ear.

"You made me almost spill my wine all over the new settee for *boys' night*?" I teasingly hissed at him.

His mouth popped open. "Oh gods, Lia, I am so sorry! Not the wine! Not the *settee!*" He clutched at his heart dramatically and fell to his knees on the floor.

"The *new* settee, you jackass," Zaela chimed in, her eyes not leaving the wooden horse she was carving.

He looked up at me with a boyish grin as he rose to his feet. "I see someone has already been at the taverns." I raised a brow, the corner of my lip kicking up to match his.

"Perhaps, my lady." He winked. "No, no! I meant, perhaps, my *queen*." He bowed mockingly.

"Oh, shut up with that," I answered, turning my attention back to my wine as Jace removed his hand from my thigh and went to swat at Gage, who was now leaning over the back of the couch.

"Is there something you need?" Jace asked with a chuckle.

Gage's mouth twisted into a sarcastic scowl. "Um, yeah. I need my best friend to join me and I came here fully prepared to beg the future ruler of the realm if I have to." He shot me a desperate look, and I sucked in my bottom lip to hold back a laugh.

My gaze wandered back to Jace and I could see the conflict in his eyes. I knew he wanted to go, but also knew that he wouldn't leave me here after we had been separated for so long.

I sat up and clutched his knee, shaking it a little. His stare met mine. "You should go," I insisted with a smile.

"But you just got here a few days ago." He paused for a moment. "As ridiculous as this sounds, letting you out of my sight seems absolutely unbearable." He snapped his mouth shut immediately after the last word left his mouth.

I was well aware that it was the mating bond talking, but the others definitely did not, and looked at him as if he had just grown a second head.

"Go," I said as I leaned forward and kissed his nose. "Go have fun with your friends. Rally them up and get them excited about heading to Alaia. I'm not going anywhere, and I will be here when you come back all tipsy." I winked.

"Thank you," he whispered as he leaned over and gave me a peck on my wine-stained lips. I pulled my legs up to my chest to allow him to stand.

"Oh, hell yeah, I knew she would be on our side," Gage bellowed. He looked over at Zaela, who was still minding her business in the corner. "Can I go, too?" he asked, and I burst into an abrupt laugh.

Zaela raised her gaze to his and looked up at him through her creased brows. "Why in the realm would I give a shit if you went?"

He laughed nervously and cupped the back of his neck with his hand as Jace stepped up beside him. "Oh, I don't know. I just figured if he needed permission, then maybe I would, too."

She rolled her eyes and lifted her hand to point to the door. "Mother of the gods, just get out."

"Yes, ma'am!" he shrieked as he whipped around and threw his arm over Jace's shoulders, which were moving up and down abruptly with his laughter at their bickering.

They both made their way through the door and clicked it shut behind them.

And then it was silent, aside from the crackling of the sparks as they bounced within the fireplace.

I took a sip of wine and glanced over at my mate's cousin, whose focus had already returned to whittling.

The unspoken awkwardness settled into the noiseless atmosphere. Zaela and I hadn't been left alone together since I returned, not to say it was *weird* to be alone with her, but before everything had happened, it wasn't as if our relationship had been on the best of terms.

I tucked my legs into my chest on the couch and took a noisy sip of wine, crossing my eyes while it slowly hooked its roots in my veins. Her stare flicked up to me, sarcastic anticipation written on her face.

"So," I dragged out the word. "How are things?"

She smirked. "How are *things?* What things?"

"You know, with Gage."

The second the words left my mouth, I regretted them.

Zaela pursed her lips and placed her knife and piece of wood down on the arm of the chair and leaned in closer to me, legs crossed.

Her eyes narrowed in on me, knowingly. "I don't know what you mean."

"Oh, come on, Zae," I started. "He follows you around like a lovesick puppy."

Her face twisted from irritation to pure rage. "My relationship with Gage should be nobody's concern but my own. Do not mistake close-proximity and friendship for love."

I flinched at her words. She was right—it wasn't my business or Jace's.

"I'm sorry." I paused for a moment. "It was just the wine talking," I lied as I took another lengthy sip.

She snorted with a sharp cackle in response, causing me to spit out the remnants of wine that hadn't been swallowed yet.

"What's so funny?" I got out through a few giggles as I wiped my chin.

"Oh, Lia. I know you well enough to know that was *not* the wine talking."

I sucked on my tongue, trying to stop my grin from forming.

"Well, fine then. Consider the wine used for courage," I admitted.

"Fine," she huffed, giving me the tiniest hint of a smile.

"I mean, I feel like he does care for you, though."

Her smile dropped instantly.

"Elianna," she hissed, and my eyes flared at her use of my full name. "Gage deserves someone who can return that love. Do you not agree?"

My eyes widened slightly once more. "I just figured he was so great, anyone could. But I'm sorry, you're right. We can talk about something else. Jace had told me that they had never seen you with anyone before, so I didn't know if it was because of Gage or not."

She tore her gaze away from me, but I continued to observe her, and didn't miss it as she nervously chewed on the inside of her cheek in the dim firelight. "For someone who pretends to not give a shit about petty gossip, my cousin sure does love to partake in it."

She rolled her eyes and got up to pour herself another glass. I sat there quietly and watched her chug the wine in a single gulp.

She anxiously cleared her throat while staring down into the empty glass. "I do love Gage, just not in that way. He is like a second, more annoying little cousin. And despite what everyone thinks, I do consider him my best friend, no matter how much he drives me crazy. I'd be lost without both of them."

"That's fine, Zae." I smiled at her. "They obviously know you care for them."

She stalked over to the fireplace and placed one of her hands on the mantel as she gazed into the flames. I observed her for a minute as she stood there in silence, clearly contemplating if she would continue the conversation.

She let out a shuddering breath, which only sparked my curiosity about the subject even further. "I cannot love Gage that way because I prefer the company of other women."

I choked on my last sip as the words flowed out of her mouth. Now *that* I was not expecting.

She turned to me and shrugged. "That's why the boys have never seen me with anyone, and it's why I always try to stomp out any lusting fire that lingers within Gage's eyes when I see it in his drunken stupors."

"Zaela, I had no idea. I'm so sorry if you just felt forced to tell me," I rushed out.

"Oh, I didn't feel forced." She let out a quiet, sharp laugh. "I just owe you a life debt, but in the meantime, I can let you hold on to my secret until I'm ready to tell the others."

A peace offering and silent plea to not let the boys know.

"I won't say anything," I promised. "And you kept Jace alive in my absence and made sure he didn't run off to do anything foolish. Consider the life debt paid."

She smirked at me. "I know you won't say anything. I just thought you should know how I feel." She moved back over to her chair and sat down, crossing one of her legs over the other as she continued to watch me.

"I truly am so grateful, and...*sorry* about everything," she admitted.

"Sorry for what?" I asked, tilting my head to the side in confusion.

She gave me a knowing look. "I was such an asshole to you. Well, I'm an asshole to everyone, but I was too hard on you for too long. I was just so astonished at how Jace acted around you, and how he had put his unyielding faith in the *leader* of our enemy's armies so easily." Her eyes lazily roamed the room. "And I never should've accused you of bringing those attackers to the village. So, I'm sorry. Perhaps things would've ended up different if we just stuck together through the chaos."

My heart twisted painfully in my chest. I now *knew* how Jace had trusted me so easily, and how his hatred for me had melted away with a single, forbidden kiss. His trust had stemmed from the mating bond, but I couldn't tell her that. Not yet, anyway.

I stood up and walked over to her, placing my hand lightly on her shoulder. She looked up at me. "All is forgiven, my friend."

As if the biggest weight had just been lifted off of her chest, she then gave me the brightest, most genuine smile I had ever seen from her before.

FORTY
Jace

Gods, I had to stop letting Gage trick me into rowdy nights out at the taverns. I opened my eyes as the blinding sunlight peered through our curtains. I groaned from the headache that ravaged through my skull and went to reach over to Lia's side of the bed and realized that her body no longer lay next to mine.

As the realization hit me, I shot up abruptly. Turning my gaze towards where she should have been, my eyes were met with only an empty space. She had definitely been there when I stumbled back home, right? She had to be. Fear quickly worked its way through my veins, my heart pounding in my chest as every fear of her being taken from me again slammed into me.

I was about to run downstairs when the sharp clash of swords slamming into each other repeatedly rang out right below our bedroom window.

As my panic was about to consume me, Lia's voice echoed through the air, "Ha! Told you I'm still better!"

Relief settled into me.

That's my girl.

I smirked and swung my legs over the side of the bed as I pulled my boots on and then made my way downstairs.

I peeked around the living room and kitchen to realize that the townhouse was empty, so I waltzed outside to see Gage and Lia sparring right in the front yard like a couple of children.

I walked over and crossed my arms as I watched the two of them go at it sloppily. Honestly, both of their forms were shit since they were messing around, but even then, Lia was still kicking his ass.

"Oh, good morning there sleepyhead!" she called over to me through a strike. "Glad to see you decided to join us!"

She swiped her new sword we had made for her through the air and Gage blocked it just in time, a little too close for comfort without any protective gear.

"And why aren't either of you wearing armor?" I grumbled as I lifted a brow.

"Ha, there's Mr. Serious." Gage laughed. "We're just messing around."

"So I see. Both of you are sparring like shit."

"Hey!" they shouted in tandem, and Gage took the opportunity to try to disarm her. She was too quick for his tricks, though.

Instead, she twirled around and swiped her foot across his ankles, tripping him and making him fall right on his ass.

His body hit the ground with a grunt, and Lia lightly placed the tip of her sword on his sternum.

"I win." She beamed.

"Wyvern's shit! I want a rematch!" Gage yelled up to her as she sheathed her sword back on her hip.

She playfully danced to me in victory to where I leaned up against the side of the townhouse, when Gage yelled over again, "If you're scared that you just got lucky and will lose, you can just say that, Lia." His grin was ear to ear.

Her eyes sharpened with challenge as she continued to stare up at me and then went back for the hilt of her sword. Only when she went to spin around to take him up on that bet, I reached out and wrapped my arm around her waist, pulling her into my chest.

She squirmed in my grasp. "Dammit, Jace! Let me go so I can make him lose again."

I put my lips to her ear and whispered, "Oh, I won't be letting this body go anytime soon. I have plans for it." Her squirming ceased, and she went limp in my arms as I felt the goosebumps form on her skin beneath my touch.

"Is that a threat or a promise?" Her words dripped with anticipation.

"Both," I whispered tenderly.

She turned to face me, my grip on her barely loosening, then she threw her arms around my neck and leaned up to kiss me.

"You know," she said between kisses. "If you're going to run around here shirtless and show the realm all the glory under your armor, it's only fair I do the same."

I pulled my lips away from hers and my eyes flared as our gazes met. An infuriating, wicked grin appeared on her face. "I think the fuck not, my queen."

Lia winked as she pushed away from my grip. She held her arms out to her sides as she backed away mockingly. "Then go find a shirt, my king."

My heart raced as the last two words left her lips, and I watched as she went back to her ridiculous sparring match with our best friend.

"Honestly, are you ever going to want to learn how to ride Nox?" Lia spat as she placed her hands on her hips, staring at me from across the kitchen.

My stare bore into hers and I rose a brow. Truthfully, I should have known this was coming. One thing was clear, and that was that Lia adored Nox, and he felt the same for her—only he certainly didn't feel that way about me, or anyone else for that matter. The beast was very protective of her.

After Lia had spoken with that frightened woman in the city, she had done just as Lia asked of her. Rumors spread that Nox was not to be feared, and the guards posted throughout the city reminded them of that if terror worked its way through the streets when he soared overhead. Our one rule for him, aside from eating people, was that he could not enter the city itself...not that we had room for him, anyway.

A few days ago, we had finally discovered where he slept. We had observed one of his flights and witnessed him find refuge on a ledge of one of the mountains that overlooked Ellecaster. Now, as soon as Lia stepped beyond our front door in the morning, her eyes instinctively sought the ledge above the city.

Aggravation rumbled through me, but this was one of the first times that I could distinguish it was not my own, and was hers coming through our bond.

I pressed my lips together firmly before I admitted, "I don't even like the idea of *you* continuing to ride Nox. I'm thankful the beast got you—"

"Absolutely not," she hissed, and my eyes flared in confusion. "You will not refer to him as a *beast*." Her stare narrowed in on me.

I cleared my throat, trying not to smirk at her demand. "Well, I'm thankful that your *wyvern* got you here safely. I don't see why you need to continue to ride around on him, though. We have horses."

"Nox will be an amazing weapon for us in this war," she answered, and I obviously agreed. I just didn't know why she felt the need to ride him into battle.

"Yes, you're absolutely correct, Lia. And he can be exactly that with your feet still on the realms' soil," I challenged.

She turned away from me as her brows furrowed in frustration, and I could tell by the look on her face that she was scheming.

"I'm going to tell him you said that."

"Tell who that I said what?" I asked, trying to hide my amusement.

"Nox. I'm going to tell him that you don't think I'm safe while riding him and that you don't trust him."

Oh, for the love of all the gods. I didn't know the wyvern very well, but I knew he understood her words enough. I didn't need a fire breathing...lizard wanting to turn me to ash.

By the look gleaming on her face, I could tell she already knew she had won this battle.

My gaze lazily strolled up and down her body. "You play dirty," I grumbled.

"It's one of my many redeeming qualities," she countered.

I took a step towards her. "Redeeming," I mimicked as I lifted both hands and motioned air quotations with my fingers. "Alright. Let's go find Nox."

Her answering smile just might have been worth the embarrassment that would surely come when I shit my pants in the next hour.

FORTY-ONE

Elianna

Jace subtly tried to hide the fact that he shook in his boots as Nox landed in front of us, but I could feel the slight ounce of fear that trembled through him down the bond. The rumble of his landing echoed across the fields and beyond the Ellecaster gates.

I observed him as he hesitantly went to take a single step toward the wyvern and then retreat his foot back to where it once was.

"Not so badass now, huh, Commander?" I teased.

"You're not funny," he responded through his teeth.

"Oh, come on! What's there to be afraid of?" I looked up at Nox as his face mimicked a smile directed at Jace, being sure to show all the numerous rows of his sharp, bloodstained teeth. "Awe see, he likes you." I strolled up to him and gave him a pat on his scaly chest.

When I went to turn, Nox lowered his head to hover directly above my own. We both stood there staring my mate down as he looked as if he was contemplating every life choice he ever made.

"I don't think him showing his teeth like that means he likes me," Jace answered, trying to keep his voice level.

I smirked at him. "Trust me, if he didn't like you, or know how much I love you, you probably would've been scorched dust on the wind by now."

I moved to walk around Nox's wing.

"What are you doing?" he asked hurriedly.

"I'm going to show you how it's done. Can't have you taking flight lessons without knowing what you're doing," I said as I climbed up Nox's side and situated myself in my usual seat at the nape of his neck.

Jace moved around Nox and was now slightly closer, staring up at me from his side. "Oh, and who gave *you* flight lessons?"

I contemplated for a moment, attempting to make myself appear as if I were in deep thought before I looked back down at him. "Myself."

"Charming, Lia," he muttered, clearly losing a bit of his patience. "Honestly, though, he doesn't have a saddle on him or anything! What happens if you were to fall off?"

I rolled my eyes at him. "Oh, okay, as if I would've been able to find a saddle that fit him, especially on such short notice."

He winced as if remembering the circumstances of my escape.

"Okay, never mind, I'm sorry, Jace." I peered down at Nox. "Let's show him how it's done!"

And with those words, Nox took my command and launched into the bright afternoon sky effortlessly.

My hair shot back from the gusting winds, and my eyes leaked tears from the force of it as we blasted up and up *and up* until we were soaring within the clouds.

I crawled forward slightly to look down over his shoulder and realized that Jace was barely visible on the ground below.

I chuckled. "Was that necessary? We are trying to get him to *want* to go for a ride sometime, you know."

He twisted his neck to try to look at me over his shoulder and when I saw the amusement fluttering within his giant, golden stare, I just *knew* I was in trouble.

Nox stopped beating his wings, tucked them tight into his sides and leaned forward, sending us shooting back down toward the ground at terrifying speeds.

I desperately clutched onto his neck as tight as I could and held on for dear life.

"Oh, you asshole!" I screamed, but it was lost in the rushing winds.

The ground was rapidly approaching, and we weren't slowing down. "Knock it off, Nox!"

He wasn't listening.

"Nox, Mother of the gods, *enough!*"

I could see Jace clearly now as he took a giant step back. The look on his face could only be described as pure horror.

"Nox. Pull up. *NOW!*" I roared at him.

Just in time, he stretched his wings out from his sides and leveled us out, sending us gliding through the air in enormous circles above where Jace stood in the green field below. The breeze from Nox's wings sent the flowers and tall grass flailing around him where he stood, threatening to knock him over as well.

Once I convinced myself that he was done messing with me, I loosened my grip on his neck.

"That was *not* funny," I muttered, clutching my throat as the nausea settled through me.

Eventually, he went to land, and as Jace made his way over, he looked far less than pleased with the two of us.

"Lia. What the *fuck* was that about?" he howled up at me.

I flinched. I assumed that the entire scene that had unfolded looked just as terrifying as it felt to be involved in it.

"He was just messing around," I answered just above a whisper.

"He could've killed you!"

Nox's head whipped to Jace, his lips pulled back in a snarl, and a deep growl rumbled through his chest as he stared him down.

Jace, to my surprise, didn't even wince at him. He stood there and held his ground. I watched in shock as he lifted a finger to Nox. "Listen! I know you obviously have protected her on your journey here, and I am thankful for that. However, as her mate, that is *my* job moving forward."

My heart fluttered in quick beats. That was the first time Jace had referred to himself as my mate. "You want me to trust you with her? Don't do shit like that," he warned the wyvern.

"It's okay, Jace," I said calmly. "Every time we have fallen, he caught me before we reached the ground." My jaw dropped at my admittance, and my hands flew to cover my mouth.

"So, he *has* dropped you?!"

"It was the first night we flew out of the gates! It was his first time flying! And like I said, he caught me. He made sure he took the impact of the fall. He saved my life and risked his own, and that was when we didn't even know each other!" I defended.

Jace rubbed at his temples aggressively as Nox and I sat there as if we were younglings, awaiting our punishment for disobeying the rules.

With one hand remaining on his brows, he pointed up at us with the other. "No more tricks, okay? No more of the shit you just pulled."

Nox turned his head slightly and his vertical pupil narrowed in on me as if he were looking to see if I agreed with the new rules being set for us.

Without my gaze leaving Nox, I said back to him, "Can we still do flips?"

"What?"

I looked at him then. "We like to do flips sometimes. They're fun." I gave him an awkward smile and shrugged.

Jace sighed and his eyes bounced back and forth between me and Nox.

"Fine. Just please wait until I get the measurements for a saddle to be made for him."

"But I don't want a saddle!" I argued, and Nox huffed out an aggravated breath, shaking his head aggressively from side to side in agreement.

He glared up at me, eyes pleading for me to work with him.

Now, I was the one sighing. "It's okay, Nox. We'll both get used to it." I fixed my gaze back on the ground where Jace stood. "If it makes you feel better, then fine. We'll get a saddle."

"Thank you!" he sarcastically shouted as his hands flew out to his sides.

"Alright, handsome, now climb on up here and let's go for a ride," I demanded as sweetly as I could manage.

He burst into a fit of laughter. "You're funny. But, after that entire show, I think I will also be waiting until that saddle is strapped on and secure." He crossed his arms.

"You're no fun," I groaned out as I dramatically threw my body down onto Nox's shoulder. I peeked out between the strands of my hair and noticed that he was standing there, smirking up at me in amusement. I realized that this was a battle I definitely would not win—at least not at this moment.

"Ugh. Fine," I huffed out.

I sat up, threw one of my legs over Nox's spine, and slid to the ground.

I swaggered over to Jace and threw my arms around his neck. He responded by hoisting me up by my thighs, allowing me to wrap them around his waist.

He gave me a kiss so deep it rattled everything within me. "Still think I'm no fun?" he mocked.

"In real life? Sometimes. In the bedroom? No," I answered, fluttering my eyebrows.

He spanked me jokingly while he continued to hold all my weight with one arm. A sharp laugh left me as I waved Nox off. The sound of his wings filtered around us as he took off into the sky.

"Let's go home. I have some...ideas I plan to act on." The tone of his voice sent a full body shiver through me.

"Yes, Commander," I answered.

His eyes flared in response and he kissed me deeply once more as he moved to walk back toward the city, holding me tightly in his arms.

FORTY-TWO

Kellan

Traveling across the continent by land had been nothing short of an absolute fucking nightmare gifted by the wretched gods themselves. Between Callius on my ass about absolutely everything, and Kai barking orders he didn't even understand, I was ready to carve myself out of my own skin.

"Adler," the prince spat from behind me. I pretended to not hear him as I led the front of the lines across the open plains. "Adler, your future king is speaking to you."

This prick.

I plastered a smile on my face as I turned my head slightly, still making sure my horse continued to move forward. "Yes, Prince?"

He aggressively kicked at Gallo's sides to make him move quicker as he caught up to me. "How much further? This is tiring."

Was he fucking serious? Some *king* this brat would be…

I cleared my throat. "Can't say, Your Majesty. I am not sure how far the traitors have traveled, but I doubt we are far behind them at this point."

"This is ridiculous," he hissed. "I'm sick of sleeping on a makeshift mattress in a tent. We should've seen something by now."

The death grip I held on my patience was about to slip when Callius trotted up next to us on my opposite side. "This is normal, Prince Kai. We will catch up to them, don't you worry."

I clenched my jaw shut to prevent myself from uttering any words I would likely regret when I saw Kai's gaze focus on something in the distance. I whipped my head forward and my eyes caught what he had seen.

"What's that up ahead?" The prince pointed to a small, dark mass on the horizon as the sun began to set in the distance.

A malicious grin grew on my lips. "I believe we found some of our escapees, Prince." I looked over my shoulder behind me. "Vincent! You're with me."

He immediately guided his horse to gallop over to us.

"What's going on, Captain?" he asked.

I pointed forward with my chin sharply. "Let's go scout up ahead."

The smile on his face grew to match my own, and then we took off as fast as our horses would carry us.

I watched our shadows move with us from the cast of the setting sun, and before I knew it, I realized that we had caught up to a group of our runaways.

We brought the speed of our horses down to a slow trot as we approached the skittish group, looking up at us with eyes full of fear and devastation.

"Well, well, well. What do we have here, Captain?" Vincent mocked as he steered his horse to the side and we both circled the group of nearly fifty as if they were prey.

I brought Matthias to a halt and leaned down slightly, gazing into each individual pair of eyes that were brave enough to meet my own. "It appears we found a small group of our traitors." I crossed my arms, letting the reins fall and rest on the front of my saddle.

"Please, sir," a stocky male in the front of the group called up to me. I watched in silence as he cradled a cowering female, that I could only assume was his wife, and a small youngling in his arms. "We were turning back to Isla. We realized we made a mistake and are completely prepared to beg for mercy from our soon-to-be king."

"You will address him as *Captain*," Vincent barked at the male as he unsheathed his sword at his side, sending the trembling members in the crowd into a full-on panic.

A snort left me as I watched Vin's eyes light up as they shrank beneath us in terror. "Now, now, Vincent. They were turning around!" I said brightly. "They wish to beg for mercy from our late king's heir. Let's bring them to him, shall we?"

Vincent's evil grin didn't falter at the threat he knew was beneath my words.

"Oh, thank you!" the female who had been hiding beneath her husband's arm shouted. "I shall thank the gods every day for the rest of my life for your kindness in escorting us all back to Isla. Back to our homes." She squeezed her son's shoulder.

"No need to thank me for escorting you less than a mile, Miss," I said flatly, and I watched as all sense of hope fell from her features as she realized he was with us.

"I'm sorry, Captain?" another male asked from behind them. "Less than a mile? Surely, we aren't that close to the city already."

"You're not," I said without a hint of amusement. "However, you wish to beg for the mercy of our future king. He is less than a mile away." I pointed behind me to our awaiting army. "Prince Kai left the safety of the castle's battlement to personally search for every single individual that betrayed him the first chance they had."

All of their faces paled before me.

"You will find that the prince has been feeling *many* things on our journey to find you, but mercy is not one of them," Vincent stated maliciously.

"Come now. Let's not keep him waiting," I urged as I turned Matthias around and led them to their certain, and likely bloody, demise.

The moment we arrived with the prisoners in tow, Prince Kai ordered them to line up, facing all of us who had traveled to find them. Each one stood before us with their arms bound behind them, trembling in their boots. Horror radiated from them as they faced certain death for their treason.

The sun had set, and darkness blanketed the sky above. Flame lit torches provided our only source of light, aside from the dim cast of the moon.

"Tell me!" the prince boomed. "Who assisted you with getting out of the city? Who was the ringleader of this act of treason?"

Silence. Not a single soul that stood before us answered his question.

"Odd," I chimed in. "Here I thought you all claimed to want mercy from your future king. He is asking you all a question and none of you have responded."

I peeked over at Prince Kai as his face contorted with rage.

"None of you shall receive mercy from your acts of treason. However, it is your duty to provide information to your *king*," the prince spat with venom.

A moment of deafening silence hung in the air as fear and rage contorted their expressions. A collective realization that their decision to turn back to Isla had been a deadly mistake. That was, until one brave soul received the courage to speak.

"You are *no* king," a male in the center of the line facing us shouted.

"Excuse me?!" Kai roared.

"I'm now realizing that the only mistake we truly have made was turning around. It does not take a genius to predict the kind of ruler you will be. You are *not* fit to rule, and you will *never* be our true king!"

The moment the last word left him, an arrow whizzed past my head and went directly through the speaker's mouth, blasting out through the back of his skull, leaving his last train of thought on the tip of his tongue as his body dropped to the ground.

Screams of terror rang out down the line from the females and younglings as Callius marched up next to me, bow in hand.

"Well, that was enough of that. Anyone else have something they'd like to say?" he announced.

A female was now on the ground, leaning over the dead body of the male that Callius had just shot down. Her head whipped back toward us and her eyes radiated fury as she rose to stand.

"Long live the rightful queen, Elianna Valderre! And long may she reign!" she screamed, the words soaked in agony.

"Fucking *shoot* her. Shoot them all," Kai ordered.

"I was hoping you'd say that," Callius answered with a menacing smile. He then raised his bow once more and launched an arrow at the female who had declared her true stance.

The arrow hit its target in the blink of an eye, protruding from her chest—from her heart. She dropped back down to the ground as blood trickled from her lips, a scream permanently etched into her cold, dead face.

Sobs and shouts of rage filled the air as our hostages that stood before us realized that their time in our realm had run out.

The corners of my mouth curved at their fear, but then my eyes locked on the boy, who fell to his knees beside his mother's dead body as he gripped his younger sibling in his arms.

My memory instantly flashed me back to over a century ago, when my own father had been reckless enough to be caught by the crown. The stubborn old fool of a pirate had been executed for his crimes, along with his crew...aside from me. I had received an exemption from the noose, offered by Callius himself because I had been considered a youngling—and the ones before us deserved the same.

I stalked up to Callius, who eyed me beneath furrowed brows as I approached.

I cleared my throat. "Spare the kids." The words left me in a huff.

His eyes flared. "Excuse me?"

My eyes narrowed in on his face. "Oddly enough, Callius, I don't recall there ever being a time in history where you found joy in executing younglings for the crimes of their parents."

His scowl lessened as recognition flashed across his features. He let out a grunt and his gaze drifted to the prince and then back over to me as the sobbing continued from those awaiting their fates.

"The prince does not wish for anyone to be spared," he said quietly, annoyed.

"Last I recalled, the queen was still the *queen*—not the queen mother. Not yet, anyway. Risk the wrath of a boy not yet mature enough to be king, or risk the fury of *your queen...*" I tilted my head to the side, my tone hinting at the secrecy of their relationship. "It is just a suggestion. At the end of the day, it will hardly matter to me. Although, one of them could become a high-ranking officer in his army one day. Let them at least decide their allegiance for themselves." My jaw locked as I lifted a brow.

He looked me up and down as Kai scoffed from behind us. "What are you waiting for?!" the prince shouted. "Kill them!"

"Dealing with one's wrath is not simply easier than the other's." Callius' voice was low, and then he turned to the soldiers behind us, awaiting orders.

He gestured with his chin to a few of my own men in the front, Vincent, another younger recruit named William, and two others behind them. "Fetch the younglings."

"WHAT?!" Kai barked.

Vincent and William looked at me, and I gave them a nod of approval. They stormed up to those in line as sobs and screams continued to ring out while the children were ripped from their parents' arms. Some of the younglings clawed at my men, kicking and screaming as they were thrown over their shoulders, but some willingly followed as their parents kissed them goodbye, with tears streaming down their faces.

"Younglings can hardly help the crimes their parents commit, Prince Kai," Callius told him. "Your mother would wish for them to be brought back to Isla and be questioned. See where their loyalties truly lie. If they are grateful for being spared, and pledge allegiance to you, they will be sent to the orphanages, and if not, then you may have your fun."

"That is not the wish of your future king," Kai snarled.

"No, but it is Velyran law. And until a new law has been set under your reign and you have been crowned, this is how it must be," Callius lied, making my eyes flare.

The prince scoffed, rage radiating from him, but to my surprise, he backed down. "A treasonous traitor at any age will face consequences under my rule."

"If that is your wish," Callius stated, and then turned to the males who held the younglings as they continued to squirm and sob. "Throw them in a wagon and be done with it!" he ordered.

We all watched as the children were tossed into a wooden wagon that once held already used supplies. Callius ordered three other soldiers to escort the younglings to the Islan orphanage, and then the two horses were set in motion, turning the wagon around to head back toward the capital.

Callius' gaze moved to Kai again, who looked as if he would explode with a tantrum, and I watched as my predecessor's jaw locked.

The blame for the younglings spared was falling on Callius, which could work to my advantage.

I stepped forward and lifted my arm to give the signal to those awaiting orders behind us.

"Ready," I boomed, and the sound of the front lines moving into their stance echoed. "Nock." Arrows were expertly placed in bows. "And loose," I commanded.

A wall of arrows were then released into the night sky simultaneously, and all of our gazes followed them as they rose and then rained down on the traitors before us, slaughtering them all.

My eyes drifted to the side, to the little shit prince, whose own stare gleamed with lusting fire at the sight of their deaths.

FORTY-THREE
Avery

A WEEK WE HAD been traveling through this gods-forsaken forest. Seven days of absolute unrest and chaos. It seemed as if the path we were following through the trees would never end.

I still couldn't believe how many among our group had abandoned us under the darkness of the night sky as we slept on the outskirts of that decimated war camp.

They had given up on finding Lia, and they had lost their faith in us leading them. My heart sank when we discovered that so many had decided that turning back and begging for mercy, which they would never receive, was a safer option than trying to travel through this ancient, enchanted forest.

Veli had been refusing to use her magic within the woods unless absolutely necessary. She had said that while using it may achieve defeating whatever creature or issue we currently dealt with, it could also attract something far, far worse. "Magic calls to its kin," she had repeated, and then immediately rejected the idea of risking even *opening* her spell book.

Finnian was thankful for her wisdom regarding the risks, but I wasn't convinced. And due to her refusal of using her magic to easily kill the beasts we already encountered, we had lost eleven of our own.

Some of those who had been killed so far were soldiers defending us from a sylis bear, a beast of astronomical size with the antlers of an elk and an appetite for flesh. This, unfortunately, was after we were forced to watch as it snuck up from the side of us and dragged off one of the females among us. The cries of anguish from her sister still radiated in my ears.

Three other males among us were found after they left to scout the area ahead. All that was left of them by the time we arrived were torn, bloody clothing, and a pile of crimson pulp.

Finnian puked his guts up for an hour at the scene. My body wanted to do the same, but there was nothing left in my stomach to do so.

Every day, more of us began to starve. Every day, more and more of us were at each other's throats. And every single day, more among us lost hope.

"Those who fled in the night before we entered the forest had the right idea." I overheard vicious, hate-filled whispers.

"We were all fools to even leave Isla, and now we will die here as treasonous traitors of the crown. The prince and princess will just receive a smack on the wrist if we are caught—the rest of us will pay for this with our lives."

These words had carried through the air to me for days, but each time they were spoken, it never lessened their sting.

The only time people were being civil with one another was when they spoke of their shared resentment towards me and my brother.

People regretted leaving their homes and families, the lives they had all built and created back in Isla. Landon and a few soldiers had to break up a physical fight two nights prior, just because of someone trying to sneak an extra bite of food. My speeches no longer served their purpose. I was even starting to believe that sooner or later, some of the soldiers would try to overthrow us as their leaders and take a different course.

I stood leaning my back against a tree while I observed everyone as they rested at the foot of a stream, attempting to wash off and drink up as much water as possible while refilling our canteens. Nyra watched over some of the younglings that remained with us, entertaining them by playing fetch with a rock they had found on the forest floor.

"How are you holding up?" Landon asked as he approached me from the side.

"Not the greatest," I answered, barely above a whisper. "There's no end to this in sight."

He shrugged. "The forest has to end sometime. We'll get there." He patted my shoulder gently and gave me the caring smile he always wore, even when there was barely anything to smile about.

"Thanks, Landon." I returned my gaze to the stream. "Have you seen Finn?"

His smile faltered only slightly at the mention of my brother. "He's over on the other side of that tree." He pointed to an area on our left.

I had to suppress my grin. I knew he was still upset with Finnian for what happened all that time ago, and maybe he never would actually forgive him for it, but it was a little funny that he still made sure to know exactly where he was at all times.

"I'm going to go find him. Would you like to come with me?" I winked.

Landon gave me a knowing look. "I'll go check on the others," he said to me and then stalked back toward the stream.

I watched him for a few silent moments and then peeled myself away from the tree bark to make my way to where he had pointed.

I couldn't believe they were both still being this painfully stubborn when it was obvious that they wanted to put everything that had happened behind them. For every whisper of self-hate from Finn, came a longing, snuck in look from Landon in his direction. They shared a love for one another that I was so desperate to experience, and they were willing to let it all go to waste.

My sister had a mate, my brother found love within the castle walls—and then there was me. Princess Avery, who had been locked away her entire existence, never knowing the touch of a male or the whisperings of sweet, tender words into her ear. It was all a myth to me—tales in a storybook that I craved more than the air I breathed.

"Finn!" I called out as I stepped around multiple bushes. My foot caught on one of the many annoying roots that stuck up from the ground.

I had never been covered in so many cuts and bruises in my life. Between walking over tree roots, climbing between boulders, and running through sharp, unforgiving branches, my body looked as if it had been to war.

Well, war for someone who had grown up within the walls of a castle and was never allowed outside of them.

Once I arrived on the other side of the trees, I realized that no one was over here and Finn must've already moved on from being in the area.

Or had he been taken by one of the Sylis creatures?...

My eyes flared wide, and my jaw popped open as I gasped for breath. Panic hit me and I frantically started glancing in every direction, looking for any sign of him.

"Finnian!" I shouted.

Nothing. I started pacing in the area, unsure of what to do before I screamed again, my voice desperate, "*Finnian!*"

"Yeah?" an echo called back from behind the trees I had just came from. "Is everything okay?!"

"What the hell?" I scoffed as I shook the nerves from me, calming my heart rate back down. I had become so jumpy at everything and automatically assumed the worst.

"Just making sure you were still alive," I called back, aggravated.

I let out a loud breath and glanced around the area, looking for anything that could help us, whether it was food or something that could be used as a weapon.

I was about to give up when, out of the corner of my eye, a massive bush covered in bunches of bright indigo-colored berries appeared.

My mouth salivated instantly. Was I hallucinating? If I were, that would be an extremely cruel punishment from the gods.

I ran over to the bush, fell to my knees and wept as I anxiously ripped the berries from their stems, building a pile on the ground beneath me. Every other pick, I popped a berry into my mouth, barely chewing them as I was desperate to get them into my stomach.

Once the rumbling of my stomach eased, I gathered the pile of berries into my hands and made my way back toward the stream where everyone awaited.

As I stumbled into the clearing, my vision blurred, and my movements slowed significantly. Dizziness took over me and my stomach suddenly felt as if it was twisting itself closed. My entire body then broke out in a sweat.

"Avery!" I heard my name called in the distance, but I couldn't get my body to move any further.

"Avery, are you...oh gods, Avery!" the same voice bellowed into the air.

Before I knew it, I collapsed to the ground. Multiple fae were kneeling over me a moment later. Between the sunlight blinding me as it shone down through the leafy canopy above and the blurring of my vision, I could barely make out the people examining me.

"Veli! Veli come quickly!" I faintly heard my brother's voice. "Where the *fuck* is Veli?!" A hand then cupped my cheek, and I tried to blink through the haze to see the outline of Finn's face as he hovered directly above my own. "Stay with me, Avery. Stay with me. I can't do this without you. What happened?!" he cried.

"Everyone *move!*" a familiar, spine-chilling voice screeched.

The silhouettes that had surrounded me one moment were gone the next and replaced by a mirage of shining silver hair.

Whimpering sounded next to my ear, and I felt Nyra's snout as she rested it on my shoulder while I lay there.

"Nyra, you have to let us help her," Finn said, and then the weight of her head lifted from me, but her whimpering continued.

"What happened?" Veli snapped, but I didn't know if it was to me or someone else. I couldn't have answered her even if I wanted to.

"I don't know, she just came out from those trees over there and collapsed! Look at her, she's as pale as the spirits that walk the realm at dusk. *Do something!*"

My eyes fluttered to a close, and as I drifted into darkness, their words continued to reach me as they frantically searched for a way to help.

"Avery, no!" Veli yelled, and I felt a sharp smack on my cheek. "Keep your eyes open."

Her gold and violet eyes roamed my body.

"Oh, mother of the gods, what are those next to her hip?" she asked.

I could only assume Finn picked up what she pointed to. "These? It looks like berries."

"Put those down, you fool!" A few tiny thumps sounded as they hit the terrain. "Did she eat those?"

"I am assuming!" he snapped at her.

Veli sighed sharply. "You idiot, Avery. Those are velaeno berries! Finnian, go fetch my pack. Quickly."

His shadow above me moved, and I could barely make out anything other than the bright sunlight that lingered above me.

I wasn't sure how much time had passed before he returned to my side—it could've been seconds, it could have been minutes. All I knew was that I could feel myself slipping further and further away.

"Hand me that vial of green liquid," she demanded. The pop of a cork sounded, and then Veli's nails pinched my cheeks as she forced my mouth open and poured the liquid into it.

I immediately choked as it slipped down my throat.

"You have to swallow it, Avery!" Finn begged.

Suddenly, Veli's hand moved from my cheeks to cover my mouth, making me swallow whatever it was she just forced upon me.

I reluctantly did as I was told, even though it felt as if my esophagus was closing in on itself. I could feel the exact moment the mysterious potion hit my stomach.

My body began to convulse, and I lost all control of myself as I sat up and violently vomited all the contents within myself, which wasn't much, but thanks to the color of the berries, it eerily resembled blood.

"Oh, gods!" Finnian cried as he threw himself back to avoid the mess that poured from me.

Once I felt that I was finally done, I opened my eyes little by little and was mortified to see that there were about a hundred other pairs of them fixated on me.

I slowly turned to meet Veli's horrified, yet surprisingly relieved, face.

"I'm sorry," I croaked out, my voice hoarse.

"Everyone get the hell away from her and give her some room!" Landon yelled at the forming crowd. They all hesitantly backed away and returned to what they were doing prior to my unexpected show.

"Here," Veli started, reaching into her pack again and shuffling through it. When her hand retreated, I saw that she held a fern-like leaf. "Chew on this."

I stared at the leaf and blinked.

"I don't know if I can stomach anything else. Especially...a plant," I answered nervously.

She rose a single brow and her lips thinned into a fine line as she stared at me, huffing through her nose. "It's just a sedaeyo leaf. Are you in pain?"

I absolutely was—my stomach felt as if a light flame was dancing within it.

I nodded twice, and she proceeded to shove the leaf into my hands as she grabbed her supplies. "Then chew it," she said through her teeth as she walked away.

I also heard her as she mumbled, "I took my eyes off of them for *two seconds*. Who knew keeping the two red-headed idiots alive would be the hardest part of this bullshit journey?"

I huffed a painful attempt at a laugh through my nose at the typical Veli response. However, I was so grateful that she saved my life that I would take a thousand more insults if it made her feel more at ease.

I warily nibbled on the leaf.

"You scared the shit out of me," Finn said as he sat slumped over next to me, and I honestly forgot he was still there.

I frowned. "I'm sorry, Finn. My body has been starving, feeling as if it's been eating at itself and I didn't think. We've been so desperate for food that I never considered something could be poisonous."

He leaned back and sat on the back of his feet, blowing out a long breath. "I honestly can't even say I wouldn't have done the same...what have we gotten ourselves into?" he said through a few sad laughs as he looked up into the trees above.

"A mess," I answered, and as we made eye contact, we both burst into laughter. "Think we'll make it out of here?" I asked through the dulling pain that still twisted my gut up as the leaf gradually took effect.

"Who freaking knows," he said as he stood, reaching his hands down to help me up.

I took his hands and closed my eyes tightly as the wooziness hit me from the sudden movement of being pulled up to stand.

Landon jogged back over to us. "How's she doing?" he asked Finn, and my brother looked as if the gods themselves had just asked him a question.

"She's, um, she's alright." He blinked.

Landon's focus returned to me. "We need to get moving. A few scouts went up ahead when we first arrived here and just returned. They think we could be out of the forest by the end of the day. They saw a clearing with sunlight towards the end of it."

That got both of our attentions.

"Well, why didn't you say anything sooner?!" I cried. As I took my first step forward, I lost my balance and nearly crashed back down to the ground before each of them caught one of my arms.

"Gods-dammit," I muttered.

Landon went to move in front of me. "How about you jump up on my back and I carry you until your strength returns enough so you can walk?"

I smirked. "Are you serious?"

"I think this is his polite way of letting you know that he doesn't want you to slow us down," Finn said with a smirk.

"This is one of the rare occasions where your brother would be correct," Landon teased, and I watched as the light finally began to return to Finnian's eyes in response.

I looked around and noticed most of the people with us had already started walking back along the trail.

"Ugh, fine."

"That's the spirit," Landon said as he bent down lower so I could easily hoist myself up onto his back.

He wrapped his arms around my legs to secure me where I held onto him.

In any other situation, a male touching me like this would be considered entirely inappropriate—especially for a princess. However, given the circumstances of being too weak to walk on my own, and the fact that he was my brother's lover, I felt like it didn't matter. And truthfully, the manners of a princess were the last thing I gave a shit about anymore.

"Alright, hold on tight," he warned as he took off into a sprint after the crowd. Nyra playfully nipped at my feet as they swung around at his sides.

I burst into a fit of laughter as Finn worked to grab both his pack and Landon's, since I now occupied his strength, and ran after us.

We were *finally* about to get out of here. I couldn't believe it.

FORTY-FOUR
Elianna

I HASTILY DODGED THE sharpened blade as it was expertly swung directly at my face, a little too close for comfort. I ducked and struck back, the clash of our swords reverberating up my arm and through my body.

"You've been practicing." I taunted Zaela as she swung once more.

"Hey!" Jace shouted from the sidelines of our sparring. "Easy over there, you two."

I twirled and kicked out from under her legs, one of my favorite moves, but she easily leapt over my foot as it went to take out her ankles.

"Your cousin is no fun, you know," I joked, but she was all business.

"I heard that!" he announced, and I looked over at him as he stood with some of our younger recruits while they observed us.

I lunged toward her, catching the wrist of her sword arm with my hand, and squeezed. Her face twisted as she tried to hide her pain.

"Tap out." I smirked.

"No!" she shouted, but her fingers had loosened too much on the hilt and her sword clattered to the ground.

The smile remained on my face. "I win."

"Oh, I don't think so!"

She tackled me to the ground, and we rolled together. I was laughing, but I could tell she was determined to win.

She punched me in the side, barely hard enough to bruise, and I returned the same kind gesture to her face.

"Gods, you two! Finish this!" Jace shouted. "You're supposed to be setting examples!" All the young soldiers' eyes remained on us, watching intently.

"We are!" Zae and I yelled in unison.

She swung at my face, but I blocked it as I wrapped my thighs tightly around her own and rolled us, putting me at the advantage of now being above her.

"I was disarmed!" Zaela yelled as she tried to swing up once more, but I caught her hand and shoved it down into the dirt next to her face. "Recruits, this is what happens on the battlefield. You *continue* to fight!"

I unsheathed the dagger at *her* side and placed the tip under her chin as I continued to hold down her arm with my other hand. My knee then dug into her remaining hand on her opposite side.

"If you break my fingers, I will be pissed," she hissed.

My grin was ear to ear as I leaned over her, now pushing up onto my feet in a very low squat. "I win. Again."

She let out a sharp laugh and shoved me off of her, causing me to stumble onto the backs of my heels and land flat on my ass a few feet away. Both of us sat there chuckling for a few moments as Jace brought over the teenagers that he made observe us.

"Glad you two think this is funny," he grumbled.

I reached my hand up toward him, a silent ask for assistance. His face softened as he reached down and pulled me up. I stood up on the tips of my toes and gave him a quick kiss, causing the trainees to make cooing noises at us, teasing their own commander.

His gaze whipped to them, and I watched as the tiniest look of fear flashed across each of their faces.

"Alright, that's enough from all of you. Go do a lap around the field if you think mocking your own leader is funny. We're done for the day after that," he ordered.

They all groaned and complained as they took off into a sprint together under the heat of the early afternoon sun, following his order.

"And you," he said as he grabbed my waist and pulled me into his chest. "I have plans for *you*."

"Gross. I think I'm going to be sick. See you guys at home later," Zaela announced with an abrupt wave as she turned away from us and headed up the hill, back to the city.

"So, what are these so-called plans?" I asked in a sultry voice, raising a suspicious brow.

He huffed out a laugh. "That will come later, but first, I want to show you something."

My brows furrowed as he pulled away from me, interlocking his fingers with mine, and led me beyond the field.

We finally came to a stop about a half mile from the front of the city gates. The entire walk over, I begged him to give me even the tiniest of hints, but he refused every time.

I pulled my arm from his grasp and stared at him. "Are you going to tell me *now?*"

He winked at me in response, which infuriated me as much as it turned me on.

A moment later, the pulsing beat of Nox's wings rumbled through the air above, and when I looked up, I was in awe of what I witnessed.

He landed a few feet ahead of us and I ran over to him to see a beautiful, massive leather saddle had already been crafted and somehow strapped around him.

My smile was beaming and laughter escaped me as I was left speechless, observing the saddle from the ground below.

"I can't believe you were able to have one made. It looks amazing!" I screeched at him in excitement. "How the hell did this get done so fast?! It's barely been a week."

"We have extremely talented artisans here in Ellecaster, and let's just say I paid a hefty fee to have this bumped to the top of their list." I frowned at him, wishing he hadn't felt the need to spend so much money. "Oh, don't give me that look. That was hardly difficult for me to do. The hard part was…getting it on him." His tone dropped on the last sentence.

I rotated my body to face him where he stood behind me. "How *did* you get this on him?" I gradually looked up at the wyvern's face and raised a brow when I saw what could only be described as pure satisfaction radiating from his golden eyes.

"Yeah, not as smooth as I would've hoped. Gage almost got fried, but we got it done. It took a lot, and I really do mean *a lot,* of constant reminding him that it was for your safety." He shot a glare up at Nox that had me suspecting that he was giving me the nice, less dramatic version of how the event truly occurred.

My focus returned to the wyvern beneath a raised brow. "Gage? Really? You know he is the nice one." I placed my hands on my hips.

"Thanks," Jace hissed from behind me.

"Well, he knows not to hurt you." I shrugged and then started towards Nox's side.

Jace appeared directly behind me, and I crawled up under Nox's wing, easily pulling myself onto the saddle using the straps that hung at his sides.

I looked down at Jace. "Are you coming, or what?" I shot down at him.

"Ugh. Fuck it," he muttered as he grabbed hold of one of the saddle's straps that buckled in beneath the wyvern's belly.

A growl rumbled beneath me. "Easy, Nox," I warned, and the rumbling ceased instantly. I patted the side of his neck. "Thank you." I smirked.

My mate worked to climb up himself, and the sight was honestly hysterical, until he finally gave up and reached his hand up to me for help.

"Don't tell the others," he hissed jokingly, and I snorted in response.

Once Jace had finally made it up, he promptly situated himself behind me, my back resting against his front, and his legs cradled around mine.

As I glanced down, I was struck by the beauty of the massive saddle and couldn't help but run my fingertips over the intricate patterns etched into the leather. A gorgeous, dark gray color, laced with champagne thread. Every stitch had a purpose. The saddle was strong, expertly made, and absolutely magnificent to look at.

My gaze fell to the horn of the saddle, an extra precaution to grasp if needed in battle, and my eyes widened as I noticed the design that was stitched into the leather directly below it.

The head of a wolf, nearly identical to the one that had once been at the top of my dagger, rested at the center of two wings. However, they weren't just any wings; they were the wings of a wyvern.

My mouth parted in awe, and I was left speechless as I sat there in silence, admiring the unique design.

Jace pulled my hair back and tucked a few strands behind the tip of my ear. "Do you like it?" he whispered.

"Like it?" I gasped. "I love it. This is incredible." I paused as my heart fluttered. "Thank you so, so much for this."

"Anything for you, my Lia," he said as he wrapped his arms around me in a tight embrace and my arms flew up to squeeze his forearms in return.

"There's one other thing, as well. I didn't think it would be ready in time, but I just picked it up this morning," he announced.

I turned my head back to try to look at him but realized that I couldn't at this angle. I quickly swung one of my legs over to the opposite side of the seat and replaced it with the other, now facing him.

"Another thing? This saddle alone was entirely too much. What else did you do?" I asked warily, my mind racing at what he possibly could have had time to do aside from this. We were always together. It was rare for us to be out and about without accompanying one another.

Jace looked up into the clear, cerulean sky as birds flew overhead, cooing their songs at us, and he smiled so brightly it made my heart nearly melt.

He reached down into one of the deep pockets of the saddle and revealed a long, decorative box with a ribbon of emerald green tied around it in a perfect bow.

He gently handed it to me. "This is for you, Lia."

Tears instantly stung the back of my eyes—I had no idea what was in this box, but I could see his own emotions intensely written across his face directly in front of me. They quickly overpowered my own through the bond, and as his heart thundered in his chest, the beat of my own matched as if our hearts mimicked one another's.

I took in a deep breath and pulled on the ribbon, which unraveled easily and fell onto my thigh. I pulled open the top part of the box and my breath was immediately ripped from my lungs at the sight of what lay in the center of it. My lips parted, and I felt heat rush to my cheeks as they flushed.

My dagger.

The dagger I had treasured so deeply as a gift from my father, and had never left my side until that gruesome day in the village. Kellan had destroyed it. I distinctly remembered watching in horror as I was tied to that pole and he stomped on it so hard that the obsidian blade snapped right off of the hilt. This was all after he had slashed it across my mate's face.

"How?" I croaked out and met his gaze with watery, burning eyes.

He lifted his arm and gently wiped away the single tear that had slipped. "When I woke up that day, I found it in pieces on the ground. I took everything I could and had it remade. It isn't entirely identical to what it was, but—"

I held my visibly shaking hand up to cut him off. He was right. It wasn't identical, but it was somehow even more extraordinary now.

At the bottom of the hilt, where the grip met the blade, was a small pair of wings protruding out from the sides. The unique design was made from the same onyx-hued iron that the blade was.

I carefully reached my hand into the box and lifted the dagger from it, observing it as the rays of the sun reflected off of its beauty.

"It's perfect," I choked out, voice cracking. I took my fingers and traced the line where the blade was reforged together. "I can never thank you enough for this." My voice was shaking with gratitude at how thoughtful and incredible he was.

Jace reached out and cupped the back of my head, pulled me closer to him, and gave me a breathtaking kiss.

I started chuckling as Nox grumbled beneath us.

"Sorry, Nox," I said through a smile that formed on my face as Jace pulled away from me with a smirk.

"Ready for your first flying lesson?" I winked at him as I moved to turn back around.

"I guess I am as ready as I'll ever be." He sighed.

"That's the spirit," I mocked.

As I was about to give Nox the order to take off, a loud, ominous horn sounded from within the city walls. Both of our gazes snapped toward the stone gates.

The horn rang out twice more before it ceased.

"Jace," I whispered. "What was that?"

"Someone's coming," he warned sternly. "We need to get back to the city. Right now."

A moment later, the two of us slid down the side of the wyvern and took off in a run back towards Ellecaster's gates.

FORTY-FIVE
Jace

THE LOOK ON LIA'S face as the horns sounded from within the city walls resurfaced a memory that I had no desire to ever relive again. Suddenly, as we were sprinting back to Ellecaster, my mind transported me back to the night of the attack, and the following morning with the look on her face that would permanently be etched into my mind as she watched me fall to what should have been my death.

I kept pace with her and snuck a look in her direction while her focus was set on the gates ahead. Pride swelled in my chest as I watched pure determination flash across her features as the wind whipped her long hair around behind her.

Once at the gates, we noticed a few guards gathering in front of the blacksmith's shop. Lia's gaze locked in on them and she jogged over without saying a word.

"What's going on? Why were the horns sounded?" she asked them, much more calm than I would've been.

Their concerned eyes flew up to me, as if looking for permission to grant her the information. They knew who she was, and that they should trust her indefinitely. The fact that they had the audacity to hesitate *in front* of her sent my blood to a near boil.

"This is your future queen. You will treat her with even more respect than you do me. Is that understood?" I snapped at them as I pointed my finger in their faces, my own twisting into a scowl as my jaw clenched. "Tell her what is happening."

One of them that I knew by the name of Darion took a single step forward. "Apologies, Miss," he said and flashed her a sympathetic smile. "This will all take some getting used to, but you have my sword. Now and until my body is but a speck of ash."

Lia's eyes darted back and forth between his. "Thank you, soldier." I watched as the tension in her shoulders eased.

"We sent out scouts to be stationed on our side of the realm before you arrived here. We just received a falcon stating that a large group of unknown fae wandered out of the Sylis Forest and are headed in this direction."

Her mouth popped open. "When did this happen?"

"The falcon must've been sent this morning. It wouldn't take the bird too long to get here from there, considering it's a day's ride."

"Did it have any information regarding who was among them?" I interjected.

"Sorry, Commander, but unfortunately, no. The letter was vague and only stated that hundreds of them poured out of the forest. No other information had been given."

"Fuck," Lia whispered as she shot me a look. "It must be the crown."

I peered back over to the soldiers who were standing waiting for orders. "Gather the troops and meet beyond the gates in one hour. Bring horses, weapons, and any supplies you can manage to muster up."

"Yes, Commander," Darion answered.

I reached out for Lia's hand and she turned back to face me. "Let's go find the others."

"Absolutely *fucking* not," I hissed at my mate as I paced back and forth in our living room.

My hands repeatedly flexed in and out of fists in front of me as I twisted my head side to side, cracking the tension that was built into my neck from the aggravation settling into me.

"Let me do this," she begged calmly.

My pacing halted and my eyes narrowed in on her as she sat in the middle of the settee. Gage and Zaela stood behind her, looking just as anxious and furious at her suggestion as I felt about it.

"*No.* The last fucking thing I'm doing is letting you go out there by yourself. They're either going to kill you right there or drag you back to Isla. How else do you think *surrendering* yourself is going to go?" I roared, my voice rattling the candelabra that rested above the fireplace.

My heart was ready to burst out of my chest it was pumping so hard. I couldn't even believe she was suggesting something like this. I couldn't lose her again. *I wouldn't.*

"I'm with Jace on this one," Zaela admitted, and Gage nodded in agreement.

"Ugh. Thanks a lot, you two." Lia rolled her eyes and leaned back, throwing her head over the top of the couch.

"Sorry we aren't willing to sacrifice someone we love and a better future for the realm just so you can go out there and play hero," I barked at her, tone harsher than I meant it to be.

"Play. *Hero*?!" she snapped, her eyes locked on me now in an intense gaze while her back straightened. "Thinking about something else happening to your people, *our people*, is crippling to me. I will not allow Kellan's armies to come here and level out Ellecaster again, like they had with the village."

My face softened at her admittance, and I stood before her as silence settled into the room. A moment later, I knelt down on one knee in front of her, taking her chin between two of my fingers. "You're right, and I'm sorry. That wasn't the right thing to say." She refused to meet my gaze. "I can't lose you again. We all go out together, and we *fight*. Agreed?"

Her eyes lazily found mine once more, but fear still lingered there. "Agreed."

"There's my Lia," I said on a breath as I pulled her up to her feet.

"Well then," Zae chimed in, breaking the silence. "Let's get our gear and kill those fuckers, huh?" She shot us a feral grin as she moved around the settee and stood next to us.

Lia turned to her with her chin held high, the look on her face nearly identical to my cousin's. "Yes. Let's."

"How many are there?" I asked Gage quietly as we stood before the rallied troops directly beyond the gates.

"Some have to stay here to guard the city. We have about a thousand ready to leave. Do you think more is needed?"

I peered back behind us and watched as Lia finished checking Nox's saddle straps, making sure they were still secure from when Gage and I wrestled him into it this morning, which already felt like a lifetime ago.

"We'll have the wyvern. That should be plenty." I gave him a curt nod and stalked toward Lia.

She jogged over to me once she noticed I was headed her way, meeting me halfway, and I smiled as I watched her sheath her remade dagger at her thigh.

Despite her strong, determined facade before the troops, I could sense the waves of fear and fury emanating from her through our bond. She could no longer hide what she truly felt—at least not from me, anyway.

I didn't want to risk upsetting her further by bringing it up around the men, so I opted to distract her instead.

"It appears that your dagger is finally back where it belongs." I grinned as I crossed my arms. "I'm a little jealous of it, if I'm being honest."

She gave me a questionable look. "You wish to be strapped to my thigh?"

I shrugged a shoulder. "Perhaps you're right. I prefer to be between them."

She swatted at me playfully with a smirk creeping up her lips as she went to walk toward our small, awaiting army. "Such a tease."

"The only thing that's a tease right now is you in those new fighting leathers you had made."

It was true. The second she wasn't looking at me, I sucked in my bottom lip and bit it so hard that I thought it might bleed as I watched how her body moved in her new, form-fitting attire.

She giggled wickedly. "Oh, these old things? I'm glad you like them." She winked at me.

I cleared my throat as my gaze went to the soldiers. "My fear is I won't be the only one."

"Oh, cut it out with the territorial nonsense." She waved me off.

Her fear had eased for only a moment before it radiated from her once more.

I could feel her body tense as we came to a halt directly in front of the others. She glanced at me and then focused back on the armada that awaited our orders.

She let out a shuddering breath and opened her mouth to speak. "Thank you for putting this all together on such short notice and thank you for trusting me to lead you there, along with Commander Cadoria." My chest puffed out in honor at the mention of my name from her. "We do not know what lies beyond these fields. It is likely an attempted ambush. However, I know you will all be ready for whatever lies ahead. You have received training, and the time to use it has come."

"You wait for her or my signal when we come in contact with them. Do not engage otherwise. Is that understood?" I boomed to the crowd.

"Yes, Commander." Their vigorous response echoed in the air.

I went to move toward the horses I had picked out for us when Lia's voice chimed through the air once more.

"The commander and I will be flying ahead on Nox." She threw a thumb behind her at the waiting wyvern. "We will scope everything out first, so there hopefully won't be any surprises. Ride fast. Ride well. We need to make sure they don't get any closer to the city if we can help it."

I shot her a look of annoyance at announcing that I apparently would also be taking to the skies. "Well played," I muttered, and I didn't miss it as she tried to hide her grin.

My gaze then flew to Zaela and Gage, who stood at attention next to her. "You're in front. Follow our lead."

"You got it, brother." Gage nodded, his eagerness written all over his face.

I marched past Lia and toward the wyvern, but she instantly caught up to me. "Don't be mad," she said amusingly.

"So much for getting practice," I whispered to her playfully.

She climbed up Nox's side and I followed, annoyed with myself about needing to grab hold of the straps to hoist myself up onto him. How she was able to effortlessly do this without them for this long was a mystery.

I situated myself behind her, identical to how we sat barely an hour ago, and she handed me one of the safety straps.

"Ready?" she asked, eyes gleaming with anticipation.

I pulled the strap tight and secured both myself and her into the saddle.

"Always." A throaty laugh left me, and her smile of excitement beamed so brightly that it could've rivaled that of the gods themselves.

Nox's wings burst out from his sides, and then, before I could blink, we were airborne.

FORTY-SIX

Avery

I couldn't believe we had finally made our way out of that terrifying forest a few hours ago. I almost kissed the ground beneath my feet once we ran past the end of the tree line and out into open fields that could be seen for miles.

In the interest of time, and the safety of whatever lurked between those trees, we decided to press on and not stop to rest on the outskirts of the woods.

We had done it. We had done the impossible and crossed the Sylis Forest and were now *that* much closer to finding Lia. Relief was plastered across everyone's faces.

I must've been smiling without realizing because Veli shot me a pinched expression of irritation.

"What? Are you still mad I ate some berries?" I pushed out my bottom lip on the last word, giving her an apologetic look.

She sighed sharply as she frowned up at me. "You're just an idiot."

My brows furrowed. "Well, that was a little harsh."

"Hardly," she grumbled.

"What's gotten into you?" I snapped at her, staring at her from the side as we led the group behind us.

Her head whipped to me, tension in her face and neck clear for all to see. "These are human lands, girl. We need to be careful. Just because we are out of the forest doesn't mean we are out of harm's way quite yet."

I examined our surroundings. "But we're here to join them," I muttered.

"And you think every human in the realm knows that? What makes us look different from any other fae? We will not be trusted. Not until we find Elianna, and that is *if* she is even alive."

I stopped in my tracks and tugged at her arm, halting her. She glared at me viciously as others maneuvered around us.

"She is alive," I hissed.

"Easy, you two," Landon called out to us as he stalked past. "We're almost there. No sense in going at each other now."

I bit my inner cheek to prevent a sass-filled remark from flying out of my mouth. Even with all the excitement of now being beyond the woods, we were all still starving, irritable, and weak. Landon was right; we had to keep pushing forward without causing unnecessary problems amongst ourselves.

A primal scream of pure terror sounded out from behind us, causing everyone with us to stop short in their tracks and whip around to where the shriek came from.

I rushed over to the female, who was trembling with her youngling in her arms. I stared at her, confused, as she hyperventilated while Veli frantically searched her and the child for injuries.

"What is it?! What's happened?" I shouted in her face as the look of fear in her eyes started creeping into my own. I could feel Finn and Landon arrive at the scene as they skidded to a stop behind us.

Her eyes remained fixated on the sky as she clutched her child tightly to her chest, and several other screams rang out around us.

I spun around to see what all the fuss was about, but instead of fear swallowing me, as it was the others, I was enveloped in pure *relief*.

I gasped out in shock as my eyes followed the path of the wyvern that was headed directly for us. Tears sprang from my eyes as I mindlessly took off into a run, directly toward the flying creature.

"Avery! Wait!" my brother called out from behind me.

"It's Lia!" I screamed through the tears of happiness, their saltiness coating my tongue as they slid down my cheeks and onto my lips.

"You don't know that!" I heard Landon shout, sounding much closer than Finn just had. Were they running after me? I couldn't bring myself to tear my eyes from the sight ahead to find out.

I could barely feel my feet as they made contact with the ground as I ran as fast as I could. It felt as if I was gliding through the air. The adrenaline pushed my famished, weakened body forward.

There was nothing else that I could see; everything around me became a blur as I darted toward Lia.

Toward my *sister*.

Suddenly, my eyes widened and my gut was overtaken with nausea as I realized that the closer I got to the beast, its rapid pace aimed directly at us wasn't slowing down.

FORTY-SEVEN

Elianna

"How are you holding up back there?" I called over my shoulder to Jace.

"Oh, never been better!" he shouted sarcastically in my ear over the winds that whipped around us as we soared through the sky.

I cackled softly in response as I glanced down toward the grassy fields below. We still hadn't come across anything yet. I half turned my body back, nearly head butting Jace as I peered over his shoulder to peek behind us.

The horses were doing a damn good job of keeping up with Nox. I almost couldn't believe it. They looked to be only a few miles behind us on the ground as they raced towards the threat that aimed to take away our peace—our home.

The idea of seeing Kellan again had rage surging through my veins. He tried to take my mate from me. He tried to trap, torture, and manipulate me into becoming his wife once he found out who I truly was—thinking I would ever be foolish enough to take him up on such a nauseating offer.

I would make him pay for everything he's ever done to those I love.

I gazed off in the distance for a few moments when suddenly my focus caught on a large, moving, dark mass on the open terrain ahead.

My eyes narrowed in on the mass of people marching towards us. Fury twisted my gut as I became consumed with the desperate ache for vengeance against those responsible for all the pain and suffering endured by my people.

I raised a surprisingly steady hand and pointed ahead. "There!" I said sternly, and Nox's wings halted in the air, hovering us in the clear sky.

Jace's body stiffened behind me, and he then leaned into my back.

"It appears we found them, sweetheart," he breathed wickedly as I felt him press a firm kiss to the back of my head while the wind tossed my hair around us both.

Those males in the distance, they were once my soldiers. They once took orders from *me*—respected me. And now here they were, so easily turned and ready to take not only my life, but that of millions of innocents as well.

My breathing turned heavy as the world around me froze. Flashes of distant memories rummaged through me, filled with nothing but the blood and ruin brought upon those the queen declared an enemy. My eyes narrowed in on the moving masses, and my jaw locked as the need to claim revenge for all those who suffered overwhelmed me.

My lip curled back into a predatory snarl. "Now!" I ordered, my voice booming through the sky.

Nox dove, plummeting towards the ground at lightning speed, aiming directly for the Islan army.

"Lia!" Jace called over the roaring whoosh of the winds. "What are you doing?! This wasn't the plan! We have to let our army know."

"No," I whispered, tears streaming across the sides of my temples, and I was unsure if it was from the racing wind or from my wrath.

"Elianna...*my Lia*," he pleaded, and an ache erupted in my chest. "Please listen to me. Call off Nox." He gripped my waist even tighter.

I whipped around to him. "I will *not* let a single person be harmed by them. They have suffered enough!" I shouted, and then whipped back to face forward once more.

"What are you going to do? Rain fucking hellfire down onto them?!"

I unsheathed my dagger from my thigh as my gaze narrowed back in on the approaching masses. "If it comes to that," I said, too quietly for him to hear.

We raced toward the ground below at record breaking speeds, and for a moment, I thought I could hear screams of terror ring out from them.

Good. Fucking *fear* me, you spineless bastards.

I had never ordered Nox to ignite his flames upon an enemy before; he had always been reactive to the situations at hand, reading not only my body language but also of those he deemed a threat.

My hand rose high, preparing myself to give Nox the first order to release his flames, when suddenly, a tiny blaze of fire appeared and separated itself from within the masses, running directly toward us, unyielding.

My breath caught, and my lungs nearly collapsed in my chest as realization enveloped me.

That beautiful blaze of red and orange hued hair reflecting in the midday sun wasn't just any brave rush of flames. It was *Avery*.

We were dangerously close to the ground now. I could faintly hear Jace bellowing behind me, but I couldn't comprehend his words as fear clogged my throat and wrapped itself around me.

"Nox, pull up," I croaked out, my words lost in the air as I stared down at my sister rushing toward me through the tall grasses.

He continued to dive. "Nox, pull up! Pull up!" Still nothing. *"PLEASE!"* I screamed desperately, the crack in my voice echoing through the sky.

At the last possible moment, Nox's wings shot out and leveled us out, allowing us to soar directly above the enormous group of clearly terrified fae.

My eyes locked with Avery's as we passed over her and I could see the tears streaming down her rosy, freckle-spattered cheeks as her joyous, relieved smile beamed up at us.

A sob left me as a smile simultaneously crept up my face while we circled the crowd below. I realized that this wasn't an army coming to destroy us at all. It was an army of *supporters*. Survivors. They had left Isla and traveled beyond the deadly forest to find me, and my siblings were amongst them. I couldn't believe it.

Jace reached around me and interlocked his fingers with mine, lifting my hand back towards his lips as he pressed it against them. "Change of heart?"

I let out an abrupt, nervous laugh as my opposite hand moved to wipe my tears. "You could say that."

He released my hand as Nox aimed for a spot to land, but I was too eager to get to them. I worked to unravel the safety straps from around my waist, contemplating slicing them open with my dagger when they wouldn't move quick enough. My hands shook with anticipation, making the act almost impossible.

Jace's arms shot out toward me. "Lia, we're almost there. Just wait!"

I half turned my head to face him. "You should know better than to tell me that." I smirked as I jumped up, finding my balance as I stood on my new saddle while Jace worked to bring me back down.

Once we were close enough to the ground that I was sure I wouldn't embarrassingly snap an ankle, I ran up the front of the saddle, onto Nox's shoulder and dove off of him.

I hit the ground running, barreling through the thick, lush grass and weeds as I made my way to Avery. She matched my pace, a look of determination plastered across her flushed face, and before I knew it, our bodies slammed into each other.

I wrapped her in the tightest embrace I could muster as we fell to our knees. The two of us were laughing and smiling uncontrollably as the crowd behind her hurried to us.

I wiped her tears away as she wiped my own, and we stared at each other in silence with childlike grins for several moments.

"Holy gods. You left Isla," I said, chuckling in disbelief.

She nodded rapidly. "Pretty crazy, huh?"

"I have so many questions," I answered in a hushed whisper.

"Gods, Avery. You're not the only one who wants a hug, you know!" I heard as footsteps came to a halt in front of us.

I looked up from her and saw Finn's silhouette form from the blinding sun as he stood directly behind her.

"Finn!" I screeched as I reached up and pulled him down to the ground with us. I threw my arms around both my siblings and held them tightly as we rocked back and forth, enjoying the embrace that none of us thought we would have ever again.

"I missed you guys so much," I whispered as I sniffled into Avery's shoulder.

She pulled away from my grip and held both of my arms as she took me in. "We missed you, too." She gave me a soft, grateful smile.

My heart leapt in my throat as a loud howl sounded off only feet away from us. My gaze whipped to the noise, and tears of happiness sprang from my eyes as I gasped out in shock at the sight of Nyra.

They brought her. They traveled all this way and even brought my wolf. She ran up to us, trampling them out of the way, and jumped up onto me. She placed her paws on my shoulders, forcing me down to the ground completely, while Avery and Finn continued to kneel, smiling as they watched us.

She licked my face continuously as I held her tightly to me and scratched her ears. "I missed you too, my girl." Tears threatened to burn my eyes again as she whimpered with joy.

Once she calmed down, we all rose to our feet as people approached us cautiously.

I turned and couldn't believe what my eyes beheld.

Veli, of all beings, was among them, and Landon. My heart skipped a beat as I scanned the crowd, desperately searching for one more familiar face that I was aching to see.

My lip trembled when I realized he was nowhere in sight.

My eyes met hers once more. "Lukas?" I asked, already knowing that I couldn't bear to hear the answer.

She sucked her bottom lip in between her teeth and shook her head. "This was all possible because of him, though. His final words were used to tell the kingdom who you truly are." She paused for a moment, her words becoming a whisper. "And they listened to him."

My lips parted and my eyes stung at what she had admitted to me. If it weren't for the absolute shock and adrenaline coursing through my body, the news would've sent me back down to my knees in anguish, but time for grief would hit me soon enough.

Someone cleared their throat behind me, and my ears perked up as I realized I had forgotten about Jace.

I twirled to face him and watched as he leisurely approached us, leaving Nox further back in the field, likely to avoid everyone screaming any more than they already had.

I smiled at him, joy beaming from me, and his face matched mine once our eyes met. I reached out my hand as he approached, and he took it and pulled me into his chest.

I turned to them. "Avery, Finn, this is—"

"The human mate!" Avery shrieked, cutting me off as she threw her arms around his shoulders and forced me out of the way.

An uncontrollable laugh left me. "Yes, that's him. His name is Jace." He raised a brow at me as if to say *she knows you have a mate, but not his name*...while he awkwardly hugged Avery back. I shrugged my shoulder in response.

"It is so very wonderful to meet you!" she said to him, eyes wide with curiosity.

"You too, and you must be Princess Avery," he said sweetly.

She took a step back from him and started fiddling with a rock on the ground with her foot. "Meh, I'm currently not very proud of that title. Avery will do." She shrugged.

Finn reached out his hand toward Jace. "I'm Finnian, Lia's brother."

My heart swelled as the words left him. It was as if the weight of the realm had lifted off my own shoulders now that everything was known and out in the open. Secrets no longer clouded my relationships with the ones I loved.

"You're my brother, too," Avery chimed in.

"Yes." Finn sighed. "How could I forget?"

Jace was laughing at them already. "It's a pleasure to meet you both."

He reached out for my hand once more and pulled me close to his side as his other hand patted the top of Nyra's head in greeting. "Before chaos ensues, I would like to personally thank you for saving her life while she was in the dungeons," he said.

Avery's eyes darted back and forth between us. "Of course," she choked out, and Finn offered him a curt nod with a smile.

"I'm sorry if we scared you with how fast we were soaring towards the ground..." I started. "We thought you were Kellan."

Darkness cloaked their gazes at the mention of his name.

"He may not be too far behind, but we can't know for sure," Finn said coldly.

I nodded quickly when suddenly the sound of stampeding hooves rumbled through the air. We all turned to face *our* army, that was now headed straight for us.

"How should we handle that?" I asked as I looked up into my favorite pair of hazel eyes.

"They were to await for our orders, but likely lost sight of us in the air, and are only now just seeing us on the ground. I'll take care of it," he said gently as he moved away from me and stalked straight toward the stampede, waving his hands aggressively in the air to get their attention.

I turned to face the crowd and Veli stepped forward, surprising me.

"Elianna," she greeted. "It's good to see you are still alive after all."

So charming, she was.

"Veli." I inclined my head to her. "I suppose you have had your hands full these past few weeks."

She rolled her eyes and grumbled, "You have no idea." She crossed her arms as she shot Avery and Finn a look.

"Gods, I eat a couple of velaeno berries, and it's like I'm enemy number one!" Avery whisper-shouted.

I turned to her, jaw gaping. "I *told* you about poisonous berries!"

Her cheeks flushed as she waved me off. "I don't want to talk about it."

"Hm," I huffed out as two of the horses that were racing towards us brought themselves to a slow trot, and then halted before us.

I looked up to see Gage beaming as he looked down at us from one of them as Zaela watched from the other. He swung his leg off his horse and jumped down, throwing his hand out for a handshake in Finn's face.

"Hello there. I'm Gage! I can see you've already met our lovely Lia," he said to them, and it sent Avery into a fit of giggles.

I cocked a brow at him. "Gage. Siblings. Siblings...Gage." I gestured to them each as I spoke.

Finn shook his hand, just as he had Jace's. Avery batted her eyelashes at him and shook his hand the moment Finn's left its grasp.

"Hi, I'm Avery! Are you a knight?" Her eyes were practically glowing with glee, and Gage's matched.

Oh, gods. My eyes flared as I watched them.

Gage got down on one knee and plucked a dandelion from the grassy field we stood in, handing it to her as he rose back to his feet. "My lady, Avery. I'll be whatever you need me to be." He gave her his charming smile.

Jace ran up to us, out of breath from being the only one without a horse. "For fuck's sake, Gage. That's Lia's sister." He threw his hand out in her direction.

His eyes lit up at what was said as if I hadn't just introduced her as my sibling, and his stare bore into hers. "Yes, and that means that she deserves a thousand more flowers than what I was just able to provide."

She twirled the dandelion between her fingers. "Thank you, Sir Gage."

I rolled my eyes playfully and turned away from them as Jace threw his arm over my shoulder.

"*That* I think we will need to be very careful of." He sighed.

I looked back at them and watched as they mingled and flirted harmlessly. My eyes moved to Finn as he remained off to the side, now near Veli, and he watched them warily.

"Maybe they both need that right now. I wouldn't worry too much about it."

"Uh-huh," he answered.

I grinned at him, but when I glanced up, my eyes locked with Zaela's as I caught her glaring at their interaction. She quickly looked away from me and started petting her horse. I focused my attention elsewhere but made a mental note to see what the hell that was about later in private.

My gaze wandered to my feet, where Nyra sat, staring at Nox curiously. Honestly, I didn't know how to feel about it. They had seen one another in the dungeons the day I had met Nox with Lukas, but they had never actually interacted with one another. My wyvern always had his eyes locked on me, making sure he knew where I was at all times, and I watched as his attention snagged on the enormous white wolf sitting on my boots.

"Come on, girl," I said, and she trotted alongside me as we carefully approached Nox.

He huffed out a breath of hot air at us, and I lifted a finger up to him. "This is Nyra. You have met her before," I stated, praying to all the Velyran gods that he understood me.

Nox tilted his head to the side curiously, and then Nyra mimicked his movements. He lowered his head towards the ground, hovering it between the height of my own and that of the wolf's.

"Easy," I whispered. They both looked to me and I carefully nodded, letting them know it was okay to trust one another.

Nyra sat down where she stood and began panting as she looked up at the wyvern, unafraid. Nox then mimicked her, leaning back on his own legs and continued to watch her curiously. Suddenly, she let out a howl of approval, making

Nox jump, but then he let out a few high-pitched chirp-like sounds—I was thankful it wasn't one of his deafening roars.

"Thank the gods you two like each other," I whispered as I turned on my heel and aimed back toward the awaiting crowd, the two of them following me.

Nox halted before the edge of the crowd, opting to linger in the distance. Once I arrived back at the gathering, I alerted all those who had fled that he wasn't to be feared, easing any lingering apprehension in the air.

After a while of mingling and introducing ourselves to people, my lips parted in awe as I observed them. There were hundreds of escapees here to support me. I knew there were hundreds of thousands of fae just in Isla alone, but support from anyone, especially those willing to risk their lives to show it, meant everything to me.

Jace and I decided it would be best if we flew ahead back to Ellecaster to alert the troops that remained that there was no longer a threat to be feared. As for those who had accompanied us here, any soldier on a horse would double up with a female or a youngling in order to travel home faster. By the looks of everyone who had accompanied them on the journey here, their aching feet were grateful.

I finally had my family back, and my heart threatened to explode with the overwhelming sense of joy that was now coursing through me.

FORTY-EIGHT
Elianna

It was nearly dawn the next day by the time the army neared the city gates. Everyone looked exhausted and irritable, and I wasn't entirely sure what to even *do* with them all. Did we have enough vacant space in the city?

As they came to a halt directly outside of the gates, I turned to my mate. "What do we do? We didn't exactly...plan for this."

He gave me a tiny smirk and reached out to tuck the front pieces of my hair behind my ear. "We'll figure it out. There are many empty rooms at the barracks and I'm sure after everyone gets some rest, we can call a city meeting and see if anyone has an open room in their homes for them. We will bring them beyond the mountains to the valley within the next few days."

I looked back at the group. Younglings clung to their mothers, some asleep in their arms. Other females desperately clutched the soldiers they rode with while trying to keep themselves sitting upright in the saddles. The males on the ground walking among them looked as if they had already been through war and back.

My heart clenched. I could only imagine what they had been through.

I cleared my throat. "Everyone! Please listen." I waited for a moment, and suddenly a terrifying number of anxious pairs of eyes were on me. "I know that you have been sitting within the unknown for weeks at this point, and I'm sure you are wondering about sleeping arrangements for the time being. Considering it is nearly dawn, and we were not expecting this...wonderful surprise of hosting you all, we will need you to bunker down in the barracks for now. The soldiers will accompany you there, and any remaining who could not find a bed will reside within the inns."

Murmurs of worry rang out, and I held up my hand to silence them. "The bill for the inns will come to me." I glanced at Jace and gave him an apologetic smirk that he answered with his own, knowing that I didn't have any coin of my own here. "We will figure out more suitable arrangements for everyone as soon as possible."

The crowd began to disperse as they exchanged nervous glances and walked through the gates to my back, following the soldiers' lead. I looked to Avery, who gave me a pretty smile as she walked up to me.

"And where will we be?" she asked, glancing between me and Gage.

I peeked over at Zaela, and watched as she eyed them warily. Interesting.

Jace stepped up to my side. "We have plenty of room for you in our home. You may have to double up in some rooms, but we do have the space, so you won't need to be with strangers," he said to them.

I watched as Landon's jaw locked, but he wouldn't meet my stare. Finnian noticed this as well, and a frown twisted his lips.

Oh gods. I'd need an update on those two later. I glanced at Avery, and she abruptly shook her head.

My eyes widened slightly as I huffed out a breath. I looked to Avery, Veli, Finn, and Landon and said, "Alright, everyone...follow us and we'll take you home."

My heart fluttered rapidly as the last word passed between my lips.

Home. We were all *finally* home.

Zaela opened the townhouse's door and immediately went to the fireplace to warm up the room. We all filed in behind her, Nyra included, and I couldn't help but smile as Avery's warm, honey-hued eyes lit up at the sight of the living space revealed.

"Oh, this is lovely," she said cheerfully.

"Bet you wouldn't have said that a month or two ago," Finn teased.

She reached out to punch him, but he dodged it. I was glad to see that they were still...well, *them*.

"Mind your manners, Finnian Valderre. Our friends' home is beautiful," she scolded him.

"Oh yes, I'm sure that it has nothing to do with having to sleep on the dirt covered ground the last few weeks." He laughed at her and she shot him a look with daggers in her eyes in response.

I tried to smother my chuckle, but it was no use.

"Yeah, I don't really give a shit if you like it or not. Feel free to go back to sleeping in the street for all I care. This is what we have," Zaela announced as she rose to her feet at the fireplace, dusting off some soot from her hands and turned to face us.

"So lovely, that one," Avery whispered to me, and my hand flew to smother a snort.

"Zae, don't be rude to our guests," Jace grumbled from behind me.

"She has a point," Veli chimed in from the doorway and Zaela's eyes flared in response.

We all turned slowly to look at Veli as she stared at Zaela from across the room. She shrugged a shoulder and lifted her eerie, long nails to her face, pretending to inspect them.

"You're all exhausting. When is the nice one coming back?" Avery asked, placing her hands on her hips.

"Oh, sure. *We're* exhausting," I heard Veli mumble behind me, and I was thankful it seemed that no one else did.

"If by the 'nice one' you mean Gage...he will be home when he's done letting the inn keepers know they will have an influx of guests for the time being," Zaela shot at her.

Oh, for fuck's sake. I was about to open my mouth to tell everyone to calm the hell down, but then Gage waltzed in through the front door.

Thank the gods.

"Ah." Zaela threw her arm in his direction. "Right on cue." She turned to sit in the chair next to the fireplace that was now roaring with flames.

I rubbed at my temples as Jace pressed a kiss to the side of my head and whispered in my ear, "Aren't you *so* happy the entire family is here now?"

I met his eyes, smirking, and batted him away in response.

"Hi, Sir Gage." Avery wiggled her fingers at him in greeting.

Gage bowed to her. "My Lady."

Zae scoffed loudly in the corner.

"Okay!" I shouted as I stormed toward the kitchen. "Who else needs some wine?!"

FORTY-NINE
Elianna

THE SECOND THE WINE slipped past my tongue, I instantly felt more at ease. After Jace closed the curtains to block out the blinding morning sun, he went around, passing everyone a glass as they settled into the living room. They all made themselves comfortable after an otherwise uncomfortable interaction.

Avery sat in the middle of Finn and Landon on the settee, and Zae was in her usual chair while Veli stood leaning against the side of the fireplace. Gage took a seat on the floor, and Jace did the same a few feet away. I wiggled my way between his legs on the ground and rested my back up against his chest, finally feeling as if we could all relax after an insane, entirely unpredictable day.

When I looked up and met my siblings' stares, their faces reflected nothing but shock at the sight of us. I winked at them as I took another sip of wine.

Nyra trotted over to us on the floor and licked my cheek. She then nuzzled up next to us in a ball and placed her big, fluffy head on my thigh. My hand moved to scratch behind her ears; she leaned into the touch and yawned. Gods, I missed her.

I took a swig of the wine and sighed. "So now that we're settled, where the hell do we begin?"

Avery's smile beamed, eyes lighting with eagerness. "How about we start from the very beginning?! Like how you somehow found your *mate!* And he is a freaking *human!*" she squealed with giddiness, but my eyes widened in horror at what she unknowingly revealed.

"Your. What?!" Zaela seethed from her chair in the corner, leaning down toward us on the floor, as her face twisted with fury.

I slammed my eyes shut and my lips pressed into a thin line. Jace gripped my wrist and gave it a small squeeze. When I opened my eyes, her stare bore straight through me. Through both of us.

Nyra let out a short growl in her direction, but Zaela seemed unfazed.

"Brother, what is she talking about?" Gage's voice echoed with hurt, which nearly killed me on the inside. "Lia?" he added.

I opened my mouth to speak, but I couldn't even find the words.

"We were obviously going to tell you," Jace started.

"When," Zaela demanded, cutting him off.

"We just haven't had the time to—" I said.

"Bullshit! Both of you!" she yelled, and Jace's body flinched behind me. Everyone else remained silent. "You haven't had the time? We are always together. We all *live* together. Yet you somehow found the time to tell them as you were rotting away in a dungeon or fleeing?! That doesn't even make sense!"

My lips parted as my eyes darted back and forth between hers, and then she continued. "And now the two of you are what? *Mates?* I've only heard stories, of course, but doesn't that mean your souls are bound together or some shit? When did you do this? Why."

"It wasn't a choice," I croaked out.

"Oh, so you're saying you wouldn't have chosen him if you had the choice?" she spat at me with pure venom as her head cocked to the side.

"That is *not* what she meant, and you know that," Jace said through his teeth.

Avery sucked in her bottom lip. "Oh, gods. I'm so sorry, Lia, I didn't know that they didn't—"

"That we didn't know? Oh, shut up, Princess. I've known you for mere hours, and I can tell that this is something you would just love to dangle in our faces," Zaela hissed.

That's it. That's fucking it.

I sat up from Jace's lap and my eyes flared as they met Zaela's. "You will *not* speak to her that way. If you're pissed at us, then take it out on *us*. Not her. Not ever her or Finn, Landon, Gage, *any* of them!" I shouted.

"Honestly, Zae, what the fuck has gotten into you?" My voice lowered into a whisper as I gave her a knowing look.

Ever since she laid eyes on my sister and Gage together, she had been lashing out. She didn't feel any love for Gage outside of their platonic friendship, so why would she be so upset about his flirting with Avery? I knew she didn't trust people she just met, but this was my *sister*. Was she worried about losing his friendship?

She stared at me coldly for a moment, and her chest rose and fell rapidly. Hurt flashed across her features, and I knew then that, in this moment at least, *that* was the true feeling she was trying to block out. Zaela was upset by us not telling them yet—she just didn't know how to handle it properly.

"We were going to tell you. *Of course* we were going to tell you. We just didn't know when or even how to say it. It's still very new, and sometimes I can't even process it myself," Jace said gently to her.

I watched as her features softened at his words and she leaned back in her chair, abruptly breaking our stare to look toward the fire. It was as if she couldn't even bear to look at us.

"When did this happen, brother?" Gage asked, letting out a forceful breath as he brought his glass to his lips.

Jace began to make comforting, circular motions on my back as I remained seated between his legs. "I don't know when it happened. It just did. Lia knows more about it than I do, but it explains why I have always felt very...*strongly* about her. And also why I couldn't kill her on the numerous chances I had when we first met."

Avery let out a brief gasp at what he said, but the corner of my lips tilted at the memories.

I looked up at them. "I could feel his pain. The entire time I could, but I didn't realize it was his until the morning after that horrible attack on the village, when they..." I hesitated. "When they sliced his face."

All of their eyes widened. Well, except for Veli's. With her arms crossed and a small smile playing at the corner of her lips, she watched the drama unfold before her, clearly amused.

"You *felt* that?" Gage asked.

"I did. And that, combined with Kellan saying that I smelled like him...it erased any doubt I had in that moment. Our scents had merged. We were mates, and us...coming...together..." I glanced up awkwardly as I intertwined my fingers. "Locked that bond into place."

I bit my bottom lip and held it between my teeth as they continued to stare at me. Finn looked like he was going to vomit, but Avery winked and started to flutter her eyebrows at me.

"I wish you told us." Gage sounded so, so sad. I couldn't take it. A single tear slipped from me, but I wiped it away immediately.

"Gage, I had no idea. I didn't know until she found her way back to us, and we've been figuring it out since," Jace told him as he pulled me back into his chest.

"So basically, you two are stuck together, no matter what?" Gage said with a half laugh.

I smirked at him. "Essentially."

"Have you two worked on the connection between you at all?" Veli asked, earning everyone's attention. The amusement that was in her stare only moments ago had morphed into curiosity. "You stated you feel his pain and emotions. Have you learned to decipher his from your own?"

"Barely," I whispered.

"We are still working through that together," Jace added. "It is all still very new."

I cleared my throat. "By all means, Veli, if you're able to teach us, that would be appreciated."

"Mating bonds are capable of expanding beyond emotions and senses, for that is just the very surface of your link to one another."

My eyes flared at her words, and the beat of Jace's heart picked up, slamming against his chest as I leaned into him.

Veli continued. "However, specific rituals must be performed to access such potential." All of us stared at her in confusion, and her violet stare leisurely wandered over everyone in the room. She cleared her throat. "A discussion for another day. This is not the time or place for such things."

The townhouse was silent as we all watched her lift her talons to her face. It was as if she was dismissing our stunned looks at what she had just revealed.

"Wait a second," Avery uttered a moment later, bringing the room's attention to her. "So, how are you mates if he is a human?"

"Gods, Avery." Finn rolled his eyes. "That is none of your business."

"What," she hissed at him. "It's an honest question." She shrugged.

My heart began palpitating as panic took over me. I was unsure of how Jace would react to discussing his lineage with them, given that they had just met.

To my surprise, he chuckled softly. "I am a halfling. We will just leave it at that if that's okay with you."

I gave her a warning look to just drop the subject, and she giggled nervously. "Oh, of course. I apologize for prying." Then she shot me a fake, angry look. "How is it that the female who didn't even *believe* in mates gets one, huh?"

"Trust me, I thought the same." I huffed out a laugh.

It was quiet for a few minutes, aside from the crackling of the fireplace, while we all processed what had just been revealed. Guilt slowly consumed me after how Gage and Zaela reacted, even if she was completely out of line.

"What happened after I escaped?" I asked quietly. I looked up and watched as my brother and sister exchanged glances, and then both of their gazes drifted to Veli.

Finn licked his lips. "We were only able to flee the city because of Veli's magic." Jace's wariness erupted down the bond, and my eyes then glanced over to Zae and Gage, who watched with wide eyes at the mention of her power. "However, after you were ripped away from us in the chaos of Kai's wedding, Kellan locked us in our rooms. Avery found a way to escape using the tunnels in the castle."

I glanced over at her and gave her a nod of approval, accompanied by a wicked grin, which she reciprocated.

"We grabbed Landon at the stables," Finn continued, and I noticed Landon's knee began to anxiously bounce where he sat. "And then we hid out at Veli's. The next day, there were...trials."

Veli scoffed. "Trials." She started shaking her head. "There was a mass hanging of the entirety of the castle staff."

My eyes flared. *"WHAT?!"* I bellowed as I sat up once more, almost spilling my wine everywhere.

Avery's lips trembled. "They're gone, Lia. All of them. It was horrifying, and they made the entire city watch it occur. We hid within the crowd."

She continued when silence answered her. "The handmaiden that helped us find Veli that night we brought her to you...her name was Lillian. She admitted to assisting sympathizers right before she was hung. I knew something had been off about her that night we met, but I couldn't figure out what it was."

"Why would she help you if she knew you were the prince and princess?" I asked.

Avery shrugged. "She whispered something about us being different from the others. Lillian must have sensed we weren't like Mother or Kai."

Jace huffed out a breath behind me. "There had been reports of executions, but not that it was the castle staff. I knew of Lillian," he admitted, and everyone's gaze swung to him. "She would often send us updates regarding whispers within the castle. She is a terrible loss for us."

The entire staff. All of them were hung in the city square. Lukas must've been among them since Avery said his final words to the realm were used to declare my true identity.

My heart painfully twisted as the thoughts of watching his body hang from a noose flooded my mind.

"How did you escape? I know you said by magic but..." My voice cracked. "How the hell did all of you get out of the city unscathed? What kind of power could even aid you in that?"

If Kai went to the lengths of having everyone hung, security must've been set tighter, too.

The three on the settee slowly looked to Veli, who appeared as if she would rather gauge her own eyes out than be here for this conversation.

She let out an abrupt sigh. "Your nosy sister found a spell book that never should've been opened. Never mind *used*," she said sharply in their direction. "Horrible mistakes were made, but we managed to get out. That's what matters."

Shock rippled through me. What in the realm did that even mean?

"Spell book?" Zaela asked cautiously, the first thing she had said since her outburst. "What, are you a witch or something?" she bravely sassed at Veli.

"Sorceress," Avery, Finn, and I said in tandem, mimicking what they had both done to me all those weeks ago when I was locked in the cell.

Veli crossed her arms once more and looked at the ceiling. "Gods."

Curiosity and caution slipped into Zaela's stare as she watched the witch intently—the boys looked slightly terrified of her.

"So, what you're saying is you used the scary, forbidden spell book to get out?" I asked.

She shot me a look, and I nearly jumped back farther up Jace's lap. "Is this a joke to you, Elianna?"

"Sorry," I mumbled. "I am just trying to get a sense of everything that went on. I haven't quite grasped the full extent of your power yet, and I just want to try to understand it. Especially if it could aid us in this war."

The witch's gaze narrowed in on me, her lips pressing into a thin line. Veli then muttered words I could barely understand under her breath and her eyes flashed their golden glow—a second later, shadows emanated from her, wrapping around her like a second skin. Power radiated through the room as they expanded, hovering as if they were her guardian.

Nyra let out a whine and ran up the stairs, snapping at the shadows as she rushed past.

"Holy gods," Zaela breathed, pushing herself further back into her chair as if trying to take a step away from the witch.

Gage's eyes were so wide that I thought they would pop out of his skull as he slowly reached for the hilt of his sword. Jace went rigid behind me as his grip around my waist intensified, and I could feel the beat of his heart as it quickened with nerves.

Veli smirked, but it was void of benevolence. "You cannot fathom the immense power that resides within me, concealed beneath my skin. I have told you once before, Elianna; it is not wise for me to use recklessly...for magic calls to its kin. Any amount of substantial power runs a risk. To answer your question, yes. I made an exception and used the book to get us out of the city, and guards were killed. Now tell me, Heir of the Realm, are you happy with that?"

My eyes were fixated on her in a trance, watching her shadows swirl around her as she stood in our living room. Everyone was silent, waiting for my answer as I contemplated everything she had revealed—everything she had done for me and my people, even if she was reluctant to do so.

"If the guards were going to harm you and those you fled with, then yes. I fully fucking support what you did, Veli. And thank you for doing so."

She went still, looking rattled by my answer. Her shadows then leisurely retreated to her, seeping back into the palms of her hands as she held them open at her sides.

"Well, the people with us did not agree." She looked away from me. "In fact, they're terrified of me now. No one would allow me to heal any injuries on our journey here. We lost many along the way as well. Some fled due to fear, and others when we came under attack by creatures of the forest. Your siblings wished for me to aid every situation with magic, but it would have only frightened the masses more."

My stare remained on her, and I couldn't help but feel awful. Veli, who rarely showed any emotion other than annoyance, seemed genuinely bothered by the escapees resisting her aid.

"How many were lost?" I asked in a whisper.

"Too many," she answered, and my heart ached as I realized how traumatizing their journey here must've been.

"Do you still have the book?" Her eyes shot to mine once more, and I swore it was as if I was a youngling again, anxious beneath her violet stare. "Okay." My hands shot up in a defensive gesture. "Never mind. We can discuss the book more some other time."

She huffed out a breath at my words and we were sitting in silence once more, only now it didn't feel nearly as tense.

"I'm just happy you're all here. I don't care what it took. You're all safe," I said as I brought my glass to my lips.

My own words hovered over me for a moment. They weren't all safe. Lukas wasn't safe. He had been forced to pay the ultimate price. He knowingly sacrificed himself to get me out of that dungeon. Avery had even whispered to me what his very last words had been. Lukas knew his life was forfeit, and still, all he wanted to do was make sure my claim to the throne was protected—and he used his final moments to tell the entire kingdom that I was the true heir of Velyra.

My jaw locked as those thoughts consumed my mind, and a pounding in my ears drowned out the noise of the crackling fireplace. As the pressure in my clenched teeth intensified, my nostrils flared. Anger surged through me as I thought of what the crown had done to my friend—my mentor and protector.

I hadn't realized how tightly I had been gripping the wine glass until it suddenly *shattered* in my hand, making everyone gasp.

The only hope I desperately clung to was that they burned his body, and he was now at peace. Those who held the realm in their grasp and wore the Velyran crown atop their treasonous heads were evil incarnate in every sense, but surely they burned the bodies of those they murdered that day.

I looked at my shaking hand as the features on my face relaxed and watched as blood trickled down my wrist—tiny shards of glass remained sticking out of the palm of my hand.

"Lia! Are you okay?" Jace yelped as he shot up from behind me, his arms maneuvering around my waist as he gently gripped my wrist. "What happened? Gage, go get some rags, please."

He held my arm lightly and began to carefully pluck out the shards of glass, but I remained silent until Gage came up and started soaking up the wine and blood on the floor surrounding us.

"I'm so sorry. My mind wandered a little, and I didn't realize how...tightly I was gripping it."

"It's okay, sweetheart," he whispered as he pressed my bloody palm to his lips. He then wrapped it in one of the towels to stop the bleeding.

"Are you sure you're alright?" Avery's anxious eyes bore into me.

"Yes." The lie slipped through my teeth in a raspy voice, and I cleared my throat. "I'm fine. It was just an accident."

Glancing around the room, I felt uneasy as I sat beneath their concerned stares.

And then my gaze met that of the witch.

FIFTY
Elianna

"Your wrath wears on you, Elianna," Veli hissed, earning everyone's attention. "Your fury pulsates through you. I can scent it—taste it on my tongue."

My jaw locked at her words, and Jace's eyes flared as she spoke this in front of them.

I worked to hide my irritation. "I don't know what you mean."

Her violet stare roamed over me slowly. "Reckless girl. I do not know where your anger just stemmed from, but it is there, sizzling beneath your skin. Is it the weight you now feel from your rightful crown, or is it the realization of what has been done and what must come next?"

She huffed out a breath and then spoke once more. "Tell me, Heir of the Realm, do you even know the truth of your heritage and why it is so important for you to take back your throne? You have already stated you do not know the depths of your bond. Your lack of knowledge is becoming bothersome." Veli's stare then swept over everyone in the room. "Do any of you know the genuine history of our world? Or has it truly been lost to both of your races?"

All of us stared at her, unblinking in silence.

Veli scoffed. "None of you even realize how this world came to be, how *you* came to be. It is alarming how indifferent both those of mortal and fae have become."

"Veli," I spoke out, my voice stern as I clutched the rag to my still bleeding hand. "You have been in this world centuries longer than those who stand before you. If you have a lesson on Velyran history for us, by all means, state it."

A click of her tongue sounded, and she stood there unmoving, appearing as if she was in deep thought. She then raised a taloned finger. "Perhaps it would be better if I showed you all instead."

A violet flash filled the room, stemming from her eyes, and suddenly, we all stood within a heavy mist. I leapt up from the floor, jaw gaping in shock. Jace brought himself to his feet, trying to pivot himself in front of my body in a protective stance as the others also rose to stand. Heavy breaths filled the air as nerves and tension rose.

The mist was so thick we could barely see each other, and the light from the roaring flames within the fireplace had been swallowed—the only source of light shone from the witch's stare as she swirled her arm in the vapor.

"Veli," her name was a whisper as it left me in awe and terror.

"There once was a time when Velyra was only roamed by the gods," her voice sounded, but it was ancient and all-knowing—that of the healer I grew up fearing, but also somehow utterly more bone-chilling.

Moving paintings formed within the mist, swirling as if they came from a distant memory, depicting a scene before our very eyes.

She continued. "The true mother of the gods, Terra, goddess of earth and life, was the first of her kind, stemming from nothing but divine power." A being with flowing dark hair formed within the mist, glowing with a supernatural grace as if the light of the very world was forged directly from her. "She roamed this realm, and all others, until loneliness settled into her bones, casting her raw power to create others like her. Soon enough, Velyra was flooded with gods—Terra serving as their primal. Their mother and monarch."

The scene Veli's otherworldly voice described played before us in the mist—Velyra forming and expanding before our very eyes, and beautiful, ancient beings roaming the lands. My eyes tore from the scene to study the faces of everyone else in the room, and from what I could make out between the foggy haze, everyone was just as entranced as I was.

"But as centuries passed, the gods' inflated egos demanded them to create beings themselves, for they wished to be adored and treasured for their power, just as Terra had been by them. Thus came the deities—the children of the gods."

My eyes flared as she continued. Everyone knew who and what the children of the gods were, but it appeared that the reason for their creation had been lost. They were not bred for love, but for oppression. The original gods of our realm birthed lesser gods to rule over.

"With the passage of time, the deities found themselves harboring the same resentment and sorrow towards their parents and rulers, mirroring the emotions once held for the mother goddess. The deities possessed even less magic than those who came before them, making them exactly what their parents had intended them to be—a people to govern. And then the war between gods commenced."

Jace's arm wrapped around my waist, pulling me closer to him as if one of the beings formed from the mist would reach out and pull me into the scene before us.

"However," Veli continued. "It was not yet a war of blood, but of power. What comes to be when all who roam the earth desire to be obeyed? They continue to make lesser beings to reign over, dwindling down the magic that was once plentiful in the realm."

"Fae and mortals." The whisper left me without permission.

"The gods no longer wished to breed their children, but conjure them from their power—morphing them into obedient servants. They approached their mother goddess with this, begging for a kernel of her power to do as she had with them, and create a new people to love, convincing her it would be what was best for the realm. After years of consideration, Terra allowed them to will these beings into light, for after all, she was the mother goddess of life."

I swallowed, the noise audible, echoing through the scene before us as everyone else remained eerily quiet while we listened and watched intently.

The mist swirled, transporting us within a thick expanse of trees—the Sylis trees. Terra stood before a cluster of gods and held her hand out before her, where a blinding light erupted from her fingertips.

All of us took a hesitant step away as if we were truly part of the history playing before us.

Light burst as if it came from the sun itself, and a figure formed before her—the terrain's soil rose, the shadows of the trees drifted, the dew from the earth hovered, and soon the form became a tangible being.

A being of pristine grace and lethal beauty—a being with pointed ears and sharpened canines.

The first of the fae.

"For you see, Elianna..." Veli's voice startled me from my trance as it came from the mist. "The realm responds to your bloodline, for you are a descendant of the first of the fae—the only lineage that Terra herself conjured."

"Holy hell," Avery breathed, and I mindlessly nodded in agreement as my lips parted in disbelief.

"This is insanity," Jace stated from my side, but Veli shushed him, and everyone went silent once more. Shock and awe reverberated through him, coursing down the bond.

The scene before us changed once more, and the witch continued her story. "It did not take long for the gods to conjure more of the fae, mimicking what their mother had displayed with her blessing. Soon, the realm was overrun with those grateful to have been created by the all-powerful Velyran gods."

"What about the humans?" Zaela's voice sounded, and Veli's eyes flashed.

"The deities feared that they would dwindle away, become extinct in their world since they were no longer desired by their makers—they had even become *hunted*—killed for sport. So they did what any jealous, desperate fool would and worked to conjure their own. Only the deities did not—"

"They did not possess the same magic as their parents," I finished for her on a breath.

"Precisely." The witch's wicked grin shone through the mist. "Thus, the creation of the mortal race. Ordinary beings that lacked any form of magic with a significantly weaker lifespan. They were flawed and easier to kill—just as their makers had been from their own."

Her glowing, violet stare then slid to mine, peering through the haze. "And this was the beginning of the end of the gods' war."

A flash in the mist illuminated everyone's appalled faces, and suddenly the scene contained nothing but a realm engulfed in flames. Beasts of nightmares were conjured from the ashes—the Sylis creatures. Wyverns, centaurs, orcs, banshees, and countless unnamed horrors burst from the forest's soil.

"Terra was furious at what had commenced in Velyra. Her children had lied to her and now worked to destroy their own kin by creating armies of lesser beings to spill their blood. It was not what she agreed to, and she would not stand for it—for after all, she was the goddess of *life*."

Veli sucked in a breath, as if she didn't wish to unveil the next scene from our lost history. "The gods heard of her wrath and knew that they would be punished. Some bowed before Terra at her feet, begging for forgiveness, while others refused. Creatures of malevolence were brewed by gods as such, including the creation of the very first High Witch—hidden on enchanted isles they forged within the sea."

Her stare moved to Avery and then back to me.

"These wicked gods knew their time had run out, and Terra's damnation stalked them in the night. So, they bound a book of malice with the skin of their captured children and hid it within the realm before they were caught in her wrath."

"*Tinaebris Malifisc*," Avery breathed, and my eyes flared.

That must have been the book they spoke of earlier—the book that helped them escape.

"Aye," Veli answered, and the light in her eyes dimmed as the misty haze that cloaked the room began to disburse.

My gaze peered around the space—all I was met with were wide eyes and gaping jaws.

"Then what?" I asked quietly as the scene before us vanished completely.

"Terra eventually caught and banished the ungrateful gods and deities from this realm, leaving the creatures conjured here to start a new world, a new life. The mother goddess then crowned her one fae creation as King of Velyra, before she vanished herself. However, the hate that stemmed in the hearts of both mortals and fae persisted, thanks to their makers, causing you to remain at odds with each other even thousands of years later."

I blew out a shaky breath. "Our hatred for each other was not even our own. And it has cost millions of lives over the centuries."

"Indeed," the witch said and then sucked on her tooth. "While the gods may no longer enter our world, they occasionally peer into it, still holding some form of power over Velyra and their creations within it. Rumor claims they peer through a rift, a looking glass into our realm, from wherever Terra had banished them to. It is how their influence is still felt and feared, and also how they manage to whisper to their favored beasts when they wish to wreak havoc from afar."

Avery and Finn's heads snapped toward the witch. "The prophecy!" my sister shrieked and my eyes widened, but I remained bolted where I stood.

Veli crossed her arms. "Exactly."

"Prophecy?" I whispered, eyes darting back and forth between them all. Jace went rigid at my side.

They all stood there and explained everything regarding the prophecy they had uncovered before their journey to come find us. How our father's untimely death had set everything into motion—Kai's reign brought by blood and malice, strangers of kin, and our once enemies weeping for the rightful, promised queen of the realm—*me*.

The gods had placed this into the minds of their creations—among them had been Veli, and the crone that caught our attention in the village.

"That is...a lot to take in," I managed to get out, my voice hoarse with disbelief as I shifted on my feet.

"I'm not even sure those are the right words," Gage said softly, eyes wide as they remained on the witch.

Jace's hand began making comforting circles on the small of my back as he remained at my side. "And you're sure of all this?" he asked.

Veli scoffed. "Why would I waste my breath if it was not our world's truth?"

"He didn't mean to imply that you were being untruthful. I think we are all just in shock," I defended my mate. "You have known this for centuries, Veli. We have known for mere minutes."

Her nostrils flared. "Yes, well, it is a shame that the information and history of your own world have become lost to you." She tapped a talon on the outskirts of her opposite arm.

As I looked around the room, I could see the exhaustion etched on everyone's faces, overshadowing the lingering wariness from her words. Distant, bloodshot eyes were all I was met with. The only noise to be heard was the crackling embers that remained in the fireplace until a yawn sounded from Gage.

"Perhaps we should all try to get some sleep. It's been a long night, and I'm sure everyone who accompanied you here will sleep through the day anyway," I suggested.

They all nodded in unison as they went to move, half of them groaning as their bones ached and cracked from their journey.

"I don't know how any of us will be able to sleep after *that*," Zaela muttered, and I was inclined to agree.

I cleared my throat. "There's an empty room down here." I gestured to the door between where we stood and the hall that led to the kitchen. "And two upstairs," I offered.

Veli wasted no time and hurried to the door beyond the living room. She opened it, revealing the newly furnished bedroom, and stepped inside, slamming the door behind her as if she was running from the mayhem she spoke of only minutes prior.

Well, that answered who would get that room. I worked to push out the memory of the scene she played before us and then turned to the remaining three.

"There are two empty rooms upstairs. So, unfortunately, for now, two of you will need to share." I gave them a sympathetic smile.

"Does one of the rooms have two beds?" Landon asked, breaking his silence. "I can bunk with Avery."

My eyes widened. All thoughts of what had just occurred faded, and I didn't miss the flash of hurt that splintered across Finn's face.

What in the realm happened between the two of them?

"They each have one bed. We will have to get a second bed if you cannot bear it until we leave in a few days. For now, you'll have to make do."

Gage raised a hand. "I would never mind sharing my room with Av—"

He was cut off by Jace reaching up and slamming his arm back down to his side as he shot him a look.

"Avery will have her own room," he grumbled at Gage, and I watched my sister's hand fly to her mouth to smother a laugh.

Jace moved to Landon. "If it truly bothers you to share with Finn, I can grab some blankets for the settee for now."

"That will work, thank you," he answered politely.

Jace gave him a quick nod and walked down the hallway to grab what would be needed for him.

Interesting.

I gave both Finn and Avery a look as I motioned for them to follow me up the stairs.

FIFTY-ONE
Elianna

I KICKED FINNIAN'S NEW bedroom door closed behind the three of us once Zaela and Gage passed by, moving to their own rooms.

I turned around and rested my back up against the door, crossing my arms as I stared at my brother.

"What the hell is going on with you and Landon? Last I saw the two of you, you couldn't keep your hands off of each other." I raised a brow.

He flinched at my demand to know his business, and reached up, cupping the back of his neck anxiously as he refused to meet my stare.

"Things changed." He shrugged.

"Things changed?" I mimicked.

He threw his hands out at his sides. "Yes, sometimes that happens, Lia! Gods, now I have *two* overbearing older sisters."

An aggravated chuckle left me. "You always did. You just didn't know."

He sat down on his new bed and threw his body back—his head bounced off of the mattress at the force of it.

I glanced at Avery and gestured to him. "Well, clearly, I won't be getting anything useful out of him, so give me the details."

She sucked her bottom lip between her teeth and squirmed where she stood for a moment, her eyes darting back and forth between the two of us.

Finn sat up rapidly and shoved his finger in her direction. "Don't. You. Dare," he seethed. "It's not your business to tell."

She blew out a breath and looked back at me. "They're so freaking *dramatic*," she drawled.

"Clearly," I answered, placing my hands on my hips.

"Sorry, Finn," she said, earning an annoyed huff from him, and then she turned her attention back to me.

"Kai attacked Matthias." My body jolted at her words. "Landon saved the horse, but Finn wouldn't save Landon from Kai's wrath." She clapped her two hands forcefully and rubbed them together. "Done. There it is! Happy?" She glared at the two of us, but then shot Finn a sympathetic look.

I was going to vomit. "What do you mean Kai attacked my horse?!"

Finn stood up then. "It was just a brand. He knew you were against it, and this was shortly after you left Isla on Kellan's ship."

Just a brand didn't make me feel any better.

My brows furrowed. "And what happened then?"

"Nothing!" he gasped.

"And that's the problem," Avery chimed in, but I whipped in her direction and shushed her, hoping Finn would tell me his side of the story himself.

"Finnian." My voice softened, and he looked up at me. "What happened?"

He sighed. "There was nothing I could do. You know Kai. You know how he is. When Landon stepped in and defended Matthias, Kai was extremely livid. He had the lords that always follow him around hold me back as he pressed the brand and held it to Landon's chest until it nearly hit muscle and bone. He then denied him a healer, knowing he would seek a hidden one in the city."

My mouth popped open. Kai was a fucking psychopath.

"So you were held back, and Landon is still angry with you months later?"

"It appears that way, Lia." He sounded so defeated. "Perhaps it didn't help that I avoided him for weeks after that, though."

And there it was.

"Well then, I guess not." I sighed.

"We had to beg him to come with us when we escaped the castle and hid at Veli's. He was upset with us until we watched the hangings, realizing he would've met the same fate," Avery said.

That he would have.

"And your journey here?" I asked, not caring which one of them answered.

Avery looked at Finn, giving him the chance to speak, but he wouldn't.

"He stepped up and helped *a lot*. It was amazing, actually. Whether it was helping find shelter, comforting people along the way, or hunting for food, he definitely made sure he was useful," she said.

"And too busy to talk to me," Finn whispered sadly.

Her eyes snapped to him and then looked at me as she pursed her lips. "They constantly stare at each other. Landon's too proud to talk to him first, and Finnian's just a chicken-shit."

"Avery!" he gasped.

Okay, I've had enough.

I turned and yanked the door open behind me and obnoxiously stormed halfway down the stairs. My stare landed on Jace as he placed blankets and a pillow on the settee while Landon hovered behind him.

Both of their eyes looked up at me as I stood there staring at them. I lifted my finger and pointed in their direction. "You. With me. Now," I said sternly, and both of them slowly pointed to their own chests, looking extremely confused.

"I think she means you," Jace whispered to Landon.

"Well, that's terrifying," Landon choked out.

"I heard that!" I called back to them as I stalked back up the steps.

They both followed, and I walked back into Finnian's room and watched as his eyes widened—his cheeks flushed as he noticed Landon entering the room behind me. Jace leaned up against the doorframe and observed from the hall.

"I didn't mean *you* should come, too," I whispered, giving him a look. His eyes flared with amusement.

"Avery." I gestured to the doorway. "Would you mind stepping out of the room?"

She rolled her eyes. "I'm the one who's been dealing with their nonsense for months, and I don't even get to see them kiss and make up?" she huffed as she moved past Jace and into the hall.

"I will be right out," I called to her over my shoulder.

I turned back to the boys before me. "Listen, if you plan to hold any sort of power within my court, then you need to figure your shit out," I shot at them, surprising even myself with the words.

"You want us in your court?!" Avery shouted with glee from down the hallway.

"Mother of the gods," I muttered, rubbing my temples.

"You want me..." Landon pointed to himself, looking stunned. "In your court?"

"Not if you are all going to sit here and act like younglings." I crossed my arms.

Silence blanketed the room in response.

Finn gulped from where he sat on the bed. "I'm sorry, Landon."

I held up my hand to pause him. "This should be between the two of you. I just wanted to make sure this conversation was had, no matter where it brings you. Though, of course, I hope it is better than where your relationship currently lies."

Landon turned to me. "Thank you, Your Majesty."

I tensed in response to him, and I cleared my throat. "Landon, you can still call me Lia." I smiled softly. "But of course, as I said, this is between the two of you. You need to figure it out, though. Things are only going to get more complicated as this war continues. I need everyone sharp and ready. Always."

He nodded. "Of course."

My nod mimicked his. "Then I will see you both in the morning."

Turning from them, I moved past Jace in the doorway, and he clicked the door shut behind us.

We both came face-to-face with my sister. "Your court?" she asked with a wicked grin.

I blew out a breath and held my hand out to her. "There will be more time to talk about that, but for now, I am exhausted and we all need to rest. It's time to see your own room."

At this point, it was nearly midday, and none of us had gone to bed since arriving back in Ellecaster with the rebels.

"And which room is Gage's?" Avery asked, sounding anything but innocent, as she took my hand and paraded down the hall with me.

"Oh, I'm *so* not telling you that," I answered with a snort.

Jace's steps faltered behind us at her question, and I couldn't help the instigating smirk that crept up my face.

Finnian

I stared at Landon as the door clicked shut behind the others, leaving the two of us alone for the first time in what seemed like months.

His eyes bore into mine from across the room, making the uneasiness I felt intensify instantly. My nerves had me picking at my nails and chewing on the inside of my cheek as I sat beneath his stare.

I cleared my throat. "Landon, I—"

"Don't." He held up a hand, halting me. "You've had plenty of time to speak with me. Why now? Because Lia is forcing your hand into it?"

That was what he thought? That I was only apologizing because of my sister?

"Landon, that is anything but true. I have tried to work up the courage to see you on many occasions. *Several* times, but I couldn't do it. I was too..."

"Proud?"

"Embarrassed," I whispered. "Not of you, never of you. I was embarrassed of Kai, what he had done and how I reacted in the moment. Not sticking up for you. Not being able to help or protect you. All because I was a coward, afraid of my own kin."

My eyes slowly rose to meet his again, and his features had softened, threatening to make my knees buckle.

"I should've returned that very night with Veli or another hidden healer and dealt with Kai. He threatened your life, and in that moment and the following days, I assumed you hated me for being related to such a wicked male. I caused your injuries by not wearing a proper mask of indifference."

Landon blinked. "I have always known your brother to be cruel. We had spoken of it many times and the possible consequences."

I blew out a breath. "Yes, well, I just needed you to know that if given the chance, I would absolutely change everything about that day. You deserved nothing of what was dealt to you. And seeing you step up for those who fled, and become somehow an even more admirable male, has just made me very proud to have once considered you...well, *mine*. Even if that is no longer the case."

We stared at each other in unnerving silence before I went to move past him, toward the door.

I anxiously cleared my throat. "You can have the bed. I will sleep downstairs. I just needed you to hear and know the truth."

Landon pivoted alongside me and grabbed my arm as it was reaching for the doorknob. He continued to face forward, refusing to look at me.

"Stay," he whispered hoarsely. "Just...stay."

My heart raced in my chest, and I desperately tried to calm my nerves as the hope that he had actually forgiven me threatened to make me collapse.

I turned, and when our eyes finally met, he threw his arms around me and embraced me in the tightest hug that I had been desperate for these past weeks.

"Anything can happen in the coming months. Gods forbid we lose this war...I would rather not carry the weight of regret and allow my stubbornness to prevent me from forgiving you."

As the words left him, I allowed the overwhelming sense of relief to crash into me as I tightened my hold on him once more.

FIFTY-TWO

Kellan

I NEEDED TO GET out of this fucking forest.

My hand moved to smash a bug nearly the size of my fist against my neck as its irritating buzz sounded around me. I grumbled as I wiped its guts that clung to my hand onto my filthy pants.

More than anything, I wished we could have taken a gods-damn ship like the last time I had to drag Elianna back to Isla. We just never thought that they would've made it this far inland. And now we were stuck walking through these eerie woods the past several days, which were even worse under the night sky. It was difficult to see, even with our fae sight, as we continued to travel in the darkness, only using the slim amount of moonlight peeking in between the leafy canopy, and a few torches throughout the army traveling at our backs.

Our carriages of supplies continually got stuck on the roots that protruded from the forest floor. Sometimes, I swore I saw the roots move out of the corner of my eye as if the forest was trying to ensnare us within it. We had even been forced to leave some of the wagons behind, the soldiers unable to heave them over the elements we were forced to travel through. The horses were constantly on edge, along with the entire armada.

They could be anywhere at this point. The traitors, the prince and princess, Lia...shit, they could even be dead. Their bones feasted on by one of the beasts that roam through these trees and we would never know.

"Adler," Kai shouted at me, forcing my lip into a snarl. "The soldiers seem to think that we will be beyond the forest in a day's time."

I half turned to him and watched amusingly as he clung to Gallo's saddle, desperately trying to not fall off of it as the horse worked its way around the maze of lifted roots.

"How lovely." I gave him an abrupt smile.

"Well?"

My jaw ticked. "Well, what, Prince?"

"Easy, Captain," Callius hissed from my opposite side.

"Well, do you think that they are correct?" he growled at me.

"Callius is much more familiar with these trees than I am." I nodded to him. "Answer our future king."

I could feel his stare, but I refused to meet it. Appearing as unbothered as possible by this entire interaction.

Callius cleared his throat. "That is what we are hoping for, Prince."

"This is ridiculous," he hissed. "I never should have come along with you brutes. The only interesting thing that occurred was finding that small group of them in that field and slaughtering them for their disobedience. Everything else has been either disgusting or boring."

"Now, now, Prince Kai. To be a successful king and ruler, you must know your soldiers. Know how they work, how they move and calculate. That is how you gain their respect and allegiance."

Kai's face morphed into something animalistic at Callius' words. I watched their interaction from the side, wholly amused by the show they were putting on for Vincent and me as he rode up behind us. I shot him a smirk.

"Or," Kai spat. "They will respect me because I'm their fucking *king*."

"So, your only plan is to rule by putting fear in your own soldier's hearts," Callius said to him. "The general masses, I understand, but it is your powerful fleets that will ultimately secure victory in this war. It would be wise to treat them well."

"I plan to rule by any means necessary."

Callius shrugged his shoulders. "Well, Prince Kai, I can only advise. If it is fear you wish to place within your ranks, that is your choice."

"My mother ruled by the same teachings instructed by her own father. It isn't my fault that *mine* was a cowardly cunt. I shall follow her lead."

What a gods-damn mommy's boy.

Although, I did respect the little shit for being so bold, speaking of the fallen king like that when he had been loved so fiercely by the soldiers surrounding us. It seemed as if the terror he wished to place upon them was already set, and no one would say anything.

The thing was, all the prince could do was bark orders. He didn't have the balls to act on what he wished to be done. And that was where I came in.

"Very well, Your Highness. Your decisions as king will have my support," Callius announced, and he definitely heard my grumble of mockery that slipped past my tongue, but I didn't give a damn.

Callius brought his horse to a halt. "We will rest here for the night. It's too dark, and I believe we will be out of the woods within mere hours of leaving in the morning. We can reconvene a plan then. Pass it down the lines," he ordered me, and a quick, disgusted scoff left me.

These were my soldiers. *Mine*. I was their captain. He gave that title up decades ago, and I wasn't about to take orders from him in front of them.

So instead, I inclined my head at Vincent to take care of it. Callius eyed me with a snarled lip but said nothing further.

Vin nodded in response, and then his orders rang out through the air, forcing everyone to dismount their horse and make camp wherever they stood.

FIFTY-THREE

Elianna

I WOKE TO JACE'S calloused hand cupping my breast as he pulled me into him in my sleep. He brought his lips to the tip of my ear, sending a shiver through my spine at the gentle, teasing touch. I pretended to be asleep for a few more moments, when I sensed his lips move, tracing down the side of my neck, hovering at the nape.

A grin crept up on my lips, giving me away.

"Good morning, my Lia," his tired, rough voice echoed onto my skin.

I blinked my eyes open carefully and rolled over to face him. My breath caught at the sight of the golden flecks in his eyes, reflecting in the sunlight within their haze of green and honey.

"Good morning." I smiled at him, my voice not sounding nearly as sexy. I wiggled closer to him and gave him a peck on the lips. "Yesterday was something."

He blew out a breath. "That's definitely the word for it. How are you feeling?"

My brows furrowed slightly and my head tilted to the side. "What do you mean?"

"I mean everything. Your brother and sister, people following them here to support you, the horrifying truth of our world from the scary silver-haired one...It's a lot. I just want to make sure you're alright. You come first to me. Always."

I gave him a soft, tight-lipped smile as I cupped his cheek. "I love you." He embraced me with a tight squeeze in response. "I'm...great."

A lie.

His eyes narrowed in on me intently. "We are back to your beautiful lies, I see." Only concern lingered in his tone as he tenderly brushed a few strands of hair from my face. "You don't have to wear your mask of bravery for me, Lia. I can feel your anguish. You're not okay. Let me help you. Please."

My eyes widened at his admittance and pleading. This gods-damn mating bond.

I blinked. "I will be okay."

His stare now bore into my own. "My Lia, you were held captive and escaped after being brutally whipped. You fled on the back of a fire-breathing creature and traveled across the realm, not knowing for sure what awaited you when you arrived here." He paused to catch his breath and then his emotions flooded me as if they were my own. Pride and sorrow surged from him as he spoke of what I had been forced to endure.

"You almost ignited your siblings and their army in flames, thinking they were our enemy. You learned of Lukas' tragic end and what the crown had done to its own people, *your* people, knowing many innocents were among them. And this was all after learning of your own father's murder."

My throat clogged as he went through the seemingly never-ending list of what had happened in barely two months' time.

"It's just a lot to take in," I whispered. "But I am alright. Everything else aside, I am shocked, but in the best way. I still just cannot believe that many fae were willing to risk their lives, their *younglings'* lives, to come here."

Jace gave me a knowing look, but luckily dropped his own point. "They are here for *you*...because they believe in the true heir of the realm. It also goes to show how well they already know Kai. They thought committing treason and starting a rebellion in your name was better than living under his reign. I'm sure the situation in the city square they spoke of did not help his cause, either. But make no mistake, their fear of Kai is not the only reason they are here."

Red gleamed across my vision as thoughts of the crown's mass executions swarmed me once more. And they had done it just to set a fucking example.

"Holy gods. Lia..." His brows drew together, and his body went still as he observed me.

"I want to destroy them for what they did." My jaw locked as my hand balled into a fist between our bodies.

Jace reached down and brought my fist to his lips, pressing them to it gently. "We will. We'll end them all for what they have done. For the castle staff, your father, Lukas—"

"I wish you could have met them," I whispered, cutting him off. "They were two of the greatest males I've ever known. I would probably still be rotting in that dungeon or dead if Lukas hadn't rescued me. He was like my second father, or one who was allowed to act like one while not hiding behind closed doors. Everything that I am, I owe it to them."

He watched me intently, his love for me erupting down the bond as it gleamed through his hazel stare.

"They will pay for every life they ever touched with their wickedness. My father, Lukas, the fae lying in fear...and of course, the humans, too. I don't want you to think I forgot that part. This is for all of them," I said.

"For a better realm, and an even better queen to rule it," he stated, determination and pride lighting his gaze.

I reached out and pulled his face to mine, tangling our bodies together between the sheets as they twisted between us.

Walking out of our bedroom once we were dressed and ready to figure out how the hell we were going to house hundreds of unexpected guests, I stopped short in the hall as I watched Landon tiptoeing out of Finnian's room. I smirked to myself as I silently observed him, thinking he had successfully maneuvered out undetected.

Jace met me in the hall and closed our bedroom door behind him, causing Landon to startle and whip around in our direction as he was heading for the stairs.

I grinned as I met his gaze. He looked mortified, as if what was happening wasn't exactly what I had expected and hoped for.

Nyra rushed past us as I stepped out to meet him at the top of the staircase. I pressed my finger to my lips as I passed him, letting him know that his secret was safe with me if he wished for it to remain as such.

Waltzing down into the sun-filled kitchen, I was surprised to see that Avery was already awake and down here. What wasn't surprising at all was the fact that she was staring at Gage amorously as he cooked everyone breakfast.

"Good morning!" I cheered, startling them, as I made my way next to her, pulling out a chair at the kitchen's wooden table.

"Morning Lia!" Gage greeted me, and Avery reached over and gave me a hug.

"How'd you sleep?" I asked her.

"Amazing. Do you know how long I've been sleeping on the hard terrain? I'll never complain about a shitty night's sleep again," she answered.

I giggled, and then Veli walked in.

"Oh, thank the gods. I'm starving," she revealed.

A few moments later, Finn arrived and stood a few feet from Landon, but they both had a certain, knowing glow to them.

Zaela stormed in from the back door at the other end of the kitchen. "Gods, you're still cooking?"

"There's double the amount of us now! I was surprised we had enough eggs lying around here. It's just about done," Gage said to her, and then turned his attention back to us. "Sorry, everyone, she can get a little hangry sometimes." He winked.

"Well, a fed Zaela is typically a happy one," she said as she made her way across the kitchen.

"Key word is typically," Jace teased, as everyone funneled in to sit or lean on the counter and start making their plates.

We all ate in silence for a few moments when Gage looked up at me and Jace. "What is the plan?" he asked.

I blew out a breath. "Well, we are going to have to call a city meeting if that's possible and see if anyone is willing to house some of our guests for the time being. We plan to head to Alaia Valley within the next few days."

"And that is where the remaining humans are in hiding?" Avery asked.

Jace nodded. "It is, and it is completely undetected by the crown. Everyone will be safe there."

Avery smiled at him, hope gleaming in her stare.

"There will be plenty of room there for the newcomers. They've been expanding the housing and creating additional settlements. If they decide to look for work while there, I know we are always looking for more people to farm the lands, continue building, or add to our armies," Jace said to them, and then placed his hand on top of mine. "And you'll finally be able to see my lands beyond the peaks."

Thinking about finally being able to see what lay beyond the other side of the Ezranian Mountains was mind-boggling to me. My entire life, we had been told that there was nothing on the other side of those peaks. Unfarmable land, no living creatures, and a place that had been cursed by the gods centuries ago. Yet the mortals had somehow discovered that it was all a lie, and they have *millions* of people back there living their lives day in and day out. Not only living, but *surviving* a war meant to destroy them.

"I'm so excited." I grinned, and then nerves settled in the pit of my stomach at the thought of finally meeting everyone there. No matter what Jace believed, I knew some, if not most, would be wary of trusting me.

Even here in Ellecaster, people had seen me with Jace, and his soldiers knew who I was, but the civilians weren't informed *entirely* of what was to come. Jace had revealed to them that I had claim to the throne, and I could be trusted. Other than that, they were almost entirely clueless, but all that was about to change.

Gage shoved the rest of his plate into his mouth. "I'll go round up the troops and get everyone out. Where should we have everyone gather for the announcement, brother?" He looked at Jace.

He contemplated for a moment. "Within the city walls, right in front of the gates. It's the most open and the people that arrive last should still be able to see, even if they have to funnel into the narrow streets."

Gage gave him a quick nod and moved to go out the front door. "I'm coming with you," Zaela announced as she stalked after him, and he put his arm around her shoulders as he walked her out the doorway.

I watched as Avery's eyes narrowed in on their backs as they disappeared from sight.

Oh, gods. How could I convince Avery's jealousy to not bubble up at their interactions without giving away Zae's secret?

Jace jerked his chin in Landon's direction. "How is your sword work?"

Landon cleared his throat. "I am not nearly as talented as you, I'm sure, but I have some training from when I was a boy," he admitted, and my eyes widened in surprise.

There was definitely more to the stable keeper than he wished to show.

"Would you like to come to train with the soldiers?" he asked right before he took his last bite of food. "We could always use more men."

I glanced over at Finn to see his reaction, and his face paled with nerves.

"Absolutely. I'll be whatever you need me to be," Landon answered, and a smile crept up my face as I watched the look of approval spread across Jace's features.

"Good man," my mate said as he reached out and patted Landon on the shoulder. He looked at Finn then. "Would you like to—"

"Yes." Finn jumped up, cutting off his question. "I would also like to train."

My gaze whipped to him. "I'm sorry, what?" My eyes bulged beneath furrowed brows.

"I would also like to train."

"...I mean, I definitely heard you. I'm just confused." He shot me a look of annoyance. "You've just never lifted a blade in your life, Finn. We are in a war, and learning the basics in the short amount of time we have won't do."

Even Kai had *some* training throughout his life. Not nearly as much as I had, or any soldier on the front lines in battle, but his teachings of the ways to be king had involved a small amount of battle briefing, though I doubted he retained much of it. Callius trained with him, just as Lukas had with me. However, Finn had nothing. I could probably count on one hand how many times he even witnessed a duel. It was too dangerous for him to start now.

Sadness swept across his face for a split moment. "You don't think I can do it."

My heart stuttered, and I reached out for his arm, but he ripped it from my reach. "No, no, of course I think you could. Just not now. Eventually, with the right amount of training, but I refuse to send my brother out on the front lines with zero experience."

He stared me down in silence, and my eyes flicked over to Jace, who stood with his arms crossed, observing us. He then broke the silence. "Let him come."

I spun to face him. "What?" I gaped.

Jace shrugged. "At the end of the day, it's your choice, Lia. But my vote is to let him come and at least watch. Lift a small blade or two, get a feel for it. It's the only way he'll learn to protect himself."

He had a point. I studied my mate for a second and looked back over at Finn. "Jace is right. I would rather you be at least somewhat prepared." His face lit up with excitement. "However, you will not take one fucking step on that battlefield until I clear you. Do you understand me, Finnian?"

My brother smirked at me and wrapped his arms around my body in an embrace. "Forever the captain leading her armies. Of course I do," he said, as he squeezed me a little tighter, and then whispered, "Thank you, Lia. Thank you so much."

FIFTY-FOUR

Jace

We stood at the top of the stone watchtower at Ellecaster's gates as we observed the citizens funneling into the streets from their homes.

They looked around at each other, confused at the purpose of why a meeting would be called at such short notice. I then watched as some of them went taut and on edge as our new fae guests made their way into the crowd below.

Whispers rattled through the wind, asking what was happening and why there were fae amongst them. Mothers of each race pushed their children behind them in defense. Men and males went on edge, reaching for their swords, not knowing how to react to such a situation.

"Still think this is a good idea?" Lia asked quietly as she stood at attention at my side, gazing out at them as I was.

"It's the only way." I took her hand in mine and squeezed it gently.

I looked down at the foot of the gate to see the soldiers officially lined up and in place as Gage and Zaela stood in front of them, peering out at the masses gathered before us all.

"Ready, my Lia?" I asked as my eyes remained forward.

"Always," she answered proudly.

That's my girl.

"Good morning, everyone." My voice echoed across the city, silencing the last of their hateful, nervous whispers. "Thank you for coming here on such short notice. Part of what we need to announce is long overdue, and I apologize for the tardiness of this meeting. As you are aware, we have been diligently preparing our soldiers and young recruits for the approaching end of the war. However, we should have made time for this much sooner." I glanced to Lia. "And what will follow this is new information as of yesterday evening."

Lia blew out a breath next to me, nerves and determination rattling the bond.

"The female standing next to me, you all know by now and have seen, but you may not know the entire story of how and why she is here by my side." I paused for a moment. "Her name is Elianna Valderre, the daughter of the late king of the realm, Jameson Valderre. She is his firstborn daughter, and true heir."

Shouts rang out throughout the crowd below. Citizens twisted and turned, looking around at what to do with the information.

"*Silence!*" Zaela's voice bellowed toward them. "This is important, and you will all listen. I don't care who you are. You will respect your commander and what he has to say."

"Hell yeah, Zae," Lia whispered, and I peeked over to see a smirk line her lips as her eyes remained on the masses.

Only the shouts of concern and betrayal never ceased. They continued to grow and roar across the city, and soon enough, Zaela's orders at them were lost among the noise.

"Fuck," I growled as I faced my mate.

The look on her face was calculative, deep in thought as she observed the chaos that was about to break out down below. I didn't want to have to order my soldiers to incite order on our own citizens, but it was looking like I was about to not have a choice.

She turned around to the open fields beyond the gates, her eyes locking on Nox as he flew around in the distance. I watched her as she walked to the opposite side of the tower. She lifted her fingers to her full lips and let out a high-pitched, sharp whistle in his direction.

On command, the wyvern turned in the air on a smooth glide, heading straight for the city. Lia let out a hum of approval as she turned back to the crowd and placed her hands on the balcony's stone railing, her gaze sweeping over the masses in silence.

I stood behind her. "What are you up to?"

"Just trust me, okay?" she whispered to me as her hair whipped around her face.

"Always," I mimicked her from only minutes prior.

A moment later, a loud, whooshing gust of wind sent us all nearly flying forward as Nox perched himself up on the roof of the stone tower. Small pieces of rock crumbled from the structure, falling at our feet as his long talons dug into it, holding him there.

His depthless, vertical pupils were fixated on the crowd below as he let out an ear-shattering screech in their direction.

The sight of the beast had them all on edge, quivering with terror, and all shouts of anger ceased.

"Everyone, please listen. I won't take too much of your time," she spoke sternly into the air. "It is true. My name is Elianna Valderre, and I am the firstborn child of King Jameson. He was my father, and he was murdered by the queen."

I waited to see if her voice hesitated or faltered as she spoke about her father, but she remained resilient in her speech. My pride for her was overwhelming, beyond measure.

"I was kept a secret my entire life, as I was born of his mistress. When Queen Idina learned of my birth, she used this to manipulate my father into this war he never wanted, and her compromise to him was that he was able to keep me within the castle walls, close to him. My father loved my birth mother with every fiber of his being, and he wished to name me heir, but he had let the queen become too powerful, taking a seat on the sidelines to watch me grow up in secret, as he feared for my life."

Her voice stuttered then on the last word. I watched sorrow flash across her face, but it was there and gone in only a second. I reached down and squeezed her wrist, letting her know I was still there, right by her side.

She cleared her throat. "My father had three other children after me, who you all know as Prince Kai, Princess

Avery, and Prince Finnian Valderre. In fact, Avery and Finnian are among us right now." She smiled as she waved an arm to the opposite tower, where her two siblings stood with Veli and two other guards.

"Kai will now ascend the throne due to my father's untimely death. He will not be the same kind of ruler my father had been, and while I know you all believed him to be malevolent, he was kind—he was *good,* and never wanted this war. The realm as we know it will cease to exist, and Kai will stop at nothing until all mortals are wiped away, and he has full control over every living being within Velyra."

The crowd gaped up at my mate, eyes wide with awe and curiosity. So many of them were raised how I had been. All they had ever known of the fae was that they were all wicked, ruthless murderers. Lia challenged everything we thought we knew of them, and I was fully convinced that if she could convince me and mine, she could convince the wary humans who stood before us.

"I wish to bring the realm back to how it once was a millennia ago. Back when fae and humans worked and lived together side by side before hatred infiltrated our hearts and beliefs regarding one another. All living creatures will be protected under my rule. No race is more superior or deserving of kindness over another. The mass genocide will cease to exist and I promise to rule with grace and integrity...with your commander..." She glanced at me and then back at them. "My mate, and your future king, at my side."

Eyes flaring, my mouth fell open in disbelief at what she announced to them, and what she claimed that she wished for me to become. To rule at her side as her king consort and equal.

I let out a shuddering breath as she met my gaze and winked, giving me her adorable, infuriating smirk as if what she had just declared was something as casual as what we planned to eat for dinner this evening.

I peered down at Gage and Zaela, whose necks were cranked at a ninety-degree angle, staring up at us. Gage lifted his fist high in the air with a cheer, and even Zae had an enormous smile stretched across her face. The crowd burst into gossip and cheers the moment the declaration left Lia's lips, seemingly forgetting the looming shadow of Nox as he watched them all intently from where he perched.

She gracefully lifted a hand to halt their chatters. "This cannot happen without your full support, and the winning of this gruesome war. We will take back Velyra by any means necessary. By blade and by blood. We *will* win this—for a better realm and a better future for our children and younglings alike." She paused as her eyes fixated on the thousands of other pairs looking up at her in admiration.

"Now...what say you?!" she roared at the crowd enthusiastically, yet with authority, as she leaned over the tower's edge.

The masses below erupted into applause and cheers as they watched our future queen gaze down at them.

My stare moved to the other watch tower, and I observed as Avery jumped up and down with glee, rapidly clapping as tears of happiness ran down her flushed cheeks. Finn clapped next to her with a smile as he watched his eldest sister publicly stake her claim to the throne for the very first time.

I turned to Lia, and she faced me with a beaming smile, her green eyes illuminating with happiness and disbelief as the emotions of acceptance radiated through her—through both of us.

My arm reached out and wrapped around her waist, pulling her chest to mine in one swift movement. I then twisted both of our bodies and dipped her backwards, pressing my lips to hers in a deep, soul-consuming kiss for the city to see.

Cheering continued to ring out as I opened my eyes to see her own staring up at me. "I love you," I whispered on her mouth.

"And I love you," she answered, cupping my cheek as I straightened us both to stand once more.

Nox let out a few chirp-like clicks of approval before he launched off of the roof and into the sky once more, making a few more pieces of stone rain down on us.

"I'm ready now. This finally feels right," Lia said, loud enough for me to hear as she gazed out at the celebrating masses.

"You've always been ready. You were *made* for this. I dream of the day that I will be able to watch you become what you were always meant to be. What the gods meant for you to be," I responded, and glanced down to see her beautiful, wicked smile as it radiated in the early afternoon sun.

FIFTY-FIVE
Kellan

Well, didn't this sight look familiar?

We marched out from the forest trees and were greeted with the char-crusted remnants of the pitiful village I burned down in search of Lia months ago. I grimaced at the sight of the blood-stained post I had secured her body to when I forced her to watch me kill her beloved *human*.

"This place has seen better days." The prince scoffed as he rode up next to me. "Thank the fucking gods we're out of those woods."

For once, I agreed with him. I just gave him a curt nod in response.

"Should we camp here?" Vincent asked from a few feet behind us as his horse trotted around the rubble.

He was right—we would need a home base now that we were on the other side of the forest. How fitting would it be if it were here?

My head swung in Callius' direction. "We will set up beyond those fields." I jerked my chin in the direction. "They can't be far from here. We will need a location to bring the rebels back to before we head back to Isla. She won't go down without a fight."

"Bring back to?" Kai spat. "We are fucking *killing* them, Adler. Solus is as good as dead. If she isn't killed on sight, I demand you to only bring her back to prolong her torture and death. I want her to feel *everything*," he seethed.

Callius eyed the prince. "I believe Captain Adler meant Princess Avery and Prince Finnian."

"Kill them," Kai demanded coldly. "I don't give a rat's ass what my mother said. I will be crowned king when we arrive back to the city and I want those traitors dead. They fled and betrayed the crown. They get the same punishment."

Callius looked as if he were about to vomit as his eyes widened, nostrils flaring. "Prince," he started.

"Enough! I know you do as my mother says no matter what, but *I* am who you will be reporting to following the ascension. You will do well to remember that."

My eyes flared at what the prince demanded of us. "Prince Kai," I chimed in. "Queen Idina's word is still above yours. We cannot kill your siblings..."

Callius watched the two of us for a moment, looking horrified and panicked about speaking further. He then guided his horse to turn to the awaiting army, shouting out orders to scout the area and make camp in the far-off fields.

Kai bared his teeth at Callius' back and then turned to me, nostrils flaring. "Make it look like an accident, then."

My brows furrowed. "An accident?"

"Like I said, *Captain*, my mother will only wear the crown for so much longer. Prove your allegiance to me. Would you prefer to die amongst traitors, or work your way to your actual goal?"

He gave me a vicious sneer.

"Goal, Your Highness?" I questioned as I eyed him warily.

"You wish to be The King's Lord, do you not?" He smirked, and it took every ounce of me not to launch myself at the little fuck.

How could he possibly have known that? Had Vincent let it slip? Or had I gotten sloppy, and it was truly that obvious? Up until I knew who Elianna was, that had always been what I desired most.

"If the position were to come back, I would be interested," I answered reluctantly, every word more clipped than the last.

His answering smile didn't meet his cold, depthless eyes. He shrugged a single shoulder. "Then do as I say."

And with that, he swung his leg over the horse and jumped down, throwing the reins in my direction. He stalked off toward the camp that was being built and left me in a state of disbelief.

My gaze narrowed in on his exposed back as each step he took brought him further away from me.

That cunning little shit just threatened me.

Perhaps he wasn't exactly how he appeared...or maybe he had finally learned how to play the game like the rest of us had.

It took several of the morning hours to set up the camp, but once it was ready, it stretched across the field for nearly a mile. Every tent that would normally hold two soldiers was now forced to host at least four, thanks to losing several supply wagons in the forest.

I made my rounds with my chest pushed out and my hands behind my back as Vincent walked at my side. Soldiers straightened as we passed and I would give them each a nod to have them get back to their duties.

We made it across the camp to my own tent, which possessed a small wooden table with maps of the realm sprawled out. We were now in the old lands toward Silcrowe. Most of it was left in ruins after those first few years of the war, but I had a feeling that there was much more on this side of the Sylis Forest than we originally believed.

I poked my head out of the flaps of my tent to make sure that no one was around to eavesdrop on our conversation and then tied them shut.

I faced Vin. "You still have it?"

He grinned. "Of course. Its stench is fucking unbearable, though."

I rolled my eyes. "Don't be a bitch about it. It will do what is necessary."

"Which is?" he questioned, and my brows furrowed as my gaze whipped to him. He had no right to question me.

"Do you forget your place, Vin?"

The sternness of his face, to my surprise, didn't waiver. "Never, Captain. We have just tried to break her many times. What makes you think this will work?"

I chuckled wickedly. "It will work." I stared at the maps for a moment. "Kai had the balls to threaten me out there."

His eyes widened, and he let out a long, dragged-out whistle. "Brave lad."

"Aye. We'll need to take care of *that* soon, too."

"And Callius?" he asked.

I sighed. "I haven't decided on that yet."

Callius kept me alive when my father's crew had been executed, acting as a father figure in his absence for some years. Sure, I lived and served in the barracks until I was of age to train among them, but I survived because of him. As much as he had been on my last fucking nerve these last few weeks, dealing with him wouldn't be as easy a decision as dealing with the rest of them.

"Adler," Callius' voice boomed from outside the tent.

Shit, had he heard us?! I rolled my shoulders back, anticipating a fight as my hand drifted to the hilt of my sword, a bead of sweat trickling down my face.

"Aye?" I shouted back, my jaw locked as I stared at Vincent, who also looked tense as his gaze remained on the flaps of the tent.

"You're going to want to see this," he answered.

I scowled, my brows furrowing, as I stormed through the tent and came face-to-face with him and two others standing in his shadow.

"What's going on?!" My angry bark was met with a disapproving frown from him.

"What's wrong with you?" he spat.

Perhaps he hadn't heard what we were saying, then.

"Nothing. Is something happening?" I tore my gaze from his as I lightened my tone.

"Scouts found something. Come with me," he announced as he turned on his feet, signaling for us to follow.

We all stalked to the outskirts of the camp to see two humans on their knees, their arms bound behind their backs and mouths gagged. They also looked as if they had already been beaten to a bloody pulp.

"Well, well, well," I started as I crossed my arms. "What do we have here?"

I glanced down to the ground directly in front of them and my eyes met a lifeless falcon with an arrow shot through it laying before them.

I raised a brow and tsked. "Messenger falcon, huh? Who were you warning about us, gentlemen?"

They remained silent as they stared up at me with hatred radiating from their pores.

"Ah, well, lucky for me, it seems the letter is still attached." I reached down and plucked the rolled-up piece of parchment from the bird's talons and unraveled it before me.

I let out a short, harsh laugh.

Commander,

The fae army is here. The real army. They are coming. Prepare the soldiers. They have set up camp outside of the remnants of Celan Village.

The Watch.

They actually named that pathetic excuse of a settlement?

My focus returned to the mortals who unwillingly knelt before me. "Well, then. I have to admit that was short, sweet and to the point, boys. Well done."

I handed the parchment to Callius, and he read it and chuckled as he crumpled it up and threw it back at them.

"Morons," he murmured.

I grimaced, my eyes never leaving the captors in front of us. "Will you do the honors, Vincent?"

"Gladly," he answered as he went to move behind them, ripping the gags from their mouths as they gasped out for a full breath.

They both bowed their heads, violently trembling as fear clogged their veins.

"Where are they?" I asked calmly.

"Fuck you!" one spat bravely.

I sighed. "No, thank you. I have plenty of females for that."

I raised a brow as my eyes flicked up to Vincent's. Without hesitation, he unsheathed his sword and plunged it down through the man's spine, spearing right through his chest and into the dirt before him.

The man gurgled on his own blood, horror carved into his face, and I watched the life drain from his eyes as his body slid down the blade and thumped to the ground.

Vin put his boot to the human's back, keeping him in place, and pulled his sword from his body. The man's blood still soaked the blade.

I turned to face the remaining one.

"I mean, do I really have to ask twice?" I laughed at him and watched as conflict consumed him.

"W-will you k-kill me?" he stuttered out, and I was losing my patience.

I shrugged. "Your odds are a lot better than your friend that screamed 'fuck you' in my face."

He glanced down at his friend's body that now sat in a pool of blood.

"Alright, I will tell you everything," he stated as he audibly gulped. "Ellecaster is the city where Silcrowe once sat. They await there. It's about a day's journey from here. If your horses are fast, you could get there by midnight. Just please, don't kill me." He shook as the words left his traitorous little lips, and he refused to look up at me as he spoke.

Fucking coward.

I crouched to get down at his level and got directly in his face. "And in which direction from here is Ellecaster?"

"N-north-east," he stuttered as he jerked his chin in the direction, since his hands were still bound.

"Excellent." I smiled as I rose to my feet.

"So, you'll let me go now, right?"

I locked eyes with Vin, who stood waiting for orders. "Sorry. Who's to say you aren't a liability and won't go running to warn them? Or better yet...why would I let a traitor live and breathe another day? You show no loyalty. I have no respect for cowards," I seethed.

And as I turned on my heel, the swoosh of Vincent's blade sounded through the air as it was swung and brought down on the human's flesh. The man's scream was cut abruptly as he met his end.

"Why the fuck would I let you take half of the camp to fetch your beloved sympathizer and leave the other half here?" Callius boomed at me in my own gods-damn tent as Vincent waited outside.

My lip curled back, eyes glaring at him, as I tried to settle the anger bubbling up inside me. "Callius, I know you sometimes conveniently forget this...but *I* am the captain. You haven't been in decades," I growled.

"Be that as it may," he started. "Certain actions taken by you as of recent days have been questionable, to say the least."

I licked my lips and gave him a full toothed grin. "And what actions do you speak of?"

He raised his finger to my face and took a step toward me. "Will you just shut the fuck up? I know you and your games.

I taught you everything you know, and I know when you're being a sneaky prick," he warned.

I shrugged. "I just don't believe we need the entirety of the troop. We will be able to sneak up easier if we are in smaller increments." He continued to stare at me, unblinking. "Especially now, without warning." I smirked.

He considered me for a moment. "Prince Kai must remain here," he ordered.

No shit.

"Of course. Wouldn't want him going off and getting himself killed without the proper training."

Callius scoffed. "Kai has *some* training. We've been working on his sword work since we left Isla. It would be foolish to not have him prepared in some capacity for battle."

They had been. Every night when we stopped to rest, Callius would work on training the little shit, who was more than reluctant to entertain it. His skills with a blade had increased over the few times I watched from afar, but nowhere near what would be needed to take down an enemy—or me.

His brows furrowed. "What are you up to, Adler? Your girl *will* die. She will be killed whether it is here or back in Isla. Personally, I would prefer it here. She has a habit of escaping, and it's rather tiresome."

"I'm not up to anything aside from getting back to Isla," I snapped, hoping I was convincing. "Now, I will ask you one more time. Can you stay here and be in charge in my absence while I go and fetch these traitors, or do I have to choose from my ranks?"

"Let him, Callius," Kai's voice floated over to us as he stood in the tent's entrance with his arms crossed.

Callius sighed. "Your Highness, I just don't believe it to be wise to send half away when we have enough soldiers to wipe out whatever awaits us in the human's city of ruin."

Kai curiously eyed me for a moment. "He said it was to sneak up on them more efficiently."

"He did," Callius agreed.

"Then let the male do what you trained him to do." Kai faced me. "You want the position of The King's Lord, and here is your chance to prove yourself. Betray the crown and it will be your head." He shrugged and placed his hands in his pockets. "Simple as that."

Callius looked me up and down. "The King's Lord?" He chuckled viciously as he moved to place his hand on my shoulder. "Don't make me regret this. You were like a son to me all those years ago, and I'm choosing to trust you right now when I feel as if I shouldn't," he grumbled, and then stormed out of the tent as he shook his head in a disapproving manner.

"If Elianna is not killed in the attack, you will bring her here to me. I want to watch the light leave her eyes," Kai said, and then observed me for a moment before lazily following behind him.

Vincent waltzed in a moment later to see me standing there with a malicious grin plastered on my face.

"Everything is in motion to draw Elianna out of hiding. Prepare *our* troop," I ordered him.

A knowing smirk crept up his face as he backed away to prepare our trusted soldiers.

Now, all we had to do was set the bait to distract her and lure her out of hiding.

FIFTY-SIX
Elianna

Once the chaos of the city meeting settled down, I was stunned as I watched Ellecaster's citizens accept the fae from Isla with open arms. There were, of course, a few families that hesitated, but there was enough space where those who hadn't felt comfortable sharing their homes didn't have to.

The fae had similar reactions, but the majority of everyone involved put in an effort to set their differences aside. Everybody had been directed to alert a nearby guard immediately if the living situations were not working or if altercations ensued. We assured everyone that their comfort and safety were most important to us all.

After everyone spread out and left to explore their new, temporary homes, the eight of us took to the city streets. Jace had us stop at Ellecaster's Post to send a falcon beyond the mountains. He wrote a letter to Zaela's mother and General Vern to warn them of the influx of residents that would soon cross between the peaks.

Once that was finished, we shopped for extra clothing, supplies, and bedding for the townhouse that would now need to accommodate all of us for the time spent here.

Veli even stopped in one of the city's apothecary shops to replenish her healing supplies.

Every time Avery picked decorations out for her room, she would forget that she didn't have any money with her. I would smirk at Jace and he handed each shop owner more than enough coin to cover the cost of what she was trying to buy. She had picked so many items throughout the city that we had to borrow a wagon to hold everything outside of the storefronts to cart around.

Gage made it his personal mission to push the cart by himself instead of using a horse since we had "disrupted" him from his typical routine of working out and training all morning.

Once Avery was satisfied with what she had for her room, she moved on to the kitchen, and then the living room...and then the hallways.

"Sorry, I just have *no words* for your friend's decorative taste. Hope she doesn't mind." She gave a wicked grin.

Jace chuckled. "Zaela is actually my cousin, and trust me, she is going to mind. But this seems entirely too hilarious to not witness."

"Oh, I'm so sorry," she answered and flashed an apologetic look over to him.

"Don't be. *I'm* sorry for her behavior again last night. She was out of line, and I think, just over tired. She doesn't warm up to new people quickly," Jace answered with a sigh.

"I meant I'm sorry that she is your cousin." Avery winked at him, and I cackled under my breath.

Jace gave me an unamused look, but I just pursed my lips and tried to hide my smirk. I knew I was failing miserably.

Like clockwork, Zaela came around the corner from the other side of the larger shop. "Are we done here?" she snapped.

Avery went to open her mouth, but I intervened. "Yes, I think so. Let's bring all of this back to the townhouse, and then we can go visit Nox. He didn't get to meet all of you when you arrived here yesterday, since I didn't want to scare any of the younglings."

"You mean you didn't want to scare Finn?" Landon teased as he admired the glass fixtures displayed on a shelf.

"Exactly." I snickered.

"I heard that!" Finn shouted from across the store, making us all chuckle—even Veli.

Jace paid for everything we chose from the store, and we all waltzed out together, piling it into our wagon and headed out to finally make our little townhouse a home.

"Gods, do you always walk all the way out here when you go to see the wyvern?" Finn said, out of breath, while we all trucked through the grassy fields of wildflowers. Sweat beaded down his pale skin from the heat of the afternoon sun.

Zae and Gage stayed behind at the townhouse, setting up everything we had bought for when we returned.

I focused on my steps, pivoting around rocks, roots, and burrowed holes in the ground from the critters that inhabited the area. "He can be needy if I don't come out and see him daily," I joked. "Besides, it's not as if he can fit inside the city."

"Trust me, she wanted to try," Jace grumbled, earning quiet laughs from them.

I turned back to face the city gates, which seemed about a mile back and deemed this spot as good as any. I halted everyone behind me and let out a loud, high-pitched whistle to summon Nox.

The boom of his wings sounded and before we knew it, he was in front of us, our necks craning as we watched him soar toward us above—his landing rattled the ground beneath our feet. I looked up at him and frowned, seeing that he still had his saddle on.

"Shit, I'm sorry, Nox." I walked up to him and gently placed my hand on the outer joint of his wing. "I forgot to take this off of you." I fiddled with the straps that crossed over his chest for a moment. "To be honest, I don't even know if I know how to."

"Just leave it. Trust me, you don't want to deal with him when you're trying to get it back on," Jace said from behind us.

Nox lowered his head and tilted it, his eyes narrowing in on him.

"Easy there." I patted his giant snout, and then turned to them all, placing my hands on my hips.

"Anyone want to go for a ride?"

Veli stepped forward, surprising me. I blinked at her, but she held up a hand to stop me from speaking. "I do not want to ride him. But I would like to approach if he allows me to. I am very curious about this creature."

I eyed her warily for a moment and then looked back at Nox and gave him a curt nod.

"You may approach him," I said, and she did. I observed her as she gawked at his lean, scale-covered body. The way his wings perfectly curved into his side, and how his neck stretched out as he stood straight, enjoying the attention of her admiring him.

She stepped in closer to him and her sharp nails pointed to the underside of his stomach, where the brutal scarring was from his lack of scales to protect it. "Ah. There it is. That must be where—"

Before I could blink, I ripped my dagger from its sheath and pointed it at her, hearing the others' bodies shift uncomfortably behind me. "Where they cut him for his blood. Yes. And you will *not* be running any witchy tests on it either. I will not have him be used as an experiment," I hissed, flashing my canines at her.

She took a step back from Nox and looked up at his face. His lips were curled back, baring his dagger-like teeth in her direction. Her violet eyes met mine. "I was just curious, Elianna. Put the blade away," she hissed as she stalked back to where she stood before.

I placed my dagger back in its sheath as I worked to bring my flaring anger down. Veli hadn't shown any sign that she was going to harm him. I trusted her medicinal expertise with my life, my family, and mate's life...but the way she looked at my wyvern ignited something within me. Gold and violet eyes full of curiosity...it sent a spark through my veins. I would never allow him to be used against his will again, especially if it meant spilling more of his precious, deadly blood.

I steadied my heavy breaths as I tried to calm down and looked to my mate, who flashed me his perfect teeth. The bastard was enjoying the show—that was for sure.

"Avery and Finn," I started. "Why don't you two come up here and say hi." I forced a smile on my face as I reached my hand out to them.

Both of them quickly made their way to me, and when I turned to face Nox, any hint of that smile dropped immediately at the sight of him.

"Uhhh, Lia?" Avery whispered.

Nox's chest was puffed out and his body towered over us, looking as if he were about to combust in a fit of wrath.

My eyes widened, and I threw both of my hands in front of us. "Nox, it's me!" His breathing was so heavy that I could see the hot air flowing from his nostrils. Then, he leaned his neck down toward us, bringing his horned head level with my own.

"Neither of you move," I whispered to them both. "I don't want any sudden movements. Something isn't right."

Finn audibly gulped from behind me.

"Elianna," Jace pleaded from a few feet away, worry in his tone. I could see him creeping up on our side out of the corner of my eye, hand on the pommel of his sword, ready to strike.

"I'm okay, Jace," I assured him.

Nox's eyes were still fixated on me, and I tilted my head to the side. "It's me." I motioned with my chin behind me. "They are my siblings. We are of the same blood," I whispered as I reached out and placed the palm of my hand gently on his snout, willing my arm to not tremble from the fear flowing through me.

He leaned into my touch and sniffed my hand, blowing out a huff through his nostrils, and then he moved to face Avery. As he sniffed her, I watched the vertical pupil in his eye thin into the tiniest slit.

Suddenly, he threw his head back and raucously roared into the open air. It was so loud that it shook the terrain, nearly causing us all to lose our balance. When he brought his head back down, sparks were forming at the back of his throat as his jaw remained open, gaping at *us*.

Nox swiveled his head toward my sister, fury gleaming in his eyes.

"NO!" I shouted and dove onto her, tumbling us both to the ground and rolling away as he sent a blast of flame where she stood only half a second prior.

All of us remained frozen in shock, eyes wide with gaping jaws, as we stared at the ash-covered burn mark on the terrain. My eyes wandered around the lot of us, blinking slowly as I made sure my body shielded my sister's.

"Lia!" Jace bellowed as he snapped out of his stupor and ran to kneel beside us.

Avery's chest was moving up and down rapidly as she desperately took in breaths. "Thank you," she whispered.

Jace pulled me to my feet, and then reached down to help Avery. We all faced the wyvern once more, who now was staring at Finnian with that same lethal look in his eye.

Oh, gods.

I took a step towards him, waving to grab his attention. "What the fuck was that, Nox?!" My voice was full of rage, desperation, and confusion.

I ran to stand in front of my brother, throwing my arms out at my sides to show I didn't have any weapons, but also to protect Finn as he cowered behind my body. I watched the fury fade from the wyvern's eyes.

"They are my *family*. Which means they are *your* family. They are good people and will not harm you, I promise," I said to him as everyone else remained silent.

Nox lowered his head in shame but kept a wary eye on Finn behind me.

"Mother of the gods, *why* did you do that?!" I shouted at him, fighting tears of stress as they threatened to slip from me. I pushed at Finn to get back, and he ran to Landon. "You could've killed her!"

He sniffed the air once more but remained where he stood, looking ashamed yet distrustful.

"I think I know," Veli announced.

I turned to her, noticing that shock was still etched in everyone's features, aside from hers.

"And what is it that you think you know?" I barked at her. "Can you understand him or something?" I asked, wondering if she could communicate with him telepathically with her witch magic.

"Don't be foolish, girl," Veli snapped. "I have had a theory for quite some time, and *that* just confirmed it." She motioned toward Nox.

"Holy gods," Avery breathed. "I think you're right."

"Can someone fill me in?" I asked as annoyance worked its way through me.

Veli's eyes shifted from me to Avery, then Finn, and back again. "The wyvern does not trust them because they share the same blood as Kai Valderre."

My brows furrowed at what she said. "So do I. That doesn't make any sense."

"No, Elianna. I do not think that you do," Veli claimed.

"What?" Finn shrieked. "So, she isn't our sister?"

Honestly, what the hell was she talking about? I definitely was their sister. My father never would've gone through what he had if I wasn't his daughter.

"She is *your* sister, boy. But she is not Kai's. They do not share blood," Veli answered as she crossed her arms, tapping her long nails on herself.

"What?" I breathed, and Jace approached me then, staring at the witch the same way I was.

I glanced over at Avery to see her lip trembling. "It is a theory we discussed briefly. Kai not being King Jameson's son."

"Why would you think that?" I asked, and as the words left my mouth, visions of the past replayed in my head. All the times that he was so evil and I never could understand how he came from my father. How the queen loved him so much more than her other two children. His constant need to torment any individual that crossed his path and how he reveled in punishing innocents.

"Actually...I think I understand," I said before they could answer. "But if our father isn't his...then who?"

"Callius," Veli said sternly. "It's the only option that fits and makes sense."

All the air was ripped from my lungs as my eyes widened. "Holy fucking gods."

Jace's body tensed next to me. "A false king," he snarled.

"He isn't a Valderre." My eyes darted back and forth as I stared at Veli.

"When the hell were you guys going to tell me? What do you mean you 'briefly discussed this,' Avery?!" Finn shot at her.

Her head flung in his direction. "I didn't want to say anything to you until we knew for sure," she said calmly. "We had no solid proof. Until possibly right now. Even then, we still don't know..."

"Oh, we know," Veli said as she sucked on her tooth. "No wonder why they were desperate to crown him."

It made so much sense. Wanting to kill me, be rid of me for good after they murdered the king. They needed to eliminate the last viable threat against Kai's claim to the throne, which I now realized he had absolutely *none*. Aside from me, it would be Avery or Finn. They truly were trying to crown a false king. Someone who wasn't actually of the Valderre bloodline, which went against everything the realm had ever known.

The queen knew this whole time. She must've. It's the only thing that would explain why Avery and Finn were loved so differently by her than Kai.

I whipped around to look back at Nox, who now had his head bowed in shame, making my heart clench. My lips parted as I stared at him, unknowing of what to say.

"Nox, I'm so sorry. I had no idea," I admitted, but he craned his neck to look up into the sky as dark clouds began to move in from the distance.

My eyes flared slightly as realization hit me. If I shared Kai's blood like I always thought I had, would Nox have let me rescue him and escape all those weeks ago when I ran to him in the dungeon's cavern? Or would he have charred me right then and there once he scented the similarity within me?

The thought of it sent a sudden shiver through me.

"Nox," I breathed, but his wings shot out from his sides in response, and he slowly lifted himself into the air, and flew off into the distance. My gaze remained on him until I couldn't see any sign of him at all.

My heart raced in my chest as guilt consumed me while I continued to stare off in the direction he flew.

"He'll be okay. He's just...moody." Jace sighed as he came up next to me.

"You two have that in common."

He smirked. "Perhaps."

I turned to face them all as they stood there, staring at me.

"It appears you do not have much control over your wyvern, Elianna," Veli stated.

I shot her a look through furrowed brows. "We are learning together. He comes when he is called and typically listens to commands while in flight."

Key word was *typically*.

"Have you ever had him conjure fire by command? Or has he always done that on his own?" she asked as her violet stare bore into me.

I opened my mouth to tell her *of course*, but then I remembered that…I never had. Any time Nox had cast his blaze of flames upon anything, he had done so on his own. My first attempt was going to be when we found the fleeing rebels, but I never gave the command because I saw Avery at the last possible moment.

"I do not believe so," I answered, and she raised a brow. "Nox has always sent his flame at what he wishes, and perhaps I have just been lucky that his instincts have been…*accurate* so far. Well, aside from just now." The moment the words left me, I flinched, realizing how foolish it all sounded.

"Gods, Lia," Jace huffed, and I couldn't even bring myself to meet his stare.

Veli took a step towards me, observing me for a moment. "I may have a solution." My eyes narrowed in on her. "There are sacred texts that I have read, stating that all Sylis creatures know the ancient tongue of the Velyran gods. He may understand commands if spoken in their language."

"What?" the word left me in a whisper, and my eyes drifted over to Avery, Finn, and Landon, who watched us intently. "I do not know their tongue. It has been lost to the fae for thousands of years."

"There is a word you may try," she offered. "Though all of this is theory, and I cannot guarantee it will work, but if you wish to master the force of his inferno, it would be wise to attempt."

"What is the word, Veli?" I asked, hoping I would be able to pronounce it.

"Ignystae."

"Ignystae," I echoed, and I could have sworn power hummed through me as the word slipped off my tongue—as if the realm itself recognized it.

"Very good. You try that the next time you are atop the beast, and you may be surprised at how he responds," she offered. "That power you just felt when you spoke the ancient tongue...that is not to be taken lightly. Remember all I spoke of yesterday—the gods' ancient presence remains around us, always. And you, given where your blood stems from, may be able to will that power into being. The wyvern may listen."

I blinked at her in response, barely able to process her words as I desperately tried to take everything else in. All I could manage was a nod.

Their gazes remained on me and I blew out a breath. My hand lifted to involuntarily scratch my head, which felt as if it would explode after the events of the past few days.

"Gods, this was such an unexpected nightmare. Anyone else in need of wine?" I asked.

They all raised their hands simultaneously in silence, and we moved to head back to the townhouse as dusk crept in on the horizon.

FIFTY-SEVEN

Jace

I STOOD IN THE corner of the living room, leaning up against the walls, while I observed our newfound family. A room full of love and hope was so foreign to me that I could hardly grasp it.

Six months ago, if you were to tell me that eventually I would pledge my allegiance to the rightful fae queen, I would've laughed in your face before sending my fist through it. And if you were to have tacked on that, not only would I show her support, but I would also be irrevocably in love with her; I likely would've killed you before the last word left your lips.

Life doesn't always work out the way you planned it to, but holy gods, did mine take an unexpected turn.

I ran my fingers through my hair and smiled as I watched Lia loosen up after her third glass of wine. She pushed the tea table at the foot of the settee aside and started dancing around with Avery in the fireplace light. They both giggled and twirled around each other playfully while Gage played a tune for them with the strings of his gittern. The others were all scattered throughout the space, either chatting or watching along with me.

Lia looked so fucking happy. I would do anything to keep that light in her eyes as she carelessly frolicked around with her best friend. But I knew deep down that beneath that light, darkness still lingered in her soul-gripping eyes. It clung to all of us, just waiting for the final battles of this century old war to come. However, something in Lia had changed.

I watched my mate as she exuded this sense of joy and relief, but down the bond, I sensed nothing but lingering anguish. My Lia had the weight of the realm on her shoulders as we constantly worked to find a way to save it from the grip of the wicked, false queen. Even though it went unspoken, I knew that she also blamed herself for her father's and Lukas' deaths.

She was fraying at the seams beneath her skin, but she refused to let the others know, and I wasn't even confident in whether she would willingly let *me* know without this bond.

Would we all survive it? If some of us didn't make it, would we survive losing them? I couldn't stomach even entertaining the thought.

We would all make it. We had to. Her entire court of rebels would survive this and live to crown Elianna on that dais.

Lia caught me staring and wiggled her brows at me as she awkwardly danced in my direction, forcing a chuckle from me.

She threw her arms around my shoulders and planted a harsh kiss on my lips. "Hi." She giggled on my mouth.

"Hi," I said back, a grin on my face.

"Come dance with me," she whined as she tugged on my arm.

"But you're so good at it by yourself," I teased, and she scoffed in response.

A knock sounded at the front door, making us all crane our necks and glance over.

"Who is it?" I shouted, and Gage halted his playing.

"Uh, Commander?" a man said through the door.

I sighed. "Coming." I let go of Lia and walked over to the front door, opening it a crack. My brows rose in surprise as I was met with one of my soldiers, Brann, as he stood in the doorway. His eyes were wide and glistening with nerves.

I turned back to my family. "I will just be a minute," I announced, and Gage instantly picked back up with his tune.

"What is it?" I asked him as I looked him up and down for injuries while closing the door behind me. "Did something happen?"

He cleared his throat. "We believe we may be under attack shortly," he whispered.

"What?" I demanded on the front steps of the townhouse. "What do you mean?"

His hands shook as he handed me a small woven sack. "Open with caution," he warned.

I pulled the string, opened the bag, and bile immediately climbed in my throat. I reached in and pulled out a brutally severed hand with a feathered quill stabbed through it. A blood speckled note between the two that read a warning to us that the army of fae had finally arrived.

"Fuck!" I shouted as I shoved the hand back into the sack and whipped it across the front yard as fury took over me. "Where did you find this? Was it in the city? Where the fuck are the guards?!"

I couldn't believe they found and slaughtered our scouts.

His spine straightened, and he bravely met my stare. "We just found them at the top of the watchtowers, Commander. Arrows protruding from their chests. I found the sack at the center of the gate's opening, waiting to be found. It was addressed to Elianna Solus, and it also stated that this was only the first."

I peeked in through the window, my eyes catching on Lia as she danced around once more.

My jaw ticked. These fucking bastards were trying to rip her away from me again. I would *never* let that happen.

My head whipped back to Brann as my chest tightened. "Did you see them?"

He shook his head. "We believe there were shadows retreating far beyond the hills, but I didn't want to send scouts out without speaking to you first."

I nodded my head multiple times rapidly. "Good man." I sucked in a breath and slammed my eyes shut as I tried to think of a plan and how to leave Lia out of it for as long as possible.

She may try to cut my balls off for it later, but I couldn't risk them finding her again. She had been drinking the last few hours, trying to have some fun *for once*—I couldn't take that away from her after everything she'd been through, and I refused to take the risk of her not being sober in battle.

I blew out a breath. "Prepare as many as you can on such short notice. Empty the barracks. Anyone who can fight will need to come if they are of age. I don't want people getting frightened, so leave the women and children out of it if you can. Ignorance is bliss." I paused. "We can't let them get into the city. We go to them. We will have the high ground."

He gave me a curt nod. "Yes, Commander." And then he marched up the street.

The beat of my racing heart threatened to make me collapse, and I desperately tried to will it to slow. Lia could sense these emotions within me now, just as I had been able to with her. I had to be careful.

Once he was out of sight, I slowly opened the door of the townhouse to see everyone had resumed their activities aside from Zaela. She was staring me down from across the room, clearly knowing something was wrong.

Lia's attention flew to me, and she drifted my way. "Is everything okay?" she asked, tone bordering on worry.

I gave her the most convincing smile I could muster. "Yes, I just need to borrow Gage and Landon for a little while. There is a bit of a ruckus happening in the barracks and we need to go handle it."

She took me in for a moment. "Is it an awful fight? Why are you so nervous right now?" she asked knowingly, placing her hand on my chest.

Ugh. This gods-damn mating bond.

"My Lia," I cooed to her. "I think you are mistaking your own feelings for mine in your drunken escapades. Perhaps you are nervous because you didn't know why I had been called out there," I teased, but my stomach twisted into knots inside of me as the lies slipped through my teeth, attempting to ease her concern.

Her eyes darted back and forth between my own, making me hold my breath, but then the corner of her lips lilted. "Perhaps you're right."

Gods-dammit, I didn't know if she would ever forgive me for this.

I planted a kiss on her forehead and she leaned into the touch. "We'll be back as soon as we can."

"You better!" she shouted as she dramatically backed away from me. "Because I have some *plans* for you and me later, Commander," she said seductively.

I winked at her with a grin, and then my focus went to the two men already waiting by the door for me. I was about to leave with them when I felt Zaela's dagger-like stare digging into my back.

I half turned. "Stay here with the girls and Finn, Zae. We'll be back." She opened her mouth to protest, but I shut the door behind me as I shoved Gage and Landon through it in a rush.

If Lia didn't kill me for not including her in this, then my cousin definitely would.

"What's going on, brother?" Gage asked as our steps quickened.

Huffing out a breath through my nostrils, I answered, "We have company. I'll explain on the way."

The three of us raced down the walkway path, into the street, and through the city as fast as we could. As our feet carried us, I prayed to all the gods that we weren't too late to stop their full army from breaching the gates.

Standing before our makeshift army, Gage and Landon flanking each of my sides, I put on the same brave face I always had when met with oncoming bloodshed.

"Your wives and children are asleep in their beds, waiting for you all to return home tonight. Don't give them a reason to wake up with heartache. Fight hard. Fight for your lives, and the lives of those you love," I announced.

As the moonlight filtered through the clouds, I watched as fear slowly crept in on their faces.

For the younger ones, this would be their first true battle. Had I trained them well enough? Hard enough? I could only hope to the gods that I had, but we were about to find out.

My eyes moved to Landon. "You're sure you can do this?" I whispered to him. "I should have found a way to ask you before dragging you down here with us. It is not too late for you to turn around."

"I refuse to sit back, consumed by fear, anymore in my life," he stated as he glanced down at his chest and then fixated his eyes on the army before us. "I choose to fight. Make me useful."

My stare then traveled to my other side, to Gage. "You ready?"

"I was made for this, brother," he answered, his voice cold and deadly calm. All signs of his typical humorous self had vanished.

"Then let's fucking end this."

FIFTY-EIGHT

Kellan

FROM A DISTANCE, I watched their pathetic excuse of an army form in the shadows of the night's darkness. I couldn't help but grin wickedly as they set forth to march right into us beyond the hills.

I guided my horse back to where we waited for the fun to begin and greeted Vincent as I dismounted. "She's coming." I laughed as I shook my head. "She'll never learn."

"I saw. Their army is sizeable, though, for such short notice. More than what we brought, Captain," he said.

I raised my brow at him and tilted my head to the side. "Scared?"

"Never. Just wanted to make sure you knew we were technically outnumbered."

I rolled my eyes. "Outnumbered in bodies. Not skill or healing abilities. We'll cut through them like nothing. Do you have it?"

Vincent patted the trap we would need to set to separate Elianna from the crowd as it hung from his side.

Excellent.

I turned to face my lethal, ready soldiers. "Everyone in position!" I boomed into the suddenly cloudy night sky.

We set forth and marched until we came face-to-face with the human army with less than a quarter mile between us.

Fury flooded my vision at the sight of who had led them there.

Not Elianna, but the fucking human filth commander that she had been sleeping with once she slipped through my fingers.

A guttural growl rumbled through my chest as my nostrils flared.

Vin let out a long whistle from next to me. "Ah. Thought we killed that one."

"As did I," I said through my clenched teeth. My gaze followed him as he approached us with two others flanking his sides.

I took my own steps forward, Vincent following closely behind, until we met in the middle. Now only several feet separated us as we stood there staring each other down.

The commander's eyes were locked on me, wrath oozing from his features as his jaw ticked in our stare down.

"Adler," he said in greeting. "What brings you here to my lands? And in the middle of the night again?" he tsked. "Well, that's just bad business."

My lips peeled back to reveal my teeth in a wicked sneer. "Commander. What a wonderful surprise..." I tilted my head to the side. "You're slightly more alive than I expected."

"Perhaps I'm not as easy to kill as you originally believed," he taunted me.

"It appears so." I grinned. "Nice scar."

His eyes narrowed in on me. "I'm giving you five fucking seconds to turn around and remove yourselves from Silcrowe or face the consequences."

I looked around, bored. "Silcrowe, you say? Last I heard, this was destroyed over a century ago."

"It has been remade," he growled.

"Aye," I let out, brushing him off. "Sorry, though, I will not be leaving. Not until I pluck three little mischievous traitors from your possession. Oh, and whoever else escaped Isla."

"Three?" He tilted his head to the side in question.

I chuckled. "In addition to Elianna Solus, the prince and princess will also be taken back to their home. You see, their mother misses them dearly, and their brother, who will soon be king, has a few choice words for them."

Out of my peripheral vision, I watched as he gripped the hilt of his sword tightly. "We do not house the prince or princess here. You must've missed them. Or perhaps they were killed on the road."

This stupid prick.

My lips tilted up. "The stable keeper standing directly behind you forces me to assume otherwise," I taunted him.

Any sense of amusement he had as he tried to toy with me vanished from his face. "You will *never* have her. Or any of them ever again," he seethed as a deafening crack of thunder rumbled the sky above.

Lightning flashed brightly in tandem with the boom of it, revealing the true terror written across his soldiers' faces. The commander was such a fool—I would never keep frightened, weak soldiers in my ranks. Satisfaction filled my veins.

"See, that's where you're wrong, Commander. It appears that you need a reminder once more that I will *always* have her. For no matter what you believe or tell yourself, she is forever mine."

His face twisted with fury before me, a vicious retort working its way off his tongue.

And then, in one swift movement, I ripped my sword from its sheath and struck.

FIFTY-NINE

Elianna

THE PARTY ENDED THE second the boys left. Something didn't feel right, and the more I sat around sobering up, the more my nerves took over me.

I looked over at Zaela, whose eyes had remained on the empty doorway since they stepped through it.

Finnian had asked me why they took Landon, and I didn't have an answer for him. I had no idea. I was just as much in the dark as he was.

Lightning flashed through the curtains. I walked over to the windowsill and gently pulled them back, looking out into the down pouring rain as it opened up from the night sky and flooded the streets.

"They should be back by now," I muttered to myself.

"No shit." Zaela stormed over to me and ripped the curtains from my hand, pushing them back completely. "Something's wrong. I can feel it."

"I think you're right," I answered as Avery walked up to us and joined.

"What is that?" she asked, as she pointed out to some sort of sack that was getting soaked from the rain in the front yard.

My brows furrowed. "That's strange. I don't remember seeing that there when we got back. I'll go check it out."

I grabbed Jace's cloak that was hanging off the railing of the staircase and threw it over my head as I opened the front door and rushed outside.

My boots splashed through the walkway's puddles, and thunder continued to boom in the storming sky above as I snatched the sack and bolted back to the door.

It slammed shut behind me from the wind, and I was slightly out of breath from how fast I had to grab it.

The woven bag dripped dirty water onto the floor at our feet and Zaela came up to me and stole it from my grasp as I peeled the soaked, clinging cloak from my shoulders.

My eyes flared as the tangy scent of blood filled my nostrils, making my heart race. I cleared my throat as they all gathered around—even Veli looked curious as she remained next to the fireplace from across the room.

I bit my bottom lip as I watched anxiously while Zae pulled the strings and glanced into the sack.

Her eyes shot up to mine, and she snapped it closed. "Can we speak upstairs for a moment?" she whispered.

I looked up and saw both Avery and Finnian's eyes staring at us nervously.

"Please tell us what it is," Avery said to her. "We can handle it. This is our life now."

I gave my sister a soft smile, but truthfully, if Zaela was concerned about what was in the bag, that even made *me* nervous.

Zae looked at her. "Suit yourself, Princess." And then she handed the bag to me as she sighed.

I gulped and reached my hand into it, and my eyes widened in horror the moment I touched flesh.

Fuck. Fuck. Fuck.

I pulled out a severed hand with a note stabbed through it. I ripped the piece of parchment from the blood covered quill and read what it said.

I could faintly hear Finn gagging from across the room at the sight of what was in it.

My mate lied to me. He lied to keep me here and snuck out with the others. With heavy breaths, I crumpled the already destroyed piece of parchment in my hand as fury took over me.

"They lied to us, didn't they?" Zaela asked, forcing me to meet her stare. The anger flickering in her eyes mirrored my own.

My jaw locked, and a frightening, breathy laugh slipped from me. "It appears that way."

She huffed out a breath and rapidly spun to face Finn and Avery. "You two..." She pointed at them aggressively. "Stay the fuck here." Her gaze snapped up to Veli. "You..." She paused for a moment, and one of my brows rose, wondering how the witch would do with taking orders.

"I'll make sure they stay put." Veli crossed her arms as she nodded at the door with her chin. "Go."

A second later, Zaela and I ran up the stairs, taking two at a time, as we each grabbed our armor and any weapons we could find in our rooms.

Racing back down the staircase, my steps paused as I found several pairs of eyes on us—Nyra's included. My wolf's gaze lingered on me with intensity, as if she knew what we were about to do.

"Come on, girl," I ordered, and then the three of us quickly sprinted out the front door and into the monsoon.

SIXTY

Elianna

My hair and clothes were soaked the moment we stepped beyond the front steps of the townhouse. Rain poured down on us as we raced through the narrow, winding streets of the city. No one was out, either due to the rain or from the hour of night it was.

Where the hell were they? If the fae army had breached the city, surely they would've been wreaking havoc by now. There wasn't anything to be seen or heard aside from the sound of raindrops smashing onto the sidewalks and roofs of the surrounding buildings.

We were approaching the front gates of the city, Nyra racing between us, when all of a sudden my legs came to a sudden halt. Slicing pain seared through my forearm, causing me to stutter and almost trip from the stun of it.

Zaela swung her arm out in front of my chest to steady me and we stood in the center of the empty square. Nyra watched me curiously, concern in her eyes.

Chest heaving, I peeked down at my forearm, but my eyes were met with untouched skin. No mark. Not a single drop of blood. Nothing.

Which could only mean one thing.

My chest tightened as blood rushed to my ears. I looked up at Zaela. "Jace is hurt."

"Shit!" she shouted into the storm. She looked back to me. "What the hell do we do?!"

I pushed my sopping wet hair from where it stuck to my face and stomped through the puddles until I reached the gates.

I placed my hand above my brows to shield my sight from the drops and couldn't see a damn thing. "Where are you, Jace?" I whispered to myself.

Zae moved up next to me and mirrored how I stood, trying to see through the storm as it slammed down on us.

Lightning flashed once more and out of the corner of my eye, shadow-like figures appeared far off in the distance beyond the hills.

"There!" I pointed and took off into a sprint, not waiting for her to respond or to even check if she followed.

Each step I forced through the thick mud was more desperate than the last. My arm ached, but luckily nothing else on my body. Which meant Jace was at least still alive. I hoped.

What was he thinking? Leaving me behind? *And* Zaela. How could he not tell me about this? Why would he ever think any of this was okay when he knew how I felt about everything?

I didn't hide from battles. I *never* fucking have. I always faced them head on, and this army marched here to destroy me. Destroy *us*. I'll be damned by the mother of the gods herself if Jace thought I wouldn't throw myself into this with him and fight until my very last breath.

And he took *Landon* with him? Oh, he would be in so much trouble if we lived through this.

We continued to race towards the fields. I lifted my hand to my mouth and let out a high-pitched whistle for Nox as my eyes desperately searched the skies above, but all I was met with was darkness and blinding rain.

"Nox!" I screamed, but its echo was lost in the booming sky. I whistled a few times more, but his wings never appeared. My memory flashed to the first night we had been caught in a storm—when we arrived at the war camp, and I remembered how terrified he had been flying in the sky as the thunder sounded.

"Where is the wyvern?!" Zaela shrieked at me through panting breaths as we ran.

"I don't think he can hear the whistle over the storm!"

It felt as if we were running for miles, and the storm still refused to let up. Thunder continued to roar in the sky and as the bright flash of the gods' wrath lit the night, I could finally see the absolute madness of the battle erupting below the hills.

The three of us came to a skidding halt at the top, looking down at the turmoil before us. Bodies were already piled in the mud. Crimson ran in rivers through the terrain, staining the realm with more senseless death.

A ferocious growl sounded from my wolf at the sight of it all, readying herself to sink her teeth into the enemy.

When I glanced at my mate's cousin, she was already watching me, waiting for my signal.

"Don't die, okay?" I shouted at her.

"You too, Lia. I can't take all the fun in killing the boys for leaving us out." She winked, and to my surprise, a pained laugh forced its way out of me.

I unsheathed my sword from my hip and raised it high above my head—my focus then fixated in on the scene.

Nyra unleashed a fierce howl that reverberated through the downpours and across the battlefield, earning many glances in our direction between the swipes of their swords.

"By blade and by blood," a ghost of a whisper left my lips of what I had promised my family and people only hours prior. I roared a monstrous battle cry into the air as thunder boomed in answer.

A promise from the rightful Valderre queen.

A promise of death.

Jace

Adler's blade had sliced my forearm wide open as our swords clashed together repeatedly in the midst of the battle. Blood trickled down my wrist and into the palm of my hand, making my grip on my weapon occasionally slip.

The moment I felt my flesh break open, all I could think of was Lia. She would know now—sense it through the mating bond. I just hoped to the gods she stayed put, not knowing where we all were, but I knew better.

Our boots stuck in the mud, making it difficult to move around as quickly and efficiently as we typically would. Adler was a great fighter; I would give the piece of shit that.

Out of breath, I heaved my blade directly at his face, but he raised his sword just in time to block the killing blow.

Even beneath the splattered mud and blood that covered his face, his infuriating grin shined through.

"I don't know if you heard, Commander," he said through deep breaths as he continued to strike. "But your darling Lia and I are to be wed upon our return to the realm's capital."

My eyes flared, and I let out a roar of rage as I swiped my blade at him continually, sparks flying every time the steel clashed. He was trying to taunt me, and I fucking hated that it worked. The thought of his hands on my mate, how he viewed and spoke of her, sent me in a fit of unmatched fury.

Our swords continued to collide until I watched as his attention moved up toward the hills. I took the opportunity to swipe, but he moved just in time for me to miss his chest, and instead, my blade slashed a gaping wound through his thigh.

He roared in pain and his fierce eyes were locked on me once more. Seething, he said, "Sorry, Commander, but it appears that my bride has arrived and I now have business to attend to."

And in one sudden, precise movement, he lifted his boot from the ground and kicked me so hard in the chest that I flew backward, landing directly into a pile of bloody, mutilated bodies. Adler let out a deep, guttural bellow, the sound echoing through the air, likely in response to the pain he had just added to his already wounded leg.

The fighting continued to rage on surrounding me and I had to quickly roll out of the way to avoid being trampled or stepped on by those who were near.

I grabbed my sword, and a second one I found on the ground that had either been discarded, or was that of one of the fallen, and whipped my gaze to the area that Adler had been staring.

My eyes widened in horror, and all thoughts were ripped from my mind as a bone-chilling howl sounded through the storm. My stare shot to the source, and I watched my mate as she roared a battle cry into the air and rushed down the hills, directly into the unfolding turmoil.

"Fuck!" I screamed and sent my blade into one of the fae that was rushing past me. His eyes had been locked on Landon, who I could see was only feet away from me, surprisingly holding his own.

Landon looked up at me and nodded, confirming he had the situation handled.

Thanking the gods, I aimed for the hilltop that I watched Lia sprint down. She couldn't have made it very far into the onslaught of bodies that were fighting and piling up.

The battlefield lay before me, a chaotic scene of violence and death, as the clash of steel against steel echoed through the air. Gripping my sword in desperation to get to her, I cut down every soldier in my path.

My heart pounded in my chest as I worked to focus on the precision of my movements, while also trying to get to her. Arrows whizzed past my head, finding their marks in the flesh of soldiers from each army. My face was covered in the blood of both my enemies and my own men as it splattered from every direction. I dodged and weaved as quickly as possible, vigorously swiping my blade, while trying to avoid being shot down myself.

The battle just beyond our own city had become ruthless, but I pressed on, unwavering. I fought through the sea of bodies, reminding myself that each step brought me closer to Lia.

Rage turned my vision red while the rain blurred everything around us. Using my double blades, I pierced through the chest armor of an enemy soldier as I brought my other sword across another's throat, severing his head from his body.

My eyes locked on her then from across the way, battling her way through the insanity. Each stride, slash and stab struck true. She was cutting them down faster and more efficiently than half of my own men were. And these were once her own gods-damn soldiers.

That's my fucking girl.

They were here to take her from me again. I would destroy them all before I let them lay a fucking finger on her.

A flash of her scars that covered her back displayed across my memory, and suddenly, my wrath consumed me.

I screamed into the air as I continued to cut down and mutilate our opponents while I moved across the bloody river that had taken over the field.

I glanced to the left of her and watched as Kellan approached, cutting down our men as he snuck in from behind her. Blood from the wound I gave him was still flowing down his thigh, soaking his pants, but he moved as if he was completely unbothered by it.

My vision slowed as I watched him reach out for her from behind. Not with his blade, but with his hands. He was actually going to *take* her.

"LIA! LOOK OUT!" I screamed as I forced my way to her as fast as I could.

Her eyes then snapped up to me from across the field, right as his arms wrapped around her chest.

SIXTY-ONE
Elianna

THE DESTRUCTION OF THE battlefield lay sprawled before us as we descended the hill, running full speed into the onslaught of the madness. The air was thick with the scent of blood, steel, and rain. I had once commanded these males and now found myself amid the very chaos they had organized against me and those I loved.

Moving with deadly determination, my blade sliced through the air with precision, striking true with each swing. The warriors I once commanded, now my rivals, fought ruthlessly in a bid for their victory. Every time my sword clashed against one of theirs, it echoed the betrayal that I felt raging within me.

Nyra shot out from behind me and attacked, sinking her canines into the flesh of enemy soldiers, letting their screams ring out as their blood coated her once white fur.

As I struck another, my eyes remained fierce and unyielding, betraying no emotion as I cut down those who worked to ambush us.

"I have eyes on Solus!" The words resounded through the madness, and I whipped in their direction as my gaze landed on two soldiers aiming for me.

"Hello, boys," I hissed with creased brows, a snarl on my lips as I twirled my sword in my hand.

I charged at the soldiers with my blade extended towards them, my powerful thighs pushing me through the thick mud that threatened to slow my movements.

My sword struck the first male with lethal accuracy as it plunged through his gut, effortlessly pushing through his armor. The second soldier was there a moment later, swinging his own blade right at my face. I moved to dodge him by heaving the body of the dead warrior at him with my blade.

My opponent lost balance as the body slammed into his front, and I lifted my boot to kick the deceased free of my sword, sending both him and the other to the ground with it.

The male shoved his comrade's body off of him and sent it flying through the mud, his eyes now locked on me with rage erupting from them. A smirk tilted my lips as I raised my weapon once more in anticipation, for I knew the wrath in my own stare was far deadlier than his.

My gaze glanced at my blade as his friend's blood slid down it in waves, washing away from the rain that continued to pour on us.

"Come on, you piece of shit, we were just getting started!" I bellowed, and he charged.

Our blades met over and over, and the ringing of their clash threatened to deafen me. Grunts left the both of us each time the force of our blows collided, testing every muscle in my body as I worked to disarm and kill a soldier twice my size.

However, where he had the muscle, I had the speed. Our weapons met once more, and I slid my blade down his, right before I tucked and rolled through the mud, out of his reach. He stormed towards me and I lashed out from the ground, swiping my sword directly at his ankles. Its steel cut straight through flesh and bone, severing his leg mid-calf. The male collapsed to the muddy terrain, a scream tearing through his throat—right until I sent my blade through that, too.

Working to catch my breath, my body whipped around as I searched through the chaos of the still raging battle. My eyes finally locked with Jace's and I felt relief as it slammed into me at the sight of him still alive and fighting. That was until my body was suffocated in an unbearable, violent embrace from behind.

I knew the scent of leather and sea salt anywhere. The feeling of his calloused hands on my body that I once craved, but now made me nauseous at the thought.

It was Kellan.

One of his hands clutched my wrist so tightly that it forced my sword out of my grasp instantly. I kicked and screamed, sending my fists flying backward towards his face as he lifted my feet from the ground and tried to walk off the battlefield with me in tow.

"Don't put up a fight, love. You know there's no use." He snickered in my ear, thinking he had already won.

"Fuck you!" I seethed, and he barked out a harsh laugh in response.

My hand moved down my thigh and ripped my dagger from its strap. Moving too quickly for him to realize what I was doing, I reached up over my head and plunged the obsidian blade behind my shoulder, directly into the crook of his neck.

Kellan roared with pain, and I placed the blade between my teeth to use the force of both of my arms to shove out of his grasp. However, his pain was too great, and he released me without much of a fight, allowing me to drop to the ground below.

I whipped around to face him in a crouch as my dagger's blade remained between my lips, his blood seeping into them.

"You stupid bitch!" he raged as he clutched at his wound that was pouring blood. "I'm the only one *not* trying to fucking kill you! Perhaps I just changed my mind." He reached down for me with his other hand.

I jumped up from my crouch and punched him directly in his face, sending his body stumbling backward.

"I *will* kill you," I growled through my teeth.

The rain was finally slowing when my ears perked up, high alert as I felt the presence of someone behind me once more. With my dagger now in my hand, I went to spin and slice them down, but my wrist was caught in midair.

My pivot halted, and my rain-soaked hair, entangled with gore and mud, clung to my face as my eyes flared. A wave of devastation nearly sent me to my knees as I came face-to-face with who I had just tried to slaughter.

Hazel eyes entranced me where I stood as the hand of my mate grasped my wrist. He gently released his hold, his stare filled with longing and worry as he stood before me, taking heaving breaths.

"It's me, my Lia. It's me," Jace whispered to me between each breath he took, and my knees buckled as guilt and pure fear consumed me.

I had just unknowingly tried to kill my mate. Mother of the gods, what did I just do? An overwhelming sense of dread flooded me as my mouth popped open in horror, breathing rapidly while he continued to watch me.

Jace quickly moved to pull me into his chest. "Are you hurt?" he asked.

I shook my head, and my eyes widened as I remembered that only a moment ago, I had been standing over Kellan, ready to finally kill the bastard once and for all.

He seemed to have the same realization, and we both turned abruptly and looked at the ground below.

Kellan was *gone*.

"NO!" I roared, and frantically searched my surroundings.

They were retreating—almost all of them. I watched as the fae soldiers wearing Islan armor ran for the far-off fields in the distance, where their horses awaited them.

"You fucking *cowards!*" I shouted into the air, my voice getting lost in the now far-off thunder.

My chest rose and fell rapidly as I watched the retreat unfold. Our soldiers cheered in unison, but I was *far* from happy.

No, they *all* needed to die for what they tried to do tonight.

I turned around, searching for signs that our friends still lived, when my eyes locked in on Landon across the battlefield.

He was walking toward us, smiling in victory, when a shadow suddenly raced toward him from the side. My eyes focused on the figure running towards him, and my heart stopped when I noticed that it was Vincent.

"Landon!" I shouted. "Look out!" I moved to rush toward them, and Nyra joined me in my race, barking and growling in their direction, but it was too late.

Vincent plunged his sword through Landon's side, and I was forced to watch as my brother's love fell to his knees, eyes filled with agony and terror.

"NO!" I boomed as my feet continued to carry me to him.

Vincent raised his sword above Landon's head once more to issue the lethal blow when suddenly an arrow was protruding from his leg, and then another in his shoulder.

Still running, I whipped my head to see both Gage and Zaela were shooting their arrows in his direction.

"Fucking get him!" I screamed at them.

Vincent ripped the arrow out of his leg and turned on his heel to retreat with the others, leaving Landon sunken on his knees in the mud.

They took off after him in a run.

I watched Landon fall to the ground face first as I finally reached him, dropping to my own knees before him. Nyra whimpered next to me at the sight of him, licking the side of his cheek that showed through the mud.

"No, no, no! Come on, Landon," I cried as I turned his body over. "You're okay. You're okay!" Tears welled in my eyes as I forced him to stay awake and with us.

Jace met me and his hand flew to cover his jaw that hung open as he bellowed a curse to the gods up into the clearing sky.

My eyes slammed shut as I rose to my feet and used the rest of my adrenaline to sling Landon's limp, yet still breathing, body over my shoulder. I let out an involuntary grunt at the weight of him.

"Lia, let me—" he started.

"No!" I said sternly as I held up my hand to halt him. "I have him. I need to get him back to Veli as soon as possible. Go hunt that piece of shit down with the others," I ordered him.

His breathing quickened, looking nervous at my refusal for his help. His worry rattled down the bond, but my anger overpowered it, blocking it out almost entirely.

"I love you, okay? Everything is going to be okay," he assured me, but I watched as his expression dropped at the sight of Landon's blood as it poured from his wound and down my back.

I gave him a curt nod. "Make sure you get him and bring him to me. Alive," I demanded, but my voice cracked as nerves took over me.

With Nyra by my side, I turned and ran up the hills, rushing back to the city as fast as the extra weight I now carried would allow.

I burst through the townhouse's front door, covered in grime and blood—soaked from the storm that had finally ceased.

Finn, Avery and Veli's attention snapped up to me and they all gasped out in shock at the sight of Landon slipping from my grasp as I desperately tried to keep him on my shoulders.

Chest heaving, I stormed through the living room and placed Landon onto the settee, not giving a damn about caking it in the debris of battle.

"Oh, gods!" Finn shouted, and my heart cracked wide open in my chest. "Landon! What happened to him? Where the hell did they go?!" He fell to the floor at his lover's side as he looked up to me with eyes drowning in devastation.

I cleared my throat, trying to catch my breath. "They found us," was all I could manage to say in this moment, and then I turned to Veli. "Help. Him," I begged.

Veli quickly rushed to her room across the hall and emerged with her hands overflowing with bandages, salves, and tonics.

"Move, boy!" she shouted at Finn, who immediately moved to scoot back on the floor to get out of her way.

She took her taloned nails and ripped open his shirt above his wound. She reached for a thick salve that was in one of the many jars she brought out and slabbed a thick layer of it onto his deadly injury.

Veli grabbed a sedaeyo leaf and shoved it at my brother. "Force him to eat this."

"How? He isn't even awake!" he cried, voice booming with anger and panic.

Her terrifying eyes narrowed in on him. "Do you want him to live?" she snapped. "It will help with the pain, but I need to focus elsewhere. As in on his *wounds*, Finnian."

Finn rose to his feet, the skin bunching around his eyes in a pained stare as he sat on the arm of the settee next to Landon's head. He carefully popped his jaw open and placed the leaf into his mouth.

"If you can hear me, chew," he urged. "Please, Landon. I can't do all of this without you." Tears streamed down his cheeks in waves.

I turned to Avery and watched as her own lips trembled, and she swiped away the few tears that slipped out.

Landon's eyes flickered open. "Finn," he started. His breaths were heaving in and out, his stare glassy. "It hurts...I'm so sorry."

A sob broke through my own defenses as I watched their interaction while Veli worked to stitch him up. Nyra, her coat still soaked and blood-stained, sat on my feet in an attempt to comfort me.

"I know," Finn whispered as he pushed back the hair that stuck to his face. "This leaf will help with the pain."

Once Landon slowly started chewing, Veli gave a subtle nod, and all of us blew out a breath of relief in unison.

I walked over to the window and peered through, waiting to see if Jace and the others had caught Vincent.

That bastard was as good as dead. Not only for the acts committed against me over the last few months, but to my people, and now Landon.

Avery gently placed a hand on my shoulder as she came up next to me, staring out into the street.

"What happened out there?" she asked, voice so soft I could barely hear her.

"War," I answered in a growl, as my gaze remained fixated on the road. My hands balled into trembling fists as they hung at my sides. "War happened, Avery."

SIXTY-TWO

Jace

I CAUGHT UP TO Gage and Zaela as fast as I could as dawn crept up on the horizon.

Gage raised his bow as he nocked an arrow in place and aimed mid-run.

"Don't kill him. Lia wants him alive," I reminded him, and he released the arrow, sending it into the back of Vincent's thigh.

He tripped and fell face forward as he howled from the impact.

We finally caught up to him as he continued to try to escape by crawling from us on the ground.

"Don't you move," I seethed as I pressed my boot into his back and stomped down, hearing a crack from his spine.

"Fuck you!" he roared.

"Fuck me? Fuck. *Me?*" I shouted down at him.

I leaned down, gripping his long, blonde hair in my fingers and ripped it back, exposing his neck to my blade that I snuck beneath it. "You listen to me, you piece of shit. If it weren't for my mate demanding you be kept alive, I would slice your throat this instant and watch the life leave your eyes as the blood spilled from you," I said through my teeth into his ear, my tone promising a gruesome death.

He laughed in response. *Laughed*. The male was clearly just as sick as Adler was.

"Is something funny?" Zaela demanded at my side as she nocked an arrow in her bow, aiming it at his face.

"Mate." He cackled again. "You think she is your *mate?* She will chew you up and shit you out once she's done with you," he said to me.

I pressed the blade tighter to his throat and blood beaded at its tip. "You don't know a fucking thing about her."

His answering grin had me imagining slitting his throat right then and there. He was trying to throw me off. Trying to get under my skin and make me second guess my own gods-damn mate.

"Brother," Gage said firmly. "Alive. Lia wants him *alive*."

I blinked my rage away enough to not destroy the man beneath me as he grimaced.

"Bind his hands," I barked, more harshly than they deserved, but the two of them knew how I could be in situations like this. I had one mood. One thing on my mind—*annihilate*. Destroy them before they could do the same to you.

My gaze drifted to where the last of their survivors retreated in the distance, their mounts awaiting them. A growl rumbled through me as I cursed myself for allowing Adler to slip through our grasp once more.

Zaela got down on her knees and bound Vincent's hands behind his back.

I pulled him to his feet by his hair, and he hissed through clenched teeth. "I am counting down the seconds until she ends you. You think a death at my hands will ensure suffering? I can't fucking *wait* to see what my queen has in store for you," I whispered into the tip of his ear.

I shoved the male, getting him to move toward the fate that awaited him, but the infuriating grin remained on his smug face.

Zaela unlocked one of the cell doors in Ellecaster's empty dungeons that sat within the foot of the Ezranian Mountains.

This was one of the few structures left standing after Silcrowe was destroyed at the start of the war, mainly because it was built into the mountain itself. Nearly everything was made from rock and stone. Upstairs lay the courtroom, where trials would be held publicly, and prisoners would be held down here awaiting trial, or if they were sentenced to time behind bars for their crimes.

I pushed Vincent into the cell, leaving his hands bound behind his back, as Gage lit a few torches in the dust covered hallway we stood in. I slammed the iron-barred gate shut in his face as he stared at me through the openings.

"Hungry?" I asked, crossing my arms.

"Starved," he answered, dragging out the word.

"Good. Fuck you," I snapped, earning a wicked chuckle from the other two.

I turned to leave to finally get back to Lia when he spoke once more.

"Oh, Commander?" he said, and I pivoted toward him with a raised brow. "I do have a gift for your darling queen. Of course, this was not how we planned for her to get it, but we still wish for her to receive it, nonetheless." His wicked smile sent a shiver of panic through me, but I didn't reveal it on my face.

"A gift?" I growled. "And what might that be?"

He pointed down to his hip with his chin, and my eyes followed the path down to where a tied bag hung attached to his belt.

My expression turned into a scowl. "What. Is. It," I demanded.

He shrugged one shoulder. "You'll have to come grab it and find out. It's quite personal. A lovely parting gift from her former love, Captain Adler."

A rumbling growl erupted from my chest as he spoke of my mate and the piece of shit that believed to have a claim on her.

Zaela raised her bow once more and pointed it at our captive. "Get the sack, Jace. If he moves, I'll shoot him."

A malicious smile grew from ear to pointed ear on our prisoner's face as I unlocked the cell door once more and stepped in.

I quickly untied the bag from his side and looked up to see he was staring at me intently, right before he blew me a kiss.

I scoffed at him in disgust as I moved to exit his cell and locked him back in.

He stood there grinning in silence.

"What's in the bag, brother?" Gage asked.

I lifted the bag in front of me and was immediately overwhelmed by a horrifying, rotting stench. I carefully opened the top of the sack, and numerous, buzzing flies flew out from it.

My gaze met Zaela's, who watched me nervously as she continued to point the arrow at our prisoner, even though I was back outside of the cell. I blew out a harsh breath and as I peered into the bag, nausea roiled through me.

I felt so many things at once.

Disgust. Horror. Devastation for my mate as I realized what they had done—how they had planned to *lure* her to them.

I tried to swallow, but my throat wouldn't let me. My glaring eyes snapped up to meet his. "You motherfucker," I seethed. "And what makes you think I would give this to her for her to see, huh?"

Zaela creeped over and peered into the bag. She pivoted to the side and bent over slightly, ready to vomit at the sight...and the smell. "Mother of the gods," she murmured. "You're sick!" she shouted at him, voice cracking.

"You'll give it to her. If you are truly her mate, you couldn't keep something like this from her." I stayed silent in response as my thoughts consumed me. Lia had been hanging on by a thread as it was, and one of her greatest fears was about to become reality. "Am I wrong?" he continued to toy with me.

I forced the bag closed and stormed toward the dungeon's entrance as I roared in frustration, its echo reverberating off the walls.

"Give her my love, Commander!" he shouted after me as he cackled. "Tell her it's a very special gift, and a reminder that she's on the losing side of this war."

Gage and Zae caught up to me quickly as I strode out into the streets while the citizens emerged to start their days. Some still seemed unaware of the events that had occurred in the night.

"Are you going to show Lia what's in the bag?" Gage asked me as he tried to keep up with my strides.

I frowned. "I don't have a choice," I muttered. "But…this is going to fucking destroy her."

SIXTY-THREE

Elianna

Once Landon was somewhat stable, we moved him to rest upstairs in his and Finnian's room—I still couldn't believe he survived. Veli had said that any longer and the gods would've claimed his soul. He could barely keep his eyes open as she stitched up his wound, and I fully believed that it was Finnian's voice, filled with desperation, that kept him in our realm.

After he was settled, I updated them all about what went on and how Kellan got away, which was still making my blood boil within my veins.

Why did I have to punch him in the face with my fist? It should've been with my gods-damn dagger. They were all just relieved that the other three were alive and unharmed.

When everyone seemed to calm down, Finn decided to join Landon upstairs to keep an eye on him. Avery worked to scrub the blood stain out of the settee's cushions, which was shocking because I had never seen her scrub a damn thing in my entire life.

She frowned. "It's not going to come out." She looked up at me. "Looks like I get to buy more furniture," she said, trying to sound cheerful in her joke. A soft smile formed at her attempt.

Avery looked exhausted, though, and I wasn't foolish enough to believe that she was unaffected by what had happened to Landon. While he was Finn's lover, I knew that the two of them had become close friends in recent days.

I tilted my head to the side. "Are you okay?"

She blew out a breath and rose to her feet. "That was so scary," she admitted. "I don't ever want to experience fear like that again."

My heart clenched, knowing that it was only the beginning of the absolute storm that was about to be unleashed.

I sucked in my bottom lip. "Would you like the painful truth or a comforting lie?" I asked, my lips tilting up at the edges.

She sniffled. "Comforting lie, please."

"Zaela will absolutely not care about you picking out a new settee, and she is thrilled with what you have done to the place." I smirked.

She let out a sharp laugh. "You're the worst."

I stepped forward and pulled her into a hug. "You should go get some rest. I know the day is only beginning, but you were up all night." I pulled away and looked into her bloodshot eyes, where a tint of purple cast a shadow beneath them.

She scoffed. "I danced around and sat here waiting. If anyone needs rest, it's you. You're the badass that just blindly ran into a battle," she said as she stabbed her pointer finger into my sternum.

I shrugged. "Go rest. I'll be up once they're back."

She huffed at me, but finally turned and headed up the stairs. I looked over at Veli and watched her as she swirled a glass of wine while sitting in the chair next to the fireplace.

"You should rest too, you know. It's also a little early for that," I mocked.

She grinned at me. "Ah, but is it too early when you never went to bed? It certainly wasn't the other day." I opened my mouth to speak, but she didn't give me the chance. "It isn't. Now mind your business, Elianna."

I watched her for a few silent moments. "You were scared." Her eyes rose to meet mine. "For Landon. You were scared that you wouldn't be able to save him."

Veli's violet stare narrowed in on me. "Do you know how difficult it was keeping those three idiots alive on the journey here? It would've been such a waste if he croaked on day three here."

I pursed my lips as my eyes rolled. "Veli," I started, but she refused to look back at me. "Why are you so afraid to act like you care about people? You're a *healer* for gods' sake. Obviously you care, so why be this way? I understand that you fear the use of your magic, but—"

"I do not fear my *power*," she hissed. "I fear what will find us if I continue to recklessly use it."

"Okay," I started, voice soft. "Regardless of your use of power...why be this way?"

To my surprise, she opened her mouth to answer, but was cut off by the front door opening.

I whipped around as the three of them funneled in through the doorway.

I ran up to them and threw my arms around Jace's neck. "Thank the gods you're okay." I released him and looked at the others. "All of you."

Jace looked relieved at my words, and I turned to Veli once more and saw she had taken the distraction to get up and leave. The click of the lock on her bedroom door sounded down the hall only a second later.

Oh, we were absolutely not done with that conversation. I let out a sigh.

"Lia," Jace whispered as he took my hand in his, pulling me to face him. "I'm so sorry."

I held up my other hand. "Not now," I said through my teeth.

He blinked a few times at me. "Okay," he whispered as he searched my face. "Landon?"

I sucked in a breath. "He's alive, barely. He is resting with Finn upstairs. Veli was able to stitch him up and stabilize the bleeding with that and some salve."

"I can't believe that happened," he muttered.

"Well?" I asked. "Did you *get him?*"

Gage and Zaela shot each other a look that made my guts twist. Did he actually get away? Both him *and* Kellan? Oh, I was about to lose my mind.

"We did," he answered, and I blinked in shock as my stare bore into him.

"Excellent." I grinned wickedly. "Gods, don't scare me like that," I huffed as I walked away and made my way to the warmth of the fireplace.

It had started to drizzle outside once more. More storm clouds rolled in, blocking the sun and encasing the living room in gloomy darkness aside from the fire.

"Lia," he breathed.

I half turned to him. "Hmm?"

He swallowed. "There's something you need to see. Something he brought. For you."

The way my mate spoke made my throat nearly close. I could feel his pain—his rage building beneath his skin. What could it possibly be to have him so deadly calm yet ready to burst?

I glanced over at Gage, and he was looking down at the floor, clearly not wanting any part in this. Same with Zae.

Heart palpitations rattled my chest as I took in the sight of each of their faces. What the fuck was going on?

"What is it, Jace?"

He made his way to me and stretched out a hand that held a filthy sack—its stench instantly clogged my nostrils.

"What is this?"

My eyes shot up to him and when I reached out for it, he gently gripped my wrist with his other hand. "No matter what happens, I love you. Okay? Everything is going to be okay. I want nothing more than to spare you from this, but I cannot keep this from you."

Pure fear radiated in his stare as my eyes frantically searched his.

"You're scaring me," I whispered.

His jaw locked, averting his gaze from my own, but he finally released my wrist and let me take the bag from him. I turned to the fire, and when I pulled open the strings, I found that all of my worst nightmares had come true.

I couldn't breathe. My vision skipped red and went straight to black. All the air was ripped from my lungs as I stared down into the foggy, disintegrating eyes held within Lukas' rotting, severed head that lay in the sack.

My jaw snapped shut and my hands began shaking vigorously as I dropped the sack to the floor at my feet.

They never burned him. They mutilated his corpse and dragged it along the entire realm and continent just to make a point. Lukas' soul would never know peace now. Because of *me*. Because of their need for revenge against me. He couldn't escape that night because he was so focused on getting me out of there, sacrificing himself to ensure Nox could bring me to safety. Everything he ever did was for me or my father. He dedicated and surrendered his life to serve the Valderre bloodline, and *this* was what he was gifted from it.

An eternal damnation.

I felt my face as it contorted into something vicious while I struggled to contain my fury and devastation. My nails dug into the palms of my hands as I stared unblinking into the flames flickering in the fireplace.

My wrath enveloped me, filling me entirely until there was nothing else left. The grip on my emotions that I had desperately held onto so tightly these past few weeks shattered in an instant. I lifted my chin high and my nostrils flared as I imagined everything I would do to make them pay for what they had done to my family.

I allowed a single tear to slip from me, and my teeth were clenched so hard that I thought they might crack as I gradually turned to face the three of them. My chest was heaving, and I looked up to meet their stares through deeply furrowed brows.

My eyes drifted to Jace, and I watched him clutch his own chest as my wrath erupted down our bond, searing it in flames of rage.

"Bring me to him."

SIXTY-FOUR
Elianna

I BURST THROUGH THE front door of the townhouse and stormed into the slick, mud covered streets of Ellecaster with one thought on my mind—*revenge*.

The need for vengeance consumed my very being as I was forced to peer into the fog-hazed eyes of the only father figure I had left in the realm.

Kellan did this, and I refused to rest until I plunged my blade into his fucking heart, as he figuratively had with mine countless times now.

I marched through the city peering through pinched brows as I followed my mate to where our prisoner awaited. He had placed his hooded cloak atop my head when we left, letting himself continue to get drenched in the rain as he led the way for the four of us.

Our people waved as we passed by, but I didn't have the energy or patience to return any of their kindness. Our men got what they wanted—they left their females and women in the dark to run off into a seemingly unwinnable battle just outside of our city gates. The lividness I felt toward Jace regarding how everything played out the night prior would have to wait until we knew exactly what we were dealing with.

Vincent was trusted by Kellan; that was clear. I knew he had information regarding what was occurring within the ranks, the crown, and any plans they had for the future of Velyra. The real challenge would be extracting the information from him, for judging by the type of male he was, it would be anything but easy.

Coming to the edge of the back of the city, we stood before an enormous stone door built into the side of the mountains that Ellecaster laid before.

Jace turned to me and hesitantly took me in. "We have Vincent inside. I would prefer if—"

"And I would've preferred to not be left out of a battle that concerned my people and mate. However, we cannot all have what we prefer, now can we?" I cut him off. His panic surged down the bond.

I went to move past him, but he grabbed me gently by the waist and forced me to look back at him. "It was to protect you. *Everything* I do now is for you. You were drinking, having fun *for once*, and the thought of that being ripped away from you killed me. I would also never risk you going into battle if you weren't sober, but I shouldn't have lied to you. The second it slipped past my tongue, I regretted it. I made the wrong call, and you're right. I'm so sorry, my Lia," he whispered as his eyes frantically searched mine.

My heart fluttered in my chest, but my face remained cold and stern at his admission. I couldn't deal with this right now—too much was at stake.

I tugged out of his grasp and moved to open the stone door to their prison.

Zaela moved in front of us and led the way as Jace fell back. His panic had morphed into sorrow and I would give anything in this moment to know how to shut it out.

The truth was that I had already forgiven him the second I saw him on that battlefield.

My heart threatened to collapse as I realized that I would've absolutely done the same if he were the one drinking and our enemy was coming for him. I never would've risked him, even if I had to lie and tie him to a gods-damn chair myself. However, I needed to stay livid for what was to come.

I stopped in my tracks as Zaela started descending a set of stone carved stairs. "Where is he?" I demanded.

She cleared her throat and turned back to face me. "There are cells on the floor below. He is locked up there."

I glanced around the enormous, sculpted cavern. "Is there an open space we could bring him?"

"There is a room where court was once held," Gage cut in.

"Bring him there. I do not wish for him to know that I'm here yet," I announced, and I watched as Zaela's eyes flew over my shoulder to look at Jace. "That is a direct order, Zaela. He isn't making this call."

"Do as she says, Zae," Jace ordered from behind me.

Her eyes flared in response, and she then continued her descent down the stairs with Gage trailing behind her.

I stood there in silence for several unnerving moments when Jace finally approached me and moved to block my path. He took my chin in between his fingers and lifted my gaze to his.

"I love you. There will never be a single second of time where my desire for you, or to be with you, fades. Whatever you need me for today, and any day, I am here to be just that." He released my chin and turned on his heel without another word to guide me to the courtroom.

"I know," I whispered to his back as my features softened. I then took my first step to follow him.

I lurked in the shadows of a hidden chamber within the courtroom, waiting for the others to deliver my captive to me. Jace stood in the center of the room with a chair and rusted iron chains, waiting for his arrival.

After what seemed as if nearly a half hour had passed, Zaela and Gage finally appeared in the far hall, dragging Vincent's bloodied, limp body.

"What the hell happened?" Jace barked at them, and I was wondering the same before I stormed out there myself. My jaw locked as I crossed my arms over my chest, watching from the far corners of the room.

"Gods!" Zaela shouted as she took a breath while throwing his body into the chair. "It's not as if he is easily controllable. He tried to attack me as we were escorting him. Gage had to slam his head against the bars of his cell."

Gage shrugged at her in response.

"Well then, let's wake the fucker up, shall we?" Jace said sinisterly as he watched the others finish securing Vincent to the chair with the chains.

I eyed him curiously as he stalked out of the room and returned minutes later with a small trough filled with water that had likely been sitting in the rain outside.

Without a flicker of hesitation, he tossed the contents of the bucket in our prisoner's direction, soaking him completely.

As my eyes sparked with amusement, I felt the thrill of anticipation rumble through me—it was showtime.

SIXTY-FIVE

Elianna

"What the fuck!" Vincent roared as the filthy water poured down his face and seeped into his eyes.

He shook his head vigorously in each direction to dry off, and as he blinked his eyes open, a grin immediately formed on his face.

"Commander, lovely seeing you so soon." His gaze leisurely drifted around the room. "Is your darling queen hiding? I can smell her."

I smirked at that. He thought I was hiding? From *him?* Absolutely not. I just needed an excuse to make my grand entrance, but I could feel the grasp on my temper slipping the more I watched the scene unfold.

Jace took the trough he held and flipped it upside down as he placed it at his feet and sat upon it, now face-to-face with the evil that stared him down. I continued to observe from the shadows.

"You will not speak of her," Jace growled as he removed his dagger from his boot. "You're going to tell us what we want to know..." He twirled the blade in his hand. "And we will give you a quick death that you certainly do not deserve. And if you—"

"And if I refuse, what? You'll make sure I suffer?" Vincent raised a brow with his sneer. "Honestly, Commander, I expected something more original from you."

Jace leaned into him from where he sat, his head cocking to the side in a predatory manner. "Make no mistake, you *will* take a knee before my queen...and then I will shatter them both beyond use." The promise of death lingered in his tone.

A wicked smile tilted my lips at his threat. The only issue was that I didn't want the bastard kneeling before me—I wanted him fucking squirming.

"That will not be necessary, my love," I called out from the hall, my voice a lethal calm as it echoed across the empty court.

I stepped out from the cover of the shadows, and as I approached them, my hips swaggered from side to side, staring Vincent down as his gaze snapped to mine.

"I will not accept a knee to be taken from a traitorous, menacing snake, for he has chosen his fate," I continued as my eyes roamed over him, a snarl creeping up my lips. "As for shattering kneecaps, though, who am I to deny you a bit of fun?"

"While I would wish for nothing more than to kill you in this moment, it is not my death to claim. It is hers," my mate breathed at him viciously as he snickered and stood from his makeshift seat.

"Ah, there she is. The true heir of the realm herself. I was wondering if you would show up or if you just sent your newfound loyal dogs to do your dirty work."

I halted several feet in front of him and placed my hands on my hips. "Interesting for you to be calling someone else a loyal dog. That is exactly what you are to Kellan, no?"

He chuckled wickedly as his gaze swept me up and down. "I told Adler we should've thrown your ass overboard all those months ago. It is quite a pity he didn't listen."

"Oh, you mean all those months ago where you tried to assault me on his ship?" I spat, and I heard a deep growl rumble from Jace as he stood at attention behind me.

Vincent lifted his chin in contemplation as he looked up at the ceiling. "Yes, actually. I believe your timing would be correct." His grin appeared once more.

"Gods, and you thought *we* were predictable," I hissed as I walked up to him and bent down directly in his face.

I didn't miss his peek at my breasts as they spilled over the top of my shirt. Jace didn't either, judging by the quick spark of anger that rushed down the bond.

"Maybe I *do* know why he was hesitant after all," he said with a chuckle as he licked his chapped, blood-stained lips.

As soon as the foul thoughts left him, I reacted instinctively by unsheathing my dagger from my thigh and driving it deep into his own. With a step back, I left the blade embedded in his flesh.

Vincent roared in pain, violently thrashing around in his chains as he stared at me, chest heaving. "You stupid bitch!"

"I'm not the one who's a prisoner with a dagger protruding from my leg. Think you'll cooperate now?" I tilted my head to the side as I placed my hands on my hips.

"Fuck you," he seethed.

"Only in your dreams, honey," I taunted as I flashed him my canines.

The three of them behind me let out wicked chuckles.

"Only a wretched creature such as yourself would have the audacity to speak to another man's mate that way," Jace stated, voice lethal.

"Mates," he spat, and then turned his attention back to me. "How delusional are you? To think your mate is a human. I'm not quite sure which one of you I feel most sorry for. You, or him."

Before I could blink, out of the corner of my eye, the bucket Jace had brought in flashed by me, the wind of it making my hair flow out to the side as it was whipped at Vincent's face.

The crunching sound it made as it crushed his nose beneath it was the most beautiful noise I had heard all day.

He let out another shriek of pain as the trough clattered to the floor.

"I told you not to speak of her," Jace said from behind me, and a ghost of a smile tilted the corner of my lips.

"Just get this shit over with!" Vincent bellowed as blood poured from his nose.

Gage let out a huff of a laugh at him. "Don't speak of our queen. You were warned."

I turned to face him with a knowing grin.

"Well, Vincent." I took a step towards him. "The choice really is in your hands. Tell us everything you know about the crown, ascension, and their future plans, and we'll make your death somewhat less torturous. Refuse...and well, you can see the kind of giving moods we are in." I shrugged.

"It's adorable you think I will tell you a single fucking thing," he hissed.

I sighed. "Gods, you're exhausting. Very well."

I moved so fast that it surprised even myself. My arm reached out and violently tore the dagger from his leg, spurting blood everywhere, and I then leapt onto him. My knee dug into his groin as I hovered over him and ripped his greasy, gore-infused hair back to hold my blade to his throat.

My wrath quickly enveloped me once more as the vision of Lukas' severed head flashed across my memory. I couldn't see anything, only a haze of darkness as I whispered, "Who mutilated Lukas?" My sight slowly cleared as he remained silent. *"Who. Did. It?!"* I roared, as my fists trembled with rage while they held him in place.

My eyes stared down into his as I pressed my dagger just hard enough to only let a few drops of blood slip through. The fucker flashed his teeth at me in a sneer as my breathing quickened while trying to decide what to do.

"You won't do it," he huffed out.

I leaned in closer, our noses nearly touching. "Do you know how long I've waited for this? My only regret is that Kellan didn't meet the same fate...yet." My face twisted into something venomous, but he still wouldn't speak.

"Where is the army?" I changed the direction of the conversation to get at least *something* useful out of him before my temper slipped further.

"How should I know? I'm here with you, after all," he answered.

I dug my knee deeper into his groin and watched as his eyes bulged while he bared his teeth at me in response.

"You're proving to be useless," I hissed through clenched teeth.

He chuckled sharply, and I could feel the other three behind me as they gradually crept up and surrounded us. "You're more like the shit prince than you think. Barking empty threats that you won't act out on your own to demand information...must be a Valderre trait."

"I am *nothing* like Kai!" I screamed in his face. The echo of my voice bounced off the walls and vibrated within me. I cursed myself for showing how his words affected me.

He huffed out a laugh, accidentally pushing the blade slightly deeper into his own flesh. "Perhaps not entirely. At least you can ride a fucking horse and wield a blade half decently." He grinned, but my jaw popped open at what he had just unknowingly revealed.

A malicious grin crept up my lips as my stare continued to bore into his. "You came by land instead of sea," I breathed, and his eyes widened. "Kai is *with* you, and you rode here by horse across the continent looking for us. Looking for those who fled. That is how there were so many soldiers." Panic slowly slithered into his eyes. "That means they can't be far..."

Surprise radiated from Jace as I spoke the words.

Vincent bared his teeth at me, nostrils flaring as the veins in his neck strained. "Fuck you, Solus," he growled. "You're as good as dead the second they come back here, anyway."

"You see, Vincent...that is where you're wrong," I whispered into his ear, seething as I put all of my weight onto my knee that dug into his groin. "They'll never get the chance to return here." I tilted my head to the side once more. "I'm about to make sure of it."

"There will never be a way for you to take the crown back! Your defeat is certain, even before the final battles commence. Kai will ascend the throne and you will be put to death!" he roared, sending the frantic and anger-fueled words booming through the court.

My eyes darted back and forth between his own beneath furrowing brows, wearing a malicious smile. The word Veli spoke to me in the tongue of the gods echoed in my mind—*ignystae*. The need for vengeance hummed through me, as did the ancient power of the forgotten word, while I imagined using it upon those who came here to destroy us.

"I *will* take my crown, Vincent. And I finally have the means to do so." His eyes flared as I brought my face directly before his own. "And that is by wyvern's flame."

Before he had the chance to get one last retort in, I ripped my obsidian blade across his throat and watched as a river of crimson poured down his front. My eyes continued to bore into his, and I reveled as his stare turned lifeless beneath me while he choked on his own blood.

My thoughts were racing, swirling in a chaotic frenzy as I tried to make sense of what I had just uncovered.

The enemy fleet had retreated only hours ago, just as dawn was rising, which meant they couldn't have gotten far. There would never be a chance that Kai was on that battlefield with them. I couldn't even believe they brought him to begin with, so I could only assume that they had made camp somewhere between here and the forest. Which meant nearly all of my enemies were just a short flight away...

I twisted my neck towards my mate, who observed everything unfolding from behind me. "Care for a wyvern ride, handsome?"

His answering grin awoke something primal deep within me.

To be continued...
END OF BOOK TWO

She will reclaim her throne...
by blade, blood, and flame.

A THRONE OF WINGS AND EMBERS
THE FORBIDDEN HEIR TRILOGY | BOOK THREE
EMILIA JAE

Acknowledgements

Thank you so much to every single person who has believed in me, and my story, from the very start.

Thank you to my love, family, and friends for supporting this and cheering me on the whole way. Your words of encouragement when I doubted myself kept me going. This is especially to Celia and Tory because this never would've happened without them and their constant support.

And last, but certainly not least, thank you to the friends I've made along the way of this crazy, beautiful journey. Whether you are another author, on my Street Team (The Dagger Damsels), have sent me words of encouragement, or have been a helping, supportive hand, I am eternally grateful.

Special shout out to "me" girls: Kara Douglas, Sheila Masterson, Penn Cole, V.B. Lacey, Tay Rose, Nicole Platania, and Helen Scheuerer. You kept me sane through this journey, and I truly would not have been able to do this without you. Thank you for being the greatest hype group of barbies a girl could ask for.

Made in United States
Cleveland, OH
02 January 2025